all

the

right

notes

all the right notes

Dominic Lim

FOREVER

New York Boston

Copyright © 2023 by Dominic Lim

Reading group guide copyright © 2023 by Dominic Lim and Hachette Book Group, Inc.

Cover design and illustration by Caitlin Sacks.

Cover copyright © 2023 by Hachette Book Group, Inc.

Hachette Book Group supports the right to free expression and the value of copyright. The purpose of copyright is to encourage writers and artists to produce the creative works that enrich our culture.

The scanning, uploading, and distribution of this book without permission is a theft of the author's intellectual property. If you would like permission to use material from the book (other than for review purposes), please contact permissions@hbgusa.com. Thank you for your support of the author's rights.

Forever

Hachette Book Group

1290 Avenue of the Americas, New York, NY 10104

read-forever.com

twitter.com/readforeverpub

First Edition: June 2023

Forever is an imprint of Grand Central Publishing. The Forever name and logo are trademarks of Hachette Book Group, Inc.

The publisher is not responsible for websites (or their content) that are not owned by the publisher.

The Hachette Speakers Bureau provides a wide range of authors for speaking events. To find out more, go to www.hachettespeakersbureau.com or email HachetteSpeakers@hbgusa.com.

Forever books may be purchased in bulk for business, educational, or promotional use. For information, please contact your local bookseller or the Hachette Book Group Special Markets Department at special.markets@hbgusa.com.

Print book interior design by Jeff Stiefel.

Library of Congress Cataloging-in-Publication Data

Names: Lim, Dominic, 1974- author.

Title: All the right notes / Dominic Lim.

Description: First edition. | New York : Forever, 2023.

Identifiers: LCCN 2022047934 | ISBN 9781538725382 (trade paperback) | ISBN 9781538725399 (ebook)

Subjects: LCSH: Musicians--Fiction. | LCGFT: Gay fiction. | Romance fiction. | Novels.

Classification: LCC PS3612.I457 A45 2023 | DDC 813/.6--dc23/eng/20230117

LC record available at https://lccn.loc.gov/2022047934

ISBNs: 9781538725382 (trade paperback), 9781538725399 (ebook)

Printed in the United States of America

LSC-C

Printing 1, 2023

To Peter,
You are my Happy Ever After.

AUTHOR'S NOTE

All the Right Notes is a celebration of love and music in a variety of forms, but it also contains some sensitive subject matter. Please take care of yourself if any of the following topics are difficult for you.

Content Warnings: alcohol and drug usage; the sudden death of family members; homophobic language; nonconsensual sex.

Chapter 1—Then

EMMETT AOKI WALKED in after sixth period had already started, landing like a bomb in the middle of Handel's "Hallelujah" chorus.

As we were steamrolling our way to the final measures, he entered right in the two-beat rest before the last *hallelujah*, grinding Sunvalley High's concert chorus to a halt. Our choir teacher—who also happened to be my father—cut us off and, distracted by Emmett's sudden appearance, didn't ever motion for us to come back in.

It was super annoying.

My dad smiled the way he did every time the mailman delivered whatever gadget he'd ordered from the latest TV infomercial and indicated Emmett should take a seat in the back by pointing to it with pursed lips—a typical Filipino gesture everyone in choir had already gotten used to. Emmett stared at my dad with crinkled eyebrows and then looked around him before finally spotting the chair. He gave a big thumbs-up and walked up the choral risers.

I watched from the piano bench as Emmett made his way to the top. Unrest bubbled up around him like tar pit goo. Girls whispered into one another's ears. The boys puffed themselves up but then deflated. He seemed oblivious to the effect he had on everyone. But I wasn't buying it.

"Quito!"

I blinked twice. My dad blared into focus. He waved a baton in front of my face.

"Yeah?"

"I said *keep rehearsing them*. I need to make copies for our guest." He pointed at the papers clutched in his hand and hurried out into the hallway, mumbling to himself as he exited. He'd been begging the principal for a choir room copy machine for the past two years and hated having to walk all the way down to Mr. Drummond's band room to make copies. (Also, he hated Mr. Drummond.)

Thirty pairs of eyes locked on to me.

"Let's take it from the pickup to measure fifty-two? Sopranos and altos? At *King of kings?*" I asked, my voice rising higher and higher with every word.

No one seemed to hear what I was saying. But not because of my utter lack of authority.

Everyone had gone rigid, their bodies shaking with the effort to not turn around and gawk at the god in their midst.

"Super," I chirped at no one in particular. My hands curled into claws on top of the piano keys. "Here's your note." I forced my index finger to open and played an A.

I counted. "One, two..."

They came in on beat three.

It was horrible.

Somehow, just by sitting there, Emmett had found a way to suck the pitch right out of them. And the rhythm. And for some people, the basic ability to breathe. I should have stopped playing. Tried to fix the aural assault I was enduring. But I didn't. I was too busy trying to keep focused, to not be more aggravated by Emmett's presence than they were.

I was failing miserably.

It was the way he sat that bothered me the most. More than his letterman jacket or fancy Reeboks, his Jason Priestley hair or the muscle tone on his arms. Even more than the way he made being Asian look not only different but special, almost cool.

No. It was more than that.

What really got to me was this: the way he leaned back in his chair, legs spread, knees out to 10:00 and 2:00. Hands behind his head. Eyebrow raised just high enough to show noncommittal interest in what was going on around him. How wherever he decided to be was the right place because everything acquiesced, the brick walls in the room seeming softer around him and the fluorescent lighting making him glow like some sort of saint. Everything about Emmett expanded outward. He conquered every inch of the world, saying, *Yo, see this? Look at me. I'm hot shit!*

I could tell he was used to it.

And it drove me nuts.

My dad returned with a bundle of music. He stood by the piano, listening to us finish the chorus. "A little off-pitch this morning, don't you think, anak?" I didn't even notice it when he called me his son, something I'd asked him not to do in class. Not because he was speaking Tagalog but because I didn't like people being reminded that the choir teacher was my dad.

"Yeah. I guess. Not sure why," I lied.

Then, inexplicably, I looked at Emmett for a reaction.

Even stranger, he was already looking straight at me.

And then . . . he winked.

I felt a rush of blood to my cheeks.

"Dad," I said, "what's the deal with the new guy?"

3

"Him?" he asked, pointing his lips at Emmett. "He dropped out of woodshop. Allergic to sawdust. He is thinking of joining the choir, which is very good because we need more male voices. And"—he leaned down to whisper—"somebody of his stature can convince even more guys to join, diba?" He tapped the sheet music on top of the piano. "Laney, please give this to Emmett."

Our soprano section leader, normally a giggling mop of red hair, froze in place. My dad placed the papers in her trembling hands and gently closed her fingers around them. She was eventually able to bring them back to Emmett, though it looked as if she were learning how to walk for the first time as she did.

"He will be good for us, don't you think, Quito?"

Not only was Emmett a member of the Rally Court (the popular students who hung out in the rally courtyard, a concrete wasteland in the center of campus where they held events I avoided), but he was also the all-time record holder for three-pointers on the varsity basketball team. And was in every AP class available. He'd even been in a Sunday newspaper ad for Macy's.

For *underwear*.

But there was no way he was right for choir. I could hear him now, attempting to make a sound. Like a dying animal crying for help.

He didn't belong here. My dad had worked hard to build up the choral program at Sunvalley High, and I wasn't going to have some pretty-boy jock intrude on it. Not my senior year, and not in the one place at school I could call home.

Especially not *him*.

Out of the corner of my eye, I saw Emmett trying his hardest to not pay attention to us. His body defaulted into one of those poses guys always force themselves into: chin jutting out, one hand propped up on his knee, the other cupped against his crotch. He was a poseur, trying his hardest to seem cool in a totally not-cool environment.

But he'd have to sing at some point. He'd have to prove himself, and I knew he'd fail. We'd all see him for what he really was, someone who didn't have a musical bone in his body. Then he'd leave us alone, and we'd get back to the way things were.

I smiled at my dad. "I'm sure he'll be great."

Chapter 2—Now

HERE'S SOMETHING NOT every accompanist will admit—sometimes when we play, we're not actually paying that much attention to what we're doing. Only in certain circumstances, of course. When our heart's not in it. Or if it's something we've played a million times before.

Case in point, virtually every song I get asked to play at Broadway Baby, New York City's fifth-most-popular piano bar, is something I've already memorized. I go through the motions of looking it up on the pianists' communal iPad, but it's all already there in my head, each song tucked away for easy access and ready to be retrieved like a book I pluck from the shelf. When I get asked to play "I Dreamed a Dream" or "Memory" or any number of *seriously-this-one-again?* songs, my fingers go into automatic pilot.

So when a woman asks me, "Do you know 'Defying Gravity'?" my mind already starts to drift. It's not necessarily that it's one of the most over-sung songs ever. It's also because there's something about her that rubs me the wrong way. I've never seen her before, so I try not to judge. But it's hard. She's squeezed herself into a dress that screams *I bought this at full price!*, her makeup is layered on so thick it's impossible to tell what her actual face looks like, and she has so much perfume on that I begin to hallucinate.

"It's a song from *Wicked*, Kevin," she adds.

"It's Quito."

"No, *WICKED*."

I nod, smiling through gritted teeth. "Sure."

She points to me and demands "Two steps lower." Her eyes close. She bows her head. She's making sure everyone understands that she's preparing.

I play the intro. She sings the first line.

Well, not so much sings it as *splats* it.

To be honest, her voice is fine. It's like the voice of almost every other aspiring actress in New York, brassy and belligerent. She plows through, focusing on her own singing, not the song itself. A subtle difference. Instead of communicating the text, she dwells on every note, calculating the sound and timbre and making sure everything spins out at full velocity. She's showing off. And while a lot of people find the pyrotechnics exciting, to me they're just another day at the office.

So, for the next four minutes, I plant a smile on my face and allow myself to drift and look around. The place is super packed tonight. Broadway Baby (which is not actually on Broadway but several blocks over in the West Village) is always busy on Friday evenings, but tonight the people are angling for every bit of space. Even in the frigid February temperatures, a line of people still waits to get inside. I can see them through the window as they snake their way past Joe's Pizzeria, CVS, a perpetually closed tarot-reading salon, and a new falafel place I keep meaning to check out. Office types, show-obsessed gays, and loyal regulars all stand in line, looking forward to an evening of overpriced drinks and the chance to sing along with an enthusiastic and underpaid pianist. Me.

A lot of people are crowded around the piano in the main room. Colored drinks sit in front of them on the piano. Or rather the fake grand piano shell that covers an electric keyboard. I'd always wondered who'd fall for the facade, but surprisingly, anyone who ever gets close enough to see the actual electric keyboard is usually shocked. *Ohmigod, this isn't a real piano?* they gasp, before spilling their drink all over it.

It's their investment in the illusion of the place, perhaps. Everyone here wants to be a star, or at least pretend they are for a few hours, so they give in to the old-time feel—the pressed metal ceiling (rubber), the salvaged-wood bar tables (plastic), the mirrors marked with decades-old imperfections (new mirrors stained with acid)—and accept all of it to be real.

After a couple of the bar's cocktails, everything's real enough.

The people are still listening to the belter. She works the crowd, punctuating high notes with gesticulations and adding a superfluous run here and there.

As I motor into the climax, I notice an older gentleman sitting by himself at a table next to the piano, round in the middle and balding on top with a Caesar-like wreath of white hair. His face is red, as if just sitting on a stool is a cardio workout. There's a slight yearning in his eyes as he listens.

The singer belts her last notes, "Oh-AHAOHAOO!" and I'm snapped violently back to the song. Her yodel stretches the upper limits of the microphone. The crowd rewards her with applause, and she bows, soaking in as much as humanly possible. She doesn't thank or tip me.

"What a voice!" I say into my microphone. "What. A. Voice. Fabulous. *Just* fabulous."

I know I should work off the momentum of her performance and play something else from *Wicked* so that people can sing along. Or ask one of the regulars to share their rendition of some other crowd-pleaser.

Instead, on a whim, I whip around to the older man next to me. "Hi," I say.

His eyes widen. He looks around to find the person I'm talking to before pointing to himself. "Me?"

"Yes. You. What's your name?"

"Edgar."

"Would you like to sing something, Edgar?"

The color of his face deepens, which I didn't think was possible. "Oh. I don't think you'd know any of the songs I know. They're like me. Very old." His mouth smiles, but his eyes don't.

"Try me," I say.

"Do you know 'If He Walked Into My Life'?"

"*Mame*," I say. "Yes, I know it. It's one of my favorites. Come here, Edgar. Up to the mic."

His left hand trembles. "Oh, I'd rather not. Can we just sing it as a group number?"

"I'd love for you to do it by yourself. Why don't you come and sit next to me?" I pat the piano bench.

He hesitates for a moment before slowly sliding off his stool. His walk up to the piano is a little shaky. I can't tell if it's because he's old, nervous, or drunk, though it's probably some combination of all those things. When he sits next to me, I feel as if I've walked into a cabin. He smells of pine needles and warm dirt. And lots of whiskey.

9

I move the mic closer to him and start improvising an intro on the piano. "How's this key?"

"Just right," he says.

Edgar sings. His voice is a lot like he is. Rough-edged and worn.

Unlike the previous song, though, I don't leave my fingers to play on their own. I do the opposite of disconnecting this time. I focus on accompanying him. Sometimes guiding, sometimes following. He makes a few mistakes, fumbles a few notes. It doesn't matter. He's the opposite of the woman before him. His voice isn't impressive or technically proficient. In some ways it's even a little out of control. And yet I feel as if every word he sings is something he believes in. Like he's written the song himself. Like he's lived the story. Is living it now.

By the end of it, he's grinning, and I am, too.

"Thank you," Edgar says, breathless. "Can we do another one?"

I'm about to say yes, to ask him to suggest another song, some other chestnut for me to rediscover with him. But the energy in the room has soured. People's conversations have gotten louder. A trio of gays at a nearby table is checking their phones. One, a tall pouter with penciled-in eyebrows, puts on his pea coat and motions toward the door. The others seem ready to follow his lead.

"I'm sorry, Edgar. How about later on tonight?"

His face sinks into what looks like familiar territory for him. "Of course."

I groan inside. I want to keep making music with him, this man who has so much more to give than a loud voice and theatrics. But I have to make as many people happy as possible.

"All right," I say into the mic, "who's in the mood for some *Hamilton*?"

Cheers go up. The trio on their way out turn back around. The crowd is on my side again. As I begin to play, dollar bills get thrown into my tip bowl. The crowd starts to sing along, and I notice Edgar quietly lumber out into the cold.

After my shift, I turn the plastic fishbowl over on the bar and count my earnings in the annex, a smaller room with only one bartender and a wall-mounted television showing the NY1 news channel. It's quieter here. I can still hear the music through the velvet curtains that separate us from the piano area, but only just barely. The late-night-shift pianist, J.B., has taken over. She's opening with her Disney princess medley, a guaranteed crowd-pleaser. Once, I'd threatened to steal the idea from her. "Over my dead, lesbian body," she said, her eyes narrowing to points behind her owl-shaped glasses.

More fives and tens than usual from the tips, plus two twenties. I gave the crowd what they wanted and was rewarded for it, though the thought of it doesn't make me all that happy.

As I contemplate what fancy dinner I can now buy, someone sits down on the stool next to me.

Mark, my boyfriend, plants a kiss on my cheek. "Hi, Quito." He motions to the bartender, Jaime. "Two Manhattans, please."

Jaime, a brute with a baby face, gives me a look, knowing I won't drink the Manhattan. I subtly shake my head. He nods and proceeds to make one Manhattan and one ginger ale with cranberry juice.

Even though it's already almost ten, I can tell Mark's come straight from work. Sullivan & Cromwell went business casual years ago, but he still insists on wearing a suit and tie. "Better chances of making partner if I dress for success!" He's been working long hours lately. So long we're barely able to go out on dates anymore, which isn't optimal for a ten-month relationship recently gone exclusive. I can see the wear of stress etching more wrinkles around his eyes, though it sort of makes his Midwest-farmer-boy face even more rugged and handsome.

"I'm surprised to see you here. Why the visit?" After we'd been dating for a few weeks, he visited me at the bar during one of my shifts to see what it was like. An hour into my set, he leaned over the piano and said, "Sorry, but if I stay one more minute, I might never get the sound of this place out of my head. I need to go home and Febreze my ears with the original cast recording of *Sweeney Todd*." Mark's the kind of guy who won't go to a restaurant that doesn't have great reviews and won't see a musical or play unless the *New York Times* has given it a thumbs-up. Among other things, he's called Broadway Baby "Broadway Wannababies," "that place where broken hearts go," and "America's Got Talent?" (emphasis on the question mark). Despite my attempts to convince him the singing's a lot better than he experienced that one night, he's never come back. Until now.

He loosens his Bvlgari tie. He has news to tell me. I can tell by the way he tucks a lock of his blond hair behind his ear and how he's so distracted by what's on his mind that he doesn't complain once about the out-of-tune sing-along of "Part of Your World" from *The Little Mermaid* happening in the other room.

"How'd you do tonight?" he asks me.

"Not too bad." I *frap* a cluster of bills against the bar top, straightening them into a manageable stack. "And you didn't answer my question. I thought you couldn't stand this place."

"So, remember how I was telling you about this attorney at work? Dinesh?"

He's mentioned a Dinesh to me before, but I struggle to remember when or why. "I don't—"

"Get this. When he's not cranking out contracts, he writes plays. He's writing the book to a new musical, and he's looking for a composer."

I already don't like where this is headed. "Okay," I say cautiously. "What's it about?"

"Picture it," Mark says, framing my face with his fingers, "a musical based on *Peter Pan* at the height of the disco era. And it's an immersive experience. Can't you just see it?"

Yes, I can. And a part of me curdles inside. Disco music? Another retread of the Peter Pan story? Aren't there any new ideas? Why do we have to keep mining the same ones over and over?

"He's got some producer friends who might back the show. He needs to present a portion of it to them, partially staged. At least one full act. They want to see something on its feet by June. He's got all the scenes; he just needs a few songs. I told him you'd be perfect for that."

I decide not to remind him that I've been trying to work on a show of my own for years. Well, working on the *idea* of a show, at least.

"That is...incredible. A great opportunity. Thank you." I try my hardest to sound sincere, but my smile is too big. Mark fails to notice.

Jaime slides our drinks in front of us. Mark clinks his glass against mine. "To new adventures."

"To new adventures," I repeat and raise my drink. It slows to a stop against my lips.

On the TV behind the bar, a man is being interviewed live. A face I haven't seen in years looks at me. A face I haven't seen in person, that is, because I, and everyone else in the world, have become accustomed to it on countless billboards, movie screens, and magazine ads. Set against the red, high-gloss walls of a Salvadoran restaurant in SoHo, smiling that smile with the crooked tooth, that familiar face is in full-scale animation telling some story, punctuated by two hands carving pictures in the air, claiming all of the surrounding space.

Emmett Aoki is in New York City.

Chapter 3—Then

MY CHILDHOOD MEMORIES are permeated by music.

Sometimes, I swear I can recall my mother singing to me before I was even born—the brushing of her fingers against the skin of her belly as she sang folk songs and church music while I rolled around inside her and grew.

"Your mother's voice sparkled like light on water," my dad told me once. "They called her *the nightingale*." They'd met at a church in Echague, where he played the piano and guitar for Mass. One Sunday, she'd come up to him afterward. "You're good," she said, "but your singing could use some work. Would you like some help?"

My father was charmed by such boldness coming from the young woman, her cheeks full like a chipmunk, the wide gap in her front teeth so beguiling that it didn't even occur to him until much later that she'd just criticized him in front of the priest.

He accepted her offer and asked how soon they could meet. My mother was amused by the way he tripped over his own words and kept scratching his nose as he talked to her. She smiled and said she'd be back next Sunday, and they could start working then.

That following Sunday, they met in the small multipurpose room after Mass, the church's sacristy, office, storage closet, and rehearsal space. My mother showed him how to breathe (*fill your lungs like you fill your belly; do not be stingy*), how to stand (*back straight, one foot slightly in front of the other, as if you are about to go on a journey*), and how to use the muscles of his mouth and throat correctly (*relax your tongue, make it soft like a bed so that your voice can bounce off—not stiff or it will become trapped*).

They went for a walk together after that first lesson. The next week, they had lunch together. The week after that, dinner.

Then marriage came.

Then me.

They moved to the United States, where living a life of classical music was more of a possibility. Not like the Philippines, where, unless you were a famous actor or popular singer, the arts were often considered merely a hobby. Playing and singing wouldn't put food on the table.

They settled where so many other Filipinos had, in the San Francisco Bay Area. First with relatives in Daly City and then in a small house in Martinez, where the hot summers made them feel more at home than the fog-induced chill of South San Francisco. They took a variety of odd jobs while trying to pursue their dreams, cleaning homes, custodial work, babysitting. My father slowly built up a reputation for being an inexpensive traveling piano teacher, while my mother sang in the church choir.

By the time I turned two, they had finally saved up enough money for a used piano from a defunct community center. Even thirdhand, it was still an extravagant purchase. We'd be eating only canned sardines and rice for weeks, but it didn't matter. They had me, a home, and a way to make music in it. Everything they needed.

My mother found steady—though nominally paid—work as a cantor at the nearby Catholic church, Queen of All Saints. She sang for all the Masses, weddings, and funerals. And with a piano in the house, my father was finally able to teach lessons at home. There were days when hours would go by without a single break in the piano playing in the living room or my mother's vocalizations emanating from their bedroom. When they weren't practicing, they were listening to the radio or records they bought from the mall. Other children might have been annoyed by it— adults bombarding them with the sounds of their own lives. For me, it was the lifeblood of our family. It ran through everyone's veins, keeping us alive and happy.

As my father tells the story, he had finished with a piano student and was just seeing him out when my dad became dazed. He wondered if he was suffering from some form of aural déjà vu because he was rehearing the past hour. What puzzled him most was that, even if it were some sort of auditory playback he was experiencing, it couldn't have been of his previous student. Because what he heard was better. No mistakes. An innate sense of phrasing.

He came running back into the living room and saw me sitting at the piano. I was playing "Frère Jacques." I was three years old, and I'd never had a piano lesson in my life.

It was all just a game to me. I'd been sitting on the couch as I usually did, listening and watching my father teach. I watched his fingers dance on the black and white keys, a pattern that was simple for me to memorize. The notes manifested in my brain as a rainbow of colors. For as long as I can remember, music has always existed like that to me, like a textured painting or sculpture, something I can reach out and touch. That day, it simply dawned on me to connect the pressing of the piano keys with the colors in my brain.

All I'd done was solve the puzzle.

My father picked me up off the piano and twirled me around in the air, my insides tickling so much that I laughed until I ran out of air.

He started giving me daily lessons. By the time I was in middle school, I was filling in for the pianist at Queen of All Saints, accompanying my mother whenever she sang. I didn't think anything could feel better than playing solo piano until I began playing for her, learning how to not simply play the notes while she sang but to support her. Anticipate her actions. The synchronicity made me feel as if I could read her mind. I adored that connection to her.

Then, the summer before I entered Sunvalley High, I lost that feeling. When the unspeakable happened. When my mother died.

I started my first year of high school with no mother and no desire to make music.

February of my freshman year, signs went up around school for the Spring Talent Show.

"Your song, Quito. The one you wrote in seventh grade and played and sang for us? The one your mom..." My father looked straight ahead as he drove us home from school. We traveled for another mile in silence before he was able to continue. "Why don't you perform it for the talent show?"

I was barely speaking to him or anyone else at that point. My playing had stopped to practically nothing. If it weren't for the fact that he'd recruited me to be the concert choir accompanist and his assistant in class, I wouldn't have been doing anything musical at all.

"Pass," I murmured.

"It's a good song. Other people deserve to hear it."

I shook my head. I didn't feel like showing that, or any other part of me, to anyone. Particularly not the rest of the students at school.

"Your mother would have wanted you to."

I could see my mom when he said that. Sitting in the auditorium. Eyes as wide as the first time she'd heard my song. It was just so unfair of him to bring her up.

I kept looking out the window, watching as the scenery passed by us in a dull blur, and agreed.

Months later, at the talent show, as I stood backstage waiting to go on, I remember the scent of the packed auditorium being heavy, ripe from the heat of an unseasonal heat wave on top of the nervous energy from everyone around me.

Two acts had already gone on, a jazz combo and a garage band called Boo Yah, Bitch! I was on after Straight-Up Sexy, five girls in purple spandex dancing to a medley of Paula Abdul songs.

My palms and armpits were so wet that I was certain I'd pass out from dehydration. The exit sign glowed just beyond the backstage door. My heart pounded.

Applause for the dance team. It was my turn.

I'd been on stages almost my entire life, playing the piano without thinking twice. Now the lights felt unbearable, the sight of the audience a weight around my neck.

I whispered to myself, "For you, Mom," and began.

I get into place
Put a smile on my face

They're all waiting for me to begin
To get to this night
I've practiced all of my life
To change who I am to fit in

Halfway through the song, I began to let go of my fear. The silence in the auditorium meant they were listening. I felt my mother's presence with me, could almost see her in the backstage wing, watching. I kept going, driven by the belief that the audience loved the song as much as she did.

When it was over, everything went completely still. For a moment, I was convinced they'd understood me. They'd seen the real me behind my song.

A deep, prolonged silence.

Then a shout. "Fag!"

It was a football player sitting in the third row. I could tell from his voice, shoved down an octave. A child's idea of what a real man should sound like. His hands were cupped around his mouth in a megaphone of hate. Laughter rang out from the audience around him.

I pushed myself away from the piano and ran offstage, past my father, who'd watched me from the wings and heard everything. I knew he'd go out and chastise everyone, give some sort of stern warning about profanity or threaten to shut the show down if everyone didn't behave themselves. And I knew he'd eventually make his way back to the choir room, where I'd be hiding, not able to talk, only wanting to go home and forget about everything. The song. The audience's reaction. And what I saw as I fled.

As I was leaving the stage, I saw Emmett Aoki in the audience, right next to the football player. Dead center of the Rally Court contingent. I would've recognized him anywhere. I'd been painfully aware of him all year. He was one of the few Asian students at Sunvalley that didn't need Chess Club or Model UN or the Asian Pacific Alliance to survive in a predominantly white high school. He was an athlete, already one of the most popular kids, even though we were only freshmen. On top of everything else, he was beautiful. To be honest, he was the kind of guy I wish I could've been. He'd found a way to not only fit in but to stand out. Everyone loved him. And he was laughing at me.

The expression on his face became a poster of that year, the sum of my pain from that entire horrible time of my life. It hung in my mind. His smug, flawless face so wrenched with disgust at my song that it looked like he was in pain.

Now I was going to have to look at that same face in choir every day until graduation. A face I never wanted to look at, ever again.

Chapter 4 — Now

MARK'S SNAP IN front of my face jolts me to awareness. "Hello? Everything okay?"

I clench the stem of the cocktail glass. My hand is shaking. Droplets of cranberry and ginger ale trickle onto it and down to the bar. "I'm fine."

I glance quickly back at the TV screen; the interview with Emmett is live. I recognize the restaurant. Mark and I have eaten there numerous times. It's not far from Broadway Baby, only a few minutes' walking distance. My neck muscles tense into hard wire.

"Did you hear what I said?"

I shake the wetness off my hand and try to focus on Mark. "Something about a Dinesh?"

He traces the direction of my helpless stare and turns around to the television screen. "I didn't know you were an Emmett Aoki fan."

"I'm not."

"God, it's so unfair how hot that guy is."

The remnants of spilled drink stick to my fingers. I take a swig. "I've never noticed."

He watches the news interview, reading the slightly delayed

closed captioning. "He's doing a promo for that new Apple TV miniseries he's in. The one about bioengineered superspies."

Mark is always in the know about pop culture. Every time we do trivia night at Phoenix Bar, we slay the competition in that category. I haven't been following what's going on in Hollywood lately, so I'm in the dark about the new show. I wish I still were.

"Sounds interesting," I say.

Mark makes the sound he always does when he disapproves of something. A cross between a *psh* and a *tsk*. It makes the hair on my neck rise. Like the premonition of an imminent threat. "Personally, I think everything he does is way over-the-top toxic male," he says. "There always has to be an explosion. Or boobs. Or both."

I nod in agreement.

He turns back around to me. "So, about Dinesh's musical—"

The velvet curtain separating the back annex from the piano bar section is shoved to the side. Metallic hoops squeal as they scrape across the pole.

"Guess who's back in the house!" My roommate, Ujima, poses in the frame of the doorway. They tower over the room in clear Lucite platform heels. Colored lights and a sing-along of *The Sound of Music* stream past them into the annex.

As they catwalk toward us, they unzip their puffy pink parka, revealing a sequined Supergirl crop top, tight against their torso. The deep black of their naked belly gleams. Long legs stretch from a denim miniskirt. Their Diana Ross wig is a supersized Afro globe, and their face is a mix of *Vogue* editorial and Salvador Dalí.

They pull me up off the barstool with no more effort than picking up a handbag and surround me in a mama bear hug. They smell of flowery perfume and cinnamon chewing gum.

"Girl, that last set at Escándalo wore me *out*. I need some dinner. All I've had to eat today was a handful of Tic Tacs and— oh." Mark turns around on his stool. Sparks flare in Ujima's eyes. "How nice to see you again, Mark."

"Hello, Gerome," Mark deadpans.

To Mark, Ujima is always Gerome Jenkins. Music ed dropout and son of a Baltimore pastor. No matter how they look.

But Gerome is also Ujima. Drag superstar (in their own mind, at least) and my roommate of two years. Their face always seems to carry traces of their various gigs, smatterings of neon and glitter, hair perennially tied back and at the ready for any number of lace-front wigs. It took me a bit of time to get used to their preferred pronouns of *they* and *them* but now it's second nature to me. I also often call them "Jee," a shortened form of Ujima.

"Huh," Jee huffs. "You can see that I'm Ujima now, right? You know, for a lawyer, you don't actually seem to be that smart—"

"Dinner!" I interject. "Yes, that sounds lovely, *Ujima*."

"You can't go to dinner now," Mark says.

Ujima bristles. "And why the hell not?"

I give Mark a warning look. "We were just celebrating because Mark got me a gig."

"Doing what?"

"Writing music for a new musical," I say. "Partnering with a book writer."

Ujima twists their face into a question mark. At least *they* remember I've been trying to work on something of my own for a while now. "What's the show about? And who might this book writer be? Are they any good?" They glance at Mark with a sideways look that says *because if they're a friend of Mark, they aren't any good.*

Mark checks his watch. "His name is Dinesh. I told him we'd come meet him. Tonight. Right now, in fact. For dinner. In Hell's Kitchen."

"Oh, uh-uh." Ujima's head waves back and forth, hair sweeping the air around us like a giant gay mop. "We already have plans."

They've done it to me again. Put me in the middle of some squabble that always seems to erupt when they're in the same room.

"Let's see if we can work something out," I offer. I try to decide who to go with and who to postpone. Multiple no-win scenarios trample through my head.

Ujima points a jeweled nail at the TV screen. "Ooh, baby, look. Your favorite actor is in town."

Another one of Emmett's interviews is on. Or maybe it's still the same one. He has his arm draped around some young actress whose name eludes me. A perky millennial who seems very aware of her best angles because she keeps presenting only certain sides of herself to the camera.

"Wait a second," Mark says to me. "You just said you weren't a fan."

I eye Ujima. "I'm *not*."

They raise a heavily outlined eyebrow. "Aren't you the one always dragging me to see his movies right when they come out?"

Somehow Jee's managed to make a connection between my movie-viewing preferences and an interest in Emmett. Ujima has many talents, not the least of which is excellent perception. They've locked on to something that I don't want anyone to know. Particularly not Mark.

I try to change the subject. "What if we kill two birds with one stone? Ujima, why don't you come with us to meet Dinesh? And, Mark, you tell us where to go. Easy peasy, lemon squeezy."

Mark frowns. Ujima crosses their arms over their padded chest.

Almost an entire refrain of "The Lonely Goatherd" goes by in the other room before I finally say, "I'll pay."

Mark sighs. "Fine."

"You owe me," Ujima says to me with a glare.

In the cab, Mark texts Dinesh while Ujima checks their makeup. I sit between them, right smack-dab in the middle of a tension sandwich, with me as a slab of buffer boloney between two slices of drama.

Mark snaps his leather cell phone wallet case shut. "Dinesh is in. He'll meet us there."

"Where?" I ask.

"Mess Hall. One of my new favorite restaurants. It's kitschy but chic. It's divine."

Ujima grunts. "Sounds lovely."

We look straight ahead and say nothing as our driver weaves in and out of the lanes of traffic. The car's overly heated air sits on my forehead. "Honey, can you roll down the window a bit?" I ask.

Both Ujima and Mark press their window buttons but stop when they realize they've both responded. The winter air rushes in and flushes away the excessive warmth, though I'm more uncomfortable than ever.

After an interminable six-minute ride, we hurry into the restaurant. Strategically placed focal spots welcome us. I'm momentarily stunned by the bright lights. It feels as if we've stepped onto the set of a carefully choreographed production. The restaurant amps up the garish fluorescence of an actual military cafeteria, with aquamarine lights instead of puke green, though it feels more of an exaggeration than an homage. Like a canteen on poppers. But it's Mark's choice, so there's no escaping it.

We're led through the restaurant by a host wearing a Naval Academy T-shirt and pants so tight I fear for his health. Every detail of the place goes up to the edge of camp and then tips right on over. The servers walk around in formfitting military uniforms, homoerotic pictures of service members in different states of undress line the walls, and marginally military-related music (currently an EDM remix of Village People's "In the Navy") thumps throughout.

We go down the length of two long tables that take up the center of the main room. The dining appears to be communal, a trend that I find annoying. As if New Yorkers didn't spend most of their day trying to carve out personal space for themselves in the waves of people we get continuously drowned in.

A man checks his phone at the end of one of the tables. His hair is shiny black except at the temples, which are the type of gradated gray that looks airbrushed. He's older but still in incredible shape. Much better shape than me. Or even Mark, for that matter (and he spends way more time at the gym than anyone I know). From the way Mark makes a beeline for the man, it must be Dinesh. The host mindlessly motions for us to be seated.

Dinesh stands up. Holy hot pants, he's tall. As tall as Ujima in heels. "Ah, so you must be Quito." His accent is a mix of British and Indian. He shakes my hand confidently. "I've heard so much about you from Mark. We work together quite a lot, you know," a fact I don't think Mark has ever mentioned to me. Inappropriate scenes of them at the law firm immediately flicker through my mind: the two of them leaning in a little too closely while going over contracts, laughing while going over edits, flirtatiously smiling at each other at the coffeemaker.

"And I suppose this lovely vision is the person Mark told me would also be joining us. Uh...Gerome, is it?" Dinesh says with a bemused look.

Ujima tries not to roll their eyes at Mark. "Ujima Decadence Fabricant Jones. It's a pleasure to meet you. Hope you don't mind me crashing your little party."

"Not at all. Please." Dinesh pulls out a chair, and Ujima raises their eyebrows at me. Most of the men Jee tends to meet in New York—particularly at the establishments they work at—have zero manners. I can tell they're impressed with this rare gesture of chivalry.

Dinesh puts his elbows on the table and steeples his long fingers. His biceps bulge against the sleeves of his tailored shirt. "So, what has Mark told you so far?"

Even though the question is clearly directed toward me, Mark says, "Peter Pan at the disco! It's brilliant. And Quito would be the perfect composer for it. He's completely on board. Right, Quito?"

I smile politely and drink some water. In the background, the soundtrack to *Top Gun* has slipped into rotation. Kenny Loggins tells me I'm headed right into the danger zone. "I'm interested to hear more about it."

Dinesh looks pleased. "The book is mostly done. Certainly enough for the first act's worth of scenes that I need. But I need a partner for the music. I've got some ideas for the songs, a few basic melodies to go with the lyrics. But I don't have a musical background myself." He traces his finger over the rim of his water glass. "I've heard you're an incredible piano player. Have you done any arranging or composing lately?"

For the past fifteen years, I've been working as a pianist in New York, accompanying for auditions and voice lessons, playing at piano bars like Broadway Baby, even subbing in for a few Broadway shows. At this point, I've memorized the keyboard books for at least six different ones.

But when it comes to composing, I've been stuck. I haven't been able to finish simple songs, let alone an entire show, no matter how hard I try. The move to New York after college was meant to inspire me to get back into composing. I was supposed to swim in an ocean of creativity. But I've only been treading water for years.

I had tried to explain it to Mark once before when he asked me why I wasn't writing any music. I was missing something, I said. Waiting for the right inspiration. Truthfully, I knew why I wasn't composing.

I still hadn't gotten over the thing that had caused me to quit in the first place.

I didn't tell him that, of course.

"Oh, sure," I say to Dinesh. "I mean, I don't have any new stuff, but I've got some old pieces I can play for you."

Mark adds, "He's an incredible composer. He mostly just plays piano now, but he majored in composition in college."

"I, ah, never finished my composition major, actually," I say.

He looks surprised at this, though I'm 100 percent positive

I've told him before. Part of an annoying habit of Mark's is to only hear or see certain things about me. Only the parts he wants, I suppose.

"Oh?" he says. "Well, it doesn't matter. Dinesh, you should hear some of his stuff."

"Oh, you should," Ujima says. I didn't think they were even paying attention to our conversation. Up until now, Jee's been perusing the waiters as much as the menu in front of them. "I've only heard the stuff he wrote back in school, but trust me, honey. Quito's music is beyond."

Dinesh leans back against the metal chair. "How about this, then? We do a show-and-tell. I show you mine. You show me yours."

Ujima purrs. "Sounds kinky."

Dinesh smiles. His teeth are so white that they might actually be glowing. "We go over what I have of my play's book. You play me some of your songs. My place? Next week, perhaps? Sorry to put the screws in, as it were, but they want to see a reading of the entire first act by June. Preferably partly staged. That's about seven numbers. With a workshop cast."

My heart sinks. It's a ton of work to get done in four months. And the thought of working on someone else's story isn't ideal. Yet I've been trying to compose something of my own for years and have come up empty.

Maybe the simple truth is that I just don't have it in me to do it on my own. Maybe Mark recognizes this. Instead of looking for something to inspire me, Mark realizes I need someone to push me in the right direction. Even if the show wouldn't quite be my own, it would still be mostly my music. It's possible I won't ever get another offer like this. It might be the only hope I have of composing again. And after all, it's better to write music for Dinesh than to not write at all.

Isn't it?

Mark and Dinesh look at me expectantly. Ujima stares at another waiter. Streaming from the speakers above, Martika sings about toy soldiers falling down.

"Yeah. Let's do it," I say.

"Excellent," Dinesh says. He signals to one of the busboys passing by. "Excuse me, Benjamin? *Private* Benjamin?" It's charming that he tries to be respectful enough to address the busboy by the title on his name tag, even though it's more likely he's been in a military-themed adult film than the actual armed forces. "I think we're ready to order."

"Yes, sir. I'll go get your server, sir," the busboy says, saluting.

Ujima watches as the private marches dutifully back into the kitchen and fans themself with one of the menus. "We have to come to this place more often."

Mark, in the ecstatic mood he was in when he first told me about Dinesh at Broadway Baby, actually laughs at this.

My iPhone vibrates against my thigh. Who would be calling me this late at night?

I pull it out of my pocket to see a picture of my father staring at me. I scowl at it, confused. It's a FaceTime request. My dad barely knows how to turn his iPhone on, let alone use FaceTime.

"Excuse me for a minute." I walk to the restroom area and click to accept the call, prepared to ask him why he's calling so late. But the person I see is not my father.

Chapter 5 —Then

MY DAD STOOD at his podium as people trickled in for choir. His brow furrowed as he tried to organize his stack of music. I sat at the piano, absentmindedly going through my binder while thinking about Emmett.

The day before, he'd spent his unannounced visit just sitting and listening and looking bored, even after Laney had given him a stack of music (and nearly killed herself doing it). My father asked him afterward if choir seemed like something he'd be interested in. He just shrugged, shook my dad's hand, flashed that snaggle-toothed grin of his, and ran off to basketball practice. So I thought (and hoped) that Emmett wouldn't be back.

After the final bell rang, I relaxed, convinced that Emmett had decided to stay away.

Then, without even looking up from the piano, I knew. A cloud of cologne and briny jock sweat wafted by me, and the room went quiet again.

"Where do I sit today, Mr. C?" Emmett asked in the stilted silence, not quite looking at my dad or anything else, really. I hated that calculated nonchalance. The aggravating fakeness of it, like purposely ripped holes in jeans.

Dad rearranged sheets of music without looking up. "Nelson,

where are you?" A nervous hand went up. "Go sit next to Nelson."

Emmett jumped up to the last row of risers and offered his hand to Nelson, a six-foot jangle of limbs who was having a very visible mini anxiety attack. Emmett took the blue plastic chair and swung it around to sit on it backward.

"Emmett." My father shook his head and made a circular motion with his finger.

Without a trace of embarrassment, Emmett turned his chair back around and sat in that same, arrogant way he had the day before. I felt my neck get red and tried not to look at him by forcing myself to study my music, note by note by note, until the pages went blurry.

I was so focused on *trying* to focus that I completely missed my father's signal to start the vocal warm-ups.

"Psst. Hoy, Quito! Pay attention please."

"Sorry."

He demoed the first warm-up. The choir stood. This time Emmett did, too.

And then something interesting happened.

As I accompanied, I listened to them sing. More confidently than yesterday, as if they'd already started to get used to Emmett being there. Then I watched him. His body looked as if it had traded places with Nelson's, who was standing up straight and singing with confidence. Emmett's hands and feet squirmed, as if they were trying to escape his body. He looked at my dad, the other kids, and finally, at me, as if he'd been asked an unsolvable question and needed one of us to provide the answer.

Emmett Aoki was nervous as hell.

"Quito," my dad said, turning to me, "slow down."

"Sorry. Got carried away."

I smiled down at the keyboard. Maybe Emmett wasn't so great after all.

For the rest of choir period, he seemed similarly lost. I knew I shouldn't have enjoyed his confused looks at the sheet music or his failed attempts at watching and following along. But I did. I soaked up the sight of him flailing, savoring the moments when I could tell that he'd stopped singing altogether and was only mouthing the words.

To be fair, he did try to pay attention to everything my dad said, scribbling in his music when he stopped to give them all notes—though I could see by the way Emmett looked at everyone else's sheet music that he often didn't have a clue what my father was talking about.

Dad didn't seem to notice. I decided it was my job to tell him. It was best for everyone involved that he be made aware that Emmett was completely out of his league and had no place in the choir.

At the end of rehearsal, almost as if he'd heard my thoughts, my dad asked all seven of the tenors—including Emmett—to stay after to audition for the short solo in Moses Hogan's "I Want to Thank You, Lord." I didn't need to tell him after all. He'd get to see and hear Emmett's painful lack of abilities for himself.

"Mr. Cruz, I really should get going." Emmett had his letterman jacket on with his backpack slung over his shoulders. His body was aimed out toward the hallway, gravitating toward the rest of the choir already leaving.

"You have better places to be?"

"I'm supposed to be at basketball practice soon."

"This won't take more than ten minutes. Why don't you go first, since you're in such a hurry?" Dad said, the tone of his voice as amiable as his smile.

But I knew my father. He didn't let anyone get away with anything in his classroom. His office was a mess, his conductor's stand a disaster of sticky notes and disorganized music, but his music-making was flawless, and he demanded the same out of his singers. It was this kind of discipline and hard work he instilled in me from my very first piano lesson.

Emmett went back to his chair and flumped down on it, dejected. He slumped, looking uncharacteristically not in control of the situation. "No, that's okay," he said. "I'll go after everyone else."

"That's very gentlemanly of you," my father responded. This time I couldn't tell if he was being sarcastic or not. "Quito, stay and listen. I want to have your input afterward."

"Hells yeah. I mean, of course." I wasn't going to miss Emmett's humiliation for anything.

The tenors took their turns.

Nelson went first. Fitful and anxious about most other things in his life, Nelson was truly comfortable only when singing and delivered the excerpt with calm assurance.

As the guys sang one after the other, Emmett fidgeted in his seat, his face tighter than a surgical glove.

Second-to-last was Kenneth Sanford. If Emmett was nervous before, he was going to be a mess after this. Ken was the soloist at the nearby Baptist church as well as Oakland Youth Chorus's golden boy. He had the pipes of a million-dollar organ. And as expected, Ken didn't just tear up the solo—he chopped it into little pieces and threw it all over the room like party confetti.

My dad beamed. "Fantastic, Ken." He was proud of all of his singers. Sometimes he liked listening to them even more than they liked to sing, I thought. "And last but not least..." He turned to Emmett.

The poor guy was terrified. His eyes were dilated with anxiety.

I felt a twinge of guilt. This was pure torture for him. I saw the same look of empathy on my dad's face that was probably starting to form on mine. Why did Emmett join choir in the first place if this was so hard for him? Why was he here, when he and all his Rally Court friends thought that singing was...gay?

Well, if he was going to learn how to be in a choir, he had to learn how to perform, and sometimes that meant singing by yourself in front of everyone else. My mind flashed back to freshman year and the talent show. My face hardened. Time for him to know what it felt like to be made a fool of in front of other people.

"I'm sorry, I...I...I still haven't learned all the notes yet," Emmett stammered.

"You've heard it six times now already," my dad reminded him. "Just try your best."

"Can Quito play while I sing?"

He looked at me. I felt the full force of his fear, as if *I* were the deer about to be hit by a car.

"Happy to," I said, complaining internally. I didn't want to help him. I just wanted to be able to listen to him fail. "I can figure out something to play underneath."

"You can't just play my part?" Emmett asked.

"I'll accompany. Don't worry. I'll support you," I said, surprised I'd added that last part.

"Okay." Emmett shook out his hands. "Here goes."

I improvised an introduction, then nodded as a cue for him to come in.

He sang the first line.

And then I stopped playing.

I didn't do it on purpose. I wasn't trying to derail his solo.

But I had to stop.

Emmett had sung only one short phrase. Not even three whole measures. And yet, somehow, those ten measly words and notes had completely thrown me. I'd never felt so discombobulated. I was only vaguely aware that everyone was staring at me. They seemed so far away.

"Shit," I said, forcing myself back into the moment. "Sorry, Dad. I mean, *dang*."

I took a breath and resumed my makeshift accompaniment. I nodded at Emmett again, who looked a little more at ease. It took all my attention to not be thrown again as I listened to him sing all eight bars of the solo, a prayer of thanks to a certain someone who was both his friend and his family.

What was this sound that was coming out of him? It wasn't huge like Ken's voice or precise like Nelson's. He was tentative. And not every note was right. But each note he sang was so vibrant, so full of overtones, that I didn't just see one color per note. I saw entire rainbows. I'd never experienced that before. Not even with my mom.

By the time Emmett had finished singing, the other tenors had clued in to what I was hearing. And to their credit, they didn't react in any kind of negative way; they didn't seem intimidated or jealous. Instead, they were less wary of him now. They nodded and smiled collegially, welcoming him in, as if he'd become someone different from the interloper they'd been seeing him as. Only the rarest of singers can do this. To be self-transformative just through their voice.

"Very good. All of you," my father said. "I'll tell you tomorrow who got the solo." My dad waved them away. "Shoo. Go home."

Emmett slid back into his old self. The guys left the room laughing, Emmett tailing behind them instead of heading out first. He walked backward out of the room, nodded at my dad, and glanced at me briefly before exiting.

I picked up my backpack. I'd expected to enjoy watching Emmett flounder, to get what he deserved. Instead, he'd just earned the respect of everyone in the room. Including me.

"Quito," my dad called out just as I was leaving. "Who did you like best?"

I turned around. "They were all good. Ken's always great. You can't go wrong with him."

"What about this new boy? Emmett? Don't you think there's something *special* about him?" he asked. His emphasis on the word "special" made me uncomfortable.

"He's one of the most popular kids in school. Of course he's special."

"That's not what I mean." That look again. "There's a rawness there that is unique. Don't you agree? I think I will give him the solo."

"But he can't read music, Dad. He was messing up all over the place," I exaggerated. "He'd need a ton of work."

"Maybe you're right."

"I *am* right." I headed back out again.

"So why don't you work with him on it?" he asked from behind me. "Get him up to speed. I'll ask him to meet with you after choir. Once a week should be enough. You can also help him learn the other music. Okay, anak?"

Not only was Emmett definitely in the choir now, but he had gotten a solo, *and* I'd have to work with him on it. And probably other things. My blood rushed to my head. Without turning around to look at my dad, I said, "Whatever you want."

Chapter 6—Now

I AM DEFINITELY not looking at my dad.

My phone screen has been taken over by a girl's plump brown face. Her curly black hair is pulled back tight, and her cartoonlike eyes blink furiously. "Hello?" she says.

"You're not my father."

Background noise blares around her. She puts the phone closer to her face, and her nostrils magnify to gigantic proportions. "Are you Mr. Cruz?"

"That would be my dad," I say to what are now just eyeballs. "I'm sorry. Could you move the phone a little farther away from your face?"

"Oh. Sorry," she says, crestfallen.

"No, I mean—you're a lovely young lady."

She giggles as the phone veers closer to her face, focusing on her mouth.

"With very pretty teeth."

"Thank you!" say the teeth.

"So, again. You're not my dad. And *I'm* not my dad. Could you tell me who you are and who you are trying to reach?"

"I—"

"And move the phone back. Just a smidge. There we go."

"I'm Celeste. Celeste Gonzalez? One of Mr. Cruz's students. The other Mr. Cruz, I mean. We just had our choir concert, and he was talking about how he had seen something on TV, and it made him think of you or something. And he said he should call you before he forgot, and then I said, well, just give him a call? And he said he wished you were here because it'd be nice to tell you face-to-face and also I think maybe he misses you? And I said, well, if you have an iPhone and he has one, too, then he could talk to you on FaceTime. And then I had to explain what that was, and he got really confused about it and also sort of grumpy, and he said he, like, didn't understand, so he told me to just do it for him."

I blink.

"So I called you," Celeste says.

"Okay."

She stares at me.

"So," I say. "My father."

"Yes?"

"Is he there?"

"Right next to me."

I sigh. "Celeste?"

"Yes, Mr. Cruz?"

"Could you hand the phone to my father now?"

"Oh! Sorry."

A blurry transition on the screen. Bright stage lights flash by. They're in the Sunvalley High auditorium.

My father's face finally comes into focus. He rubs his heavy-lidded eyes. Dark circles line the bottoms of them. I remember how he'd get so exhausted after concerts, having spent the previous days fussing over every last detail. The lighting, the blocking, the bows. Not to mention the music. He'd start out full of energy, but by the time the concerts were over, he'd fall in on himself like a blow-up doll whose air had all leaked out. "How are you, anak?" he asks.

"I'm fine, Dad. Though I'm kind of in the middle of something right now."

He scratches his head. People have always said they can see the family resemblance between us. But though we have the same round face, the same broad nose like a downward arrow, and bushy eyebrows like caterpillars above our eyes, he was blessed with a thick head of hair. Grayish now but still full. While the bald spot on the crown of my head grows bigger every day. "You know," he says, "I've been a teacher here at your high school for almost thirty years. Can you believe it?"

Classic Dad, not to get to the point. "What's up, Dad?"

He smiles. Not a happy one. "I don't know if the kids even like what I'm picking for them anymore. They like such different things now. With all this rap music. Lady Gaga. You know that *gaga* in Tagalog means a stupid woman?" He chuckled. "So she is actually calling herself Lady Stupid Lady."

"*Dad.*"

"Okay, okay, you don't have to get testy." He shuts his eyes, looking even more tired. "I am going to retire at the end of the school year."

Something lurches in me, as if I've stopped too quickly at a red light. Dad retiring? I feel like I've aged years in seconds. My father is calling it quits with his career, while mine seems like it hasn't even gotten started. Maybe it's a good thing that Mark's got me involved with Dinesh's show.

"Are you sure? You've got a lot you can still teach to those kids."

"That's what I'm trying to say, Quito. I don't think that I do. I'm getting to the point where I won't be able to...when I cannot—"

Screaming and laughter erupt behind him. A group of teenagers still dressed in their concert white dress shirts and black slacks run around throwing things at one another.

"Hey! Knock it off back there, all you kids!" Dad yells. "Go home now! The concert is over! Where are your parents? Why don't they come take you away? *Susmaryosep!*" he says. "What was I saying? Oh yes. It's getting to be too much for me to deal with."

"I can see that."

Working with kids day in and day out couldn't ever have been easy, even when Dad was in his thirties and had plenty of energy. Now that he's approaching retirement age, why shouldn't he be allowed to stop? I've only ever known him as a music teacher, but some things have to come to an end eventually.

"I guess you should be able to spend more time relaxing. Maybe travel more. You've done so much for that school and all those kids over the years. You deserve to be able to do what you want. I don't know how they'll ever replace you, though."

My father stares at me through the screen. His image is so still, I think the app has frozen. He has on one of those expressions of his that I'm unable to interpret. I can't tell what he's thinking when he looks like that—his eyes looking so far past me that I can never find him.

"Thank you, Quito," he finally says. "I knew you'd understand. That's also why I'm calling you. I am going to have a special concert, okay? At the end of the school year. We are going to raise money for the choir, so I can make sure they have plenty in the budget for some nice upgrades before I go. They need new microphones. And risers. And it would be nice to get a..."

"Copy machine?" I smile.

"Yes," he says, smiling back at me. He looks away from the screen, distracted by something. "By the way, you come back to play for us. Okay? Assist me with rehearsing them. There's going to be a lot of new music. I need your help."

There it is. The real reason for the call. Not that my dad retiring isn't big news, but he could have just told me during our regular Sunday-afternoon telephone conversations. This was a special request he was making.

It wouldn't be that big of a request, normally. I try to get back to the Bay Area at least twice a year, during the holidays and once during the summer for my father's birthday. But what about my responsibilities here now? I glance back into the Mess Hall dining area at our table. Dinesh seems to be explaining his show to Ujima, who looks like they're genuinely interested, though it's hard to be sure if it isn't just because they want to sit on Dinesh's lap. If our connection works out, I'll be busy writing songs for his show. Between Broadway Baby and my other accompanying gigs, I'll need all the time I can get to compose. I haven't done it in years, and I can't afford to be distracted.

"I might be working on something soon, Dad. I'm not sure I can come out right now."

"Oh," he says and shrugs. "Sige. That's fine."

The tone in his voice now is one I know extremely well. Last year, he called asking me if I'd like to "volunteer my time" to go back and perform for the Fil-Am Community Center variety show in Walnut Creek. They were raising money for typhoon victims in the Philippines. When I told him I was going to sub in *Phantom of the Opera*'s pit for the next few weeks, he said he completely understood, sounding exactly as he does now—seemingly okay with my answer but actually not. He proceeded to send me articles about the death toll from Super Typhoon Yolanda. Every day. I couldn't stand more than a week of it before I finally caved in. Later I found out he'd already told them I'd agreed to the show before he'd even asked me. When my dad wants something, he'll keep asking for it, no matter what anyone tells him. He uses the slow trickle of guilt to work its way through the person, waiting for them to eventually yield.

I sigh. "All right. When is it?"

For a moment he looks young again. Not anywhere near retirement age. "The first week of June. Come in May. So that you have more time to work with the kids."

"I'll just be accompanying, though, right?"

"Coach them, too. Take your turn at directing. You've been working with all those Broadway singers now, anak. You can pass on your wisdom to these kids. There's one here especially that could use your help. He's having problems with his voice. I think you can help him. He reminds me of you, Quito. When you were young. He's ... special, too."

The idea of helping kids and directing a choir does not make the invitation easier to take. I've never stopped accompanying singers, but I haven't conducted them in years. Not since the last time I saw Emmett.

"I'd rather just stick to the piano, Dad. And one week might be all I can swing."

"We'll be very happy to have you," he responds, in a way that implies that he either hasn't heard what I've just said or has decided I'll change my mind about it. "You know I've told the kids all about you. They are so excited to meet such a hotshot Broadway guy."

"Thanks, but I'm not—"

"Oh," he interrupts. "One more thing. I told everyone you'll bring Emmett."

My insides seize up. "What?"

"I saw him on the news. He's there in New York right now, diba? Doing publicity for his new TV show. Have you seen him yet? He's staying with you, maybe? Tell him we need him, okay? We want to sell as many tickets as we can. And with a big Hollywood star coming out to perform, it will be a big success. A big success, talaga!"

"Uh, he's not staying in my shitty apartment, no. He's a really busy, famous guy, and I don't think he'd be able to do it."

"He's your best friend. Of course he will sing. Just ask him."

My body stiffens. "Of course," I manage. "Right. He's my best friend."

"And my favorite student, don't forget. That's why I want him here, of course."

"Right."

"Very good." More screaming laughter breaks out. "Hey. Hey! Time to go home now, you kids. My god! Don't you have anything better to do?" He looks back at me. "I have to go. Tell Emmett I said hi."

"Will do," I say to the already blank screen.

46

Back at the table, plates of fries and chicken tenders sit steaming. Ujima's favorites. They would live off the appetizer section of the Applebee's menu if it were possible. I watch as they dig in.

"Ah, Quito, I was just giving Ujima the rough outline of my show. *Our* show, hopefully," Dinesh says.

Mark puts his arm around my shoulder as I sit. The sensation of claustrophobia creeps through me.

Ujima tilts their head at me. "Everything okay, baby?"

I try to smile. "My dad's retiring. Which is kind of a surprise. I guess I just thought he'd go on teaching forever."

"He's a teacher, then? That's lovely," Dinesh says, sounding sincere. He does seem like a genuinely decent person. If there's a chance we'll be working together on this show, I don't want to have to tell him that I might have to take time out from it just to play piano for a bunch of high school kids. Better to keep my mouth shut until I can sort out all the details.

"He's a music teacher, actually," I say, "the choir director at my old high school."

"Talent runs in Quito's family." Mark removes his arm from my shoulder and takes my hand, slightly crushing it. "Quito, I'm sure your dad's going to be so excited to hear about you writing music for this new play. Dinesh, why don't you tell him more of your ideas for some of the songs?"

I pull my hand away. "Actually, I'm feeling pretty tired. I think I need to head home."

"But we haven't finished talking yet," Mark says.

"I've had a long day, and I'm just realizing now how big the prospect of this new show is." Which is the truth, albeit only partly. "I need a day or two to wrap my head around everything." Definitely true. "It was really nice meeting you," I say to Dinesh.

"Until next time, then. Would next weekend be okay for our sharing session?"

"Yes. Looking forward to it."

"Aren't you forgetting something?" Ujima waves a fry at me.

"Damn." I promised Jee dinner. "Sorry. I'll make you something at home."

"Baby, you are so aggravating," they say. "But fine. We're taking a cab home, and you're paying. Let me at least take some of this chicken home." They wave their pink patent leather purse at one of the servers passing by. "Sweetie, I'm gonna need a to-go box." They eye him up and down. "Hm, I'd like to take *that* to go."

Mark rolls his eyes. He's gone back to his surly mood. "I thought you were staying at my place?" he says to me.

I'm disappointing everyone tonight. "Tomorrow instead?" I offer, kissing him on the cheek. Then, glancing at Dinesh, "Don't stay out too late?"

"Okay," Mark says, his expression hard to read.

The server returns and practically throws the to-go box on our table from a few feet away to avoid Ujima. Completely unaware of this, Jee happily scoops the food into the box.

The strange look on Mark's face is just about to change my mind about going home when Ujima pulls me out of my chair. "Come on. You're making waffles to go with this chicken."

Dinesh says goodbye. Mark doesn't wave or smile. I sag with guilt as we walk out.

"What was that all about?" Ujima asks once we're outside.

"My dad wants me to come home to California."

"Why?"

"To help him with a farewell concert."

"Oh, good. I was worried there for a minute."

Two years ago, my dad came to visit me during his summer break and stayed with Jee and me in our apartment for two weeks. After just a few days, he was driving me crazy, but he got along well with Gerome, finding all their attention-seeking antics hilarious. Then, when he saw them in drag, not only did my dad approve, but he seemed to like them even more. In fact, even though his usual bedtime is 9:30 p.m., he demanded to go to every one of Ujima's shows, even if they didn't start until after midnight. Suffice it to say, Jee adored my dad.

"I was afraid he might be sick or something." They stick their neck out into the street to look for an available cab. "He don't eat so good, you know. Remind him to have a vegetable every now and then."

"He's old-school Filipino, Jee. His idea of eating vegetarian is having fish."

"When is the concert?"

"Early June. But he wants me to go out there to work with the kids in late May."

"And Dinesh's show? You'd have to compose all those songs *and* get it rehearsed and ready by June."

I grimace. "It'll be fine. I can do both." My brain races as I freak out about the implications of the timing of everything.

"Mmm." They give me that look that says they see something that I'm doing a horrible job of hiding. "You're still not telling me everything."

The cold air bites against my face, and a light spattering of wet snow begins to fall, making my hair damp. I close my eyes against the coldness. "He told everyone that Emmett Aoki is making a guest appearance at the concert."

Ujima's head whips around, and a clump of Diana Ross hair hits me in the face. "Why would he promise that?"

"Because he thinks we're still best friends."

"Best friends? Wait. *Still* best friends? You were best friends with Emmett Aoki? THE Emmett Aoki?"

"No. We just went to the same high school. He sang in choir. We were... We were never friends. Only acquaintances. At best."

Cabs whiz by. Without even thinking about it, Ujima sticks their leg out into the street and pulls their miniskirt up as high as it can go, revealing a wide swath of thigh. Almost immediately, a cab swerves over to our street corner. Jee gives me a wink and then says, "Now talk."

I open the cab door. We're hit by a wall of citrus air freshener. I don't want to get into my history with Emmett, though I'd normally tell Ujima everything. The past is just too complicated, and the night is too far gone. "There's not much to tell."

"Well, whatever tea you got, start spilling it. We've got about a hundred and fifty blocks to go, and Mama needs some entertaining. You pulled me away from a restaurant full of tasty snacks, and I'm not just talking about the food. It's the least you can do."

Chapter 7—Then

THAT EVENING, AS I was helping my dad cook dinner, he laid out the rehearsal schedule for Emmett and me.

"On Fridays after choir, you can practice with him. That will give you at least half an hour together before he has to leave for basketball." His face glistened from the steam spouting from a just-opened pressure cooker. He'd been tenderizing oxtails, the main component of kare-kare.

I kept my eyes glued to the chopping board, mostly to make sure I was cutting the string beans, eggplant, and bok choy into consistently sized pieces but also because I needed to focus on what I was doing so I could avoid thinking about the heartburn that had started to build up inside me.

"And when exactly would I have to start doing this?"

"Tomorrow."

"What?" I asked, nearly nicking my finger with the knife. "There's no way Emmett will say yes to that."

"He already has," he said, straining to be heard above the exhaust fan he'd turned on. Into a pan of sizzling onions and garlic, he poured beef stock, ground peanuts, and some achuete seed–colored water, which turned the stew a deep mahogany. A sweet and savory scent filled the air.

"That's not possible," I said. "Emmett left the solo auditions today without you saying anything to him."

"I called him after school. He said it's fine."

I wasn't sure which was worse. That my dad had set up a regularly scheduled meeting between me and Emmett without asking me first or that he had him on speed dial. My stomach churned, but it wasn't from hunger anymore. Despite the fact that kare-kare was one of my favorite dishes of all time, my appetite had almost completely disappeared.

I didn't want to have anything to do with Emmett. People noticed him. Followed him around. I wanted to be left alone to my music. He was everything I wasn't. And he was a jerk. Maybe he had a decent voice, but that didn't make him a decent person.

I was convinced this was the reason I was upset.

Later that night, after barely eating any of the food, I tossed around in my bed, fixated on the impending coaching session with Emmett. The thought of it blinked like a red light in the distance, never shutting off, getting brighter and more insistent.

My classes the next day went by with me completely tuned out. I couldn't think about anything else. I walked through the hallways scanning my immediate vicinity, afraid of running into him. I wanted to delay the inevitable as long as possible.

I managed to avoid Emmett except for a special combined gym period outside. A massive all-hands-on-deck one-mile run test. I'd been dreading it all semester. During the run, with my insides on fire and my legs screaming at me to stop, slow down, turn around, start crawling—do anything but keep running—Emmett ran by me. Even though I'd started in the first group and he was in the fifth. I could've sworn I felt him come up from behind me without seeing him, like prey sensing the impending leap of a wolf. As he passed, it seemed as if he looked over his shoulder at me. He resumed his five-minute mile, or whatever it was, while I tried not to collapse into a hyperventilating mass on the track. In the locker room later, hurrying to get changed and get the hell out of there, I told myself that I'd imagined it. That he didn't actually see me.

For some reason, this just made me feel worse.

Then, finally, choir.

At the piano, I sensed it again. Emmett's presence, almost vibrating through me. Or maybe it was just the Drakkar Noir cologne he wore, which I'd never really liked before. Though I had to admit, on Emmett, it smelled different—something about the way it interacted with the leather of his letterman jacket, or his clothes, or the smell of basketballs, or—

He slapped me on the back. "Wassup, dude?"

I jumped off the piano bench.

"Me and you after class, right?"

A sting began to creep out from between my shoulder blades and down my spine, to the tip of my tailbone.

"You gonna drill me hard?" he said.

It was several moments before I realized my mouth had dropped open without saying anything in response.

He squinted, probably wondering what the hell was wrong with me.

Then he punched me on the shoulder. A jock move I'd never been on the receiving end of before that he'd probably done to other guys a hundred times. "Take it easy on me, okay, dude? I'm a virgin," he said with a completely straight face.

Overwhelmed with a fear that I'd just blushed, I turned away and tried to come up with an excuse to escape or at least cover up my face. Was he messing with me? He must have known that everything he was saying was a double entendre, right?

I looked back at Emmett just in time for him to wink at me.

The bell rang, the sound coursing through my frayed nerves. My dad emerged from his office. "All right, you crazy kids. Let's get to work."

"See ya afterward." Emmett punched me on the shoulder again and waited for some kind of response. When I did nothing again, he shook his head and strolled back to his chair to sit in that exasperating Emmett way of his.

The class period had an indefiniteness to it, seeming both interminable and fever-fast at the same time. No matter what I did, I couldn't focus. All during the rehearsal, I made way more mistakes playing than I usually did.

Which is to say, I actually made mistakes.

Wrong notes clunked out left and right, incurring bitchy looks from Laney. Emmett seemed to find my blunders hilarious, though. Whenever I messed up, he chortled. Something about this made me acknowledge the gaffes by crossing my eyes and cringing visibly. This only made Emmett laugh louder.

"Focus, please," my dad said.

"Sorry," Emmett and I said at the same time.

Emmett raised an eyebrow at me. *Maybe we should get our shit together?* the look seemed to ask, though why I thought I had any idea what was going on in Emmett Aoki's mind was beyond me.

"Let's go over the pronunciation again," my father said. We were working on Mozart's "Ave verum corpus." "Ah-veh, not

Ah-VAYEE," he pointed out to everyone. "Veer-jee-neh, NOT virgin-ay."

All of it melted into note-and-word mush as I watched Emmett, who had actually resolved to pay more attention, it seemed. He was doing some variation of the same sequence of actions over and over: listening to my dad's instructions, scribbling something in his music score, shaking his head, and then erasing what he'd just written. The day before I'd found his Sisyphean efforts amusing. Now I was starting to feel sorry for him.

I kept looking at him. Again and again. Compulsively. I convinced myself it was just to observe. To see what he might be struggling with so that I could address those issues in our coaching sessions directly, thus minimizing the time we had to spend with each other. That's all it was.

The bell rang. My father made his way back to his office as everyone exited the choir room engaged in loud conversations.

I pretended not to pay attention as Emmett made his way to me at the piano. He stood next to me, backpack over one shoulder, thumb hitched underneath the strap. "Dude, you were fucking up all over the place today."

Now he was making fun of me. The idea that we'd found a connection during class suddenly seemed ridiculous. I began putting sheet music in my binder. In the wrong order.

"Me? No, you," I offered pathetically.

"There's no way you heard me mess up."

"Because you're perfect?" I said, then regretted I had. I didn't have the talent for witty banter. Or even middling banter.

"Because I wasn't singing most of the time." He grabbed one of the blue plastic chairs and set it close—too close—to the piano.

The smell of him bloomed as he leaned into me. "You need to teach me."

Had I remembered to put on deodorant that morning? My body itched with the instinct to scoot farther away from him, in case I didn't smell as nice as he did. "All right, hang tight," I jabbered.

He stared at me oddly, not sure of what I'd just said. I wasn't so sure myself. I scratched the back of my neck, wet with sweat, and then quickly wiped my fingers on my jeans. "Let's start with your solo on 'I Want to Thank You, Lord.'"

His face cracked. "Wait. I got the solo?"

I paused, trying to think. Dad said he'd talked to Emmett on the phone. I assumed he told Emmett that he'd given him the solo. Apparently not.

"Uh, yes?" I responded.

The crack in Emmett's face widened. "Oh, no. No."

"You deserved it."

"I can't do it. That's not why I—"

"I'll help you."

He was looking off into space. He didn't seem to hear me.

"Hey," I said. For some inexplicable reason, I felt compelled to pull him back to earth by putting a hand on his knee. "I said I'll help you." My stomach reeled when I realized what I'd done. Did I just grab hold of a Rally Court jock's knee? Guys didn't do that to other guys. Certainly not ones who barely knew each other.

I didn't know what to do. Jerking my hand away from him would only bring attention to it. Make things more awkward. But I couldn't just keep it there.

I decided it was best to pull away slowly. Very, very slowly.

As I began to slide my hand off Emmett, he refocused and looked at me. "Okay." He'd hardened his face with determination. "I trust you."

I stared back at him. With my fingertips still touching his knee.

I was seconds away from dissolving into a pool of embarrassment when he punched me in the shoulder.

My third shoulder punch of the day. I needed to do something this time. Punch him back? Kick him in the shins?

Not knowing what else to do, I just said, "Oww?"

Emmett snorted. "Dude, you are such a weirdo."

Shooting shoulder pain aside, I was grateful he'd done it. It gave me an excuse to take my hand back. I rubbed my shoulder and felt the pain burn in a not altogether unpleasant way. "Um. Let's start the song from the beginning."

He pulled his binder out from his backpack and flipped through the sheet music. "You'll have to play it a couple of times for me," he said. "I can't really read the notes, but once I get something in my ear, it never leaves."

I tapped a finger to my lips.

"What?" he asked.

"Hold on a sec." I hopped off the piano bench and went to my father's office. He was reading the school newspaper.

"I haven't heard any practicing yet," he said without looking up.

"Do you still have that old tape recorder?"

"It's on the top of the bookshelf. What do you need it for?"

I reached up and swiped my hand back and forth. My fingers made contact with hard plastic. I jumped and grabbed the tape recorder, something he'd gotten at RadioShack for taping our rehearsals but never got around to using.

"I'm borrowing this." I ran back out to the choir room.

Emmett was hunched over on his chair, slowly balling a fist into his other hand. I wondered if he practiced things like this. He always managed to make his poses look so natural. So effortlessly masculine. Something I would never be able to pull off, no matter how much I practiced.

I clicked the eject button of the recorder, checking it for a tape. A cassette jumped out with a plastic pop. I pushed it back in, set the tape recorder on top of the piano, and pressed record.

"I'll play the part. You sing it back," I explained. "We'll do that a few times, and you'll have it all on tape so you can have it to practice with at home."

"Cool," Emmett said. "Hey, thanks for doing this, by the way. I'd be lost without you."

Instead of a wink or an upturned chin or another punch, he gave me a smile. Small and subtle yet unmistakably sincere. Not an ounce of posing. It startled me.

"What?" he asked.

"Nothing." I shook my head. "It's just—you're not exactly what I thought you were like."

"That's funny. Because you're exactly like what I've always thought you were like."

I couldn't have heard him correctly. "Like—what?"

"Funny. Super talented. Hella smart."

"No. What I mean is, you've been thinking about me?" The words stumbled out of my mouth and fell to the floor. I immediately wanted to bend down, scoop them all back into my mouth, and swallow them all whole.

"Your song at the talent show freshman year?" he said. "I was really impressed by it. I couldn't believe you'd written that by yourself."

My head was spinning with too many thoughts. He'd been impressed by me? He thought I was talented? The fact that he'd thought about me at all was throwing me for a loop. "You actually liked it?"

"Dude, it was rad. The music was great, but the words, the lyrics... they were amazing."

Did he understand what the lyrics actually meant? What I had been trying to say with them? "I thought you and the other athletes were laughing at me."

"Trevor. That idiot," Emmett said quietly to himself. "That fucking sucked, what he did."

I thought back to that moment. The look on Emmett's face. Did I mistake his disgust for delight? Had I been misjudging him this whole time?

"That was really hard," I admitted, surprising myself. I hadn't talked about that evening with anyone. Not even my dad. It was a memory I wanted to crumple up and throw away. "I haven't even thought about that song since that night."

"That's too bad. Because you were awesome."

I tried to look at him, tried to thank him, but I couldn't. My mouth was so dry it was stuck shut.

I could sense he was waiting for me to respond. To say something. To compliment him back. At the very least, to thank him. Maybe even something more. The more I thought about the possibilities, the more it felt as if I'd break into a hundred pieces if I did anything.

The last time I said something nice to a guy that good-looking in choir...didn't go so well. The thought of opening myself up only to be humiliated wasn't something I wanted to go through again.

So I just sat there. Getting more dry and brittle by the second.

After a silence that seemed to last hours, I managed to move my hands to the piano. My fingers slowly plunked out his solo part. "After I play it, you sing it back. Got it?"

He said nothing.

I managed to turn and look at him. He nodded slowly, his face shadowed. Most probably from concentration. At least that's what I made myself believe.

Chapter 8—Now

"SO YOU WERE his little choir buddy," Ujima says.

My head presses against the window of the cab as I look out. The storefronts and apartment buildings of Manhattan's Upper West Side zoom by in a multicolored haze. Even this close to midnight, the streets are still buzzing—people smoking in front of neighborhood dives, ducking into bodegas, sitting at the windows of twenty-four-hour diners and late-night cafés. After fifteen years of living in New York, I still can't get over how nighttime burns as bright as day.

"It was a long time ago," I say. The smell of car freshener has mellowed to that of a lemon drop. "And I wasn't his buddy. Just a tutor."

"You never hung out with him?" Ujima asks.

"With the most popular kid in school? Nah."

"Mmm-hmm."

"What?"

"Nothing." The cab turns off Broadway and onto our street. "You can stop right at the corner, honey. Thank you."

Ujima says nothing as we walk up the stairs to our fifth-story walk-up, which is unlike them. Even after a long night of performing, they normally still manage to talk my ear off, going on about how much they hate living in a walk-up and why the hell don't we live in a building with an elevator and wouldn't it be wonderful if we could have a doorman who would greet us every day, preferably one who's swarthy and Puerto Rican?

I unlock the door to our apartment and flip on the lights. We enter into a familiar mix of smells—candles, laundered clothes, half-emptied take-out containers, and the dregs of coffee and cocktails in various glasses and mugs.

Jee commences their daily ritual. A transformation from Ujima back to Gerome. They kick off their high heels, look at themself in the floor-length mirror by the door, and pluck the humongous wig off their head, revealing their own hair. I'm surprised at how full it's become. At some point, they might not even need a wig. Jee tilts their chin up and examines the effects of the evening on their meticulously painted face. Ujima's makeup tonight, as always, was flawless. *Beat for the gods*, they like to say. Applied with such thick, masterful strokes that even heaven can't miss them.

I've noticed lately that they wait longer and longer at the mirror before resigning themself to the bathroom, not wanting to say good-bye to the person they see. As if they'll never see them again.

I sense that familiar sadness in them and try to cheer them up. "You looked gorgeous tonight," I say, trying to support the instinct they have to delay their change back to their less femme self. For a little while, at least.

Ujima's reflection in the mirror gazes at me, their eyes like flints. "Get those waffles crispy," they say and wander off to finish unmaking themself.

I start gathering ingredients for the batter and listen to Jee singing in the shower, washing themself back to the form I was introduced to first. The one who, eight years ago, sashayed half an hour late into the first rehearsal for an off-Broadway (off-off, actually—as in Park Slope, Brooklyn) production of *Pippin*.

I was playing rehearsal piano. Our director, Kelly, an ex-actor whose biggest Broadway credit was playing a dancing plate in *Beauty and the Beast*, was undeterred by Jee's fashionably late entrance. "Call was one thirty, Gerome," she singsonged.

"Sorry, girl. Late night. The boys just couldn't get enough of Ujima."

Kelly exhaled audibly, paused for dramatic effect, and then continued with rehearsal.

Gerome dragged themself to the last open chair, crossed their legs, and put on a pair of reflective sunglasses. As Kelly went over the rehearsal schedule, I sat at the piano, sneaking glances at the new guy and wondering who the heck "Ujima" was and why Kelly didn't seem to care that Gerome had so obviously fallen asleep.

The answer to the latter question came after just one sing-through of the score. Gerome was not only the best singer in the cast, but they were also the most prepared. They'd memorized nearly all their songs as the Leading Player.

Then dance rehearsals began. Gerome could move in ways I'd never seen before. They'd clearly had a classical background— I found out later they'd trained in ballet since childhood— but there was also something else. Something I couldn't quite describe. When they danced the choreography, they imbued all their movements with a sensuality that was both masculine and feminine at the same time. Their movements went beyond my own simplistic concept of gender, being neither as much as both. They were absolutely mesmerizing to watch.

Then, when the cast dragged me out one afternoon to go dancing at Body & Soul, I finally met Ujima.

We'd all been there for over an hour when they waltzed into the club. The crowd instinctively parted for them as they came toward us. I knew at a glance who they were. That afternoon, as I watched Ujima conquer the dance floor, glowing with sweat and looking like an outer space goddess in their sparkling silver outfit, I almost fell in love with them, pulling them aside and monopolizing their time, wanting to be near them constantly.

But later, after floating on a high from hours of dancing, after we'd stumbled into the alley for some fresh air, the brief kiss we shared was more confusing than satisfying. We looked at each other and laughed after we'd done it. Then we hugged, somehow knowing we'd fallen into something that would take a bit more practice before we would figure out how to get it right. We'd realize that we did belong together, but as friends—eventually sharing a home, if not a bed.

Gerome emerges from their bedroom, wearing a lime-green kimono. A pink sash corrals their burgeoning Afro. They close their eyes and inhale the steam from two freshly pressed waffles filling the kitchen. "Now, that's what I'm talking about."

They perch themself on one of the high stools at the counter separating the kitchen from the living room.

I place a plate of waffles in front of them. The pat of butter I've put on top of the stack is already melting into glistening rivulets down its sides. I set out a bottle of maple syrup and the Mess Hall chicken, which I've warmed up and recrisped in the oven and then soused with Jee's favorite hot sauce. "Bon appétit."

"Admit it. You love taking care of me," they say with their mouth already half-full of waffle.

"Don't flatter yourself. I just love to cook." I pour them a glass of orange juice as I continue waiting for my own waffles to be done. "Cooking might be the biggest love of my life besides music."

"Not Mark?"

I pause, my head briefly blank. "And Mark," I manage. "Besides Mark. Of course. Besides music and Mark. I love Mark and music." I see excess batter flowing over the side of the iron and onto the counter. "Shit." I grab a kitchen towel.

Jee tears the sauced chicken into pieces and pops them into their mouth one by one. "You know, I always thought Emmett Aoki was gay. He's too damn pretty to be straight," they say, chewing.

"He's not gay."

"Bitch, please. That wife of his, the reality star? The opposite of real, honey. Fake as a sack of Swarovskis."

"Ex-wife."

"Wait, are you sure?"

"Yes," I say, bending down to the floor to clean up some of the batter, which has somehow ended up there. "Positive."

"Oh. You're right. I remember now. Damn, they weren't married long. Is he dating someone new?"

"No. I don't know. I don't care. Why should I care?"

Gerome continues to eat in silence. Then, "Is something burning?"

I sniff the air and look up. A tiny tendril of black smoke unwinds from the waffle iron. I run to it and pull it open, hoping some of it will be salvageable. "Goddammit." My waffles are a goner. I slam the iron shut.

"Here," they say, pushing their plate toward me. "Have some."

"No, it's okay." I reach for a bag of tortilla chips next to the kitchen sink, grab a fistful, and lean against the counter, munching sullenly.

Jee watches me as I try to quell my hangriness. "So, you're really going to do this? Ask a movie star to sing for a high school choir concert?"

I swallow and cough. Bits of chips irritate my throat. "I guess."

"How are you going to get in touch?"

"No clue."

"Will he even remember you? It's been a long time since high school. At least for you, old man."

I sit down on our cracked pleather couch in the living room. My reflection in the flat-screen television stares back at me from the gaping blackness. My hair is tufted and wild, and my eyes are as puffy as my cheeks. Why didn't anyone tell me I looked like shit? I've been stagnating in every part of my life. My career, my music, my relationship. It's only natural that my body would fall into the same rut. What's in motion tends to stay in motion, and what's at rest stays lazy and bloated.

I think about Emmett's interview on the TV screen back at Broadway Baby. In the years since I've seen him, he's added bulk to his lean frame. Gotten bigger, more muscular. A decade of constant preparation for blockbusters has sculpted him into a high-speed chasing, fistfighting action god. Age has only had beneficial effects on his face, his only wrinkles the fine lines that crinkle in the corner of his eyes when he smiles for the camera. His smile is the same as I've always remembered. Unchanged. Imperfectly perfect.

"It *has* been a long time. I haven't talked to Emmett in almost twenty years."

Jee pats their tiny belly. They belch. "Oh Lord, excuse moi." The fogged-over look of satiation sits happily on their makeup-free face. "Even if you do manage to get in touch with him, how are you going to convince him to do it?"

The truth is, I don't think I *am* going to be able to convince Emmett. Not because, as I told Ujima, we were only acquaintances in high school. There's a reason we haven't spoken in almost two decades. And I don't want Jee, or anyone else, to know about it. In fact, the more I think about it, the less I want to go through with the whole thing. Why dredge up the past?

I get up to pour myself a stiff glass of iced tea to clear my throat. "Doesn't matter. It's not going to happen. On that TV interview, he said he's leaving town Sunday night. After he hosts *Saturday Night Live.*"

Jee perks up. "He's hosting *SNL* tomorrow night?"

"Yes. Why?"

"I know exactly how you are going to get a little face-to-face time with your choir buddy."

Chapter 9—Then

WE STOOD AT my doorway facing each other awkwardly for a few moments until Emmett held up a gift bag.

"My mom told me to bring this."

"What is it?"

He opened the bag, letting me peer inside. A green bottle of some kind of liquid and something else wrapped in tissue paper.

"Sake," he explained. "Rice liquor. We brought it home from our last trip to Kyoto to visit my grandparents. My mom saved it for a special occasion. And there's a glass to go with it. Normally, you're supposed to use a tiny one, but we didn't bring any home from Japan, and my mom didn't think a shot glass would be right. It's just a regular-size glass. But we got it from Macy's. So it's fancy."

"Uh, cool." I motioned for him to enter.

He thrust his free hand deep into the pocket of his trousers and followed me into the living room. His blue Oxford shirt was buttoned up to the top, and his usual pompadour had been slicked back. He smelled more of himself than usual—that mix of cologne with his own natural scent, one I've learned doesn't come from his jacket or clothes but somehow emanates from his body, earthen and outdoorsy like a tree that's absorbed hours of sun and is radiating it out again. A scent that doesn't even remotely smell like mine.

I grabbed his collar and flipped it up. "What, no tie?"

"Quit it," he said, turning red. "Dinner at a teacher's house. I don't know. I have to be on my best behavior and everything. Make a good impression."

"It's just my dad. And me."

Emmett opened his mouth but then shut it again quickly, looking like he was swallowing some sort of response.

I decided not to give him another chance to say anything. "This way."

Even though our house wasn't big, he stayed close behind me, as if he might get lost. I'd grown accustomed to the way constant proximity to him felt—a live wire–like energy that used to paralyze me. We'd had several weeks of coaching sessions together by then, and in the beginning, hours would go by after our time together without me ever successfully shaking off the sensation, like a permanent second skin on top of my own.

We walked through the living room, past the brown corduroy couches, the matching walnut end tables, and the entertainment center straining to contain our monstrous television and stereo system with its many cassette decks and speakers.

Emmett paused. The array of framed pictures on our upright piano had caught his eye. Photos of all the stages of my life sat there: me as a baby, a toddler, a teen. And in the middle, a black-and-white picture of a woman sitting on concrete steps, exotic foliage standing at attention in the back. In the portrait, she is young, her hair short, her cotton dress simple and suffused with tropical light. The words "Your Nightingale" are scribbled on the bottom corner of the picture in swooping, dramatic cursive.

"Is that your mom?" Emmett asked.

I stopped for a second. Then I nodded and kept walking to the kitchen, silently willing him to keep following me.

He didn't move. I felt the invisible line between us stretch and detach.

I turned back around and watched as he scanned the surface of the piano, the living room walls, the other tables in the room. "You don't have any other pictures of her."

A familiar ache inside me rose. A sensation I'd thought would lessen over time but always proved me wrong when it resurfaced, just as heavy as before.

"My dad says it's the only one she ever liked of herself, so it's the only one we keep out. She used to be really harsh on herself. Looks-wise, at least."

"Why? She's beautiful. She kind of reminds me of you."

So much sadness was rising in me that Emmett's comment didn't register at first.

"Ah, Emmett." My dad emerged from the kitchen. He wiped his hands with an old kitchen towel.

Emmett presented the gift bag to him with outstretched arms, his body bending slightly at the waist. How he was able to make this look graceful and not at all weird was yet another example of how complete the control of his body was as it moved. "A gift from my mother." My dad eyed it with skepticism. "It's sake. A Japanese liquor," Emmett said. "Made out of rice."

He lit up. "Well, if it's made of rice, then it must be delicious!" He took the bottle and rolled it over in his hands. He inspected the label closely, as if that would somehow render the Japanese comprehensible. He eventually shook his head. "Please tell your mom I said thank you. I'll put this in the refrigerator for now.

Dinner will be ready in about ten minutes. Just spend time together for a while, and I'll call for you. Okay?"

"Cool. Thanks, Mr. Cruz," Emmett said. "Hey." He bumped into me lightly. "Want to show me your room?"

"Uhhhh..." My heartbeat quickened. "No, my room is messy. Which is stressy," I blurted out, which was bizarre and not even remotely true. I'd spent an hour earlier in the day tidying it up, making sure it looked presentable and didn't smell of dirty socks and pork rinds. The real reason I panicked was because the prospect of us actually being alone in my room together gave me a horrifying shiver up and down, like the feeling I'd always get right at the crest of a roller coaster's first drop.

"Why don't I show you more pictures of my mom? Here," I said, walking to the bookshelf next to the couch, "we have a crap-load of photo albums."

His smile diminished. "Cool."

I pulled down one of the albums, green and bulky with too many pictures. I sat on the couch. Emmett plunked down right next to me. The air whooshed out of the couch cushions and my lungs, and breathing became arduous and non-automatic. I tried not to think about his thigh, muscular and surprisingly hot, pressing against mine. My fingers quivered as I opened the album.

The corrugated cardboard pages were covered with cellophane-like plastic sheets, which made them stick together. I peeled two sheets apart, and images of past lives unfolded: my parents dressed in white linen, my mother's hair hidden by a turban-like headpiece; in another picture, my mother stood in front of our house, belly protruding; in another, my father was seated at our brand-new piano, bouncing an infant me on his lap; and then one of me, a toddler, watching my mother by the piano as she clasped her hands to her heart, mouth open wide.

"Did she used to sing?" Emmett asked.

"She didn't just sing," I said quietly. "She was a singer."

"What's the difference?"

I traced the outline of her face carefully with my fingertips, as if I might be able to feel real flesh if I did it correctly. "Anyone can sing. But not everyone can be a singer."

"You're lucky. Your mom and dad raised you with music."

"Not lucky." I frowned and pulled my hand away from the picture. "Not lucky at all."

"Did something bad happen to her?" Emmett asked.

I said nothing. I hated when people asked about my mother. Hated having to tell the story. Because recounting it made it more real in my head, when instead I wanted it to stay a distant memory. To become more indistinct and fuzzy over time.

"I'm sorry," he said. "You don't need to tell me if you don't want to."

I touched my mother's face again. She deserved to be talked about. And I wanted to share the last memories I had of her with Emmett. Even if it was hard.

"It happened right after middle school. The summer before our freshman year at Sunvalley, I'd gotten this gig playing at the new Grayson Creek Mall. They'd hired all these kids around the district to play songs for a ceremony of the mall's opening. My mom had been encouraging me for weeks to perform more for other people besides just church and my piano recitals. So even though I knew she'd be tired all week from work and volunteering, I told her to come see me. This stupid mall concert. She said yes, of course. Especially since my dad was in Riverside that weekend at a choral workshop.

"I got a ride to the mall ahead of time with some of the other kids. When we were performing, I looked all over for her everywhere in the audience, but I couldn't find her. I thought maybe she'd decided to not come for some reason. After the ceremony was over, one of the other kids' parents came up to me with a cop. A drunk driver had hit my mom. On her way to come see me."

Emmett exhaled. "Shit."

"I was waiting for her to get out of surgery. My dad had to drive all the way home from Riverside. Which is really far. Too far. By the time he got to the hospital, the doctor was already done and waiting to speak to us. That's when she gave us the bad news that my mom didn't make it." Tears pooled in my eyes. I wiped them away with a quick swipe of my fingers. "You're the lucky one. You still have both your parents."

Emmett stayed quiet.

In the silence, I started flipping the photo album's pages. I forced them apart, one after another. My mother smiling at me, my mom laughing, my father holding her hand, my parents holding me in an embrace. At a party. At Christmas. At a park. Happy. Alive. The pages kept turning, the months and years passing by.

Emmett rested his hand on one of the pages before I got the chance to turn it. "Is this when Mr. C started teaching at Sunvalley?" In the picture, my dad stood with one hand on top of the choir room piano, his smile so infectious I instinctively mirrored it. His tie was crooked. His hair was still all black, his cheeks full and youthful. "He looks super young here."

"He was," I say. "He's been teaching at Sunvalley since I was in first grade."

"That's a long time. He's really good, you know? The best teacher I've ever had."

There were more photos to look at, but something about what Emmett had said—or rather, how he'd said it—told me to stay with that one for the moment.

"I'm really sorry to hear about what happened with your mom," he said. "But at least you still have your father. And he's totally awesome. Mine—he never talks, never smiles. Just wants everything to be perfect all the time. Stereotypical Asian dad. And my mom worships him. So if *he* wants me to get straight As, then that's what *she* wants me to do. And I do it. No discussion. I barely get to do anything *I* want to do. Just basketball and that one modeling gig for Macy's sophomore year. And choir." He suddenly smiled. "Well, maybe I *am* lucky. Because my mom has a soft spot for music. She managed to get my dad to allow me to join you guys. Without her, I'd never have been able to do *this*."

Emmett moved closer to me. Why did he emphasize *this*? And what exactly did *this* mean, anyway? Choir? Singing? Why did he look at me so intensely when he said it? Was I just imagining that? I felt myself get sucked into that limbo I always felt with him, where every action I could conceive of would lead down some road from which I was afraid I'd never be able to return.

"Boys," my father called out from the kitchen, "come in here now."

Emmett hopped up off the couch. "Let's go!" he said. I put the album back on its shelf, reminding myself to look at it more often.

We pushed the kitchen's French-style folding doors out of our way. The smell of seared meat filled our noses. I immediately recognized at least one dish, longganisa, a pork sausage we usually reserved for breakfast. My favorite brand was tinted red from paprika and beetroot and sweetened with pineapple juice. The familiar scent made my mouth water.

My father stood at the stove, lifting the lids of each of the pots and peering into them. On the counter next to him, a rice cooker stood ready. White steam billowed from the small hole on the top of the lid.

"Anak, ipasok mo sa loob." He handed me Emmett's sake and pursed his mouth, motioning toward the refrigerator. It was already stuffed full of food and drinks, plastic containers full of leftovers, and various bottles of sauces—A.1. steak sauce, soy sauce, oyster sauce, bagoóng, Jufran. I stuck the sake into the only free spot I could find, behind a large bottle of Sunny Delight.

Dad had put out party-style place settings. A spoon and fork (no knife) on a paper plate placed inside a wicker holder, each on top of their own tacky plastic place mats. Emmett tried to decide which seat to take.

"Here." I pulled out the chair at the head of the table, its seat covered with a worn fabric cushion tied to the chair's wooden slats.

"You sure? Wouldn't want to take someone else's spot."

My dad brought a saucepan to the table and set it on top of a pot holder. "You're the guest here, Emmett. That is your place tonight. Francisco, help me."

Emmett looked at me. "I thought your name was Quito."

"Francisco's my real first name. Quito's just the short version."

"How is Quito short for Francisco? I don't understand."

"Well, my cousin Tony is Boy, my cousin Soledad is Choleng,

and my other cousin, Roque Jr.'s nickname is Onyong. And Paquito is short for Francisco, which I shortened even more to Quito. I don't know—it makes sense to me."

"Yes, I agree. It's only common sense," my dad said and put an entire roll of paper towels on the table for us to use as napkins.

Emmett shrugged and waited for the food.

We set out three pots total, as well as the rice and a bottle of RC Cola. Dad lifted the lid off the first pot, revealing chicken adobo. I knew that its marinade of garlic, soy, and sugar cane vinegar would be tempered by the sweetness of my mother's secret ingredient, a hint of coconut milk. The second was full of the longganisa, the plump little sausages so juicy that all their casings had burst. The third was beef sinigang, which, from a quick glance at the empty seed pods on the kitchen counter, I could tell would get its characteristic sour tang from real tamarind instead of the common shortcut ingredient of lemon juice. I was surprised by the extra effort my dad had put into everything. Usually, I would have assisted him with food prep by chopping up the vegetables or at least cooking the rice, but this time he'd insisted on doing everything himself.

Emmett seemed overwhelmed by the choices.

"I hope you like meat," I said.

"Oops. I probably should have told you I was a vegetarian," Emmett said.

A look of horror washed over my dad.

Emmett struggled to keep a straight face before finally laughing out loud. "Just kidding."

"Don't ever joke to my dad about something like that," I said.

My dad's wide eyes shrank. "I think maybe we have some pickles I could give you."

I smiled to myself. Once, back in middle school, after learning about the US government's new food guidelines at school, I'd told my parents at dinner that we needed even more vegetables in our diet. My mom offered to make a tortang talong or pinakbet for dinner the following night. My dad responded by saying *too much trouble* and put a jar of dill pickles on the table.

"Seriously, do you guys always eat like this?" Emmett asked.

"These are some of Quito's favorite foods. I usually make them for his birthday, which is not until late December. But this counts as a special event."

Emmett whispered to me, "See, I told you this was a special occasion."

"Okay, a prayer first. Then we dig in." My father lowered his head and reached out for our hands.

I automatically did the same, with one eye slightly open.

I snuck a glance at Emmett. He looked flustered. It was apparent he'd never said grace before. I held his hand as neutrally as possible because I wanted to make sure no extra communication was being transmitted with my grasp, that it was firm enough to convey confidence but didn't have too much affection-filled grip.

My dad started with his usual grace. Then added more to it. The prayer went on forever. He mentioned me. The choir. Emmett. Emmett's family. The bottle of sake. The food on the table. The food in the fridge. Even the band teacher, Mr. Drummond (*Please, God, give him the wisdom to see how unreasonable he is*), and almost everything else my dad could think of. My hand in Emmett's was getting warmer and warmer. I began to mouth my own prayer. That my hand wouldn't be completely drenched in sweat before Dad's prayer was over.

When my father finally finished, I squeezed both his and Emmett's hands, a conditioned response to the end of grace, and then immediately pulled away. Emmett flashed a quick grin at me. I smiled back and wanted to deflect with something witty.

"Kain na!" my dad yelled out, inviting us to dig in, before I could say anything.

My father patted his bulging belly and belched.

"Good one, Mr. C," Emmett said.

"Dad!"

"What? I'm not allowed to release gas in my own house?"

"Oh my god." I covered my face with my hands while they snickered. "Okay, time to clean up." I started clearing the dishes.

"Just leave it, anak," my dad said while nonchalantly undoing the top button of his jeans. "I'll take care of it."

"Are you sure?"

"Yeah, Mr. C. Let us help," Emmett added. "It's the least I can do in return for dinner."

"It's okay," my dad responded. He started taking the paper plates out of their holders and throwing them into the trash can. "Go figure out what you're going to do for the holiday concert."

Emmett and I looked at each other.

"What do you mean?" I asked. "Emmett's solo? We got that down weeks ago."

"Not that. I want you to do something together. A voice and piano piece."

Emmett looked as if all the food he'd just eaten might come back up again. "Uh, Mr. C, there're a lot of great singers in the choir. Like Ken. How about giving him a chance?" He was being sincerely generous. I'd gotten to know him well enough to know. But I also knew he was anxious. An eight-bar solo in a choral piece was one thing. Doing an entire song all by himself was another.

My dad rummaged through the cabinets for plastic containers to put the leftovers in. "They'll all get their chances in due course. You're both seniors. This is your time to do something special."

"What, like a Christmas carol?" I asked.

"It doesn't have to be holiday themed," he said, scooping the food into the containers. "Choose a song that means something to the both of you."

Emmett's face wilted. "But I don't—"

"Come on," I said, heading out of the kitchen. Knowing my father wouldn't take no for an answer, I decided to spare Emmett the effort of trying to get out of the assignment. "We'll figure something out."

My dad nudged Emmett out of the kitchen. "Go. Enjoy this wonderful gift I'm giving you," he said, holding a dirty pot. "And when you're done, I'll have some leftovers for you to take home."

"Thanks, Mr. C." Emmett caught up to me and whispered as we left the kitchen, "Do we really have to do this?"

"Look, if there's anything you need to know about my dad, it's that, when he gets something in his head, he won't let it go. I didn't want to be the choir accompanist, but he wouldn't take no for an answer."

"You didn't want to accompany the choir?"

"It's not that. I just felt kind of weird about being the pianist for my own dad's class. I thought it'd be awkward, but it turned out fine. Just like he said it would." I sat down at the piano, lifted the keyboard cover, and slowly slid it back, revealing the polished keys. "Actually, I enjoy accompanying. A lot. More than playing solo piano."

Emmett's body sagged. He leaned against the top of the upright piano. "Don't you get more attention when you're a soloist?"

"I'm not into music for the attention. I don't really care if anyone sees me. I'm more interested in the way I feel when I play. When I play a solo, it's nice. But when I accompany someone, it's way more than that. I hear them sing, and we become, like, one instrument. We're able to make something together that we couldn't have on our own."

Emmett just kept looking down, his eyes floating and slightly lost, as if he were listening to an incomprehensible conversation going on in his head. He knocked the piano's body with his knee by mistake, which caused the strings inside to vibrate softly. I felt the hum of them through the keys into the tips of my fingers, which I had rested there by instinct. I let the feeling of it resonate through me.

"The song you did at the talent show," he said.

"That's one of the only times I've ever done a vocal piece by myself. It was a mistake."

He shook his head. "No, I mean—well, first of all, it wasn't a mistake. Second, maybe we can do it for the holiday concert."

"You want to sing my song."

"Yeah."

"Emmett, I got called a fag for that song."

"By an idiot who thinks that, when a girl says her Aunt Flo is visiting, it's actually her aunt," he said. "Besides, it'll sound buttloads better when I sing it."

"You're a dick."

"Well, if we're talking percentage-wise, that *is* my biggest body part, so..."

"Gross." I tried to not give in to his jokes, but it was impossible. Even crass, Emmett had a way of charming me into forgiving him for it. Or maybe I forgave him more readily now. More than I did when I first met him because I knew him better. "I don't know. The lyrics are—"

"Perfect. They describe how I feel all the time."

A bundle of nerves right behind my belly button began to twitch. Was he trying to tell me that he was...like me?

"My dad is always expecting me to be perfect. To be the best at everything. And it's, like, I'm tired of always having to live up to that. You know?"

"Oh." My nerves flattened back out. "I see."

"Just play some of it for me."

I hesitated. Even just thinking about the song dredged up unpleasant memories from that night.

"Please?" His long lashes blinked slowly. Was he trying to be charming? Or flirtatious?

Whatever he was doing, it was working.

"Okay."

I reached inside and accessed the song, letting it out through my fingers. Slowly, at first. As if I were allowing each note to wipe away the bad thoughts associated with it. Intro gave way to verse. Then another verse. It was coming back to me. Not just the music, which was always just a breath away, but the faith I'd had in it. The pride. And the memories tied to my mother, not the disastrous talent show.

Still, something was holding me back.

"Why aren't you singing?" Emmett said, as if reading my mind.

I stopped. "I . . . I don't know."

"Start over. Don't just play it. Sing it to me."

The demand made me feel dangerously close to being naked. The piano was the only thing protecting me. If I sang the words, too, I'd reveal too much of myself. Again.

He must have sensed the fear in me. He sat down next to me on the piano bench. Like earlier on the couch, his presence was almost unbearable. Too many sensations careened through me.

Just as I started to become too lost to do anything, he pressed his body into me. Gently. Instead of ramping up the sensory overload, the physical contact with him somehow grounded me.

"What are the words?" he said. "I'll sing them."

I heard a click inside as something in me unlocked. That gesture of wanting to take on my story and make it his own somehow felt right.

I opened a folder of music on top of the piano, where I'd put the sheet music for my song. "A Part I Play" stared back at us in my scratchy script. "I know you can't sight-read. But the words are here."

"I think I remember the tune well enough," Emmett said. "Let me try it."

I began the song again, bringing the melody out to guide him.

I get into place
Put a smile on my face
They're all waiting for me to begin
To get to this night

I've practiced all of my life
To change who I am to fit in

He didn't need my help. Whether Emmett remembered the melody from the one time he'd heard it at the talent show or was able to feel it instinctively, his singing of the first verse was uncanny. Like he'd already known it by heart. The second verse went even better than the first.

I'll do what they want
And try not to flaunt
To be something I'm not supposed to be
Do it just so
So they'll never know
Deep inside I just want to be free

Emmett sang faster, almost on top of my playing. I accelerated. Not to try to match him, I realized, but because my heartbeat was quickening, pumping the blood to my fingers.

When we got to the refrain, I felt everything slide into place, the two of us matching each other's tempo and phrasing. Even our bodies seemed to be moving at the same time.

They tell me the show must go on
So I'll try to be strong
And I'll say what they want me to say
But the person they'll see
Won't really be me
It's only a part I play

By the end, we were nearly out of breath. Neither of us said anything. We just sat there, the last page of sheet music looking at us. All I wanted was to stay wrapped up in that moment, locked in my link to him.

"Ahem."

Both of our bodies jerked. We stood up from the piano bench on opposite sides. My dad was standing in the frame of the kitchen door, drying a plate with a worn dishrag. He regarded us with that inscrutable look of his. "I see you've picked your piece."

"It was my choice, Mr. C," Emmett said quickly. "I wanted to do Quito's song."

My dad kept wiping the plate and looking at us.

"What do you think?" Emmett asked.

My dad focused on me. I was certain he'd say no. The song was so tied to me and my mother—and him—I was sure it was disapproval that obscured his eyes.

"What do your ears tell you?" he asked.

"That we need to work on it some more," Emmett said.

"That we shouldn't do it at all," I said.

"No. That's not what I meant." My father finally stopped wiping the plate. "Yes. You will need to practice it, of course. Then listen to what you are making together. Really listen. If what you hear sounds good—if it sounds *right*—then you have my approval." His eyebrows lifted slightly, implying something I didn't quite understand.

He turned around and walked back into the kitchen, resuming his wiping of the dish, which must have already been beyond dry.

Emmett punched me in the shoulder. "Dude. We are so doing your song."

"You're not anxious to be doing a big solo? To be doing...this?"

"Not if I'm doing it with you." He stroked the sheet music. Tiny pins pricked up my body, as if he were touching me instead.

A horn honked from the street. Emmett's mother was here.

"Hey." He tapped his fingers on the music. "You don't actually need this anymore, right? You've got the song memorized?"

"Yeah. You can take this and use it to practice with." I pulled the music out from under his hand, straightened the pages on the piano with a quick tap, and handed them over to him.

My dad came out of the kitchen and gave Emmett a brown paper bag stuffed with plastic containers of leftover food.

"Thanks, Mr. C."

"If you want more, just let Quito know, okay? We'll bring you some at school."

We walked outside. On the street, his mother was in the driver's seat of a gray BMW, while a girl sat in the back seat, roughly college-aged. She looked, like Emmett, to be a mix of his Japanese father and white mother—her hair shiny, black, and unmistakably Asian and her eyes and nose more like Emmett's mother's, perky and patrician. Emmett had never mentioned having a sister before.

He saw me watching them and tensed. "Tell your dad thanks for the food. And thank you again for the sheet music. I mean, yeah, I'll practice with it. But I'm also thinking, if I framed it, it could be a great present. For a special birthday coming up." He waved at the idling car. Two slender arms waved back in almost the same exact manner. He turned back, patted me on the shoulder, and winked. "One day, when you're famous, it'll be super valuable and worth a lot of money."

Planning ahead for my birthday? Making something special out of something I'd written, something we'd soon be working on together? It was so thoughtful I wanted to hug him. Which of course I didn't.

Instead I said, "Enjoy, my boy." Then I hung my head in embarrassment.

Emmett bared his crooked-toothed grin and got into the car. "You won't regret it, dude!" he shouted from the open window.

But later on, I did.

Chapter 10 — Now

A LONG QUEUE snakes down the block at 30 Rockefeller Center.

"Lines." Ujima groans. "Why can't we just do it like it's Black Friday at Walmart and rush it? Survival of the fittest."

"Whatever, Mx. Pilates," I say, giving Jee a sideways glance. "Not everyone has your physique." Their body looks stunning in a close-fitting cheetah-print dress and bedazzled sandals. A silk scrunchie holds up their wig into a ponytail.

Jee taps an older woman on the shoulder. "Excuse me. What is this line for?"

"Oh!" The woman, sporting high-waisted denim and a fanny pack, is momentarily speechless. It's obvious she's never met someone like Ujima before. "*Saturday Night Live*. Just waiting to go through security. Emmett Aoki's the host. He's very handsome, don't you agree?"

Ujima pulls her aside. "Girl, he is to die for. And get this, he just so happens to be the high school buddy of my good friend—"

"Thank you, ma'am. Hope you enjoy the show." I pull Ujima away. "Let's not cause a scene."

"Fine. I won't. Unless someone offers to pay me for it." They pop open a red fan with SHADE written across it and begin fanning themself, despite the fact that it's ten o'clock at night and still February.

I follow Jee inside to the lobby of 30 Rock, toward a beefy Middle Eastern man. His uniform says SECURITY in bright yellow. When he sees Ujima approach, his face becomes almost as bright as the letters. Jee notices this, of course, and takes their hair out of the scrunchie, letting the long, magenta curls wave behind them like a waterfall.

Security Guy smiles. "How can I help you?"

"Are you the man in charge here?" Their voice, already normally low, takes on a ragged huskiness. "Why am I even asking? Of *course* you are. Anyone can see *you're* the person I need to get to know better..." Ujima bends toward Security Guy's chest to read his name tag. "Tariq."

He stands up straighter and sticks his thumbs into his belt loops. "Yes. That would be me. Tariq. Miss...? What can I call you?"

They offer a hand to him. I get a little nervous waiting to see what the man's reaction will be to Ujima's hand, broad and thick, maybe the only thing about them that doesn't quite pass in drag. "You can call me Ujima. Miss Jenkins if you're nasty," they coo.

Tariq looks down and blinks. He grabs hold of their hand. I relax when he kisses it. An almost imperceptible look of apprehension on Ujima's face extinguishes once his lips make contact with their skin.

"What can I do for you, then—*Miss Jenkins?*" Tariq says, with so much loaded innuendo that his beard hairs engorge.

Jee bats a row of fake eyelashes. "Bradley Rose is expecting us. To take us to the VIP section."

"I'll call him." Tariq pulls out a small two-way radio from his vest. "You just stand there and keep looking beautiful."

I notice that people at the front of the line waiting to get into the lobby are watching us as if we were the warm-up act. "How do you know this Bradley guy again?" I ask Ujima.

"From Escándalo. He comes every Sunday night to see my act."

"And you're sure he'll be able to get us in?"

"Honey, he's one of my biggest fans. After I perform, he always *conveniently* runs into me in the bathroom and tries to get some alone time with me in one of the stalls. That pervert," they sneer, though I can tell they're impressed by his depraved tenacity. "Anyway, he'll do us good. He's *SNL's* audience wrangler. One of the many little things he keeps trying to impress me with."

I don't want to know the other little things he tries to impress Jee with.

One of the elevators opens onto the lobby floor with a ding. A cute, slightly pudgy frenzy of strawberry-blond hair pops out of it, frantically clutching a clipboard and sipping coffee. He looks like what would happen if Prince Henry and Elmo had a very gay, very hyper child.

Tariq waves me over to the elevator. "He will take you to Studio 8H." He kisses Ujima's hand one last time. "It was a pleasure, Miss Jenkins."

"You rascal." They pull their hand away playfully and then pat him on the chest before we walk away from him. I think I hear him moan as we leave.

"Hi! Hi! Follow me." Bradley ushers us into the elevator. "So glad you were able to make it, Ujima. So beautiful. As always." He looks Ujima up and down. His body holds an incredible amount of tension, as if he's having a hard time restraining himself from doing something. Like touching Jee. Or howling at the moon. "Wow. Wow. What a dress." He pivots to me. "And you're Quito. Interesting outfit. Very simple. 'Cazh Friday' for a Special Saturday."

I thought I was dressed up. I'm wearing my favorite cardigan and a classic white button-up shirt. I have on jeans, but at least I'm wearing nice brown Oxfords. Maybe too brown. Are they the color of crap? Am I wearing poop-brown shoes?

"Stop worrying," Ujima says, stroking the back of my neck. "You look fine."

"Yes. Agreed. You do. The look suits you," Bradley rapid-fires, not making it clear if what he's saying is actually a compliment.

The elevator opens up to the main hallway leading to the studio. Walking down it, we glance at the walls lined with photos of *SNL*'s best sketches before entering Studio 8H through the main doors.

Bradley shows us our seats. In the VIP section. The very first row.

"Here we are. And don't worry, Quito," Bradley says. "From where you'll be sitting, no one will be able to see your outfit. They'll only see the back of your head. All five million of our viewers." More audience members start filing in. "Got to go." He spins around and looks over his shoulder. "I'll text you the after-party address. See you both there. Ta-ta!"

Ujima immediately befriends the people sitting next to us, a ridiculously attractive hipster couple, all tattoos and piercings and mismatched thrift store clothing that somehow look like they spent a fortune. I sink into my chair and wish our seats were anywhere but where Bradley put us.

As the NBC pages seat more people, the atmosphere in the studio begins to ramp up. Expectancy whirls around us, especially when the band starts to play. It's hard not to get caught up in the moment. I start to relax a bit. After a few songs, longtime cast member Kenan Thompson comes out to give the audience instructions, peppered with a few jokes. They're tepid at best, but I laugh nervously at almost everything he says.

"Oh. I like this one," he says, pointing a finger at me. "And my, my. I like your friend, too." Kenan rubs his hands together and makes a cartoon awooga face at Ujima, who smiles regally. Jee is, as always, a cool goddess, while I am a tittering, poorly dressed loser.

After Kenan is done, the cast gets into places for the cold open—the sketch that starts the show. This one takes place in the White House. Mostly unfunny, it plods by without a single appearance by Emmett.

I begin to worry. Did we come on the wrong night? Is he not tonight's host? No. Midwestern Mom Jeans confirmed he was. Was he replaced at the last minute? I ping-pong internally, not knowing whether I want him to actually show up, when everyone onstage starts chanting the intro, "Live from New York, it's Saturday NIGHT!!"

And boom. The set bursts like a dam.

Stagehands in black shirts come running out of every corner. They shift the set, tucking the Oval Office away and replacing it with something else. Props and sets go flying while the band plays its familiar *SNL* theme music and the announcer lists off the names of the cast members and musical act, some new band I've never heard of (although I never seem to recognize any of the musical acts these days).

"Ladies and gentlemen, your host. Emmett AOkiiiiiiii!"

The upstage door swings open.

Emmett appears.

He jogs downstage toward the audience, looking more relaxed in a fully tailored suit than most people do in sweats. His shirt is unbuttoned to almost midway down his torso, which reveals the edges of his pectorals, and the fit of his pants is surprisingly revealing. Everyone can easily see what God gave him. Ujima clutches my hand and says "mm-mm-mm" into my ear, confirming that I'm not the only one impressed.

He looks up toward the audience in the upper level, plants himself in the center, legs spread, back arched, arms stretched out, and takes everything in like the petals of an unfolding flower drinking in the sun.

I'm within inches of him again, for the first time in years. It's surreal. As if reaching out and touching him will make the illusion shimmer, waving outward in concentric circles like the dropping of a pebble on water.

I completely forgot what it feels like to be near him.

"Thank you. It's so great to be here! I've always wanted to host *Saturday Night Live*, and here I am tonight, living—" He stops midsentence.

He's looking straight at me.

He swallows audibly and continues. "—my best life."

He doesn't say anything else.

Emmett is frozen in place.

I feel the entire studio tense. Some of the musicians behind him look at each other. Emmett just keeps staring at me, unable to speak.

I don't know what to do. Should I smile and wave? Say

something? Encourage him to continue? Pretend he hasn't seen me? Run out the side entrance?

Mercifully, Kenan comes out from one of the wings. "That's what you get for being in all those Michael Bay movies, man. All those explosions did a number on the old noggin." He raps Emmett on the skull. The audience lets out a cathartic laugh.

Emmett's gaze snaps away from me. He looks out and smiles broadly. "Yeah, but now I'm so good at jumping from burning buildings and running away from dinosaurs. Basic skills that everyone should have."

He goes on to casually mention his new TV show, his upcoming movie, and the fact that he's the first Japanese American to ever host *Saturday Night Live*, all of which is met with enthusiastic applause.

I think.

I'm only marginally aware of what he's saying. Mainly, I try not to go into cardiac arrest over the fact that my mere presence has almost derailed the live taping of a show on national TV.

"We've got a great show for you tonight," Emmett says. "WonderBelly is here! Stick around. We'll be right back!"

The main camera operator waves them out, and Emmett walks toward me, mouth open, but is yanked away at the last second by a stagehand who literally drags him off the set as two others start undressing him. Others move set pieces into place for the first sketch. In less than five seconds, he is gone. Whisked off to wherever he needs to be.

Ujima turns in their seat to face me. "What are you not telling me?"

"Sorry?"

"I might not know a lot of things, but I know men. I can read them like a community theater playbill. And that man—that *demigod* of a human being—was destroyed after one look at you." Jee turns my face toward them. "Just choir buddies, my flawless black ass. What went down between you two?"

"Nothing."

"Quito."

"Nothing."

"Francisco Calimag Cruz. Tell me the truth."

I sigh. "We were friends. At one point. And..."

"And what?"

The band leader waves his hand and cuts off the music. The stage area to the left of center has been transformed into a house in the suburbs. Emmett, along with a few other cast members, walks on.

"I'll tell you later," I whisper.

"Yes," Ujima whispers back. "You will."

We watch Emmett play a salesman. He holds knockoff Tupperware parties and makes a fortune selling the products—which are clearly inferior—only because all the women (and some of the men) just want to have sex with him. He plays it as if he's unaware that everyone is attracted to him. It's the only funny thing about the sketch. That and the way Kenan keeps breaking character when the plastic containers make fart-like noises when Emmett opens and closes them.

Afterward, they do Celebrity Jeopardy! with Emmett as Kim Jong-un. His impression is...not great. The same goes for the sketch after that. A reality dating show spoof. Everything he's doing seems a little detached. The audience laughs generously, but I can sense things are falling flat.

The more I watch, the more I begin to see that I'm responsible for his mediocre performance. He's disturbed that I'm here.

More than disturbed.

Angry.

WonderBelly, a retro-punk band that steals all the wrong things from the eighties, plays a midshow song. During the commercial break, as the stagehands put things into place for whatever follows, I find myself floating out of my seat and leaving the audience area.

"Hey!" Ujima hisses. "Where are you going?"

I don't answer. I don't know where I'm going. I only know that I need to get out of there. That I don't want to be there when Emmett returns to the stage.

I wander into the outer hallway. The faces of past cast members and guests stare at me from framed photographs, laughing.

Bradley comes running after me. "Quito!" He jogs beside me, clipboard still in hand. "Bathroom break?"

I keep walking, staring straight ahead. "Yep."

"Okay. Follow me." Bradley rushes on ahead. "But hurry. Commercial's almost over. Weekend Update next!"

"Wouldn't want to miss that."

He shows me to a unisex bathroom off to the side of the main corridor. "I'll wait. Take you back when you're done." He looks nervously at his watch. "Two minutes to do your business. Hope it's not too *in-depth?*" His left hand mimes air quotes.

I shut the door in his face and lock it.

I stare at myself in the mirror. In the bright light, the face looking back at me glares in high definition. My eyes are tinged with red. My pores seem larger than usual. My lips are dry.

This was a mistake. This whole thing was a mistake. I don't want to let my dad down, but I should've just let things lie. Not poke at the past. I don't have it in me to face Emmett. To tell him that I'm sorry. Certainly not now, when I'm being watched by the entire country.

I lean my back against the wall. Then I slowly slink down and end up on the tile floor. The ceramic feels cold against the seat of my pants. I pull my knees in and hold my legs close.

Bradley knocks on the door. "Finishing up?"

I don't respond. I'm seriously considering just curling up into a fetal position on the floor of the bathroom. It doesn't seem that dirty. It's miraculously clean for a semi-public restroom. So I tip my body over and let gravity pull me down. The floor is freezing. Strangely, that's all right with me.

"Quito? Look, are you ...? Is everything okay in there?"

Through the crack underneath the door, I can hear Bradley's feet nervously tapping. Finally, his footsteps recede into the distance. Good. Now I can lie in peace, inhaling the strangely comforting scent of bleach and antibacterial spray.

The footsteps return. More knocking on the door. Less urgent this time, though. I decide to just tell him I'm having stomach problems and won't be able to catch the rest of the show due to leaky bowels or something equally disgusting. Years ago, I learned that the more explicit you can get with excuses, the more likely it is that someone will believe that you're sick. That little trick I got from listening to all the messages other kids would leave on my dad's office voicemail. *My snot is yellow! I'm having a heavy flow day! Ear wax isn't supposed to be green, right?* I push myself off the floor and unlock the door. "Geez, I'm sorry," I say. "I think I might have soiled my pants."

The door opens. Emmett's face stares back at me, changing from concern to amusement. "Well, hello to you, too."

"Shit."

"In your pants, apparently." He holds the door firmly, quashing my best efforts to close it.

The coldness from the floor evaporates in a flash. "Ha. Ha. You're a funny bunny."

"Is it safe to come in?"

I strongly consider bolting out of the bathroom and back into the studio, but instead say, "Sure. Step into my office."

"Nice place you got," he says, looking around. Then, squarely at me, "I'm surprised you're here."

"I needed to use the bathroom." The more he looks at me, the more true that is. I'm certain he's about to lay into me, tell me all the things he's been holding back all these years, and my bladder isn't reacting kindly to the eventuality.

"No, I mean, *here* here. At *SNL*. I wouldn't have thought...I didn't know you liked the show," he says, not as upset as I thought he'd be.

I run my fingers nervously through my hair but regret it instantly as I encounter hardened gel. I continue to push through the crystallized mass, feeling everything fall apart with a crunch. "Sure. I watch it all the time. I've always wanted to see it live."

"And you just happen to be at this one."

"I know, right? Wow. What a coincidence."

"I saw you from the wings, leaving the audience. I thought you might have left."

Emmett smiles that crooked-toothed smile. I'd always assumed that, when he hit the big time, he'd get it fixed. But it's survived.

A welcome holdout from an earlier time. Back when *my* Emmett Aoki hadn't yet become the world's Emmett Aoki. A time when I couldn't help but think about that tooth every day. How it was one of the things I loved the most about him.

"My agent keeps harping on me to fix this," Emmett says, pointing to the tooth.

"What? I wasn't—"

"Quito, you were staring."

"Nope. Wrong." I feel the urge to close the door again. The coolness of the bathroom floor beckons.

But it also finally feels like Emmett is actually here. Real. Not a thousand miles away, untouchable. He's in front of me. Close. So close I could just reach out and—

"Mr. Aoki, we have to go!" Emmett is yanked back out of the bathroom by a stagehand. "Weekend Update is almost done, and you're up next after the break!" I watch as he's dragged, again, down the corridor.

"Meet me at the after-party. After the show," Emmett calls out before disappearing.

"Oh god. You're all right." Bradley comes back to the bathroom in a tizzy. "Emmett wandered out here. He said he knew you? Is that why you and Ujima wanted to come tonight?"

I straighten up, feeling more like myself again. "I knew him in high school. He used to be...a friend. A really good friend, in fact." It surprises me that I admit this to a complete stranger.

It surprises me even more that I feel good saying it.

Bradley motions with his head. "Come on, they're about to start again." He accompanies me back to the main stage in a hurry.

"Hey," I say as we run-walk. "Tell me more about this after-party."

I take a sip of my virgin mojito. It's smooth, sweet, and latently assertive—the lime tang kicks in at the end. Can a drink be passive-aggressive? If so, I'm in the right place for it. A prohibition-themed place in Chelsea called Speakeasy, this week's *SNL* after-party spot. I've passed by it a couple of times on my way to other places in the neighborhood without ever noticing it was there. That's the whole point of it, I guess. To be hidden from people who aren't in the know.

I kind of hate it here.

The seats are lined with expensive leather. Wrought-iron chandeliers force shadows onto the brick walls, and bartenders in bow ties and Vandyke beards mix cocktails behind the bar. Everything is haughty, aloof. As if we should all be glad we were even able to find the damn place.

A stick of a woman in a flapper dress stands by the door. She's in charge of the guest list and looks miserable, although she does sport her four-inch stilettos admirably. If I pointed the shoes out to Ujima, they might be impressed, but they're in a banquette on the other side of the room, trying to feign continued interest in Bradley. He's wound up way too far, his body jerking with each point of whatever it is he's talking about. (Himself, most likely, from the way Ujima mindlessly twirls a chunk of magenta hair.)

I've been roaming around, reliving my run-in with Emmett in the bathroom in my head, trying to process the fact that he wasn't upset to see me like I'd been dreading. He was thrown off by my appearance, yes, but only because he was surprised.

And . . . happy?

Maybe time does heal everything. There might actually be a

chance of me being able to get him to sing for the concert. And for us to have a relationship again.

A friendship, I mean.

After an hour of waiting, he still hasn't shown up. So I decide to make myself useful and rescue Jee from Bradley.

Several choices for an emergency excuse run through my head. Exploding toilet? Sick cat? (We don't actually have a cat, though we do have an aggressive pigeon who keeps shitting on our fire escape.)

So many little lies fill my head that I don't see Emmett step in front of me.

Virgin minty goodness splashes all over his chest, pushing the drink over into the more aggressive side of passive-aggressiveness. "Oh crap."

"No worries," Emmett says, unperturbed.

His shirt becomes transparent straight through to the hardened pecs. I grab cocktail napkins off a nearby table and furiously dab at his chest. It takes a long time. There's just so much to dry. He's so much more of a man than when we were kids. Broader and thicker in every direction. Then again, action stars don't get paid the big bucks for looking like the scrawny kid on the beach. Pleasant thoughts of sand and sun on his skin start to swim around in my head when it slowly dawns on me that I'm rubbing Emmett's right nipple in tiny little circles.

I grin and pat him one last time. "Yep. All dry now." I shove the damp napkin mound into my pocket. A wet chill hits my crotch.

"I can toss those for you." He reaches for my pants.

I push his hand away. "I'm good. Truly cooly."

He laughs. "You still do that."

"Do what?"

"Rhyme when you're nervous."

"I'm not nervous!" I say too loudly. "I'm not nervous," I whisper. I have absolutely no idea why I can't modulate my voice correctly. So I punch him in the shoulder.

He reels backward. "Ow. That hurt."

"Sorry! I—"

"Just messing with you."

He unbuttons his shirt, sticks his hand inside, and pulses it in and out, trying to breathe air into the damp fabric. Classic Emmett. Doing something that seems absentminded but is actually meant to focus attention on him. It takes everything I have not to stare at the tiny goose bumps rising to attention on the surface of his skin. Thank goodness for the cold shower in my pants.

"So, how have you been?" he asks me.

"Oh, you know. Busy doing the piano thing. Teaching lessons, playing for shows. I sub in on Broadway shows every now and then."

He nods as I talk, as if he somehow already knows all this. Is it because I'm babbling?

"And I play at a piano bar. Broadway Baby. Two times a week. Fridays. And Sundays. Fridays and Sundays. Is when I play piano," I say, babbling.

"Broadway Baby. In the West Village? What a coincidence. I was near there last night, taping my NY1 segment. I would've come to see you if I'd known you were playing."

"The West Village, yes. I'm on again tomorrow at three."

"Playing the show tunes. Just like old times."

"Just like old times," I repeat. The past comes flooding back. All those afternoons and evenings spent sitting at the piano together, playing and singing. It feels like we've been doing it for the past twenty years, uninterrupted, almost as if we'd never parted at all. I'm wary of holding his gaze for too long, so I look at something else to distract myself.

Unfortunately, that ends up being his bare chest. "I see you're keeping in shape."

Dammit. Thanks for nothing, cold crotch.

"It comes with the business." He takes his hand out of his shirt, rests it on my shoulder, and then massages it, casually, as if it were the most natural thing in the world to go from fondling himself to stroking me. "You look great, by the way."

Everyone else around us—the *SNL* cast members, the random VIPers, the band whose name I absolutely cannot remember—fall away, and I'm back someplace familiar, somewhere where we aren't complete strangers to each other, where he and I are connected by more than just high school choir.

His fingers massage harder. They dig into my shoulder, just skirting the edge of pain.

It feels incredible.

He lets go and slides his hand back into his shirt. "Hey, how's your dad doing?"

I inhale deeply, not realizing until then that I'd been holding my breath. "He's, uh, fine."

Emmett's given me a way to bring up the concert. But I hesitate. He's been in the movie business for so long, stopped singing years ago. That's not a part of him anymore. And I'm not sure he wants to bring it back. "Uh, how're *your* parents?"

He smiles sadly. "Not really talking to my dad at all. They finally got divorced about ten years ago. But my mom is doing well. She's getting remarried. Next month, actually."

"That's great! I mean, great for your mom. And you. For not talking to your dad. I mean—"

"I know what you mean, Quito. Don't sweat it." He laughs, flashing his smile. "It's great you're doing so many things. You must've composed a ton since I last saw you."

I don't respond to that. I don't want to tell him how wrong he is. "So . . . how come you haven't done a musical? Every actor seems to be doing one these days."

"A musical? I've thought about it. No one's ever pitched me anything I've been interested in."

"Waiting for the right project?"

"You could say that." Emmett raises an eyebrow. "Any suggestions?"

He hasn't changed. Still flirting his way through life. That's all it is, I know—just his hopelessly ingrained habit of flooding all lines of communication with his hormones. I have to keep reminding myself it's not a specific message to me.

I decide to use it to my advantage. It's becoming clear now that I don't have to bring up our disastrous last interaction in college. He's either forgotten all about it or forgiven me. Now is the time to bring up Dad's request. "I do have a suggestion, actually, something to get you singing again. My father—"

Ujima swoops in between us.

"Hello there," they say. Bradley is nowhere to be seen. I wonder how they managed to get rid of him. "I'm Quito's roommate and BFF. Ujima."

Emmett takes his hand back out of his shirt and shakes Ujima's. "I saw you in the front row next to Quito. You're a hard one to miss."

It's rare to witness Ujima speechless. After nothing comes out of Jee's hanging, half-formed mouth for a few seconds, I kick them in the calf. "OH," they shout, "thank you, dear. You're a hard one yourself. I mean a hard one *to miss* yourself."

I stifle a laugh.

"So," Jee says, giving me a quick look, "Quito tells me you two used to be quite close."

"We were," Emmett says. "We met in high school." He turns to me. "Speaking of which, you were about to say something about your dad?"

The question feels loaded with something I can't put my finger on. "He's retiring."

"Wow. Really? Time flies."

"He's putting on a farewell concert for his last year. A benefit. He wants me to play. And for you—"

"There you are." Bradley comes up to us holding drinks. "Thought you said you'd join me at the bar, Ujima."

Jee takes a drink and gives him an air kiss. "Bradley darling," they say, rolling their eyes at me behind his back.

"You friends with Emmett, too?" Bradley asks.

"Of course. I came over here to catch up with him. We go way back." Ujima gives Emmett a look that says *Go with it.*

"Eeexactly," Emmett says. "Old high school chums. In fact, Quito was just catching us up on his dad. Our old choir teacher."

"Choir?" Bradley says.

Before someone else can interrupt me, I say, "Yes, and what

I've been trying to tell Emmett is that my dad is retiring. He's putting on a benefit concert, and he wants me to play and Emmett to sing."

"I'm sorry," Emmett says. "What?"

Oh no. I was too concerned with being able to get a face-to-face with Emmett and what he might possibly do when he saw me that I haven't worked out an actual strategy to get him to say yes after I've asked him.

"It's a lot," I say. "I get it. You're too busy. Maybe we can pay you or something? No, we can't do that. Rename the auditorium after you? No, that won't work. Name the new copier after you?"

"Hold on a second," Emmett says, laughing. "When is it?"

"First week of June? With rehearsals in late May."

His eyes flicker, like he's scrolling through a mental calendar. "I might be able to make it work."

"Seriously?" I share an incredulous look with Ujima.

"Get the old dream team together again?" He laughs. "Yeah. Why not?"

"Fantastic! I'll tell my dad—"

"Wait." He snaps his fingers. "Late May? I think I have to be at the Cannes Film Festival." He checks the calendar on his phone. "Yeah, I do. I'm sorry. I forgot."

Ujima, clearly agitated by Bradley's presence, has already finished their drink. "Debuting a new movie?"

Emmett squirms. He scratches at his chest and fumbles with the buttons of his shirt. "Yes, but . . . not one of mine. I'm supposed to be there for Emma's new release."

Bradley gasps. "The gossip. It's true. You're dating Emma Chen."

"Who?" I ask.

"Emma. Chen," Bradley says, clearly annoyed. "*Road to Canberra*? Last year's Best Supporting Actress Oscar? Hello?"

A TV ad starts playing in my head. A young woman with a tennis player's body, her muscles taut, walks along a desolate dirt road somewhere in the Australian outback wearing hiking boots and carrying the remains of some dead relative in an urn. She glistens with exhaustion. Her pale skin and long black hair remind me of another girl. Someone from our past.

"You're dating her?" I ask.

"Yes. And no. We're not official. Yet," Emmett replies. "We were waiting to announce it until after we're seen at Cannes together." He doesn't look at me. "Look. My agent plans all my social activities. I mean, he picks all the important things I need to go to."

"Does he pick your girlfriends, too?" I mutter.

He gives me a smile that really isn't a smile at all. "Why are you here, Quito?"

"You invited me here."

"That's not what I mean. Why were you at *SNL* tonight?"

"My dad needs you."

"That's it? That's the only reason?" He shakes his head. "And after all this time, you thought it'd be that easy to ask me? When we haven't talked to each other for twenty years?"

So, he hasn't forgotten. He hasn't let things go.

"I know. I'm sorry we fell out of touch. I'm not sure why that happened."

"You know exactly why that happened."

The big band jazz music being played in the bar sounds as if it's been turned all the way up. The twenties roar into my ears. There are too many people here at the party. Too many conversations, too many people looking at us. Everything engulfs me.

"Excuse me." I walk toward the bar, seriously considering an alcoholic drink for the first time since college.

My phone buzzes. A text from my dad:

> Quito this is your dad. Kamusta ka? OK? Did you talk to Emmett yet? My god, the students and the parents and even the other teachers are all so excited. The concert is already sold out! I think we will have to add standing room only in the back of the auditorium. Text mo ako ha. Ingat! Love, Dad

Then I see that Mark has left me a series of texts. I didn't even notice my phone vibrating all night.

> 10:15 pm: How's your evening out with Gerome? (j/k) Ujima?

> 11:40 pm: Where did you guys go? When are you thinking of leaving? You still coming to my place after?

> 12:50 am: Excited for the musical with Dinesh. Just know you're going to write amazing stuff for it.

> 1:20 am: You must be having a good time. Going to bed now. Miss you.

I stare at my phone. The light of it blazes. A bartender finally acknowledges my existence and indicates he's ready to take my order.

I put the phone in my pocket, wade through the crowd of people, and exit into the predawn darkness.

Chapter 11—Then

I STOOD IN front of the mirror second-guessing my clothes for the third time (third-guessing them?) and wondered if it was too late to buy something new. Jeans and a short-sleeve polo shirt. The outfit I wore nearly every day. To school, to church, to the movies, to the comic book store. My closet was full of a variety of tasteful polo shirts to suit every occasion.

At that moment, for example, the one I was wearing had a thick stripe across the front, blending from sky blue to dark black. It made me seem more broadish in the chest area. There wasn't a lot of pec matter to accentuate, so every bit helped. It was a good shirt, in an optical illusion kind of way. Perfect for a simple get-together. Except Laney's Christmas party wasn't just a simple get-together.

Laney was a choir geek like me. But her older sister, Deborah, captain of the varsity cheerleading squad, was Rally Court royalty. Like Emmett. At their party, I'd be surrounded by people I didn't like being in the same school with, let alone the same house.

What kind of dressing up did they do? Or did they...dress *down*? I should've asked Emmett. Or better yet, I should never have said yes to his invitation in the first place.

I blamed it on the post-performance glow of the holiday concert.

I'd been singularly open to the idea of braving the unknown because of how well everything went.

The concert had started with "I Want to Thank You, Lord" and Emmett's solo. His basketball teammates (who'd originally come out to heckle him) were so genuinely surprised by how good he was that they jumped to their feet before the song even ended and gave us a standing ovation. They pumped their fists in the air, chanting Emmett's name. *EmMETT! EmMETT! EmMETT!*

My father scowled at all the shouting. Then he saw the effect this had on the choir, and his face softened. He realized what we were all feeling.

Pride.

He must have felt it, too. Not because of the response from a pack of hormonal athletes but because the choir sounded amazing. We usually performed well, but somehow Emmett improved everything. It wasn't just his singing. His very presence galvanized us. He gave us a sort of credibility, a visibility, we'd never had before.

I still had a brief moment of panic when Emmett and I took the stage to perform "A Part I Play" and looked out into the darkened auditorium to see, shadowy but unmistakable, many of the same faces I'd seen at the talent show three years before. The same ones who'd laughed at me. Were they going to make fun of me and my song again?

As soon as Emmett started to sing, I knew I wouldn't be living a repeat of that night. The audience, already firmly on our side from the beginning of the concert, was enraptured. I attributed it completely to Emmett's singing, of course, not to my song, though it didn't matter. It didn't matter that they might not be going on the journey I'd intended when I composed it. He was taking them somewhere totally different, and that was fine. That was the magic of music. Every performance of the same piece can be something new. Especially in the hands of someone as talented as he was.

When we were done, there was no booing. No insults. Just long, enthusiastic applause.

Emmett pulled me from my incredulous stupor on the piano bench, put his arm around me, and made me bow with him. Three years ago, they'd all laughed at me. Now they were cheering. I should've known everything would be fine with him at my side.

After, in the choir room, Ken blasted "We Are the Champions" from the sound system. My dad busied himself with putting the chairs away and pretended not to watch a room full of kids hugging, laughing, and dancing around him. He just shook his head and went on about his business as if everything were normal.

"Dude." Emmett tousled my hair. "Your song was a hit."

"Pshyeah. It was all you," I said. "You could've peed onstage, and they would've loved it."

Emmett stared back at me quietly. A stillness formed around us in the middle of the choir chaos. My thoughts spiraled. Was that the wrong thing to say? *Thank you. Say thank you.* He paid me a compliment, and like an idiot, I deflected it when I should've just said—

"Thanks, by the way. For giving me the sheet music of your song." He walked to the back of the room and put his folder away in the cabinet. "I framed it all nice and shit. It's gonna be hella rad."

"Oh. Cool."

"By the way, Laney's sister is throwing a party this weekend.

You're going, right?" he yelled over his shoulder, straining to be heard over all the noise.

I was about to respond by saying, *Sorry, no thanks, not my kind of thing, I'd rather hang out with my dad, or anyone else, really*, when he winked at me and my brain short-circuited.

I shouted back, "I'll be there!" as he melted into a crowd of his adoring public in the hallway.

At the party, I sat on a worn-out couch squished between two bulky and oddly baby-like seniors from the wrestling team, wishing I hadn't been an impressionable idiot after the concert and agreed to come.

The only thing keeping me there, still waiting for Emmett to show up, was the fact that he'd brought up the gift of my framed sheet music right before he'd invited me. My birthday *was* next week. It was the reason he'd asked me to come. He was going to give me my gift. It had to be here. It was going to be the last chance we'd see each other before I turned eighteen.

Lumpy and Dumpy nestled red cups to their chubby chests, watching as people walked past our couch. They weren't drinking very quickly. Probably because the drinks weren't their first. That's the way they smelled, at least. The whole house smelled this way, actually. Fermented. Like hard water stains and yeast. I briefly considered getting up and moving someplace else, but there was really nowhere else to go. And besides, the weight of Lumpy and Dumpy had sucked me into the couch like a black hole, so I sat there and tried not to think of how I looked like a loner with no drink and no one to talk to.

Some of the varsity swim team members were playing billiards in front of us while a handful of girls made out with the other swimmers. I recognized the girls as a team of some type. A dance troupe or flag squad. Or from the way they were using extra tongue, French Club.

The guys really sucked at playing pool. The balls rarely went into the holes. And when they did, it was usually by mistake. One guy, his skin more acne than not, got frustrated, lined his cue stick up, and used all his arm strength to plow through the ball. With a loud crack, a red billiard flew through the sky and straight at my head.

In middle school once, forced to play softball during PE (despite my best efforts to convince the teacher my fingers were an insurable commodity), I'd failed at catching a pop fly. It slipped through my hands and hit me. I ended up nursing a raised red welt on my forehead for two weeks. This was going to be much worse. Unable to dislodge myself from the Lumpy and Dumpy fat-trap and knowing I'd never be able to catch it, I covered my face.

A hand plucked the ball out of its midair arc. I looked through the safety net of my fingers to see Emmett gripping it. "Do I get to keep this?" he asked the swimmers.

"Thanks," I said, relieved on several fronts.

Emmett tossed the ball back onto the pool table. "That could've been bad, dude. Good thing I was here to save your face." He had on a turtleneck and fancy acid-washed jeans I'd never seen before.

I tried not to fixate on how the clothes hugged every part of his body. "Yeah. Thanks. No balls in this face, please," I said, then closed my eyes as a wave of mortification washed over me.

Emmett laughed. "Come on, let's go get a drink." He grabbed my hand and yanked me out of the quicksand couch.

I watched as the dozens of people who had crammed themselves into the crevices of Laney and Deborah's house moved aside when Emmett shepherded me through them, his arm tight around me. It felt as if I were back on the auditorium stage performing, on display again. I didn't know if I liked the feeling or not.

"There are so many people here. I don't even recognize most of them," I said to Emmett.

"They're not all Sunvalley. Some are Sycamore High. And a bunch of Valley Creek Community College students, too."

"I'm at a college party?"

"Welcome to adulthood."

He pulled me in closer as we maneuvered our way through a crowded hallway. He smelled like high-end shampoo, the stuff they sold at hair salons. "So...ummm...why'd you ask me here?" I asked.

"It's a party. We deserved a good time."

"You didn't ask me here to...I dunno. Give me something?"

He looked, briefly, as if he'd just been caught telling a lie, before edging us to the front of the line for drinks. "Well, duh." He handed me a clear plastic cup full of beer. "We're here so I could give you this."

I took the cup but didn't drink from it.

"I've seen that look before," he said. "I thought it was because you didn't know what sake was."

"I didn't. But I've also never had beer before," I said.

"No time like the present. Cheers." He clunked my cup with his and waited.

I put the cup up to my lips. It smelled like the house did. I tried not to gag as I sipped. Bitter bubbles gathered in my mouth. As I swallowed, I felt my insides roil.

Seemingly satisfied that I'd passed my first rite of adulthood, Emmett took a long sip of his own drink, which looked like it went down significantly more smoothly than mine. A small mustache of foam formed on his upper lip.

"What do you think?" he asked. He noticed me staring at his lips and licked them.

Something rose inside me, catching in my throat, and I was pretty sure it wasn't the beer coming back up. "Delicious," I replied without thinking. Then I pretend-coughed into a clenched fist. I took another drink of my beer, trying to hide my reddening face by turning away, only to cough for real this time. A big, wet, hacking one.

He shook his head with disappointment. I hoped it was only at me not being able to handle a beer and not my response to his question.

He looked past me. Behind, through the glass doors, winter sun lit up a patio and a lawn that looked as if it had been hacked at with a machete. At the very back of the sorry yard, vaporous steam issued from a large outdoor Jacuzzi. A few people had already gotten in.

"Hey, you want to go out back?" Emmett asked.

"Depends," I said. "Will the beer taste better outside?"

"Nah." Emmett stuck out his tongue. "Nothing could make this cheap shit taste good."

Outside, shrieks of laughter erupted as one of Emmett's fellow basketball team players stepped into the Jacuzzi fully dressed.

Whether it was because of a dare or full-on drunkenness, I couldn't tell.

Emmett eyed me. "Want to get into the hot tub?"

"I didn't bring a swimsuit."

"Yes, you did. So did I. Look." He reached down into his pants and pulled up the waistband of his underwear. A black Calvin Klein label came into full view, along with a long stretch of the lower part of his abs. The sight imprinted itself into my brain like a lightning bolt leaving scorch marks. Heat flooded my crotch area. I stuffed a hand into my pocket. "Okay. Yeah. Let's go outside. Swim, swim, everybody in!" I yammered, hoping to distract attention away from the tenting going on in my pants.

"What's going on over there, Quito? You that excited about the hot tub?"

"What?"

"Can't wait to see me in my underwear?"

"What? NO! I would never—I mean, I'm not like that!"

"Dude," Emmett said. "Chill out."

He paused, did an about-face, filled his cup with more beer, and made his way toward the patio without another word to me.

I felt as if I'd narrowly averted some disaster.

Or else, maybe, pushed something away that I shouldn't have.

The patio door slammed behind him, the sound of it shockingly loud. He said hello to the guys outside with fist bumps and ass slaps—all that coded language of masculinity that was completely beyond me.

I hesitated, confused about whether I should follow Emmett outside or stay indoors. Around me, people drank or stuffed their faces with snacks from multicolored plastic bowls as they swayed to Bon Jovi blasting from a boom box sitting on top of the avocado-green refrigerator. Two girls smoked cigarettes in the corner while a couple of woodwind players from the band made out sloppily at the dining room table. *Nice embouchures*, I thought to myself, retching slightly.

Gas bubbles gurgled in my stomach. I burped up rotten apples and vinegar. I wanted to be behind my piano at home, not in a moldy-bread-smelling house trying to be friends with the most popular guy in high school.

Who was I trying to fool?

I looked out into the backyard expecting to see Emmett there, tossing a football with his buddies or stripping down to his underwear to jump into the Jacuzzi. Instead, he just stood in a semicircle of people, beer cup in hand, seemingly not listening to what anyone was saying. He looked agitated, distracted.

He was looking at me.

He seemed to be trying to communicate something across the expanse of concrete and through the glass patio doors.

I couldn't make myself look away.

The more we stood there staring at each other, the more I became convinced I was just imagining things. Emmett wasn't looking at me but at something near me, or through me, or nothing at all. Or it was a hallucination. A fun house mirror refraction of my point of view.

I took another sip of my beer. It was the same drink. But now, for some reason, it didn't taste half so bad. Was I imagining things?

No, the beer *was* better now. It wasn't an illusion.

And Emmett was definitely still staring at me.

I finally tore myself from my spot and crept toward the glass doors when I felt a tap on my shoulder.

"Are you the composer?"

I turned around. A pretty young woman stood behind me. She wore a baggy knit sweater over cotton leggings, her hair clipped on the side so that it cascaded like a wave over one ear. She had on thick-rimmed glasses that didn't look nerdy on her at all.

I'd seen her before. Somewhere. There weren't many Asians at Sunvalley, and I didn't recognize her as one of the juniors or seniors, though she was old enough to be one of them. Was she a college student?

She waved at someone across the room with a willowy gesture of her long arm when I remembered: the girl from Emmett's car. His sister.

"I'm sorry, what did you ask me?"

"You're Quito, right? Emmett's composer friend?"

"I am. You must be Emmett's sister."

She giggled, her creamy white cheeks flushing faintly. "Oh no. I'm not his sister. I'm his girlfriend, Angela," she said, offering me her hand. "Nice to meet you."

I stared at her hand in horror, as if it had suddenly turned into an octopus tentacle.

His girlfriend.

"He never told me he was seeing anyone."

"Oh." She pushed in some loose hairs that had escaped from her hair-sprayed bangs. "I go to UC Berkeley. Between my biochem classes and all his basketball practices, I hardly ever get a chance to see him. I've been looking forward to this party. I knew you were coming, and I wanted to meet you. He talks a lot about you."

Her words entered my ears and promptly turned into mud. The fact that I was one of Emmett's favorite conversation subjects should have made me feel amazing. Instead, all I wanted to do was toss what little remained of my drink at her, refill the cup, and then walk outside and throw the entire thing at Emmett.

"I know a little bit of piano, you know. I was out of town, so I wasn't able to go to your concert. But I did play through that piece you gave to him. It's gorgeous." Angela's left eye was smaller than the other. She tried to compensate for this by adding more black eyeliner to its outer edges. It made her look like a raccoon. "It was so nice of you to let him have it to give as a gift. He put it in a black frame from PrintPlus and everything. It looks really nice."

I'd been a complete idiot. Of course it wasn't *me* he'd wanted to frame the sheet music for. It was for his pretty little college girlfriend.

The beer in my gut was threatening to resurface. I swallowed the bile back down and looked outside. Emmett's buddies were still there, but he had disappeared.

I turned around to see him standing next to Angela.

"You finally made it," he said, giving her a peck on the cheek. "Quito, this is Angela Asari."

"We've met," I said.

"Looks like you seem to be getting along."

"I've seen you before," I said to her blankly. "With Emmett's mom. That's why I thought you were related."

"We both have Japanese dads and white moms," Emmett explained.

"I was just telling Quito how amazing his song was." Angela placed her arm in the crook of Emmett's.

"So this is why you invited me here," I said to Emmett.

He looked confused. "No. That's not—"

"Dude! Is this your girlfriend? She's hella fine!" The gang of basketball jocks had made their way back inside, some of them dripping wet.

"Hold on a sec," Emmett said. He started pushing them back toward the patio, which swiftly devolved into a wrestling match. Angela's eyes widened. She looked to me for guidance.

"Sorry. Nice meeting you. I have to go." I put my cup in the kitchen sink.

"Should I tell him you're leaving?"

I started winding my way through the throng of people, all of them lost in conversation, moving to the music, carefree and oblivious to what I was going through.

"No," I shouted back at her. "He won't care that I'm gone. He won't care at all."

Chapter 12 — Now

I WALK FROM the Christopher Street subway station to get to my Sunday shift at Broadway Baby. Trudging through the uncleared snow, still fresh from a noontime snow flurry, I think about how I nearly let history repeat itself by holding on to that tiny little hope, again, that I could ever be more to Emmett than just a friend. That's already gotten me into one too many messes. I can't afford another one.

Now that I think about it, it's just as well that Emmett can't do the concert. I'll figure out an alternative for my dad. Maybe Ujima'd be willing to guest star instead. Jee's not famous, but they sure as hell can command a stage.

By the time I get to the bar, I'm wet and cold. I place a hand over one of the nearby radiators. Barely a hiss of steam.

"Hey," I call out to Jaime, "where's the heat?"

"Dunno. Been like this all day. Someone's working on the pipes. I'll make you a hot chocolate."

I wait at the bar, shivering. Everyone has their winter coats on inside, cutting down on the amount of wiggle room, so no one's moving around much. They look cheerless and aggravated. Common for New Yorkers at most times but rare for Broadway Baby.

J.B. is finishing out her shift at the piano. She's working her way through a set of Patti LuPone's songs. A little *Les Miz*, some *Gypsy*, some *Company*, a bit of *Sweeney Todd*. She's currently pounding out "Don't Cry for Me Argentina." With a red and white winter cap on to keep her head warm and her glasses and boyish face, she looks exactly like Where's Waldo.

She still manages to play impeccably despite the freezing temperature. After I finish my hot chocolate, I maneuver my way to her and find out why her hands haven't completely frozen. There's a space heater plugged in by her feet. It's old and rickety. If she kicked it over by mistake, it would probably burn the whole place down.

"Has it been like this all night?" I ask her.

J.B. nods. "Jaime texted to warn me, at least. That's why I brought the space heater. Thank god, or else my fingers would be icicles by now."

"Everyone's so quiet. They usually belt the crap out of this song." There are a few women singing along to J.B.'s playing. Most everyone else seems to be contemplating whether they've had enough of the frigid room.

"They're not happy," J.B. says.

"And the tip jar's not very happy, either."

"Hey," she says, segueing into *Anything Goes*, "I heard you might be working on a new show?"

"News travels fast."

"You know how it is. Everyone knows everything in this town."

"Mark got me the gig. I'm not that into the concept, though."

"What's it about?"

"Peter Pan," I say. "Except it takes place in the seventies. Peter

Pan is gay. And so are the Lost Boys. Wendy's a lesbian. Or a stripper. Maybe both. I can't remember."

"Interesting." I can't tell if she's being sarcastic or not. She seems to linger on some thought while continuing to play the Cole Porter from memory. "I might have a song or two that could fit."

I believe her. J.B. has more right to call herself a composer than I ever could, having written songs for at least three of her own shows, including one that made it to the Fringe Festival a few years ago. J.B.'s the person I want to be when I grow up. Minus the having-sex-with-girls thing.

"Maybe you should do the show instead of me," I reply. "Want me to talk to the guy?"

"Really? You won't mind?"

"Nope."

"What about Mark?"

I hesitate. Of course Mark would mind if I handed off the opportunity he was so excited about to someone else.

"Maybe I can just give you some ideas. Free of charge." Not only is J.B. more prolific than I am, but she's also more generous. In fact, she's the one who introduced me to the owner of Broadway Baby. She'd asked me to fill in for her while she was away musical directing a non-Equity tour of *Joseph and the Amazing Technicolor Dreamcoat* with a cast that was, in her words, "gayer than the goddamn coat." After my tryout stint, I was hired as a regular pianist. I still owe her for that.

"Sounds good," I say.

"Great. Now"—with the edge of her thumbnail, she glissandos down the length of the keyboard, her usual ending flourish—"take over. I'm done freezing my tuchus off."

"Can I borrow your space heater?"

"Be my guest. I never actually use that thing at home. It's a fucking fire hazard." She bundles her puffy parka around her as she waits for the tip jar to come back from one last go around the crowd. She sticks her hand in, takes out the few bills, stuffs them into her backpack, and hugs me. "Tell Mark I said hi."

Everyone in the bar is quiet as I take my place at the piano, their conversations blunted by the temperature. My internal Rolodex runs through the songs most likely to get them going. I start off with some *Mamma Mia!* But despite the fact that ABBA is always a dependable crowd-pleaser, barely anyone sings along.

It's going to be a long night.

I look over to the bar and notice Jaime handing a familiar old man a hot chocolate, steam rising in the cold air. I smile when I realize that it's Edgar and that it's not a hot chocolate but a hot toddy. He sips happily, his face plum red, and waves at me with a hand covered in a tattered wool glove.

Behind him, Jaime catches my attention with two muscular thumbs-up. Has the heat been fixed? Over my crowd's half-hearted sing-along of "Dancing Queen," I hear what I think is the banging of pipes being forced full of new steam. The crowd hears it, too. People turn to one another, looks of hope growing on their faces. I feel the place slowly warm up as the hiss of heat starts to issue forth from the radiators.

Then the room explodes.

It isn't the pipes that have erupted. It's high-pitched squeals and shrieks, which peal out from men and women both.

Emmett Aoki is in Broadway Baby.

He brushes snow off his winter coat near the entrance. The

crowd draws close to him like he's the resurgent source of heat. He sees me at the piano and waves. Then he tries to work his way through the mob of onlookers filming him with their phones.

I close my eyes. Maybe if I stay still, he'll forget where I am. I'll just disappear into the wood-paneled walls like a brown chameleon.

"You ran out on me last night," Emmett says, standing in front of me. He takes his jacket off and places it on the fake piano cover. A few people eye it with desire, probably contemplating petty larceny. "Seems to be a habit of yours."

"Habit?"

"Leaving without saying anything. You did it to me at that Christmas party in high school, too, remember? It's a pattern."

"It's not a pattern," I say. "Twice is not a pattern."

The room seems to shrink as everyone closes in on us, straining to hear our conversation. "What are you even doing here?" I ask as quietly as I can, though getting softer only makes everyone nosier.

"Thought I'd left town already?"

"*That* would be a pattern, wouldn't it?"

A tiny muscle in his jaw tenses and untenses. The clanking of the radiators ratchets up to full volume. I feel sweat collecting at my hairline, about to drip onto my face. I quickly wipe my forehead with the back of my sleeve.

The left edge of Emmett's upper lip lifts into a tiny half smile. "Good thing for you I'm not dependable enough to form any kind of habit."

"Yeah. Good thing."

His half smile grows. That wonderful, crooked tooth appears.

"So, what were we talking about last night before you bailed?" he says. "Oh, yes. The concert."

"Which you can't make. Because of Emma Chen."

Somebody says, "So you *are* dating Emma Chen?" A chain reaction of chatter flares up around us.

Emmett ignores them and leans over the piano. He says to me, his voice steadfast, "I'm not dating Emma. That was my agent's idea, okay? He was trying to set us up as a thing. I didn't say no. Maybe I should've. I will now. Since I'm not going to Cannes anymore."

The clanking around us stops abruptly. Jaime props open the front door to dispel some of the excess warmth. Cold outside air floods in and mixes with the radiator heat, stabilizing the temperature inside. Only then do I remember that J.B.'s claptrap heater has been on this whole time. I reach down to turn it off and instantly feel much better. "Wow. That's great. That's really—just great."

"The me-doing-the-concert thing or the me-not-dating-Emma thing?"

"Thing shming." My cheeks are burning. Still flushed from the surplus of heat, I decide. "So, what will you sing?"

"Don't know. I have a few weeks to think about it, though, right?"

"No. I mean, what will you sing," I say, getting louder with each word. "Right. NOW?"

"Oh." He shakes his head. "Quito, no."

It's too late, though, and we both know it. Everyone has heard me throw down the gauntlet.

"Look, everyone, I don't have anything prepared. I'm sorry," Emmett says.

He clearly underestimates the crowd's desire to hear him sing. He has to give them what they want now. They won't let him out alive if he doesn't. "Sing! Sing! Sing!" they chant.

Emmett cranes his neck around, toward the front door, the annex, and the fire exit, literally looking for any way out of his predicament.

When he finally realizes he can't escape, he raises his hands. "Okay, okay. Just one." He looks at me. "Pick something. Something easy!"

Really, I should listen to him. Pick something simple. Ubiquitous. Let him off with an easy standard, something any person in the bar could do, even after a long night of drinking.

I look over at the bar and see Edgar. His face is so red with excitement that it looks as though he might keel over. And I decide. Edgar deserves a show. Everyone in the bar does. They've been suffering for the past few hours in the miserable cold.

Plus, I kind of want to pay Emmett back for the Emma Chen thing.

I grin devilishly to myself and start playing a familiar six-note theme in two groups of three, instantly recognizable to everyone in the room.

Emmett blanches.

"Something's Coming" from *West Side Story*. A song everyone knows but very few can sing. It's deceptively difficult, both rhythmically and range-wise.

I keep repeating the same two intro bars over and over, needling him with the theme. "Come on. We used to do this at my house all the time," I say.

"That was a long time ago, Quito."

"Just like riding a bike."

Emmett covers his face with his hands and groans. "You're a bastard."

"You're welcome."

He focuses on my accompaniment, lining himself up with the vamp to begin at just the right moment. All conversations around us cease.

He breathes.

He sings.

Now, the patrons at Broadway Baby are used to good voices. Trained voices. Professional ones. New York is full of them, and many of them find their way to the piano bar at some point or another. But there's always been something more to Emmett's singing than just a nice voice. It's the way he delivers the text. There isn't a trace of tension in his body, no raised veins on his neck, no strain on his face, his mouth as relaxed as if he is using no more effort than to whisper directly into your ear, as if he's delivering the song to you and you alone. And even though "Something's Coming" is one of Leonard Bernstein's trickiest pieces from the show, Emmett doesn't miss a single note, syllable, or beat. He makes it all feel effortlessly real. True.

I feel the piano keys give way underneath me, responding to his singing on their own, his breaths manifesting in my fingers.

He sings about possibilities. Urgency. The hope that the one great thing he's always wanted to happen to him will, indeed, happen. Maybe tonight.

As the song winds down, Emmett comes around and sits down next to me on the bench, which I somehow sensed he would do. On the last word—*tonight*—he opts for the high variant G on the last syllable, floating in the air so ethereally that everyone questions themselves: Have I even heard the note? Am I dreaming it? Even after I'm done playing, long after he's finished singing, everyone waits for that last note to fade. None of us wants to let go of the feeling of it sounding in our ears.

Applause finally ends the silence.

Emmett beams. He reaches his arm around me and pulls my head into his chest, mumbling into the top of it. I can't hear what he's saying exactly, but it doesn't matter. The message burrows into me.

The past is behind.

We can move forward.

I look up, past the crowd of people, and see a pair of eyes laser-focused on us from across the room. There, hanging on the periphery of the crowd near the entrance, his coat slowly being zipped back on, is Mark. He's leaving.

And unlike Emmett, he is definitely not happy.

I push my way through the crowd and out onto the street. In my hurry, I leave without grabbing my jacket. Streams of late-afternoon sunlight peek through a bank of clouds, refracting through the slow but persistent sprinkle of snow.

"Mark, wait!"

He continues to trudge down the street, shoulders square, face straight ahead.

"Christ, it's freezing out here," I mumble.

"Go back inside, Quito. You'll get sick."

I manage to catch up to him. "I thought I was coming to meet you at your apartment after my shift."

"Dinesh and I had lunch." He stops but still faces away from me. "He's nervous about you not being serious about the show, so I came over early to convince you to meet with him before next weekend. Maybe take you out to the dinner we didn't get to have on Friday. But I see you have other things on your mind."

"It's not what you think. Emmett—"

"Knows you. Clearly," he says.

"Let me explain."

"You told me you didn't know him. That you weren't a fan." His voice is hoarse. I recognize that sound. The stress that creeps in when he's mad.

"I'm *not* a fan of his. That much is true," I say softly.

"But you know him. Were you and him ever—"

"Friends," I say. "Just friends. We went to high school together."

He finally turns to face me. "You went to school with Emmett Aoki?"

"Yes." I rub my hands together. "Can we just go back inside? I'll introduce you. I know everyone sees him as this big deal. To me he's just a guy I knew as a kid, okay? Nothing else. Just, please. I'm freezing."

He sees me shaking in the snow. The frown on his face melts slightly. "Fine."

I hurry back to the bar, turning every few seconds to make sure Mark is still behind me. He takes his time. And despite the warm temperature inside Broadway Baby, he doesn't take his jacket off when we get back.

An unrelenting crowd has trapped Emmett behind the piano, waiting for him to sing something else. I motion to Mark to follow me to him.

"I'm fine right here," he says.

Emmett notices that I'm back, waves at me. Mark's glare hardens.

"Hey, Emmett," I shout over the bar's buzz. "Come over here. I want to introduce you to someone."

He extricates himself from the crowd's clutches. All eyes follow as he makes his way over to us at the entrance. "Hey there. I'm Emmett," he says, offering his hand. "You are...?"

"Mark." He takes Emmett's hand firmly. "Quito's boyfriend."

Something flits across Emmett's face, like a moth obscuring the light. In a nanosecond, his face shines again with a brightness that feels more forced than usual. "Very nice to meet you."

"You look surprised," Mark says. "I take it Quito hasn't told you anything about me."

Without a pause, Emmett says, "He didn't tell me how handsome you were, that's all."

Watching Emmett handle Mark, I'm reminded of how he's always been able to read people, how he's so quickly able to glean what a person needs and respond accordingly. It makes me wonder how often he's done that to me.

"Thank you," Mark says, his face less tense. "You two went to school together?"

"Good old Sunvalley High."

"How come you never told me this?" Mark asks me. Beads of sweat line Mark's forehead. He still doesn't take off his jacket. He's ready to jet at a moment's notice.

Emmett replies before I can say anything. "Because I asked him not to. I like keeping my personal life private. It's better off for them that way. Otherwise"—he leans in closer to Mark, looking peripherally at the people around us—"you have all these idiots trying to get the scoop on any crazy behavior from my past. Besides, school was hell. I mostly put it out of my head. I'm sure Quito did, too."

I force a grin and say nothing, leaving the smoothing over of things to the professional.

"You just wanted to keep the past secret? What kinds of things?" Mark's neck is sweating heavily now as he tries to dig deeper.

Don't I owe him the whole story? We've been together for almost a year now. A lifetime compared to my other relationships. I lied to him about knowing Emmett, and he found out. He could find out about everything else. It's not too late to just come clean about our past, to bring it out in the open, right here, right now, for us both to accept. It's what's best. Not just for Mark. For me and Emmett, too.

The truth begins to form at the base of my throat, but it feels painful and gets lodged there. All around us, videos and pictures of Emmett are being taken. Ours is not a private conversation. In the end, no words come out at all.

"Look," Emmett says, "Quito and I used to sing together. His dad was our choir director. They invited me to sing for a benefit concert in June since he's retiring. That's all."

"Really?" Mark asks me.

My throat constricts even more. I nod.

Mark turns back to Emmett. "And what did you say?"

"I said yes." He turns to me, sealing the deal with a wink and a smile. "Quito's dad was like the dad I never had. So, yes. I'm doing it. And," he adds, for emphasis, "I'm going to have to tell my *girlfriend* that I won't be able to go to her Cannes movie premiere like I promised to do. Just so I can help out Mr. C. And our old pianist, here, of course."

Mark scans his face for a trace of deceit. He won't find it. Emmett is an actor. This is what he does. Making you see what he wants you to see.

Mark finally begins to take off his coat. "And your girlfriend won't get mad?"

"I've got her wrapped around my finger." Emmett wreathes his right index finger with his left fist and thrusts it in and out. Then he laughs his jock laugh—the one that used to both infuriate and turn me on in high school. "Emma'd do anything for me. You've heard of her, right? Emma Chen?"

"Emma Chen is your girlfriend? Hey," Mark says admiringly, nudging me with an elbow, "did you hear that?"

"Well, I hate to run, but my flight back to L.A. leaves soon," Emmett says. "A pleasure meeting you, Mark."

My stomach lurches. We haven't even figured out the details for the concert yet. When he's coming. What we're going to do. We haven't worked anything out at all, really.

He pauses as he buttons up his coat. "Quito, we should probably exchange numbers so we can get in touch." We trade phones to put our numbers into them. "After my mom's wedding next month, I'll give you a call so we can go over the logistics of your dad's concert. And thanks for the tunes, by the way. Some things never change. Right?" He raises both hands to everyone. "Remember to tip your pianist!"

A chunk of the crowd, their phones still recording Emmett's every move, follows him toward the exit. He turns to wave at us before he's pushed out of it.

"You never told me about this concert for your dad," Mark says.

"I didn't? I thought I did. I'm pretty sure I told you he was retiring. I must've told you about the concert."

He gives me that look that tells me he's caught me in a lie.

"Look, I wasn't sure I was even going to do it. And I had no idea I'd be able to convince Emmett."

"But you managed to find a way," he says. Not with bitterness or envy. But with something approaching awe. Whatever other problems we've had in the past, Mark has also believed in my musical abilities. And I've been lying to him this whole time.

"You'd still be able to do Dinesh's show, though, right? June's the backer's performance, too," he says.

He's been trying to support me by giving me this opportunity with Dinesh. I can't bear to see him lose faith in me. Not after all I've done to give him reason to doubt me.

"I'll make it happen," I say, not entirely sure that I can. "I won't be in California for long. Just for the concert and a few rehearsals beforehand. A week or two, tops. The concert's in June and I don't need to be in California until the end of May. I'll be done writing and arranging all of Dinesh's songs by then. I might even have some ideas already." I do, in fact. They're J.B.'s, but he doesn't need to know that.

"Hey, maybe you can convince Emmett to be involved with our show. Have him make a demo of one of the songs? Or be one of the backers?"

"Sure, yeah," I say, barely registering the fact that he called it "our" show. "I'll see if he's interested."

"I knew this was going to be the right project for you. This is going to be your big break. You're going to get what you deserve. Finally."

He rubs my fingers with his. His face is glowing with sweat from wearing his coat too long indoors but probably also from excitement.

The crowd no longer pushes in on us now that Emmett is gone. It thins out, giving us more space. Mark hugs me. I breathe in the familiar scent of designer cologne covering a slightly acrid musk. "Thank you," I say.

As we hold each other, I sense the crowd's attention shift to the window outside, as if catching sight of someone looking in. When I turn to see who it is, I see nothing. Whoever it was is gone. If there was even someone there at all.

Chapter 13 – Then

AFTER MY VANISHING act from Laney's Christmas party, I walked out into the cold and thought about the colossal mistake I'd made. I'd misread my relationship with Emmett and built it up into something it never was. When I got home, I locked myself in my bedroom and sank into a general funk of low-level depression.

I thought he really cared about me.

But I was wrong.

I was just a means to an end. Someone to teach him how to sing, how to get better at one more thing in life. Someone to provide a one-of-a-kind birthday gift for his college girlfriend. A gift I'd given him first and was hoping to get back in return, a circular symbol of what we meant to each other.

But I didn't get anything from him. Nothing at all.

When classes started back up again after the holiday break, I kept as much distance as I could between us, steering clear of him in the halls, coming to choir late, leaving early, never looking up from the piano during rehearsals in case he was watching me.

I stopped helping him with choir music. My excuse, if he were to ask me, was an increased homework load in English. Not that he ever asked me. Emmett seemed to be okay with me disappearing from his life. Further proof that we were never as close as I thought we were. It was a relief, as well as—though it killed me to admit it—a disappointment. The petty part of me had wanted to punish Emmett by giving him the silent treatment; I wanted to see him suffer. But he went on with life as if nothing had ever happened. As if he'd lost nothing.

In fact, my dad was more upset over my silent treatment than Emmett was.

"Why are you avoiding him?" he asked me at dinner one evening.

"I'm not," I lied.

"Then why doesn't he come over to the house anymore?"

"Because I never invite him."

"Why? Why don't you ever practice together?"

"I don't know. Ask him."

Though it seemed as if my dad might actually take me up on my suggestion, he never did. Instead, he resorted to assigning Emmett more solos he'd need help with, hoping that would make us work with each other again. Unfortunately for him, the ploy never worked. Emmett had gotten the hint and kept his distance from me, asking my father directly for help instead. They'd work on music after class, and I'd slip out, thankful that they were keeping each other busy.

The new status quo worked for everyone. I got space to think. Emmett got someone to help him who wasn't obsessing over him. And my dad got to work one-on-one with the son he'd always wanted.

It was the only thing that made sense. Why else would he have tried so hard to get Emmett into choir? To have me teach him? To get him to come over for dinners? Emmett was smart, talented, confident, athletic, popular. Someone my dad could be proud of in endless ways. Unlike the shortish, average-looking Filipino loner whose only redeeming quality was the ability to magically play stuff on the piano. My parents had always been happy with my musical abilities, but I'd long suspected my dad wanted more from his only child.

In middle school, he'd tell me to take a break from practicing sometimes and drag me to my older cousin's soccer games. We'd spend an hour driving all the way to San Bruno in our beat-up Subaru and then sit in the bleachers while he'd cheer for Manny in his (admittedly festive) green uniform. "Isn't it fun, anak? Wouldn't you like to be like your pinsan?" I wanted to tell him that running around chasing a ball, kicking and jumping and getting grass stains all over my clothes, was the last thing on earth I wanted to do. Not wanting to hurt his feelings, though, I said, "Sure, Dad," and feigned interest while I retreated into my brain to let Mozart and Sondheim take me someplace else entirely.

After a while, when he'd gotten the hint that sports bored me to tears, he stopped trying to get me interested in soccer. And Oakland A's baseball games. And basketball. And boxing matches on pay-per-view. I was relieved. Though a part of me always felt like I'd let him down in some way by not being the kind of son he wanted.

Well, now he had the perfect son. Emmett. And he could have him all to himself.

As the spring semester went on, I got used to not spending time with Emmett. It hurt at first to see him during choir rehearsal forming bonds with everyone else, but I kept reminding myself that the piano had been my closest companion almost my entire life. I didn't need anything or anyone else.

Then one afternoon, after we'd returned from spring break, he snuck up on me in the hallway after third period.

"Can we talk?"

I would've refused, but the shock of having his voice so close in my ear, warm and muggy, caught me off guard. What's more, his whole body was strangely off-kilter, his back bowed from the weight of sagging shoulders. I'd never seen him so upset. My defenses dissipated. "Okay," I said.

He led me to the end of the hallway and crammed us between two banks of lockers. "I need your help."

"For what?"

"Look. I just need a friend right now." His body was almost on top of mine. There wasn't a lot of room between us. For weeks, I'd managed to allow the intangible connection between us to fall away. Now every second of being close to him was building it up again, link by invisible link.

I needed to stop it. "You've got more friends than anybody I know. Any one of them could help you out. Give you moral support. And stuff." I couldn't look at him. "Why not ask Angela?"

"She can't help me with this. Just you." He forced a smile, which cracked. And through this chink in his armor, I was able to see him. The true him.

My heart, already racing because of our closeness, was making it hard for me to stay calm at his assertion that there was something only I would be able to understand.

"It's my mom. She's not doing well."

The thumping in my chest lessened and then shifted into a different gear as I realized what he'd just said. "Oh, is she sick? Did she get into an accident?"

"No, no. Nothing like that. It's just...well...she's really unhappy. My dad is treating her like crap."

The story came rushing out of Emmett. A month prior, his father came home early, suitcase in hand, his breath reeking of alcohol. It took his mother almost an hour to pry it out of him, but eventually, in a torrent of screaming and profanity, he admitted he had gotten fired from his job. Some sort of "impropriety," although he declined to go into any further detail. He went on to yell at Emmett's mother, blaming her for not being a better wife—as if that had anything to do with him losing his job—before finally passing out on the couch in a drunken haze. Almost every evening since then had been some sort of variation of the same event.

"He yells at her all the time. Telling her that she's useless. Stupid." I watched as the crack in Emmett's smile grew, tiny hairline fractures of concern taking over his normally flawless face.

"He's not, like, hitting her, is he?"

"Oh, hell no. I'd hit him back if he did that." The lines on his face burned, and I knew Emmett would do exactly that. He'd defend his mother from anyone, including and especially his father.

"When I'm around and hear it happening, I tell him to back off. He just storms off and locks himself in his office. But I'm not always around to stand up for her. My mom says it's fine. He's going through a rough patch, she says. But I can see what it's doing to her. She's not sleeping. And sometimes, late at night when she thinks I'm asleep, I can hear her crying in the kitchen."

My hand started to raise instinctively to touch him. I forced it back down to my side. "I'm so sorry."

"I keep telling her she should just leave. Go somewhere else, maybe stay with my aunt in San Francisco. I told her I'd go with her. I mean, there's no way I'd stay with my dad and leave her alone."

"What did she say?"

"That she needs to stay. For my sake. Since it's my senior year. She's willing to put up with my dad's crap for a few more months, at least until I graduate. But she says it's only because he's out of work, anyway. She's convinced that once he finds another job, he'll go back to normal." He shook his head and frowned. "Not that *normal* was that much better."

The space between us had shrunk to nothing. I could feel the pain inside him as it flowed outward and blanketed us both.

He needed something from me. But I wasn't sure what I had to give, what I had to share with him besides our love of music.

"My parents had problems sometimes," I said.

"No way. I can't see your dad ever treating your mom badly."

"He didn't. But he didn't always have steady work. And even when he did, there were times when it wasn't enough to pay the bills. Musicians don't make a lot of money. My mom told me once that my lolo and lola—her parents—didn't approve of her marrying my dad. They said he'd never be able to provide for her. That he needed to get a *real* job. They tried to get her to convince him to give up his dreams of being a musician and become an engineer or a nurse instead, or else he'd never be a good husband to her and a good father to me. She told them she knew my dad, that he'd take on a hundred jobs if that's what it took to take care of his family. She fell in love with a musician. He'd never give up his dream, and she never wanted him to. She saw that in him."

I allowed my hand to rise this time, to rest itself on Emmett's shoulder. His eyes, glistening, locked with mine.

"Your mom sees that in you, too, Emmett. She supports you in everything, but especially in your love of music, right? She's staying because she knows that if she left, you wouldn't have someone on your side at home. Or, if you went with her, then you'd be away from . . . um—choir."

Emmett's shoulder, at first iron cold under my hand, warmed up and loosened.

"And you," Emmett said.

I felt the heat from Emmett's shoulder run down my arm, up my neck, and straight to my face. "I mean, I guess we make pretty good music."

The lines of hurt had disappeared from Emmett's face. "The best," he said.

A crowd of people walked by us on their way to class, chattering. Out of the corner of his eye, Emmett noticed them. A hardness veiled his face briefly, and his eyes shifted subtly to my hand on his shoulder. I let go of him. He turned to the people passing by and gave them a chin nod.

When they disappeared, he turned back to me, the momentary callousness and the earlier despair now gone. He smiled his slightly flawed smile.

"Would it make you feel better if we worked on some new stuff together?" I offered.

Emmett pushed his fist against my shoulder. A kinder, gentler version of his usual punch. "Hells yeah."

I didn't want him to know how much I'd missed it, so I shimmied out from our cramped quarters together, clamping down on the growing smile on my face by gritting my teeth, almost painfully. "Meet me after choir," I said and hurried to fourth period.

Emmett needed a friend. That was all.

That's all I was going to let it be.

I needed to make sure I didn't ever get carried away with him again.

Later that day, my father noticed that things had changed. "You're friends again? That's good."

Emmett and I had simply walked into the choir room together, sat down on opposite sides of the room, and took out our music, ready to begin.

How could he tell? What exactly had he seen?

I ignored my dad and leafed through my sheet music, careful to keep a mask of tedium on my face. I needed to keep denying the fact—to everyone, including myself—that I felt more stoked for rehearsal than I had in weeks.

After choir, lacking anything from our upcoming concerts to work on, Emmett and I decided he'd just come over to the house for dinner and work through some new solo repertoire, songs I'd been keeping in mind for him.

He poked me in the ribs. "Nice to know you've been thinking about me."

"Don't flatter yourself. It's just some stuff I think you'd be good at. That's all," I said with such disinterest that I even managed to convince myself.

My father, of course, was thrilled his prodigal son was coming back over. He cooked up an entire Filipino feast for us to have for dinner. And even though it all smelled delicious, we were so engrossed in our music-making that we had to be dragged away from the piano to eat.

There were so many new things to try that evening that Emmett came over again the next evening. The following week, after his dad had calmed down a bit (feeling more hopeful from some promising interviews, Emmett said), he felt freer to come over, sometimes as many as three or four times a week. Which was good because a surfeit of music had been trapped inside me, pent up since December. I hadn't realized how much it all needed release.

I made Emmett listen to the original London cast album of *Les Miz* and taught him some of the songs. The next week, we worked on *Into the Woods*. Then *The Phantom of the Opera*. Even *Rent*, which I didn't have the vocal score for but didn't need because I'd been listening to the new cast album on nonstop repeat and had every song memorized. It ended up being Emmett's favorite. We'd often sing through the entire show, even the girls' songs. I tried not to make a big deal in my head over the fact that Emmett's absolute favorite was "I'll Cover You," a duet between the two gay lovers, Collins and Angel. I just let myself enjoy his singing and the look on his face when we'd sing through it together.

One Sunday afternoon in late April, while we were playing through the *Little Shop of Horrors* songbook, my dad brought out plates of leche flan and insisted we take a break. One look at the caramel sauce dripping over the creamy mounds of custard was enough to get us to agree.

He sat with us in the living room as we shoveled spoonfuls of it into our mouths. "Sounding good, you guys," he said. "Emmett, you're picking up music very quickly these days."

"Aw, thanks, Mr. C. Honestly, it's all Quito. He's a natural teacher. I mean, he doesn't even need to look at the music. He has it all in his head. Like, sometimes he makes it all sound better than it does on the CD."

As compliments went, that was a pretty good one. Too good for me to acknowledge with any sort of grace. "As if," I said, embarrassed.

"You know," my father said, "Quito has written some new songs that he could share with you. They are even better than all the stuff you have been doing so far."

I was baffled. How the hell did my father know about my new songs?

In the weeks after Laney's party, they'd started coming out of me, showing up uninvited in the shower, at breakfast, or during boring stretches of English class, when Mrs. Hempstead would drone on about totally irrelevant books like *A Separate Peace*. I'd write the songs in my head, sketching out chord progressions and basic melodies. A few lyrics here and there. Most of the songs didn't have titles, and some weren't even complete. There was no possible way he could've known about them.

"I don't have...I mean...they're just dumb songs. They aren't any good," I said, flustered.

"Don't be so dramatic, Quito. I think they're excellent. And I have the best taste." He took a bite of his leche flan. "Mmm. Like this, for example. It's very good, diba?"

"How would you even know? I'm pretty sure I never played through any of them while you were home."

"A little birdie told me," he said. I think. Hard to tell since his mouth was crammed full of custard.

A chill went through me. Was that a reference to my mom? Like most old-school Filipinos, my dad had an unwavering belief in the hereafter and in ghostly visions. He used to tell me that my mother would sometimes appear to him at the foot of his bed at night, watching him sleep. The first time he confessed that to me, I made him promise not to ever bring it up again. It saddened him, I know, for me not to want to know about my mom's supposed visitations. But the thought of a ghost appearing in my bedroom, even if it was my mom, scared the crap out of me.

Emmett tapped his fork on his ceramic plate with a clink, startling me. "First of all, Mr. C," he said, "this Filipino pudding is hella dope. Secondly—dude, you have to play me your new stuff."

"Let's just do more *Little Shop*. You can be Audrey II this time."

"Quito." My dad glared at me, clearly unhappy. "Don't hide that part of yourself. You know your mother would not have liked it."

I was trying to think of more excuses to give myself time to get the songs into more presentable shape. My music felt safe where it was. Inside. Where no one could touch it, criticize it, or hate it for being less than perfect. Where no one could call me names because of the meaning behind the words.

But Dad was right. My mother would have wanted me to share my songs. If not with the world, then at least with one other person.

"Okay, but just so you know, they're not really finished yet," I said.

"Whatever." Emmett set his plate down on the coffee table and wiped his mouth with the back of his hand. "I'm gonna like it all anyway."

"You don't even know what they sound like yet."

"Don't have to. You wrote 'em."

My dad smiled at this and then packed his mouth with the rest of his leche flan. "Go. Practice," he mumbled while pushing us both to the piano.

Later that afternoon, after I'd played my songs for Emmett, he surprised me and my father by insisting he help prepare dinner.

"No," my dad said. "You're a guest here."

Emmett responded, "Am I just a guest, though, Mr. C? Or don't you consider me more, like... one of the family?"

My dad stared at him, saying nothing. But in his eyes, I could see a change in the way he saw Emmett, as if Emmett had suddenly turned a brighter color or grown an inch. "Well, I suppose. Just this once."

I accompanied Emmett, intending to help guide him through the food prep. But surprisingly, he had skills in the kitchen. He knew how to properly peel ginger by scraping the skin off the knobby roots with a spoon. And he was decent with a knife, able to mince garlic, onions, and ginger with ease. I sautéed those together with hunks of chicken and poured in rice and water, which would simmer down into one of my favorite comfort foods, arroz caldo. Meanwhile, my dad cooked diced pork and fried cubes of tofu. He had Emmett and me make a sweet vinegar dressing, which he combined with the pork, tofu, and chopped red onions to make tokwa't baboy, an ideal complement to the arroz caldo.

When we sat down to eat, we were quieter than usual, only speaking to ask for the food or drinks to be passed around. Part of this was probably because we'd already spent the past hour shoulder to shoulder, talking, giving each other instructions on how to create the delicious meal we were now eating. But it also felt as if familiarity and comfort had settled into us, making general chitchat unnecessary. All we needed was the food and each other's company.

Afterward, Emmett and I sat outside in my backyard to take advantage of the warm weather we'd completely ignored the rest of the day. Even with the shouts of neighborhood kids, dogs barking, and the hum of the BART train all around, the calm still stayed with us. We drank from cans of RC Cola and watched as the sun sank. Neither of us said anything for a long time. The quiet between Emmett and me felt just as natural as all the singing and playing that had come earlier in the day and the cooking after that.

"Thank you," he said, finally breaking the silence.

"For what?"

"Sharing your songs with me this afternoon. I know you said they weren't done, but it didn't feel that way to me. They felt, I dunno, right, somehow."

"You learned them super fast. Even faster than any of the musical theater stuff."

"I know. Almost like you wrote them for me."

At that, a part of me came loose and was set free—a part I hadn't realized needed freeing. I'd written those songs in my effort to *not* think about Emmett, when, really, they were the part of him inside me that I couldn't deny, wanting to come out.

"Hey," Emmett said, turning to me. "Why did you stop talking to me after Laney's party?"

A small child's shriek from next door pierced the air. I flinched and swished the remainder of my cola around in its can. "I got really busy," I said.

"You were mad at me."

"No, I wasn't," I said, which was only half-true. I was more mad at myself than him.

"Quito, don't lie to me."

"How come you never told me you had a girlfriend?"

"She goes to another school. I didn't see a reason to."

"I thought you were my friend."

"I was. I am," he said.

"Look, she told me you never had enough time with her, that she barely saw you. So I thought—as a *friend*—I shouldn't be taking up too much of your time," I said, lying. "You shouldn't have to choose between us. I just did what I thought was best. For you."

"For me," he repeated.

"Yeah."

"Well, it doesn't matter now. She's out of the picture. We've got all the time in the world to chill." Emmett stared out across our yard as the sun dipped down. The sunset flared brightly, all of its being concentrated into a glowing crescent of light.

"What do you mean?"

"I broke up with her."

"What? When?"

"Right after I started hanging out with you again."

I said nothing at first, letting what he'd just said settle in the air.

"I'm sorry it didn't work out," I finally said.

"Thanks."

We sat in silence, watching the sunset overtake everything.

"I got into Oberlin, by the way," I said. "I was going to tell you before, but I never found the right time."

He punched me in the shoulder, sloshing the contents of my soda on the concrete porch. "Dude!" he said.

"Full ride, too," I added.

"Sweet!"

"Yeah."

"And I heard from USC," Emmett said.

"You got in?"

"Yep."

My eyes stayed fixed on the horizon, trying to hold on to the sun as it faded.

"Congratulations," I said.

In a few weeks, we'd graduate. After the all-too-brief summer break, we'd be going our separate ways. We *didn't* have all the time in the world.

Emmett said, "I'm gonna miss our jam sessions."

"We'll hang out during vacations," I offered. "And you could come visit me."

"In Ohio? Not."

The colors of the sky were changing quickly now. Blue morphed into pink, purple, magenta. They were undefinable. Never settling on one shade or another.

"What if I made it so you had to come?" I said.

He turned to me. "What do you mean?"

"If I end up being a composition major, I'll have to pass a jury at the end of my freshman year. That's how they decide if you're good enough to go on. They're going to want a recital of my stuff. I'll be writing a bunch of vocal works, of course. What if I wrote some songs for you? Things that would fit your voice. Then you'd have to come visit me at Oberlin to sing for the recital."

"Hm," Emmett said. "Sneaky."

"The songs that run through my head, you're always the one singing them. I can't hear anyone else. I write for you because that's all that will come out. So you have to come. Or I won't be able to finish my degree." I felt my insides seize up. I hadn't planned on telling him how much he inspired me. Up until that moment, I hadn't even realized it myself.

He held out his can of RC to me. "Here's to me being your Musetta."

I snickered. "You mean *muse*. Musetta's a character in *La Bohème*."

"I thought that was Maureen."

"You're thinking of *Rent*."

"Same difference."

"Right."

"Anyway, here's to me being your *muse*."

I clunked my can against his. "And more." My fingers closed around the can, making it crinkle. "Like, you know," I stuttered, "to your visit. And to me writing songs for you. And stuff."

On Emmett's face, something revealed itself briefly, like the ruffle of a stage curtain. Then, just as quickly, the curtain fell back into place.

"Yeah. And stuff." He chugged the rest of his soda, burping loudly afterward.

We laughed and looked out as the sky settled into a single tone of darkness.

Chapter 14—Now

"THIS IS WHERE Ujima's show is?" Mark asks.

A warehouse wall stretches down the block. Electronic dance music thuds from inside, spilling out of the entrance and onto the sidewalk.

I put my arm around Mark's waist. "This is it."

It's been a while since I've been in the Meatpacking District. The neighborhood has changed since the last time I was here. Gentrification has taken over, claiming its stake with shiny restaurants, art galleries, and condos, while a new stretch of the High Line park watches from above. Compared to everything else, the warehouse next to us is a relic, a reminder of a seedier past. The gamey smell of meat even seems to still linger in the air around it.

"I always wanted to come to this club back when it was still open. Never had the guts, though. I was too intimidated by all the muscle boys," Mark says. "Did you ever come here?"

"Not a lot." I rest my head against his shoulder. "A few times."

"Did you like it?"

"Not really."

He watches as people walk inside. His face is lined with a trace of yearning. "I think I would've loved it."

Originally a slaughterhouse, then a skating rink, the building beside us was best known as Twixxy—a discotheque that opened in the early eighties. At the height of its popularity, it lured in huge crowds. People came from all over the world for its celebrity DJs, hordes of shirtless men, and nonstop dancing that went into the early hours of the morning. I managed to catch the last few years of its notorious run after graduating from college, right before it closed in the mid-2000s. By then it had fallen victim to the rising popularity of the internet, its more convenient chat rooms and dating sites eventually replacing the gay megaclubs.

A black Tesla drives up to the sidewalk. Puddles of spring rain splash at our feet. Dinesh emerges from the Uber. He's dressed in a tweed overcoat that looks as if it costs more than I make in a year.

"First working note," he says, waving his printed-out e-ticket at us, "let's make sure the title of our show isn't rubbish. *ONE-derland*? Really?"

"It's a remake of *Alice in Wonderland*," I tell him. I'm about to add, *yet another one*, when I remember that his Peter Pan show isn't exactly the apotheosis of originality. "Would it make it better if I told you that the score is made up of one-hit-wonder songs?"

"You're joking."

"That makes it worse," Mark says.

"Well, I think it'll still give us good ideas for our show," I say. "Let's just try to keep an open mind."

Mark puts both hands to the side of his head and expands them like blooming flowers. "I'm sure it'll be *one*-derful."

At the entrance to the club, we're greeted by a large THIS WAY DOWN THE RABBIT'S HOLE! sign, which seems appropriate in several ways. The pink neon TWIXXY sign by the box office window is turned off and dusty with age, though the ticket sellers are just like the old Twixxy ones—inexplicably angry at us for making them do their job.

Once we're in the main part of the club, subwoofers saturate us with ultra-low bass frequencies, and memories come flooding back to me. Every Saturday night for two years, I'd wait behind the Twixxy velvet rope for the privilege to pay too much entrance money and be ignored by the half-naked bartenders and everyone else. I've never had a body like a sculpture, never been famous or well connected or into ludicrous levels of substance abuse. So the odds were against me. Not to mention the fact that, as an Asian, I was on the lowest rung of the NYC gay male desirability chart.

Not really sure of where to go, we lean up against one of the walls where several other people have decided to wait. The wallpaper is scuffed and tearing away in some places, revealing older wallpaper and even older paint. The urge to pull at the layers to see what's underneath gnaws at me, to see if, maybe, I'll find the actual wall and see what the place really looks like.

A couple of people are brave enough to be the first out on the floor. They dance awkwardly to the music. Above them, the disco ball still sparkles as if it has never stopped spinning. The DJ works her equipment at the booth on the side, though there doesn't seem to be any sort of stage for the show—just a bunch of black box platforms of different sizes and shapes scattered about, like the ones the Twixxy go-go dancers used to dance on, thrusting and gyrating in their thongs. I used to be transfixed by the dancers but always made sure I didn't watch them for too long, afraid it would make me look desperate. Not that that helped me be more attractive to anyone.

I squeeze Mark's hand. He squeezes back. We've had a good few weeks. I'd never seen him as jealous as he was at Broadway Baby, when he caught me with Emmett. But that's behind us now. He believed me when I told him that we were just old classmates. Nothing more. And while that wasn't exactly right, the truth was that there was nothing between Emmett and me. There never has been, and there never will be.

In a strange way, our run-in with Emmett actually brought us closer. I wasn't sold on Dinesh's musical at first. The project didn't seem like the right fit for me, and I couldn't understand why Mark was pushing me so hard to write music for someone else's show when I barely had the inspiration to write for myself.

But at Broadway Baby, I saw how scared he was to lose me. He was only trying to do what he thought was best by setting me up with Dinesh. It was the kick in the ass I needed to start writing again, even if it was for someone else's idea.

So far he's been right. I have to admit to myself that it feels good to compose again. I've managed to write two of the songs Dinesh needs, plus arrangements for four others that he'd already come up with melodies for. We just need one more new song to round out a decent first act to show the producers. After that monumental writing effort, I felt myself running out of creative steam, so I suggested a group field trip to Ujima's show as a way to get some more ideas. It felt like the perfect thing to get my juices flowing again. Not to mention the fact that I wanted to support Jee's first official off-Broadway show.

I see Ujima emerge from a side entrance. Even if they didn't wave at us, they would be impossible to miss. Their costume is a ruby and ivory sculptural dress that takes up most of the space around them, the shoulder pads so big that they could be used to serve food. People jump out of the way as Jee comes toward us, pushed aside by their dress. Or maybe it's because everyone is scared of the object they're carrying—a flesh-colored staff that's topped with a heart-shaped tip, which is, for some reason, upside down.

It's basically a massive dildo.

"Hello, boys."

"Wow," Dinesh says.

"You like?" they ask, waving the staff over themself.

"Er . . . y-yes," Dinesh stutters.

They sigh. "I can see you're not gagged by my divine eleganza. Just this enormous—"

"Power rod?" Dinesh offers.

"Sex scepter?" Mark says.

"Wig in the shape of a crown?" I say.

Ujima rolls their eyes at me. "Bitch, please. Don't pretend you can't stop looking at this thing like everyone else. I can feel your sphincter muscles tightening from here."

"So you're the Queen of Hearts, I presume?" Dinesh asks.

"Miz Queeny Hart. Owner and MC of the Croquet Club." They bow low, showing off the center of their crown-wig, which is filled with stuffed hearts. It really is a phenomenal hairpiece. "Thank you all for coming," they say, to Mark in particular.

He nods. "You can thank Quito for that."

"Well, you didn't have to say yes. I appreciate your support."

"You're welcome." Mark is being sincere. I know that he's been trying. For me, at least, if not for Ujima.

"Oh. I have presents for you all." Jee hands us heart-suited playing cards. "Entrance to the VIP lounge behind the bar. Drinks are gratis in there," they say, pronouncing it *graTEES* in their best incorrect French.

I give Mark a quick peck on the cheek. "You two go ahead. I want to catch up with Jee." As Mark and Dinesh head back to the lounge, I take a closer look at Ujima, touching different parts of their costume. It's surprisingly decadent for a show I didn't think had a huge budget. Then again, there seems to be no set, so maybe they've saved money that way. "So, where is the stage? When do we get to see Wonderland? I mean, *ONE*-derland."

"Honey, you're already in it. The main tunnel where you came in? That's the rabbit hole. So, technically, you've arrived."

"And how does this whole interactive thing work? Are we part of the show? How are we supposed to know what to do?" Past nightmares run through my head, the ones where I suddenly find myself onstage for a concert without knowing any of the music I'm supposed to play.

"Don't worry. We're going to guide you through everything."

I survey the club. It looks as if some of the other cast members are also starting to mix in with the crowd. I'm not entirely sure about all of them, but some—like the white boy in dreadlocks and a green trench coat smoking a vape pen and the man in an ivory fur coat twirling a watch on a gold chain—are definitely part of the show.

"I'm along for the ride, Jee, whatever this ends up being. It's your first off-Broadway gig. I know how much this means to you."

They look down at their dress and touch the sides of it, as if they're reassuring themself that everything is where it should be. "It does feel right somehow. Like this role was written for me."

"It was. I wouldn't have missed it for anything. Not even your scary stick could've kept me away."

They wave it at me, and my butt cheeks automatically clench. Dammit. Jee was right about the sphincter thing.

"So has you-know-who called you yet?" Jee asks.

I shake my head. It's been seven weeks and four days since Emmett and I last saw each other at Broadway Baby. Not that I've been counting.

"Girl, why don't you just call him?"

"It's fine. He's busy. He'll call when he can. We still have plenty of time."

They shift their attention off to the side, and a flash of light goes off. A photographer gives us a thumbs-up. He's just snapped a candid of us.

Jee pulls me in close to them, filling my nose with the smell of stage makeup, hair spray, and lavender perfume. "How's my face?" they ask through their teeth. I give an okay sign. "Do me a favor, sweetie, and take one more of us," Jee says, standing in bevel and presenting their other side to him. "Promo pictures for the website," they explain to me. "Look pretty for the camera!"

I give a closemouthed smile and then wriggle away so that the photographer can't take another picture. I've never been fond of getting mine taken. My dad always used to lug his camera with its complicated lenses and attachments to my recitals, snapping endless shots of me while I played. When we'd pick the developed pictures up from the drugstore, I'd refuse to look at them. They always seemed like someone else. Someone whose eyes were too far apart, with a nose that was too big and a chin that was too small. He'd frame his favorite ones and put them on the piano. Whenever I'd practice, I'd turn them around so I didn't have to look at them.

"I should go find the boys." I kiss Jee. "Break a leg. Both legs."

"Honey, these are my money makers," they say, pulling the sides of their dress up and slapping their padded hips and thighs. "Mama's in big trouble if these break."

I wade my way through the crowd, now thick with audience and cast members. The lights flicker briefly. The DJ begins to play the theme song to the old TV show *Alice*. No doubt a cue that the show is about to begin. I hurry back to the VIP lounge and almost miss the dark glass door behind the main bar. Back when Twixxy was open, I never had the connections or the money or the drugs for VIP access. I show my red playing card to the bouncer and slip in.

Some of the people are already starting to leave, meandering out toward the main dance floor for the show. Even with the thinning crowd, I have a hard time finding Mark and Dinesh. Finally, I spot them at the very back near the mini-bar area. They're not talking to each other. They stare at their drinks like they're both concentrating on something. As if someone's just asked them both a question and they're still trying to come up with the answer.

"Hey," I say. "I think the show's about to start."

Mark looks up at me, startled. "Great. Let's go." He starts walking toward the exit immediately without looking back at Dinesh, who follows us without a word. I make a mental note to myself to check in later with Mark to see if they've gotten into a fight of some kind. If they have, I hope it doesn't have anything to do with our show. Or my songs. I'm the first person to admit they're not my best work, but they're still decent. My heart sinks with the possibility that Dinesh hasn't been happy with them, that Mark might have been trying to stick up for my music. He's already done so much for me.

159

I take his hand when we arrive back out on the dance floor. He doesn't hold on to it quite as tightly as when we first arrived.

Four of the movable boxes have been smooshed together, forming a makeshift stage on the dance floor. A spot lights up Ujima, standing in the center of it. "Ladies and gentlemen and everyone in between, welcome to...ONE! DER! LAND!"

The crowd roars. The show has begun.

Ujima explains that everyone is now part of the show as ONE-derland clubgoers, witnesses to Alice's evening of adventures. The story will unwind in different parts of the club. We'll be nudged along to where we need to be by cast members as they move the platforms in and out of formation, creating an ever-changing set.

Once the actual show begins, I become distracted. Unmistakable tension runs between Mark and Dinesh, standing on either side of me. Mark can't seem to enjoy himself. Not even when the Alice character, a whiny bridge-and-tunnel girl, starts crying over not being able to get into the VIP lounge and a slew of chorus boys in bathing suits perform "It's Raining Men" as a response. Mark's got to be truly upset not to enjoy being surrounded on all sides by endless abs.

When Alice befriends a bunch of club kids dressed in animal-themed costumes, I ask Mark if he's doing okay. He looks confused. And not just because the cast members are now instructing us to dance the Macarena with them in a big circle. "I'm fine," he says. "Why?"

"No reason," I say as I pat each of my ass cheeks and shimmy my hips. "But is Dinesh having problems with my songs? I can fix them up. And the last one, which I'm almost done with, will be the best one yet." Not a lie, exactly. More of a hopeful exaggeration.

"Oh," he says. "No. He loves your songs. Don't worry about that." He rubs my back briefly before returning to the dance steps.

I'm happy they haven't been arguing over me. And I am surprised at how much Mark is getting into the Macarena.

As the story unfolds, it becomes increasingly clear to me that this Alice isn't as sweet and innocent as other versions of the character. In fact, she's kind of a sloppy drunk drama queen. She keeps taking other people's drinks and asking everyone for what she calls "happy cakes," which, from the strange ways they affect her, are infused with questionable substances. When Off-White Rabbit—a tweaked-out dealer on way too many uppers—gives her one, the seat of her pants inflates, making it look as if her ass swells up.

Naturally, he sings, "Baby Got Back."

The three of us look at each other and burst out laughing. We decide the best thing to do is to give in to the sheer ridiculousness of the show.

We dance along to the song and everything that comes after, including Mr. Caterpillar's rendition of "Ice Ice Baby," Chester Cheshire singing "I'm Too Sexy," and, finally, Ujima's performance of "Bitch," which is the highlight of the evening. It's such a tour de force I completely forget that we're watching a show and give Jee as big a hug as my short arms can around their massive costume after they're done. I don't care if it's not allowed. I don't even care that the heart dildo is only inches from my face. I just want Ujima to know how proud I am of them.

After the cast bows at the end of the show, the Off-White Rabbit announces that ONE-derland will stay open. The DJ will spin more one-hit wonders until midnight, turning the venue into a real club. "At that point," he says, "the Rabbit's Hole will close!" Talk about tightening sphincters.

We manage to pry Ujima away from a group of appreciative audience members so that we can celebrate with a round of drinks in the VIP lounge.

"I have to admit, that was quite a show," Dinesh says. "I'm genuinely impressed by how they managed to make 'Tubthumping' work. That song has never made sense to me until now."

"I can't believe I'm saying this, but I agree," Mark says. "Congratulations." He raises his martini to Jee.

"To the queen," I say, clinking my soda to everyone's glasses.

Ujima lets out a throaty laugh. "Long may I reign!" they pronounce, before sipping their fruity cocktail through the tiny stirrer stick.

I feel my cell phone buzz in my pocket. Maybe Emmett is finally reaching out.

I don't want to check it with Mark sitting right next to me. "Excuse me," I say, "just have to use the little boys' room." I run to the nearby bathroom, where the booming beats aren't quite as loud.

By the time I get to an empty stall, my phone has stopped buzzing. I check the caller ID. Not Emmett.

Dad.

I call him back.

"Mr. Cruz?" responds a familiar girl's voice.

"Celeste? Why do you always have my dad's phone?"

"Um, I'm at his house? Your house, I mean. In your old room, bee-tee-dubs. You have super-cool taste! All these framed posters of old musicals. Did you actually get to see any of these? Like the original production of *Into the Woods*? I mean—"

"Celeste, what are you doing at my house?"

"I stopped by to bring your dad some chicken soup. My mom makes some really amazing pozole. Not too spicy. In case it irritates your dad's condition."

"What are you talking about? Why are you bringing him soup?"

"He didn't want to tell you." She brings her voice down to a whisper. "He's asleep right now. Recovering. Us choir kids have been taking turns visiting him."

I pump up my phone's volume to maximum and press a finger to my free ear in order to be able to hear her. "Please. Tell me what's going on."

"Mr. Cruz. I mean, our Mr. Cruz. I mean, your dad. He's been gone from school for the past two weeks. He's been sick. Like really, really sick. Mr. Drummond, the band teacher, is subbing, but all he does is put on DVDs of movie musicals. And not even good ones like *Hairspray* and *Dreamgirls*! Terrible ones. Like *Seven Brides for Seven Brothers*. We haven't had a real rehearsal since Mr. Cruz left. He's never been gone this long before."

She takes a ragged breath before asking, "Can you come earlier than you were supposed to, Mr. Quito? We could really use your help."

Chapter 15 – Then

"YOU'RE SURE YOU'RE okay? Did you get someone to help you like I suggested?" I asked.

Outside my dorm room, rain was coming down in torrents. Our tenth straight day of spring showers. Yay, Ohio.

Emmett *tsk*ed on the other end of the telephone line. The noise of rushing cars and honking horns echoed in the background. "I got this, Quito. Just chill."

"You've been practicing all three songs?" I'd mailed him the sheet music for my song cycle two months ago. Then, after stress-obsessing over it for a week, I'd followed up with a tape recording of me playing them overlaid with a separate track of me singing the vocal line on top. Just to be sure. Emmett wasn't an expert at reading music, and I wasn't at USC to help him.

"It's all good. I found someone here to run through them with me. She's more of a jazz pianist, but we got through it all right. Your practice tape helped a lot. Plus, most of the melody lines by themselves aren't that hard."

I'd done that on purpose. Not because I didn't trust Emmett's natural musicality. It was one of the defining aspects of my cycle: setting simple melodies on top of an accompaniment that constantly changed. The texts I'd chosen, excerpts from Filipino national hero José Rizal's poems, were easy to read and absorb—while the themes behind them were complex and myriad. I wanted that to be reflected in the piano and voice.

"That's great," I said, relieved. "How are things in L.A.?"

"Good. I booked a couple of modeling gigs. The agency's thinking of sending me out for some other types of auditions."

"Awesome. And classes are going okay?"

"Still getting straight As."

"Show-off. Rehearsals for *Guys and Dolls?*"

"Oh. I had to drop out. Conflicted with basketball practice."

"You're still in choir, though, right?"

He laughed sadly. "Yeah...so...I dropped out of choir, too."

"What? Are you really that busy?"

"It's not that. For choir, at least. It's just...I don't know. I didn't like it. The director picks interesting music. He's just not like your dad. He's kind of, I dunno. Boring. And, like, *you're* not there."

"Yeah, well, no one could possibly replace me," I joked.

"Exactly." He stretched the word out, filling it with unspoken things. "It's just not the same without you."

We tended to end up like this during our phone calls. I'd find myself maneuvered into a place where I had to choose carefully what I said next, mindful not to cross over into a misunderstanding of our friendship again. The things he said and the way he said them to me—they always felt as if they were some riddles to solve. When he'd do that, I'd force myself to think back to Laney's party. Him and Angela. Side by side. A perfect picture. I'd think: What girl was he dating now? Or fooling around with? Because there had to be one, of course. Or more. Maybe the pianist was one of them. But while it wasn't something I wanted him to tell me, not knowing about that part of his life bugged me. It always crept in on the edges of my mind, no matter how hard I tried to keep those thoughts out. So I did what I always did in those situations. I pivoted the conversation back to him.

"So you're not in choir. You're not doing the musical. Are you singing at all? You must be out of practice. I should have just asked someone here to do my recital."

Emmett's stay wouldn't be long. The fact that we'd only have a day to prepare together before my composition jury stressed me out. This wasn't us going through nonconsequential music back at my house just for fun. We'd be in front of people whose job it was to judge me. There'd be no room for error. The comp professors would be holding my future in their hands.

"Don't be a spaz," Emmett said.

"Just be ready," I said. "I don't want you fucking things up."

"Dude."

I gripped the phone in my hand. "I'm sorry."

It wasn't just the jury. My anxiety level was growing the more I thought about the coming weekend. Two whole days of nerve-racking events. Emmett would arrive next Saturday afternoon, which meant we'd only have an hour or two to practice my compositions before Acappellooza at Finney Chapel that night. It would be the first time for the Obertones—Oberlin's premier all-male a capella group—to host the event and my first time directing them. Then, the next day, the Tones would have to sing again for the Alumni Luncheon. Right before my composition jury with Emmett. We'd have to run from the luncheon to the Conservatory just to get there on time.

But the thing that made me the most nervous? Emmett. We hadn't seen each other since Christmas break. Just enough time for a brief dinner at Red Robin, doing our best to catch up on a semester's worth of first-time college experiences over the all-you-can-eat fries. This time, he'd be coming to stay with me for an entire weekend, sleeping just a few feet away in my roommate's bed while my roommate would be visiting his cousins in Cleveland. The thought of spending that much time with Emmett—and being that close to him at night—made my head swim with anxiety.

"It's gonna be okay. I promise," he said, the confidence in his voice as powerful as ever. He always had a way of convincing me of almost anything.

"Okay," I said. "Well, thanks for agreeing to do this. Coming all this way just for my exam."

"I'm not coming just for your exam."

"And for Acappellooza."

"You know what I mean, Quito."

The line on his end went quiet. He must have closed the windows of his room to the riot of Los Angeles outside because I couldn't hear a thing.

I felt him growing impatient on the other end. As if this were a scene in a play and I was missing my cue to say the next line.

I had to keep reminding myself: Emmett liked girls. Not me. Not that way.

Remember.

"I. Um. I'll ... see you in a week," I barely managed to say.

Silence.

Finally, Emmett said, "Yep, see you," and hung up.

I listened to the dial tone for a while, letting it drone in my ear until the busy signal took over and drilled into my head. I knocked the receiver end of the phone onto my forehead a few times before finally putting it back on the hook.

Next door, in the adjoining bedroom, Jayesh was talking to his computer science study partner, Melina, a trust fund kid who tried to hide her privilege with dumpster clothing and had questionable personal hygiene. They were arguing about subroutine programming. Or ASCII dots. Or something. I couldn't make it out and wouldn't have been able to understand it even if I could. All I knew was that in order to get out to go to the bathroom, I had to walk through Jayesh's room, and I wasn't eager to do that.

Melina kind of had a thing for me.

The first time Jayesh introduced me to her, she grabbed me by the hand and regarded me as if I were the biggest stuffed animal prize at a carnival booth. After that, she started making a habit of bumping into me in Dascomb Dining Hall and then staring at me from across the room while she gnawed on her whole-grain breadsticks. Not that I was any expert at flirting, but I'm pretty sure she was the absolute worst at it. I steered clear of her as much as possible to avoid giving her the chance.

The ache in my bladder was building up. I knew I didn't have much time before pee started to leak out of my body, so I decided to chance it. They'd stopped talking. Maybe they were studying so intently that I could slip out unnoticed.

I tiptoed through Jayesh's room. Only to walk straight into Melina. She was almost six feet tall, so she was pretty hard to miss.

"Hey, Quito." Her eyelids blinked slowly and heavily as she

looked down at me. Either she was on barbiturates, or she was trying to seduce me.

"Hey...you," I said, avoiding her gaze at all costs. "Sorry to disturb you. Just have to use the little boys' room."

She planted herself right in front of the door. "You were so very, very quiet. Like a little mousy. I didn't even know you were in there. Trying to hide from me?"

The main door opened, and Jayesh sauntered in, holding several bags of barbecue potato chips from the vending machine. I took advantage of the distraction to sidestep Melina and escape. She yelled out behind me, "God, Quito! You're so *random!*" while I sprinted down the long hallway, filled with panic and built-up pee.

Later that afternoon, after hiding for at least half an hour in one of the bathroom stalls, I tiptoed back to my dorm room, peeked to make sure Melina had finally left, grabbed my music portfolio and practice binder, and hightailed it to the Conservatory. Not only did I need to make sure my composition jury pieces were absolutely perfect, but I also had to practice my conducting on the Obertones pieces we were doing for Acappellooza and the accompaniment for a bunch of voice recitals in the coming week. I had a ton of work to do and only a few days to do it all before Emmett came.

The day Emmett arrived, the sun had finally come out. The air smelled of wet grass and budding flowers, everything fresh and full of potential. It almost pained me to rush him to the practice room building straight from the airport shuttle. He'd spent several months in smog-congested Los Angeles. Being in suburban Ohio must have felt like an environmental detox.

"Do we have to practice right now?" Emmett asked. "It's so amazing out. I saw some people playing Ultimate Frisbee out on the lawn in the park. Can't we go join them first?"

"Emmett, we only have two hours. Then I have to get ready for Acappellooza."

"Pfft. Plenty of time to rehearse."

"No. This is too important."

He took the only chair in the practice room, the one for the piano, and sat back in it, putting his hands behind his head and stretching himself to the outermost limits of the tiny room. I strained myself trying to ignore him and focused instead on the sheet music I was spreading out onto the piano's stand. He knew I was trying to avoid looking at him because I saw him smile out of the corner of my eye.

"Quito," he said. God. I'd missed that crooked-toothed smile more than I'd realized. "Chillax. We used to learn entire musicals in an hour. And not just because I'm a fast and incredibly gifted learner. Which I am. Because you're an awesome teacher."

I shook my head and sighed. "Let's see how much we can get done in an hour. And if we're good enough, I'll let you go do ultimate freestyle or whatever. Deal?"

He got up, took my hand, squeezed it, and shook. "Deal."

Even though I hadn't seen Emmett in months, I hadn't forgotten how it felt to touch him. Like watching infinite sunsets setting at the same time and feeling the accumulative warmth of them in my body.

I shook it off. I had to.

We got down to work.

Thankfully, he hadn't lied. He *had* practiced. A lot. So much that he almost had things memorized. At one point, I almost stopped playing when I realized he was singing the songs without looking at the sheet music. Instead, he was watching me, keying into movements, my playing. Just like I'd always done with his singing.

We went through the first song twice before moving on to the second. It was just as well prepared.

My fingers became looser. I played more freely. We were able to have more fun with the music, to work on nuances I didn't think we'd have time to address.

He'd really done what he'd said. I never should have doubted him.

Then we tried the third song.

Halfway through, Emmett stopped singing. He tilted his head at me. "Am I messing up that much?"

"Nope. You're fine."

"Quito, I see that vein in the middle of your forehead. It only throbs when you get anxious."

"I have an anxiety vein? Why did nobody ever tell me this?"

"It makes you look more mature." Emmett laughed. "So tell me. What am I messing up?"

I tapped a finger on the sheet music. "Let's go over the first verse again."

"That part's the trickiest for me, for some reason."

It was the complex accompaniment. Maybe too complex. I had wanted the poem's theme of conflict to come across in the music. So I filled it with runs of chromaticisms paired with syncopated cluster chords. Of course he was having a hard time singing the melody correctly. I was throwing him off.

But I had built something into it that he probably hadn't noticed. Something that might make things easier. "Let me play it for you again. Don't sing. Just listen."

I started from the beginning. This time I brought out certain notes. They never appeared in an obvious string. They jumped from hand to hand and sometimes even from octave to octave. It took careful listening to discover the harmony I'd hidden, one that paired perfectly with the melody. "What do you hear?" I asked.

He shook his head. "I don't—"

"Keep listening," I said. "Close your eyes. Let yourself really hear it."

I kept going, bringing the hidden line out even more. Playing it as if it were the actual melody.

Emmett's eyes popped open. He laughed. "You hid a duet in there."

"See. I'm with you every step of the way. You just have to listen."

He stared at his music, tracing the notes with the tips of his fingers. At first I thought he was trying to locate the hidden harmony. He wasn't. He was caressing the pages. The same way he'd touched my copy of "A Part I Play" when I'd first given it to him. As if it were something precious.

"So you think you got it?" I asked.

He nodded. "I got it."

"I know you do. Actually, I think we *will* be able to finish early. You can go have some fun before Acappellooza."

"Cool! And, Quito, we're going to be fine," he said. "More than fine."

But, unfortunately, he was wrong.

Chapter 16—Now

I'M FLYING.

The New York skyline is barely recognizable from up here. As I ascend, the island of Manhattan melts into the rest of the Eastern Seaboard. The sun is so bright that I can feel it searing into my eyes, leaving a corona-shaped imprint. The clouds are cool and bracing against my skin. Shouldn't the air sting more this high above the ground?

Someone squeezes my hand. Mark is holding me aloft. He takes me higher, into the dark reaches of the sky, out into space. I can see the entirety of the United States. An expanse of valley greens and mountainous browns.

We keep climbing.

A pull. Coming from my other hand.

Emmett.

He turns and shines me that smile of his and then tugs me down back to the earth. Heading westward toward California.

Mark pulls us back up. The fringes of his tunic flutter in the wind, and his feathered cap escapes and flies away. He's... Peter Pan?

He lets out a mischievous laugh.

I'm stuck in midair. Like a human rope in a game of tug-of-war. My arms cramp up.

A woman materializes ahead of us. Her hair is pixieish and

dark brown, her eyes obsidian black. Her dress sparkles with every color of the rainbow. Her mouth, beak-like, lets out a beautiful, silvery tune. It sounds like a bell. *Tinkle, tinkle, tinkle, tinkle—*

"Hoy! Francisco!"

I force my eyes open. "Dad?"

"Your alarm has been going off for the past ten minutes." His face, prickly with several days' worth of stubble, hovers above mine. "Halika na. Gutom na ako." He scratches his behind and lumbers out of my childhood bedroom. "I want some Spam pancakes."

I stare up at the ceiling above me. Splotchy in all the same spots. My old desk and bookshelves still hold the same books, the walls the same Easter egg blue I'd wanted for my fifteenth birthday. My blanket and pillows even still smell like my childhood. Layers of generic laundry detergent struggling to rein in years of messy, musty adolescence.

White noise crackles in the living room, followed by loud conversation. Like clockwork, my dad is tuning in to his favorite morning news show. A host tries unsuccessfully to get his guest to shut up and gets cut off by a commercial for fibromyalgia pills.

Grunting, I throw my legs over the side of the bed. My toes poke around everywhere, trying to find my tsinelas. I get them on after the third try but still can't muster the will to get out of bed. I've gotten used to a schedule of going to sleep around 2:00 a.m. and not getting up until ten o'clock the next morning. I'm resentful that I now have to get up at 7:00 a.m.

As if to spite me, my phone alarm goes off again. I grab it off the bedside table and carry it with me to the living room.

I rub my eyes with the heels of my hands and flop down on the couch. "Can you turn it down a little? It's so loud."

My dad sinks lower into his recliner and begrudgingly points the remote control at the wide-screen TV, one of the only things in the house not originally from the eighties or nineties. "I have a hard time hearing what they're saying sometimes." His disheveled hair is more gray than I've ever seen it before.

"All right," I say. "You can put it back up a few notches."

I pull out my phone and check my texts. Still no word from Emmett. Just a reminder about an upcoming dental appointment and a check-in from Ujima.

My emails scroll by. In among the junk is a message from Mark.

Hey. Hope your dad is doing okay.

I've been working feverishly with Dinesh to get *The Forever Boys* (working title) on its feet. The auditions went better than expected. We found some great people. Including the PERFECT guy to play Peter Pan, touring and regional credits and a fantastic voice AND looks like he's 12 (though he's probably around 30, that bastard).

Anyway, we start rehearsals soon . . . sooooo we're hoping you've managed to get some work done on the final song? I reattached the lyrics here, just in case. Oh, and we changed a few words here and there, to tighten it up.

We miss you.

-Mark

PS: when are you back?

With me here and the producers' audition coming up, Dinesh needed logistic help. So Mark offered to assist. Not that he's ever been a director, actor, singer, or dancer—but he knows more about musicals than even I do. He's got plenty to offer.

I just hope it isn't anything more than that.

We.

A ten-sentence email and he used the word four times, each appearance of it brighter than any of the other words on my phone screen.

I force myself away from the main body of the email and open up the attachment. The lyrics to the Act I finale. A song about Tinker Bell's magic fairy dust. The changes they made did nothing to improve it; the allusions to cocaine are still clumsy and the rhymes are beyond lazy. *"Soaring so very high. When we are so very high?"* Really? It's no wonder I can't manage the motivation to finish composing the last song. I've got shit-all to work with.

Still, I know Dinesh is getting nervous. We're running out of time. At least he was kind enough to not get upset when I told him I needed to come back to California to take care of my dad. Unlike Mark.

"Is he really that sick? It doesn't sound so bad. One of the partners at work had walking pneumonia, too, and she was back to work after two weeks or so. Why do you have to fill in for him at school? Aren't they supposed to get a substitute for that?"

"They do have a sub. He's the band teacher. And he hates choir. Plus, they need to keep preparing for Dad's concert."

"What about our show?"

"I'll finish the last song in California. I promise."

"Fine. Just don't be gone too long. We can find someone to

play the songs while you're gone, but it'll be better if you're back in time to music direct. It's your stuff, after all. This show is your big shot. You don't want to mess it up."

I didn't know how to respond to that. Not in any way that wouldn't start a fight, at least. The truth was, they didn't need me like my dad did.

"You just got out of bed and already you check your phone," my dad says to me. "You kids these days. I'm always confiscating the students' phones because they're like you. As if you all cannot live without it. Is there really something so important there you have to check it all the time?"

When I arrived back in California two weeks ago, I gave in and texted Emmett. I didn't tell him my dad was sick. Only that we needed to start figuring out when he should come up to the Bay Area to start rehearsing for the concert. The Emmett I knew from school would only need a day or two to practice with me and the choir. But as far as I know, it's been years since he's sung in a public concert—not since high school. So I sent a text suggesting he come up at least a week in advance. More than one text, in fact.

He still hasn't gotten back to me. I'm starting to panic. Though, of course, I can't tell my father this.

"Nope. Nothing important," I say. "Did you say you wanted Spam?"

"Yes."

"And pancakes?"

"Spam pancakes."

"You want Spam pancakes? Is that even a thing?"

"Trust me."

"How do I make them?"

He taps a finger onto the outstretched palm of his other hand, as if this gesture is enough to explain.

"What the heck is that supposed to mean?"

"Put Spam inside the pancakes."

"Like, as a sandwich, or...?"

Dad sighs. One of the deep, weary kind that only parents seem to be able to make.

"I'll figure something out."

I plod into the kitchen. At least now I can make some coffee.

The coffeemaker's insides are crusted over with so much residue that I can't even make out the original material. It's like the rest of the kitchen, unchanged from my high school days. I'd suggest remodeling, but Dad is a creature of habit. *So what if everything is old? Why waste the money when everything still works fine?*

The Last Supper woodcraft relief on the wall stares at me as I wait for the coffee to brew. A serene and lopsidedly carved Jesus watches, just as it did every time I'd sit at the table and beg for McDonald's instead of the food my parents made. It took me years of living without home-cooked Filipino food to realize how good I had it back then.

"Maybe Dad's right," I say to wooden Jesus. "Sometimes the old stuff is best."

Feeling renewed after a sip of hot caffeine, I root around in the cabinets looking for flour. All I see is a box of Bisquick. After checking the expiration date to make sure it isn't as old as I am, I mix a cupful with eggs and milk to make a batter and then pop open one of the many cans of Spam from the cupboard. I chop it up into small cubes and, not knowing what else to do, toss them into the bowl with the batter.

I pour chunky, decidedly non-pancake-shaped blobs onto the frying pan. After flipping them over, I tear off a piece of one with a fork to test it, dipping it in some syrup before popping it into my mouth. Dad was definitely onto something. It's delicious.

There's still fresh orange juice left in the refrigerator. I pour some in Dad's favorite glass. The same one Emmett had given to him with a bottle of sake so long ago. The multicolored Mondrian-like block pattern on it still looks as good as new. It astounds me how, after so many years of constant use, he's never once so much as scratched it.

I bring the OJ and pancakes out and set them on a TV tray table. "Here you go."

"Did you try it already?"

"I did."

"What did I tell you? You should always trust my judgment." He closes his eyes as he chews, and his face takes on a satisfied, sanguine look. When I first arrived, he was still in pretty bad shape—always exhausted with barely any energy to get up in the morning. And although he wasn't coughing or sneezing, he complained of minor chest pains often enough that I never forced him to do anything more than eat his meals, even in bed if he wanted, which he usually did. Seeing him almost like his usual self makes me more confident that he's well on the road to recovery.

"Dad, do you think you might be able to go back to school soon? I don't want to push you, but you seem to be doing a lot better. You're not even coughing at all, and I don't think you've had a fever since I've been home."

He keeps eating and watching the television.

"Dad?"

He says, still not looking at me, "I'm sick."

"Okay, fine. I'll see if I can extend my visit for a little longer. But I was only supposed to be here for a few days and not until later in the month. If I stay too long, I might lose my job at the piano bar. And I'm supposed to be working on a show."

"Show? What show is this?"

"Oh." I'm immediately sorry that I've brought it up. "Just this new musical. I'm writing a few songs for it."

"Why didn't you tell me, Quito? A new musical? Wow, that's good news! Ang galing talaga ng anak ko!"

"I guess."

"You haven't composed in so long. I've been wondering why you haven't been using your gift."

"Playing piano has been enough."

"You didn't have the right inspiration. And now you have it."

I swirl the remains of my pancake around in a puddle of syrup. "I know I should be excited, but I'm just not that into it."

"You don't like the project?"

"Not really."

"Why did you agree to it, then?"

"Mark got it for me. I owe it to him," I say. My chest tightens. "I'm sure I can make it work somehow. The more energy I put in, the more I'll get into it. That's all."

My dad mutes the TV. The sudden absence of noise startles me. Growing up, if music wasn't being played in the house, the TV was on. There was always a near-constant stream of sound. Silence was reserved for sleeping time and sometimes not even then. "Francisco. You know that's not how music works. When something you're working on is worthwhile, it gives *you* strength, not the other way around. If you don't find it with this show—with Mark—maybe you should be looking elsewhere. Maybe you should be focusing on something you really love."

Something breathes its way into my lungs. "Maybe."

"Why don't you write a song for our concert?"

The tightness comes back. Emmett hasn't been in contact, so we haven't worked out any of the details of what he'll be doing. "You mean for Emmett? I'm not exactly sure what he had in mind. He probably already has something he wants to sing."

"No. I meant for the choir. Why don't you write something for the kids?"

"Those kids wouldn't want to sing anything I write for them."

"And why is that?"

"Because they hate me."

"They don't hate you. You're *my* son, and they love me." Dad laughs.

"They miss their Mr. Cruz."

"You are a Mr. Cruz, too."

"Just consider going back to work soon. Okay?" I get up to bus his plate. Dad hands me his empty glass. I hold it firmly in my hand before putting it on the tray. "The sooner the better."

"Anak, speaking about Emmett, I should probably tell you something—"

The doorbell rings. At seven o'clock in the morning?

I open the front door and see Emmett standing there holding a carry-on bag and what looks like a gift-wrapped painting.

"I heard you could use a little help," he says.

Chapter 17—Then

I STOOD IN the wings of Finney Chapel's stage, watching the Tufts University Beelzebubs obliterate the audience with their rendition of "Motownphilly" at Acappellooza.

When they'd first arrived, I wasn't expecting much of a show. They seemed like a boring collection of geeks in buttoned-up jackets and matching ties. Nowhere near as cool as the Obertones, dressed in our jeans and untucked shirts. In fact, when their soloist had taken the stage, I thought they'd made a mistake and announced the wrong song. There was no way that this guy— a skinny kid with the sex appeal of a saltine—could be the lead vocalist on a Boyz II Men song.

Then he started singing. With one thrust of his bony hips, he completely upended my brain. His baritone voice oozed more sex and white-boy soul than Rick Astley. I peeked out into Finney and saw everyone's faces light up. The rest of his group backed him with tight harmonies and slick dance moves, almost turning Finney Chapel, however briefly, into an actual place of worship.

How the hell were they this good?

And how were the Obertones supposed to follow it?

Just an hour before, I was in great spirits. Emmett and I had run through my song cycle twice, perfectly. After watching him chase a Frisbee in front of Harkness Co-op for a while, I'd even managed to squeeze us in some time to grab food at Wilder Hall before the concert.

"This place is nothing like USC," Emmett said in between bites of his chicken sandwich.

"Is that a good thing?"

"I mean, it's such a tiny campus. There's nowhere to go. But you kinda got everything you need here. And the...Con? Is that what you guys call the music conservatory? It's amazing. We have, like, twenty times the students you do, but our music department sucks compared to yours."

"We do have great music here. The best in the country."

"I bet the Obertones are incredible."

"We're pretty solid," I said.

"There you go again. Downplaying shit." He grabbed a french fry from my plate, dipped it into the mound of ketchup there, and popped it into his mouth. "Look at you. You're already leading the number one a cappella group on campus, and you're just a freshman."

"*First-year*, thanks. *Freshman* is way too sexist for Obies."

"Oh, excuuuuse me."

"And I don't know. I feel like I just lucked into it. I didn't even try that hard to get into the group in the first place. This senior voice major that I accompany, Shane, he sort of fast-tracked me in. Then, when their director Brett left all of a sudden, they just unanimously voted to make me his replacement."

"Why'd he leave?"

"For selling pot, I think. To a student he was tutoring. Or having sex with a student he was tutoring," I said. "Anyway, I think he was also a seventh-year senior, so they probably just got tired of him being here."

"Maybe that's why Shane got you in so fast. He saw the writing on the wall."

"Yeah, maybe." I took a sip of the last dregs of my soda. "You know, the weird thing is, my dad predicted I'd be leading the Tones within the year."

"He said that?"

"Yeah. He said I helped him conduct a choir for years. I was meant to be a director."

Emmett chewed, swallowed. "They're lucky to have you." He smiled.

I responded by finishing my sandwich and tried not to get too wound up by his compliments.

I was excited, though. This was going to be my first concert as the Obertones director. And Emmett had flown all the way here. To sing for my recital, yes, but also to hear our concert. After we'd finished eating, I made sure to seat him in the front row in Finney before heading backstage to warm up the Tones. I was fully expecting to lead them to success, to give Emmett a one-of-a-kind performance that no one would forget.

But Saltine Boy and the Sex Gods in Suits were messing up my plan.

They ended their number and were rewarded with cheers.

For their second song, the Beelzebubs got into a tight clump and put their heads down. Their director blew into his pitch pipe and counted them off. As each guy entered, they lifted their head, creating a visual road map of the song, an arrangement of Toto's "Africa." Each part bubbled along, accompanying the lead line, splitting into different solos among the group. There was no central soloist or flashy moves this time. Just great singing. Great enough for me to continue doubting myself. How was I going to make sure the Tones brought it all home and justified being the closing act of our own event?

The Beelzebubs finished their song to enthusiastic applause. They walked off the stage grinning at us while they passed. They'd transformed into rock stars right before our eyes, and they knew it.

"Let's do this!" one of the Obertones shouted. Shane, I think. I was too nervous to be able to tell. They bunched up around me, howling, and pushed me out onto the stage like a tide carrying a body out to sea. I fought back the sensation of drowning and tried to look as confident and excited as they sounded.

We got into our standard semicircle formation: tenors on the right, baritones on the left, and basses in the middle with mics in front to capture their low notes. I stood on the outer edge of the tenors so I could direct. I hummed an E-flat. Shane took the center of the stage. I counted off a measure for nothing, and we were off.

They *da-da-da*'d in a syncopated harmony—the intro to my arrangement of "Kiss from a Rose" by Seal. Shane, stout and blindingly blond, was the physical polar opposite of Seal. It didn't matter when he started singing the solo, though, because his voice was perfect for the song. Light and flexible with a craggy edge. He maneuvered through the solo's extreme interval jumps like an acrobat leaping through circus hoops. The rest of us felt his confidence and returned it to him with rock-solid accompaniment.

I glanced out into the audience, looking for Emmett's reaction.

But from where I stood, the dim house lights made it too hard to see him.

Then, sooner than I'd expected, we arrived at the end of the song. Everyone held on to their notes while Shane slipped back into place with the tenors. Their eyes shifted to me while sustaining the chord. They were waiting for me to conduct them into the segue for the next song. "Father Figure," by George Michael.

My solo.

Whose idea was it for me to sing this song?

Oh yeah.

Mine.

I'd auditioned for it, knowing we'd be performing it for Acappellooza, knowing Emmett would hear it. For some stupid reason, I thought it would be the perfect time to show off a little. Impress him like I did the first time I sang "A Part I Play" for the Sunvalley talent show. I wanted him to be proud of me.

The tips of my ears began to heat up so much that I was certain they'd ignite. The rest of the Obertones stared at me, looking as if they might pass out soon from singing the chord for so long. They weren't going to be able to hold on for much longer.

I took a deep breath. With as much calm as I could manage, I motioned with my hand for them to let go of the chord and move on to the next piece. Their faces melted with relief. I crept out to the center of the stage as they sang the beginning of "Father Figure." Why did such a slow song sound like it was moving at a hundred miles per hour? My throat was starting to close up.

They got to the eighth and last measure of the intro. Time for me to sing. I stared blankly out into the audience. Not a single thing came out of my mouth.

Confusion rippled behind me. Some of the guys stopped singing momentarily. Quickly, they realized they needed to regroup. They repeated the first four bars of the verse accompaniment. Then again. Over and over. They kept vamping until I could find my way back when I was ready. *If* I'd ever be ready. With all of the moisture now totally gone from my mouth, I was positive that moment was never going to come.

Then I saw Emmett. He was leaning forward out of his seat so much that he was falling out of it. He mouthed something to me. I shook my head. I was horrible at reading lips. I couldn't understand what he was trying to say.

The Obertones tensed behind me. Their singing became more rigid. They were losing faith that I'd be able to do this.

Emmett pointed to his ear.

Oh.

"Listen," he was saying. *What do you hear?*

I closed my eyes. The Tones sang louder, singing my own arrangement back to me. I heard them trying to buoy me up. I felt their support. I listened even harder and heard Emmett in my ear.

We're going to be fine.

I opened my eyes. All I could see was him. He'd been telling me how much he believed in me. I waited for the right beat and started to sing. In that moment, I felt as if Emmett were singing with me. Just the two of us onstage. Together.

I sang, pleading for the object of my affection to put their hand in mine. I'd be their preacher. Their teacher. Anything they had in mind.

The words rang with crystalline clarity. I'd never really

understood the song until that moment. Emmett was watching me. Looking out for me. Somehow fueling my voice as if he were somewhere deep inside me. I'd never felt so good in my entire life. I wanted the strange symbiosis to keep going—me on the stage singing and him out there supporting me. The opposite of how we usually were.

The last refrain. I gave a vow to love until the end of time.

Everything went quiet. I looked out to see Emmett's reaction. He smiled and winked.

The bubble of silence popped, and sound flooded in. Cheers and clapping echoed in my ear. Only then did I even realize that the song was over.

Emmett jumped to his feet. In typical fashion, everyone followed his lead.

I'd done it. I'd made it through my solo *and* led the Tones through a fantastic performance. As good as, or hell, maybe even better than the Beelzebubs.

And I knew that it was all because Emmett was there for me.

We bowed and ran off the stage. All fifteen of us bunched up together in the wings.

"Nice work, guys," I said to them. "We did good."

"Better than good! We were the fucking bomb! Booyah!" Shane said, punctuating it by punching his fist in the air.

This set everyone off like firecrackers. They ran around yelling and grabbing one another by whatever body parts they could hold on to. Someone threw their arms around my chest from behind. Shane, I assumed, until I inhaled the familiar smell of tree bark and leather.

Emmett.

He'd come running up to the backstage area. He engulfed me in warmth, with a feeling that everything in the world was perfect. The same as I'd just felt out onstage. He spun me around to face him and pulled me in close.

And then I felt it.

A stiffening. Down there.

Not from me. (Although my body mirrored his *very* quickly.) My instinct was to pull away, to avoid the embarrassment of what was happening.

Emmett pulled me in even tighter. Did he have any idea what our bodies were doing? Was it just, I don't know, friction?

Whatever it was, *why*ever it was, Emmett didn't seem to care. In fact, it seemed as if he wanted me to know. He was holding me so close that I could hear his heart pounding. Or maybe it was mine. Whoever's it was, it was telling me something.

It was telling me it was time to stop denying how I felt about Emmett.

It was time for me to be honest and tell him.

Chapter 18—Now

"WHAT ARE YOU doing here?" I ask Emmett.

"Nice to see you again, too," he says. "Can I come in?"

My dad brushes past me. "Yes, come in! Come in! Oh my god, Emmett. It's so good to see you again." He throws his arms around Emmett, who hands me the gift-wrapped picture or whatever it is he's holding, to better return the hug. My dad rests his head on Emmett's chest, smiling so hard that his eyes water.

"Mr. Cruz, you haven't changed one bit."

My dad pulls back and laughs up at Emmett. "Naku, what a flatterer!" he says, and pulls Emmett into the living room. "Quito, get the suitcase."

I drag Emmett's carry-on inside and close the door. "Would someone please fill me in, because I am clearly being left out of the loop. Emmett, you haven't responded to any of my texts. Why are you here all of a sudden?"

He and my dad look at each other and grin sheepishly.

"Anak, why don't you sit down? I'll get some coffee for Emmett while he tells you everything."

"Gee, thanks, Mr. C," Emmett says.

He unzips his track jacket, sits down on the couch, and motions for me to take a seat next to him.

I eye him warily, not moving. I sit, finally, in my dad's recliner, a few feet away.

Emmett looks at me for a second before erasing all the space between us by scooting over to the end of the couch closest to me.

He leans over onto his knees, which are now so close that they almost bump mine. I smell the leather of his high-end running shoes and the soapy-clean detergent smell of his pants.

"Your dad told me you might need some help with the kids while he's out of commission."

"No. Yes. I mean, maybe—but I can handle it on my own, thanks. More importantly, how the hell did my dad tell you that?"

"He called me."

"He has your phone number?"

"He's *had* my phone number."

"What? For how long?"

"For many years now," my dad said. He's holding an oversize mug of coffee, steaming and so sweet with sugar and cream that I can smell it from across the room. He sits down next to Emmett.

Emmett takes the coffee from my dad, blows on it, and sips. The super-sweetness of it makes his eyes widen. "Yeah, we talk every few months, actually."

"So you—you've both been...?"

A years-long hidden history exists between Emmett and my father. An entire relationship I've never been aware of.

"Dad, you knew Emmett and I hadn't talked in years. But you never said anything about it to me."

"I knew you stopped talking. Emmett would never tell me why. That was your business. I didn't want to get involved."

My face burns. I don't want to talk about our college fallout in front of my dad. "So, if you two have been so chummy all these years, why didn't you just call Emmett and ask him to sing for the concert yourself?"

"He did," Emmett says. "The day before you and I ran into each other in the bathroom."

"The bathroom?" my dad asks.

"Long story," I say. I think back to *Saturday Night Live*. I knew there was something funny about the way Emmett asked me about how my dad was doing. Like he already knew. The same for when I filled him in on my life—as if everything I said were things he'd already heard. Which he probably had. From my dad.

"Wait," I say. "So, then, why did you make *me* ask Emmett?"

"It was long past time for you two to start talking to each other."

My dad had decided to just go and manipulate the events in my life. As usual.

"Unbelievable." I fall back so hard in the chair that the back reclines and the footrest pops up. I nearly go flying off it. Both Emmett and my father start laughing.

"Hahaha." I pull the chair back up. "Yes, very funny. The joke's on me."

"I'm sorry, anak. I should have told you. But now that Emmett is here, why don't you talk? Decide how he can assist you with the concert."

I turn to Emmett. "You couldn't be bothered to answer my texts, but now that my *dad* asked, you've come all the way here to help?"

"Help with the choir, yes. But also with your dad."

"Susmaryosep! I'm fine. Don't worry about me. I don't need a babysitter."

"Hold on," I say. "That's a great idea."

Taking over for my dad at school has been rough. The kids barely respect me as it is. If I brought Emmett into school early, they'd be focused on him, and I'd lose any of the attention they had for me completely. There's no way I'd be able to get them ready in time. Best to work with Emmett on music separately and bring him in for just the last few days, after the kids are in good enough shape to risk being disrupted by his megastar presence. Plus, if he were at school, the choir kids wouldn't be the only ones affected. The teachers, the staff, and the rest of the students would be distracted for weeks. Everyone at school.

Including me.

With Emmett at my side, I'd have every eye on me. It's an occupational hazard of being friends with him that I learned about a long time ago. You can never just recede into the background. With Emmett, I'd always be in the spotlight. And I've never been comfortable with that.

But if he stayed at our house instead of going into school, he could keep an eye on my dad during the day, so I wouldn't have to worry about how he was doing. Emmett could relieve some of my stress *and* not prevent me from doing my job.

"How long can you stay?" I ask.

"I cleared my calendar," Emmett says. "Rehearsals for the play I'm doing at the Mark Taper Forum are coming up in late June, but I've got my script so I'm good."

"I can handle the choir alone," I say.

My father begins to open his mouth.

"For now," I say to him. "But maybe...you could stay with my dad for a while, Emmett?"

"Huh. Yeah, sure. How about it, Mr. C? Want to help me learn my lines?"

"So what, you will just hide here with me all day long?"

"Well, I generally try to keep a low profile when I'm visiting friends and family. You don't know how the paparazzi can get. Those guys can be real assholes."

Paparazzi. I hadn't even considered that. In New York, people tend to be respectful of celebrities' space. We get excited about them, sure, like at Broadway Baby when Emmett showed up unexpectedly. But there are so many famous people in New York City that the antics of gossip sites angling for a good scoop are pretty well dispersed among everyone, so no one gets too hard of a time. It'd be different in the Bay Area. Our celebrities are mostly boring tech moguls. Once word got out that Emmett was around, he wouldn't be left alone. *We* wouldn't be left alone.

"And then you will just go back to your hotel room at night?" my dad asks. "People will see you coming and going there."

"I'm at the St. Regis. They're pretty good about being discreet. They set me up with an entrance through the back."

"Forget all that cloak-and-dagger stuff. You just stay here, in the spare bedroom."

Oh. No. I shake my head uncontrollably. That's not a good idea at all. Emmett definitely cannot stay here. That is a horribly—

"Great idea!" Emmett claps his hands together.

"But...the spare bedroom has all your exercise equipment in it, Dad."

"Yes, yes, most of those things are still in their boxes. Easily moved. Good thing I never got around to using any of them."

"Come on Quito. It'll be just like high school," Emmett says.

"You never lived with us in high school."

"I mean, I basically did. I was here, like, every other day."

Not quite, I think to myself. Even though I wanted him to come home with me every day.

Emmett's long arms go wide as he gets more worked up. "And it'll be way easier to practice music for the concert together. When you're done with the kids at school, you and I can go over our songs here. Just like old times." Emmett snaps his fingers. "Ah, speaking of which—" He grabs the gift-wrapped picture leaning against his luggage. "This is for you, Quito."

"For me?"

"My mother cleared out most of the old stuff she had in her condo when she moved in with her new husband. She gave it to me, but I thought you should have it."

I pull back the wrapping paper and see sheet music displayed in a wooden picture frame.

"'A Part I Play.' How did your mom get this?"

"Don't you remember?" Emmett asks. "I gave it to her as a birthday present our senior year."

Sunlight through the living room window glints off the glass covering, making the song glow.

"You gave this to your *mom*? I thought you gave it to your girlfriend. Angela."

"Angela? Why would I have done that? Nah, it was for my mom's fortieth birthday. Music was this bond that we had because it was the one thing she defied my dad to support me on, remember? This was my first solo performance ever. I figured it'd be the perfect gift for her."

"Angela said ... I just thought ... " She said she'd seen the music and had played through it. I had assumed the gift was for her.

All these years I thought he'd given a part of me away to a girl.

The notes come alive in my mind as I scan them. I look up from the music, and Emmett is smiling at me knowingly, as if he can hear the song, too. I want to go over to him, hug him, thank him for giving my song to his mother—not Angela—and for giving it back to me. But my dad's flip-flopping stares between the two of us are making the back of my collar itch, so instead, I just say, "Thanks, Emmett."

"You're most welcome."

"And I don't have any problem with you staying here."

As I get up to finish getting ready for school, I notice my dad and Emmett glance at each other briefly and nod, but since I'm running late and have a ton of work to do before choir starts, I don't think about it too long.

That afternoon, when I get back from yet another unproductive day at school with the choir kids, Emmett and my father are sitting on the couch together, eating Hawaiian pizza and watching the opening scene to *The Catwalk Killer*.

"Oh, Quito. Nandito ka na pala. You're just in time. Do you know what this is?"

"Yes, Dad." I toss my messenger bag next to the coffee table. "Emmett's movie debut."

"The best acting of my entire career," Emmett says.

"I wouldn't go that far."

He throws a chunk of pineapple at me. I try to dodge it, and it hits me on the forehead.

Emmett laughs, almost choking on his pizza. "Wow, you still have zero athletic ability."

"Yeah, we can't all be action movie studs like you."

"A stud, huh?"

"What?" I say, sitting down at the far end of the couch from Emmett. "Stud, spud. Whatever. Just saying, I've always been athletically ungifted, that's all."

"One of the many things I like about you," Emmett says. "Anyway, you've got your talents, and I have mine."

I glance at my dad, who doesn't seem to be as embarrassed as I am by our interaction. He hasn't been listening at all, in fact. He's too busy watching the movie. A busty brunette model is taking her shirt off in a room filled with creepy dress form mannequins and ancient-looking sewing machines. Emmett's character, a young fashion student, watches her, although one could argue the target of his passionate gaze is actually the intricate lace of her see-through bra, not what it conceals.

"I remember watching this back in college." I sit down on the couch next to Emmett. "You and I hadn't...ah...talked in a while, and I didn't know what you'd been up to. Then one day senior year, I walk into the Apollo Theatre off-campus to watch the new horror movie that had just come out, and there you were."

Emmett and the girl on-screen, both nearly naked, are going at it hot and heavy in the dark fabric warehouse. I try not to notice how engrossed my father is by the scene.

"All three minutes of me," Emmett says.

"You managed to do something with this dinky little appearance, though. It launched your career. There were practically no famous Asian American actors back then. Barely any on TV and less in the movies. But when I saw you there, larger than life, just like I'd always remembered you, I knew you were going to buck the trend. You were always going to be a star. It was only a matter of time before the rest of the world realized it."

The girl screams. On-screen, Emmett grabs her hand and flees with her down an empty hallway. After a few seconds, he trips and falls. The girl, pausing briefly, screams and keeps running off without him. Emmett turns around to see a masked killer holding a pair of bloody scissors and then turns back. The camera zooms in on his face, filling the screen with his utter terror.

Emmett grunts. "Kind of embarrassing how bad I am in this."

"You were great," I say.

My dad, mindlessly chewing on his pizza, waves in our general direction without looking at us. "Shhhh."

"America fell in love with you with a single appearance," I whisper.

The movie's soundtrack swells, and movie-Emmett's scream rings out and ends with a ripping sound. The music stills to nothing. A gush of wetness fills the silence.

"Well, looks like I'm done. Want to go talk about music?"

"Sure," I say.

"Shhhhh!!" my dad hushes.

Emmett smiles and shakes his head. He takes another slice of pizza and motions for me to follow him into the kitchen. I close the folding door behind us, leaving my dad to watch the rest of the *Catwalk Killer*'s designer do-ins.

"Your dad cracks me up."

"I'm glad someone thinks he's funny."

"You know you've always had the best dad ever." Emmett pulls out one of the wooden dining chairs, swings it around, and straddles it as he sits. "He's always been more of a father to me than mine."

"I knew that was true back in high school. But, apparently, he's been parenting you for a lot longer than that." I lean against the kitchen counter. "So, how *did* you guys start talking to each other? How did he even get in touch with you in the first place?"

Emmett takes a bite of pizza, chews thoughtfully, and swallows. "He wrote me a fan letter, believe it or not. Right after *The Catwalk Killer* came out. Remember when people still sent actual letters? He said he was proud of me. My own dad never told me that. But yours did. I reread that letter so many times, my fingers smudged the ink on the sides of it." He pauses, staring off into space for a moment. "He scribbled a phone number at the end of it and told me to call him anytime I needed someone to talk to. So I did."

"Why?"

"I was lonely. I'd call my mom, but she's never been great on the phone. I was still feeling out of my league in Hollywood. It's a tough town. Big and isolating. I guess I needed someone to remind me of home."

"Then you told him that we weren't talking to each other anymore."

"Not at first. He'd ask me if I'd spoken to you, and I'd just say we hadn't talked recently. That I was too busy. I skirted around it. Then one day I was... thinking about you. So I called him. Asked him how you were doing. I told him the truth. That we hadn't spoken since college. But he never asked why. I think he could tell I didn't want to talk about it. He didn't want to force anything."

The edge of the counter digs into my lower back. I straighten up and lean my elbow against it instead, but for some reason, I can't find a more comfortable position. "Emmett. About that night at Oberlin—"

"You know, Quito, I was thinking I should sing 'A Part I Play' for the concert."

He doesn't quite look at me when he says that. His body seems to be in two different places at once, slouched over the chair, amiable, eager to talk about music yet also hiding rigidity in certain parts—his neck and shoulders, his balled-up fists. He doesn't want to talk about that night together. He wants to move on.

"Um, all right," I say. "Well, actually, I had another idea for you." I've been mulling something around in the weeks since he'd agreed to participate in the concert. I know that denying Emmett the chance to sing my song again will upset him, but I also know he'll understand.

"You don't want me to sing your song?"

"That's not it. I just have other plans for it."

"Okay." He attempts to extinguish the look of disappointment on his face. He compensates, in that very Emmett way, with extra swagger. He jumps up and stands next to me. "Well, if I can't sing *your* song, how about another song that reminds me of you?"

He closes his eyes and begins nodding his head, bobbing in time to some internal metronome. He's so close to me that I can feel him as he prepares to sing, taking in all the air around me.

He sings George Michael's "Father Figure" to me, all its lyrics sensual and pleading. My face flushes. A feeling I definitely do not want to be having in my parents' kitchen roils in my lower regions.

I cut him off. "Yeah. How about something not so much about sex for a high school choral concert? Thanks."

"Am I wrong, or are you looking a little bothered there, dude?"

I want to tell him the truth. That yes, anytime he sings to me, it feels as if he's located the pent-up longing inside me and set it free, out in the open for all to see. That thinking about that night after the Acappellooza concert, even with all the unsettled drama, still sends a shiver down my torso and into my groin.

But I can't. I have a boyfriend. And Emmett has...Emma Chen. Maybe. I still haven't figured out if they have any sort of real connection at all.

"What about 'True Colors' instead?" I ask. It's a simple song, but one I know Emmett could really deliver well. It feels so appropriate for him. And—in some ways—for both of us.

"Ooh. I like that song. It could work."

"And maybe for a second selection—"

"I already know what that second one's going to be. I'm keeping that one a surprise," he says.

"How are we supposed to practice it if you don't tell me what it is?"

"You won't need to accompany me."

"You're singing it a cappella?"

"You'll see." He cocks an eyebrow. "You've got your secrets. I have mine."

"Tease." I poke him in the ribs.

Emmett freezes.

Oh. I shouldn't have touched him like that. I've overstepped a boundary. I...burst into laughter as Emmett digs all of his fingers into the sides of my body and tickles every inch he can find. "HAHAHAhahahahaha!"

"Hoy!" My dad's yell pierces through the kitchen door. "Ang ingay nyo! Quiet, please! I cannot hear the TV!"

We cover our mouths, trying to smother our laughs, which end up bubbling through our fingers.

"The movie will be done in about an hour and a half," Emmett says, still half giggling. "We can work on 'True Colors' then, right?" He pulls one of my dad's San Miguel beers out of the refrigerator. "Want me to grab some more pizza from the living room?"

"Actually, I need to take care of something really quick. I'll meet you in the living room when Dad's done watching the movie." I've forgotten that I needed to answer Mark's check-in email from earlier this morning. Plus, I need to tell him about the whole Emmett situation. I wasn't going to make the same mistake twice in not coming clean about all things Emmett-related. There was nothing to worry about, anyway. Emmett was just here to help me with my dad and to prepare for the concert. He's just staying at our house to avoid being seen. That's it.

But as I head back to my bedroom, I pass by the spare, where Emmett has settled in. His track jacket is draped over the side of a chair, and his clothes are all already unpacked and hanging in the closet, organized by color. A black binder lies open on the desk, its pages marked with pink highlighter. The room already even smells of him, sweet with an underlying dusky warmth. Only one thin wall will separate me from Emmett and the space he's already saturated with his essence. Tonight I'll be sleeping in the room right next to his.

Just like what happened that night in college.

Or, rather, how it was *supposed* to have happened.

Chapter 19—Then

I TORE THROUGH all the clothes hanging in my closet, going through everything at least twice, and I still wasn't able to decide on anything. Why hadn't I brought more options from home? I'd packed an entire suitcase full of music scores to bring to Oberlin. I should've left some and brought more polo shirts instead.

It was only after I pulled out the same shirt for the third time that I noticed my hands were shaking.

After I finally broke off my awkward embrace with Emmett backstage at Finney Chapel, he went around congratulating everyone whose hand he could manage to shake.

"Party at Love Shack!" one of the Tones had yelled at us as we all filed out of the church.

"Hey," Emmett said, "we're going to whatever club that is, right?"

"It's not a club." There were no clubs near campus. Oberlin was in the middle of absolutely nowhere. "Love Shack's an off-campus house. A few of the Trebs live there," I said, meaning members of the all-girl group Nothing But Treble.

"Sounds fun."

My head was still reeling from the performance. And our hug. The hundreds of different thoughts running through my head were hard to manage, but they were slowly coalescing into something. A plan.

"You go on ahead," I said. "Just tag along with Shane. I want to drop by my room first."

He looked slightly confused but let it go. "Okay. Just don't be late."

"Later, gator."

He ran after Shane, leaving me standing on the sidewalk, already going through my clothes in my head and obsessing over what to wear.

In the end, I settled on black jeans and a shirt with a red horizontal stripe, one button left unfastened at the top. It made me feel scandalously slutty.

I examined myself in the mirror. Rolled my sleeves up. Unrolled them. Rolled them back up again. Buttoned the top button. Unbuttoned it. Added extra gel to my hair. Splashed on more cologne. Decided it was too much and wiped it off with a towel.

The bedside clock glowed eleven o'clock in bright red. The party would be in full effect now. Emmett hadn't really had a chance to see my room yet. We'd dumped his suitcase off on Jayesh's side before running to the Con to rehearse my song cycle. My desk was a mess of music manuscript paper and theory books strewn haphazardly across it. A half-eaten cheeseburger stolen from Dascomb Dining Hall was wrapped up in napkins and sat on the corner.

My bed was made, though. The sheets and pillowcases had just been washed. I formed my music into a single stack and threw the cheeseburger in my garbage can. Good enough.

On the way out, I grabbed a small case of mints from my desk. Just in case.

Love Shack was crammed by the time I arrived. People had been squeezed out of the house like toothpaste, forced onto the porch, patio steps, and the sidewalk. Cigarette smoke wafted in the colorful lights still trimming the patio some five months after Christmas.

Inside, Nolan Botts, a jazz guitarist from the Con, was DJing a set of early-eighties dance songs from behind a faded couch. Everyone's conversations were several decibels above normal in order to be heard over Katrina and the Waves blasting from the speakers. I smelled hard alcohol mixed with patchouli and marijuana smoke, all tinted with the funk of spring fever hormones.

One of the Obertones waved at me from the kitchen. "Yo, Maestro!" Jordan was a sexually ambiguous women's studies major with consistently fresh-smelling breath and even better-smelling hair, so he was lusted after by pretty much the entire college. Singers from several of the visiting a cappella groups surrounded him, still wearing their concert outfits. "Wicked concert tonight, right?" he said. "You did a great job leading us."

"Thank you."

"We're doing the same songs again tomorrow for that alumni lunch thingy, yeah?"

My nerves, already frazzled, sparked at Jordan's reminder. But the benefit luncheon wasn't going to be as nerve-racking as the concert. We'd be the only group performing besides a string quartet from the Con. And besides, Emmett would be there again. I'd managed to get him a ticket to the lunch, which had cost me most of my spending money for the month, but I needed him to be there. "Yes. Same set."

"Cool beans." Jordan nodded affably. "So, what do you want to drink?" His big baritone voice boomed even above the blasting music. He opened cabinets to look at the available liquors. I vaguely recalled that Jordan's sister, Alex, was one of the Trebs living in the house.

"Have you seen Emmett anywhere?" I asked.

Jordan poked through the bottles, sorting through and organizing them. Not by type but by color. He burped and then giggled at himself. "Uh, I think I saw him go upstairs with a bunch of girls from that Wooster group."

I couldn't help but frown. "Make me a Long Island Iced Tea. Super strong."

"You got it, Maestro," Jordan said, pouring with abandon.

Though the house was Treble territory, the Tones had been entrusted to run the show. They were infamous for their parties. Hallmarks of an Obertones-hosted party were surprisingly competent DJs, tons of weed, and generous open bars, courtesy of Jordan, who was super rich, another reason so many people wanted to get into his pants.

At first their bacchanalian culture wasn't something I jibed with. My last experience at a high school party certainly wasn't something I wanted to live through again. But things were different at Oberlin. As an accompaniment and composition double major, I'd made a ton of friends playing piano for people's lessons and writing music for various ensembles and soloists to play and sing. Being in the Conservatory felt as comfortable and safe as being in Sunvalley's choir, except on a much bigger scale. I learned to let go a bit and enjoy. I never developed the taste for beer, but the Tones were more into mixed drinks anyway. And pot. Lots and lots of pot.

Jordan handed me my drink. "Here you go."

I took a sip. Jordan, even as blasted as he already was, made a damn tasty concoction. I tilted my glass at him before making my way through the crowded kitchen to the staircase at the back of the house. It was a typical off-campus student home with outdated appliances and furniture all on its last legs. Everything worn at the edges but homey. Certainly good enough for college students.

The top of the stairs leveled out into a small corridor with two doors on each side. Two bedrooms on the left, bathroom and another bedroom on the right. The bedroom on the right was bright with laughter.

Emmett was sitting on the floor, his legs stretched out in front of him, his arms propping him up from behind as he leaned back. He watched as a girl from Wooster took a too-large hit from the bong in the middle of a circle of people and coughed it back out, laughing afterward. Emmett looked up and practically launched himself at me in the doorway.

"Where have you been?" he asked. "I thought you'd never get here."

I couldn't help but smile. He put an arm around me and led me into the room. "Guys, the amazing Quito Cruz."

I was greeted with kind faces smudged with stupor. I was pleased to see the room wasn't just Wooster girls. There were people from all over, though no other Tones. Mostly visiting a cappella singers and other non-a-cappella Obies.

Emmett pulled me down to sit next to him and immediately rested his head against my shoulder. He must've been completely blitzed to openly do that in front of strangers. I wanted to put my head on top of his but couldn't. Not with so many people around.

One of the Beelzebubs, a linebacker of a guy with a crooked buzz cut, pushed the bong toward me. Pot wasn't really my thing, so I was about to turn it back to him. Then I felt the weight of Emmett's body against mine. I ached to lean in to him, to pull him down on the floor right there and just lie next to him. I changed my mind and took the bong. I brought it to my mouth and inhaled.

Emmett pulled his head up and examined me, brow furrowed. I looked at him as reassuringly as I could. He squinted and then smiled. He must've already had several hits from the bong. I took another hit, smaller this time. Emmett seemed satisfied and put his head back on my shoulder. His body heat amplified the sensation of warmth growing in the center of my chest.

"You okay?" he whispered to me.

"Yes." I was okay. Everything was exactly how it was supposed to be.

One of the Wooster girls noticed that I'd been eyeing her drink. I was, but only because I'd become fixated on the swirling colors, the orange juice mixing with the red cranberry, all swimming around the melting ice cubes like an expressionist painting. She offered it to me. I nodded and took the cup from her hands without saying anything. Talking felt overrated. Better to just ease into the flow of things. Things were so flowy.

I drank. Sour. Sweet. Delicious.

The girl noticed the smile widening on my face. She waved the cup to me. *Keep it*, she mouthed. Hey, I could actually read her lips. Cool.

I drank a little more and offered the rest to Emmett.

The bong was passed around one last time. I went to go for

another hit when Emmett took hold of my hand. *You sure?* his face asked.

I nodded silently. *Yes.* I was sure. I was feeling free. More than I had in a long time. I needed that feeling to keep going. Now more than ever.

I inhaled.

The night went on. Emmett and I whispered nonsense to each other while the circle of people got smaller. That was the only way I could tell that time was actually moving forward—the change in the scenery. Eventually, it was just us and two Oberlin girls who had been talking to each other on a pile of cushions on the floor, their legs and arms tangled around each other. They looked as if they might move on to whatever came next. Probably in that very room.

I swallowed. My head felt like it was filled with cotton. In the middle, a white glow pulsed. I tried to poke at it with my consciousness but wasn't successful.

Emmett rubbed the top of my head. "You ready to go?"

"Mmm." His fingers were massaging my brain.

We stood up, balancing against each other. I was pretty sure I was supporting Emmett's full weight, but it was no problem at all. Like I'd been carrying him my whole life.

Downstairs, the music had wound down to a soft stream. Most of the house had cleared out except for a few people on the threadbare couches talking softly to one another.

Outside, Shane and Jordan were sitting on the patio stoop, taking long, languorous drags of a shared cigarette. Shane let out a steady stream of smoke into the now-cool air. "You calling it a night?" he asked.

"Yep," Emmett said, almost tripping down the stairs.

"Don't kill yourself," Shane said.

I pointed at him. My finger felt longer than usual. "I thought voice majors weren't supposed to smoke."

"I thought musical geniuses were supposed to know how many bars of intro there were before the beginning of their solos," he responded.

"Touché."

Jordan took the cigarette from Shane's fingers. "Good thing you guys are going home together. I don't think you'd make it on your own," he said to Emmett. Though, for some reason, he was looking at me.

"Thanks," I said. "Good night. Great work. On the concert."

Shane laughed and gave me a two-finger salute. "You got it, Maestro. See you at the luncheon tomorrow." Their continued conversation lilted behind as we made our way to my dorm.

It was almost morning. The air was wet with dew. We walked into a bank of mist, and droplets clung to us. My lungs filled with coolness as we walked so close to each other, we were almost holding hands.

What was my plan again? I was going to talk to him. About me. Us. How was I going to do it? I tried to focus, but time was mercurial. At one point, I was convinced that we had been walking for hours. Then, before I knew it, we were back at South Hall.

I was out of time. As I unlocked my dorm room, I realized I'd soon be putting Emmett to sleep in Jayesh's empty bed while I drowned myself in my sheets in a different room. I needed to say something before we'd be separated.

The door unlocked with a click. We entered—and a snore ripped through us like a gatling gun.

Jayesh was asleep in his bed, covers tucked up to his chin. Someone was sleeping next to him, an anonymous series of lumps. Whoever it was was the one snoring.

Jayesh stirred. "Mm," he grunted. "Sorry. Trip canceled," he murmured before falling back asleep. The person next to him kept snoring.

"Shit," I whispered.

"What do we do now?" Emmett asked.

"I guess you're taking my bed," I said, not thinking clearly. We went into my room and closed my door behind us.

"Where are you going to sleep?" Emmett asked.

"The couch. In the lounge." The air in my room felt thick and gauzy. I waded my hand through to reach for the doorknob.

"No." Emmett grabbed my arm. "Stay."

"You're the guest. You get the bed."

"No. I mean, stay here. With me."

This was what I wanted. Right? Or...god...Why weren't my thoughts sticking...? Was he just being a friend? A good friend? My *best* friend. Saying we should just crash in my twin bed. Because that's what buddies would do. Without even thinking twice about it.

He was still holding my hand. For how long? I couldn't remember. All I knew was, I said, "Okay."

I didn't look at him. I couldn't. I tried to take my shoes off and lost my balance, almost falling on top of him. I sat down on my bed. Kept my eyes focused on my feet.

Emmett stood beside my messy desk, not moving, regretting his suggestion (probably). Or he was too drunk and too high to move.

He sat down next to me. We sat there for a minute. Or ten. Doing nothing.

I unbuttoned my shirt, reached down to take off my shoes and socks and threw them on the floor.

Emmett did the same. The unzipping of his pants was so loud that it made the hairs on my neck stand up. He tossed them onto my desk.

I slid behind him, into the bed and under the sheet. I tried to hide myself. I turned on my side, facing the wall.

Breathing was hard. I had to think to make it happen. My head pounded. I clutched the edge of my bedsheet and crumpled it in my hand.

Emmett eased beside me, turning on his side, facing the opposite direction.

We had no room. His back pressed against mine, making a map. The expanse of it went on forever, extending out of our bodies, into the air.

He breathed in. Out. I tried to match him. *Calm down*, I thought. *You're not nervous. Everything is fine. Natural.*

Only, the more I tried to slow my breathing, the more ragged it got. My own body fought against me.

Emmett breathed slower and slower. Was he falling asleep?

"Hey," I whispered. "You still awake?"

No answer.

He'd passed out. The moment was gone. I'd missed my chance. I had to wake him up. Should I shake him? Make some kind of noise?

I started to spiral. All the space in my head funneled into a tiny black hole, sucking me down into it.

Then Emmett said, "Do you have anything warmer than this sheet? It's kind of cold in here."

"You're, uh...you're cold?"

He cleared his throat, likely dry and scratchy from the pot. "Yeah."

I stared into the wall, boring holes into it with my eyes.

I knew what I had to do.

I turned over onto my other side. Slowly. Achingly slowly. My tummy pressed against Emmett's back. I snaked my arm up and over, casually draping it over the side of his body.

I clutched his chest.

My heart exploded.

I realized I couldn't match Emmett's breathing anymore because I'd stopped breathing completely. I was paralyzed, waiting for him to throw my arm off, jump out of bed, move away.

Except he didn't do any of those things.

We stayed that way for so long that I lost all sense of myself. Where I was. When I was. Who I was. I found myself muttering incoherently into the darkness. I tried to hold on to everything in my head but felt it all slip into the black hole now growing, turning into a gaping maw.

In fact, when I looked back on that night, what I'd remember most is how much of it I couldn't really remember at all.

Chapter 20—Now

I WAKE UP to the ping of a new email notification from my phone. I've had only three hours of sleep. Not only did I toss and turn all night, excited by how fruitful and familiar my rehearsal of "True Colors" with Emmett was (and still unnerved by the fact that Emmett was sleeping less than three feet away from me), but it's also only five o'clock in the morning.

Mark's written me back. A quick message before work.

Hey—

Thanks for letting me know about the situation with Emmett. It's cool that he's helping out with your dad while you guys work on the concert together. You're still going to be okay getting our final song done, though, right?

Hey, maybe you and Emmett can work on it together? Maybe even talk up the show to him? Any involvement from him would help us out tremendously. Just think about it.

Quito, what if you could convince him to come sing for the producer showcase? We'd have to give the current Peter Pan the boot, but who cares. It'd be worth it.

Anyway, just a suggestion.

Can't wait to hear what you come up with. Tell Emmett I said hi and that I think he's a star for helping you guys out.

Miss you,

Mark

He doesn't seem to be concerned about my and Emmett's close quarters at all. That makes one of us, at least.

I turn on my side in the bed and set my hand against the wall. Just on the other side of it, Emmett lies sleeping, completely unaware of the excitement and anxiety that have kept me awake all night.

Mark doesn't care that Emmett's here, so why should I?

Why *should* I?

I can't give in to that hopeless fantasy again, the one where Emmett and I end up together. We're fantastic as friends. And as musical collaborators. Anything more than that...we tried before.

Or rather—*I* tried.

And it didn't work.

Besides, I have a boyfriend. One who's depending on me.

If I can't get back to sleep, I might as well do something productive and work on the last song for, ugh, *The Forever Boys.* (I can't even think of that horrible title without gagging.) I pull up the lyrics on my phone and read through them a few times, trying to let some sort of melody come to me.

Nothing presents itself. First of all, the lyrics are hopelessly banal. I don't get any inspiration from their meaning. Second, the words don't quite scan right—they fumble and halt, never quite attaining any sort of musicality on their own, so trying to come up with a decent line to go with them is almost impossible. I need to try to rework the words to make something actually singable. If Dinesh would be open to that.

Dinesh and Mark, I mean.

But I lack the energy to alter the lyrics. The words just lie there lifeless on my screen.

I decide to text Ujima instead.

I haven't had a chance to tell them about Emmett yet. I could use their advice on that. And maybe Jee can give me some tips about how to get the kids to pay attention to me. They did study to be a music teacher in college for at least two years before switching to a performance major. And Ujima is a master of attention-getting. They know how to command a crowd. And more than that, they've always known how to buoy me. To get me to believe in myself.

Besides, sending texts to Jee is way more fun than altering someone else's bad lyrics.

> Quito: Hey, boo. You'll never guess who's sleeping, like, right next to me (kind of)

. . .

[finger on chin emoji]

Emmett :)

My phone vibrates. It's Ujima. Which is impossible because, unless they're attending an open-call audition, they never get up any earlier than 10:00 a.m.

"Explain yourself." Jee's voice is so raspy that it sounds like the signal's being broken up by static.

"Hey," I whisper, "I didn't mean to wake you. Go back to sleep. I'll text you the story."

"Girl, I don't know what possessed me to look at the text you sent me, but now that you've tittie-lated me and ruined the rest of my beauty sleep, you better tell me everything. Why are you sleeping with Emmett? How did you manage to get into his pants? And what are his measurements?"

I crawl into the closet on the other side of the bedroom and slide the door closed. "He's not in my bed. He's in the room next to me. He flew here early to help with the choir. Except I'm not letting him. So he's keeping an eye on my dad instead while I'm at school. And my dad made him stay here. With us. In the room next to mine."

"Have you notified the nineties? Because this sounds like the setup for a bad sitcom."

"I know. But at least I already told Mark, and he's fine with it."

"Well, thank *god* Mark's happy."

"Be nice, Ujima. I thought you guys were friends now."

"Honey, we ain't ever gonna be actual friends. Friend-adjacent at best."

"Look, I can't think about it right now. I have to focus on the kids. Which I definitely need your advice on, because now that I'm trying so hard not to think about Emmett..."

The closet door slides open. "Why are you trying so hard not to think about me?" Emmett asks. He's wearing boxer shorts and a tank top, and even with a colossal hairlick sticking out from his head at a vertiginous side angle, he looks breathtaking. "And what are you doing in the closet?"

"I'm not in the closet. You're in the closet."

Every single drop of blood in me gushes to my head as I wonder if it's actually possible for my heart to overtax itself and give me a cerebral embolism.

"Hello? Hello?" Ujima says from my phone, which is now hanging lifeless from my hand.

My eyes close slowly. "Jee, I'll call you back."

I hang up and manage to look up at Emmett, who is smirking at me. He yawns. "Want some coffee?"

"Coffee, yes. Please."

He pulls me up from the closet floor, and we head into the kitchen.

"I'm sorry I woke you," I say, watching as he moves around the room, easily locating the coffee grounds, the mugs, the sugar. As if he's lived in our house for years. "I was trying to be quiet."

"It's cool. I'm usually up early to go running anyway. Probably better to do it now before most people in the neighborhood are up, so I can do it in-cog-NEE-to."

The warm, roasted smell of percolating coffee fills the air. Emmett sits down across from me.

"Quito, do you not want me to be here?"

"No. I mean—no, that's not it. It's just...I need to keep focused on helping my dad with the choir. And it's good to see you. Really, really good. But it's also been a long time. We're not the same people we were all those years ago. I just have to remember that we're not those kids anymore."

Emmett looks away, back over his shoulder, and nods, as if agreeing to something some invisible person behind him has just said.

The coffeemaker dings. He pours two mugs full of coffee. "Cream and sugar?"

"No thanks."

"Black it is." He brings both unadulterated mugs to the kitchen table. "I love your dad, and he makes amazing food, but his coffee is not good."

"It's just a little too..."

"Dramatic?"

I smile. "Yeah."

Emmett takes a sip and watches me as I drink. "Quito, your dad wasn't the only reason I came up early, you know. I wanted to see you again."

"Oh. Okay."

"Look, I know we haven't been close in a long time. We didn't exactly part on the best of terms, back in college."

"I've been wanting to talk to you about that—"

"Hold up. Let me finish." He puts his hand on top of mine. The coffee I've just sipped intensifies into something too hot for my mouth. "What I was going to say is that, when I saw you in New York, sitting right in the front row of freaking *Saturday Night Live*, it was both completely surreal and also—I don't know—right? Like we'd both been there before. Or had always been there. You and me, together. Does that make sense?"

I swallow, feeling the coffee burn as it goes down my throat. "Yes, it does."

"Quito, singing that song with you at Broadway Baby? That. THAT made *me* happy. And after I left, watching my mom get married, seeing her be with someone who was actually right for her...I kept thinking how I wish you could've been there with me. My mom was always a fan of yours, you know? She always saw you as a positive influence on me. And you were the one who helped me to see that she was just trying to do her best back then. For me. Because you've always known me better than anyone. That's the me and you I want to remember. Everything else, I just want to let go. I've just been trying to figure out a way to tell you that for the past few weeks."

Emmett watches me. And waits. His hand, still on mine, is bigger and heavier than anything I've ever felt. As if nothing could separate it from me.

"I'm happy you're here," I finally say. "I promise."

My hand squirms for a second. When Emmett lifts his off, I turn mine over and quickly grasp his, bringing it back down to the table.

"But can we just make sure my dad gets the send-off he deserves? And also enjoy the time we have together? Just...let's not think about it too hard?" I say, as much to myself as to Emmett.

He smiles. "Deal."

A hacking sound comes from down the hall. We let go of each other's hands.

"Hoy, no coffee for me?" my dad says as he wanders into the kitchen.

"Go for your run, Emmett," I say. "I got this."

Evenings at home fly by. Sometimes when I get back home from school, I continue to chip away at the final song for *The Forever Boys*, but mostly, I spend it with Emmett and my father. As my dad's energy has improved, he's been cooking more. He started with easier dishes like tinola—chicken soup with garlic, ginger, green papaya, and fresh watercress—and has gradually been making more intricate dishes and desserts for us. Sometimes he permits us to help him, like when we chop vegetables to be mixed with shrimp, chicken, and Chinese sausage for Emmett's favorite noodle dish, pancit. Or when we roll a savory meat mixture into spring roll wrappers to make lumpiang Shanghai, fried until they're so crispy and addictive that we can't stop eating them until they're all gone. But usually he insists he's fine on his own and pushes us out into the living room to rehearse for the concert.

We continue to practice Emmett's "True Colors." He's asked for a jazzier rendition, something like the way he'd heard Michael Bublé sing at a recent Hollywood Bowl concert. I oblige him, but I also throw him a few curveballs and sometimes segue into different styles. Reggae. Doo-wop. Classical. He always manages to keep up, though he swears at me the whole time.

After that song feels solid, we move on to other songs. Older songs. Things he hasn't sung in years. Not for the concert, but for the simple joy it brings the two of us to be making music together.

I spend less and less time working on the song for Dinesh and Mark. Even though Mark's told me they already have the cast up on its feet, learning the other songs and working on simple blocking for the rest of the first act, I can't bear to pull myself away from the fun Emmett and I are having—him singing by my side, filling a space that's been empty for so long.

One that Mark or this new musical should be filling, though neither of them really do.

I try not to think about it too much. I can't. Watching over my dad and rehearsing for the concert must be my main priorities. In some ways, they're almost the same one—making sure Emmett and the choir are fully prepared is the best way I can think of to make sure Dad is happy and healthy.

But while the evenings with Emmett are a joy, the days with the kids continue to be a struggle.

My father still doesn't believe I'm having any problems with the choir, even when I beg him to give me some pointers. When I tell Emmett about the situation, he's the same. Their unwavering belief in me is nice, but I'm still in the same situation: in a slowly sinking choir boat with me at the helm.

After a few more days of me struggling and failing to get the choir to a level worthy of the most important concert of my father's career, I text Ujima again to get the advice I'd been meaning to solicit from them.

Quito: Jee, please tell me how to get these kids to listen to me.

Ujima: They are. Kids just always look like they hate you, but they don't. Mostly. Just put your big girl panties on and stop complaining.

How much longer do you have to sub, anyway? I thought your dad was doing ok?

Quito: He is. At least I think he is. But he says he's not ready to go back. It's weird, he loves his job. Not sure why he's avoiding going back.

Ujima: hmmmm

Quito: Yeah.

How are things with you, btw?

Ujima: Good news and bad news. Pick.

Quito: Bad first.

Ujima: Of course :-P

Quito: You know me so well.

Ujima: ONE-derland is closing.

Quito: What? When?

Ujima: Well...

yesterday.

Quito: Oh no! I'm SO sorry.

Ujima: But some good news—

I got some business in the Bay Area, so I can come visit y'all! I'll get to see you and your dad. And my future husband, of course.

Quito: Slow your roll, there, Jezebel.

Ujima: ;-)

Also, maybe I can help you with those kids while I'm there. I wasn't the best music ed student but I remember a few things.

Quito: Yes! Please! When are you coming? Also: why??

Ujima: More deets later. I'm taking a red-eye, getting into SFO early next Tuesday morning. Will be there about a week. Maybe longer.

Can you pick me up from the airport?

Quito: Of course.

Ujima: Good. Thank you! Ta-tas!

A visit from Ujima would be a true gift. For the kids *and* for me. Jee could provide a different perspective on things. Give me a supportive boost. Get the students to open up. Something. Anything to help me get through to them.

When I first arrived at Sunvalley High School, the situation seemed much more positive than I'd envisioned. The choir kids were so glad I'd come to save them that they broke out into an impromptu rendition of *The Wiz*'s "Brand New Day"—like those videos of the cast of *The Lion King* suddenly breaking out into "Circle of Life" at the airport, or the subway, or at Filene's Basement, any place they happened to all be together. (Why were they always together?) I'd never believed people actually did that sort of thing. But there they all were, harmonizing their silly teenage faces off.

They had several reasons for celebrating, I guess. I was Mr. Cruz's son. I had big-time New York experience. And because of me, they'd soon be meeting Emmett Aoki. Not to mention the fact that my arrival meant their nemesis, Mr. Drummond, was done for, melted into a puddle of mismatched socks and bad comb-over hair. It must have felt like a brand-new day for them indeed.

Then things started going astray. As if their acne-prone noses could smell that I was anxious, slightly resentful of needing to be there in the first place, and had no business taking over for my dad. I tried to use their initial enthusiasm to hold positive rehearsals. But nothing I did seemed to work.

Now, on this overcast Friday morning in the choir room, there is no breaking out into song. No celebrating. Just a bunch of faces broadcasting at me: *You suck.* I wrestle with a mass of music from my messenger bag and finally just toss the pile on top of the piano before it can all fall apart.

Celeste springs from her seat. "Can I help with any of that, Mr. Cruz?"

I wonder if she knows that her oversize polka-dot dress does absolutely nothing for her, hiding her body instead of showing how beautiful she really is. "We've been over this before, Celeste. Just Quito is fine."

She winds and unwinds her brown hair around her finger and keeps balancing from leg to leg, never quite finding the right position to stand still in. I worry that, if I don't give her something to do, she might burst into an explosion of polka-dot dress confetti.

"Actually, why don't you help me reorganize these copies and start handing them out to everyone?"

"You got it, Mr. Qui—uhh, Quito. Cruz. Sir!"

One of the sopranos in the front row rolls her eyes and keeps scrolling through whatever she's reading on her phone with her painted-black nails.

While Celeste and I sort the sheet music, I see that one of the boys is sitting in the middle of a ring of empty chairs. I noticed he hadn't spoken a single word to anyone since I arrived, but he's even more self-isolated today. He's a tiny kid with hair so blond that it's almost white. I wish I could remember his name. Melvin? Merlin? I've tried to memorize everyone's name. So far I've only been able to remember Celeste's.

She stands at attention next to me at the podium after handing out all the music.

"Thank you, Celeste."

Her body pulsates with the need to do more, help more. I sigh and use my lips to point to her chair. She dwindles with resignation as she takes her seat.

We've managed a complete run-through of almost every song on the concert program at least once. And they all sound...competent. I can never get them past a basic level of mediocrity. I decide to tackle the "Gloria in D." It's especially tricky in that I have to play the piano *and* somehow conduct the choir at the same time. My dad's always been able to do this by using graceful head gestures as he plays and looking at the choir to cue them at key musical moments. I've been mostly doing a bunch of nonsensical lip and eye movements while I jerk my head around. Not surprisingly, the kids just ignore me.

As I'm about to begin, I hear someone behind me clearing their throat.

"Working on the Vivaldi, I see?"

Someone cries out. Celeste runs past me to the doorway. I turn around to see her tackling my father in a bear hug so forceful that he almost tips over.

Though his face is newly shaven, I can tell he's not here to take over. He'd have worn his standard button-down shirt and khakis instead of the sweats and 49ers hoodie he's thrown on.

The rest of the choir follows Celeste's lead and runs over to him.

"I wasn't expecting you, Dad. Everything okay?"

"I'm fine. I'm fine. Aray! Not too tight, kids," he says. Then, out of the corner of his mouth, "You-Know-Who wanted to run an errand here at the school, so I decided to tag along."

"What?" I whisper. "He's here?"

"Don't worry. He's got on a disguise. He said he only needs about ten minutes or so. I'm just killing some time before we go get some Taco Bell for lunch."

"And you wanted to check on me?"

"Of course not."

Most of the kids have given my dad space, but Celeste is still hanging on for dear life. I'm both touched and a little resentful of the fact that they look like they're on the verge of tears. It's no surprise how much they love him. I was one of them. I remember how much of an impact my father makes on everybody. No matter how many students he has, he's always managed to make a connection with each one, always seeing through to the very core of each kid and finding the potential waiting there. He's turned the most tone-deaf students into competent singers and just average musicians into proficient ones. He empowers them. Shows them how to find joy in music. He makes them happy. How he does this completely eludes me. The very last time I led a group of singers was a disaster—the Benefactors' Luncheon with the Obertones the day after Acappellooza. The day Emmett left me. The day I decided I didn't have any business trying to show other people how to make music. Or to make any of my own.

"Mr. Cruz, are you coming back?" Celeste asks my dad.

"Soon. Quito will still be your teacher for a while."

"Aww." Celeste sags. "I mean, yay." She pumps one fist into the air and smiles at me half-heartedly.

I give my dad a look. *See, I told you.*

He pushes them away. "Go sit down now. Go on. Just ignore me," he says, attempting to shift attention back to me.

I try to strike the right balance between authority and coolness. "All right, all you excellent song makers. Let's all please take our seats. If you don't mind." My words are limp. A poor echo of my dad. "Let's skip the Vivaldi for now. Let's do an a cappella piece—how about the 'Hiney Mah Tov'? From the top." As the kids re-arrange their music to switch to the madrigal, my stomach sours in anticipation of my father's inevitable disappointment of what they'll sound like. "Remember to breathe in with the vowel."

Dad drags a chair over and sits next to me. He closes his eyes and tilts his head upward, the state he always settles into when he prepares to listen to something important, as if readying himself to receive signals from above. Memories of him in this exact pose flood my brain—attending my piano recitals, listening to records of great choral works, and sitting in the church pews as my mom would sing.

I smile and inhale. "And . . ."

The choir breathes with me. A solid entrance. More than solid. It's confident, almost brazen. Their sound is better than I've ever heard it. It takes me by surprise at first. What happened to the lackluster droning from every other rehearsal we've had? Has my conducting really improved that much? Is it because I'm more aware of my technique, now that Dad is—

Ah.

That's it.

They *are* better now, singing their very best.

Just not for me. For him.

I try something. I pull back a little, making my gestures a little less overt. More inelegant. Their energy is the same as before. I do even less. To the point where my hand movements are merely ornamental. A basic bobbing in time. It doesn't make a difference. The choir still sings with everything they have, leaning in or backing away when the music calls for it, almost instinctively. I know it's not instinct, though. It's muscle memory. They're calling up instructions they've been given before. They're imagining my father in front of them. Not me. Why can't Dad see that?

Well, for starters, he's not watching. His eyes are still closed, his face calm throughout the entire song, though his body moves ever so subtly in time to the singing, weaving to and fro with the kids. When it's over, he pops his eyes open. The choir has delivered a prize-winning performance. Too bad nothing I did had anything to do with it.

"Very good, everyone," my dad says. "I see you're in very good hands with my son."

Their faces radiate pride. How do I tell my father that the only hands they should be in are his?

My phone vibrates. A call from Ujima.

"Hey, Dad, can you step in for a second?"

He gives me a look, probably thinking I'll just abandon him completely, a gambit to make him take over.

"It's Ujima. They're planning a trip here . . . It might be important."

"Oh! That's wonderful!" My dad turns back to the kids. "Okay, kids. That sounded so good. Why don't you sing it for me again?"

They do an encore performance of the song as I go into the office and shut the door.

"What's up, Jee? You can just text me your flight details if that's easier."

"Baby, I just saw something you need to see."

I wait for Jee to continue.

They sigh.

"You're making me nervous," I say.

"Get onto Instagram. I'm gonna text you the name of the user you need to look up." My phone chirps with the text message: *photodabomb_nyc.*

"Should I know this person?" I ask.

"He was our *ONE-derland* photographer."

"Okay."

"Quito! How could you forget an ass like his? Anyway, it's not about him. It's something he happened to take a picture of."

I scroll through the first few lines of pictures until I see familiar faces—including me and Ujima, posing for the camera the night of their show. Then I see it, a picture taken in Twixxy's VIP Lounge. In the foreground, two women, their smiles straining against the unfortunate effects of one too many Botox injections. And directly behind them, not as sharp, but distinct enough: Mark and Dinesh.

Locked in a kiss.

So that's what was going on that evening. I knew I wasn't imagining the tension between them. And even before that I'd sensed there was something more to Mark wanting me to work with Dinesh. Something sublimated. That evening at *ONE-derland*, those underlying currents broke the surface, spilled out, and resulted in the spectacle captured on film now being displayed on my phone.

Was it their first kiss? Possibly. But probably not their last. Not after all the "work" they've been putting in on the show together these past few weeks while I've been gone.

"You still there?" Ujima asks.

The choir has finished singing through another effortless run-through, prompting plaudits from my dad. "I gotta go."

"That's it? No cussing Mark out? I just showed you the receipts that he's a cheating pig. At least let me hear you lose your temper."

"I'm not going to get mad about this, Jee."

"Hmph. And I know the reason, too. Because now you're free like a bird, baby. Spread your wings. Fly on over to that bedroom next door!"

"BYE, Ujima."

I hang up as they yell, "Go on and get yours!" into the phone.

The kids have devolved into boisterous chatter when I reenter the choir room. My father pushes off his chair to stand, his face twisting with effort. "Excellent job, everyone. I see you're in good hands with my son. You're very close now to being able to work with the famous Emmett Aoki. Maybe closer than you think," he says, winking at me. "Quito, I'm going now."

"Wait," I say. "They're not—"

"You were exaggerating, anak. I knew you'd do a good job." He pulls up his sagging jeans. "I think our *mutual friend* must be done with his little errand by now. Besides, I need to take a nap."

"You sure you're okay?" I walk him to the door.

He pats me on the back. "The office told me the concert is oversold now. Principal Higgins says many of the parents are so excited about Emmett that they spent some extra to get the best seats. We will make so much money for the kids. All thanks to you and Emmett." He turns back around to the choir. "Keep it up. See you soon. I promise."

The students wave and yell back goodbyes as my dad shuffles out of the choir room into the empty school hallway. I listen as the slapping of his flip-flops against the floor tiles fades. I want to follow him down the corridor, out into the parking lot, and into the car for Emmett to drive us both home. Or anywhere else. I still have no clue how to direct this choir.

And my boyfriend cheated on me.

What am I going to do?

When school gets out, I find myself filled with an excess of free-floating anxiety. I'm not ready to go home just yet.

I call my dad and tell him to not expect me for dinner, that I need to get a couple of things related to the concert done. Instead, I get into my car and just drive around aimlessly. I venture out beyond town, find myself on the freeway, and end up driving westward through the Caldecott Tunnel and onto the Bay Bridge, trying to sort my thoughts as I go.

Ujima had expected me to be mad at the picture of Mark and Dinesh kissing. But all I felt looking at the two of them together was a smallish, dull thud in my stomach. Not much more. It did hurt me that he'd betrayed me but in a general way—like the pain one feels when someone close to you has lied. Not the bone-crushing agony of my one true love proving himself to be anything but.

Ujima was kidding, but they were probably right. I'm not that upset because I do feel like I've shed something that was holding me back, not lifting me up.

How happy have I actually been with Mark?

The truth is that it doesn't surprise me that Mark cheated. For all the months we've spent together, I always had the feeling that I never made a deep connection with him, never really knew who he was. And, more importantly, that he didn't really know me.

No.

That wasn't exactly it.

Mark has never really known me because I've never truly been myself around him.

Other people are like mirrors. If you look at someone else, you can see your own reflection in them. Or at least a piece of it. And the closer that person is to you, the more pieces of yourself you're able to see. With Ujima, I can see nearly all of myself. My dad reflects back a lot of what I know to be true about me. But with Mark, I don't ever seem to add up. He brings out parts of me that don't feel as if they should go together. Maybe because his vision of me isn't quite right anymore. Maybe it never has been. Maybe it's my fault because I've never shown who I really am to him. Then again, Mark has never brought it out in me, either.

My eyes should be welling up with tears from the betrayal. But they're dry as a bone.

As I cross the bridge into San Francisco, the setting sun filters through the buildings, throwing columns of light my way. It's beautiful. I can't help but smile.

I wind my way through the city and end up at the top of Twin Peaks. It's been years since I've seen this view. I step out of the car and look out on the landscape of lights all just beginning to twinkle awake. The wind up here is merciless, but I don't mind. The cold feels good. Invigorating. A reminder of the human capacity to feel pain.

And the ability to overcome it.

Chapter 21—Then

IN THAT SPLIT second upon waking, I had no idea where I was. The bedsheet in my hand felt unfamiliar, the furniture in my dorm room strange. I sat up quickly in a panic and then immediately regretted it. Light and sound converged into a tiny point in my frontal lobe and exploded like a shrapnel grenade. I grabbed my forehead, leaned over, and threw up on the floor.

"Gross." I wiped my mouth with the back of my hand and looked around for something to clean the mess with. A used bath towel on my dresser was the nearest option. My legs nearly gave out as I made my way over to it.

The person looking back at me in the mirror was unrecognizable. My hair stood up at awkward angles, and my eyes flamed red with a maze of veins.

I blinked. Then blinked again.

Emmett.

I threw open the door adjoining my room to Jayesh's. The sound woke him and the person sleeping next to him on the bed. Insanely, I hoped it was Emmett.

The lump of unflattering clothes and clumpy hair lifted its head up and looked at me with lazy bedroom eyes.

"What's up, cutie?" it said.

Melina. The sight of her and Jayesh in bed together triggered my gag reflex.

"Are you okay?" Melina asked, her voice ruined from a night of drinking and smoking and who only knows what.

"Have you guys seen my friend? Emmett?" There was no sign of his stuff in my room or Jayesh's. "He was staying with me this weekend. He's supposed to sing for my composition jury today. But he's gone."

Jayesh yawned. I could smell his rotten beef breath from where I stood. "Yeah. I think he, like, left early this morning."

"What do you mean, left? Like, went to get breakfast or—"

"Naw, man, like, *left*, left. He threw his stuff into his suitcase and went out and never came back."

"What time was that?"

"Right after we woke up and had some freaky early-morning sex. Right, babe?"

"Yeah, lover." She looked at me with puckered kissy lips. "Around six o'clock."

I looked at the clock on Jayesh's wall. It was 11:52 a.m. Emmett could be anywhere. I could check the Conservatory. Maybe he just wanted to practice my songs some more. Left early to get some coffee, took his stuff with him so he didn't need to come back here. Or maybe he was already at the Benefactors' Luncheon. Which was at noon.

Eight minutes from now.

The bottom of my stomach fell out. I ran back into my room and, unable to hold it in any longer, threw up again. At least this time I managed to get it into the wastebasket. My knees slammed down onto the plastic tiles of my bedroom floor, and the room spun around in tight circles. I was supposed to have warmed up the Obertones for our performance at the luncheon at eleven thirty. Hopefully, Shane took over for me. We were last on the program, after the lunch had been served. But even that gave me less than an hour to get sober, clean up, and most importantly, find out where the hell Emmett had gone.

"Are you all right?" Jayesh yelled from his room.

"Do you need any help? Some water? A back rub?" Melina added.

"No!" I screamed back. I threw on some clean clothes, tried to wrangle my hair into something more presentable, slipped my shoes on, and ran out.

"Hey! You gonna clean up your acid chowder?" Jayesh's voice trailed behind me as our door slowly shut. "Smells like ass!"

There was no sign of Emmett in South Hall. He had to still be on campus somewhere. I had to believe that he was. I ran around outside aimlessly. The sun high above was bright, digging daggers into my brain. The humid Ohio air was cutting off my flow of oxygen.

I made my way to the Carnegie Building, where the luncheon was being held on the second floor in the cavernous Root Room.

The Tones stood around waiting on the first floor. Shane was pacing back and forth when he saw me come in.

"Jesus, Quito. Where the fuck have you been?"

"Have any of you...?" I could barely make it out, breathless. "Have any of you seen Emmett?"

"Who?"

"Emmett? My friend from USC? He was at the party last night."

"Keanu Reeves?" Jordan asked. Unlike the others, he lay back comfortably on the staircase, probably high.

"What?"

"That's what we were calling him at the party last night. He's got those movie-star looks."

I shook my head, trying to get the nonsensical dribble out of it. "Have. You. SEEN. Him? He's supposed to be at the luncheon."

No response.

Shane said, finally, "I snuck a peek at all the people upstairs. I didn't see him."

"You're sure?" I asked.

"He's hard to miss, Quito. Not a ton of hot people at Oberlin, and that guy is Brad Pitt level."

"Forget it." I tugged at my hair. "Warm up. Then a run-through."

I should have just taken a moment. To breathe, to relax. To focus on the task at hand. The Benefactors' Luncheon was an important event for the school. It usually raked in tons of money from wealthy alumni and other donors. Especially after they listened to the impressive slate of young, world-class musicians from the Conservatory. The Obertones were the uplifting, feel-good dessert served at the end to seal the deal.

But my head was pounding so hard that I couldn't hear my own thoughts. I couldn't center myself. All I could feel was confusion, anger, and resentment from Emmett's absence. The throbbing in my forehead hammered like a series of red-hot rails between my eyes. I couldn't stop it, no matter how many times I tried to blink it away.

"We're gonna rock this!" Shane said.

"Shut up," I said. Shane flinched. "Be serious for once in your life. I don't want you all screwing up and making me look bad."

Jordan's placid smile disappeared. I intoned the starting pitches for "Kiss from a Rose." But my throat was an arid mess. All the notes I sang at them wobbled out of tune precariously. Some were completely incorrect. They looked at me confused, not sure of what to sing. I raised my hand to cue them, "One, two, three, four, five—"

The tenors started singing in two different keys.

"No, no," I said. "Wrong. Start again." Shane started to say something. I cut him off with my hand. An even faster cue this time. Without regiving any pitches. "Four-five—"

An even worse entrance this time.

"What the hell? Get your act together, tenors!"

"Dude," Jordan said, putting his hand on my forearm, which was already raised, ready for yet another doomed start. "They're confused. You need to give better starting pitches."

"I don't need to do anything. They're the ones who sound like crap. Just do your job and sing. Four-five—"

Somehow, maybe through panic, or sheer will, or, more likely, a unified need to vocally kick me in the nuts, they sang—crashing their pitches together for the intro until they met in the middle. We kept going. They managed to make it for another eight measures before I clapped my hands together like a hyperactive walrus. "Stop. Stop. STOP. We can't go on sounding like this. Why does it sound like a hyena orgy? Did you all get completely wasted last night?"

Shane stepped out in front of the circle of Tones, his pointed finger accusing. "Quito, *you're* the one who got hammered. And high. And whatever else you ended up doing with your friend. You're the one making us sound like this. We're all fine. You're clearly not."

Shane was right. I wasn't okay. I was going to mess them up again. Except this time Emmett wouldn't be there to save me.

They stood there, waiting for some kind of apology or reconciliation. Something that would reassure them that whatever was happening to me was just some fluke. That I could shake it off and focus and be the leader they needed me to be.

My skin felt translucent. Like they could all see to the very core of me. Weak. Rotten. My head was killing me. I grabbed the sides of it and tried to squeeze the pain and anxiety and hurt out of it. None of it disappeared. Nothing came out except me saying, "I'm out."

I turned around and left.

"Quito! Hey!" Some of them called out to me as I walked. I kept going and didn't turn around. They were better off without me. In the state I was in, I was only going to lead them into a performance that would sound as horrible as I felt. That's what I told myself, at least, as I made my way to the Conservatory to look for Emmett. I had two hours before my composition jury. Two hours to try to make at least one thing turn out all right.

I crossed through Tappan Square to get to the Con. A few South Hall residents saw me and waved. I ignored them. It was taking all my energy just to keep moving forward.

Why the hell did Emmett leave? What had happened? I tried to focus on remembering the night before and managed to call up a few muddled recollections. Flashes of things I thought I remembered. A party at Love Shack. To celebrate the Tones' performance at Acappellooza. Music. Drinking. A bong. I was there with Emmett. Next to Emmett. I wanted...I wanted to be *with* Emmett. I was trying to figure out a way to let him know how I felt about him. The alcohol and the pot—I did it to loosen myself up, to find some courage. And since Emmett was drunk and high, too, maybe, just maybe, he'd be open enough to my confession.

I couldn't recall the walk home, yet we ended up there somehow. Jayesh was in his bed. Emmett had to sleep with me. Everything was lining up for us to be together.

Then what? What did we do?

What did *I* do?

Emmett was cold, he said. Though I remember his skin burning against mine. Or maybe that was *my* skin. My arm against his chest. Rubbing. Moving downward.

Oh god.

It was coming back to me. The friction of my hand against his erection. Me behind him, trying to focus. To register every second in my head as if I needed to somehow catalog the bits of memories, afraid they'd be gone forever, and failing as almost all of them slipped away, disappearing into a muddled haze.

Wetness in my hand. Between my legs. Someone rolled over. Me or him? As I tried to recall, pain hit me behind my eyes. I blinked hard. The only thing that came back to me was the absolute stillness during all of it. As if we were scared to be heard. As if engaging any more of our senses would have been too much for us to handle in that tiny bed.

Or did we not talk because we were ashamed of what was happening? If we weren't talking, then I wasn't checking in. Which means I didn't ask his permission. The first-year students laughed at the amateur skits during Orientation Week, all the steps required for safe, consensual sex drilled into us by our Resident Coordinators. And yet one of the scenarios had emblazoned itself onto my brain. The one about date rape. Mainly because it had involved two cute upperclassmen. The message came across loud and clear. *No* meant no. And we couldn't automatically assume that silence meant everything was okay. We were supposed to be on the same page at every point during the encounter.

But I'd never asked him if he was okay with what I was doing. I was too far gone. And too afraid he'd say no if I did ask. So instead, I just took advantage of him in his drunken state.

I sprinted the rest of the way to the Conservatory, barreling into the building to retrieve my composition portfolio from my locker. Clutching it tight to my chest, I skidded through the hallway joining the lounge to the practice room building, almost careening into an open door. Emmett *had* to be there. Practicing my songs. The more I thought it, the more important it became for me to believe. Though with every step I took, the plausibility of him being anywhere but the Cleveland airport waiting to get the hell out of Ohio was becoming infinitesimal.

I checked every room on every floor. Peeked through all the diamond-shaped windows, not caring who I was disturbing.

He wasn't in any of them.

I looked up at the clock on the wall. An hour and forty-five minutes before my fate as a composition major at Oberlin would be decided.

A wave of acid sloshed up into my mouth. I kept it closed and forced it all back down. I needed to make this work somehow.

The nearest empty practice room had one of my favorite grand pianos. A small piece of luck.

Half of my compositions were piano only. Those would be fine. It was the song cycle that needed a singer. Too late now to try to recruit anyone. Even the best sight-singer was never going to be able to sing the pieces; they were too confusing against my seemingly unconnected accompaniments.

I would just have to sing them myself. Which was going to be a challenge for me, given how tricky the piano parts were. All my composition's faults would be magnified. All my vulnerabilities laid out for the professors to pick up, point out, and note on my jury sheets. Only Emmett's singing could have smoothed out my inconsistencies, saving me with his ability to make me better than I had any right to be. When Emmett sang, all my problems disappeared. There were no mistakes. No strange segues or unjustified dissonances. He managed to make my broken parts into something beautiful. Without him, the songs weren't good enough.

But he'd left me no other choice.

Maybe what I had done crossed a line last night. Maybe what I'd done was inexcusable. But for him to leave without a word, without giving me the chance to explain myself, apologize, grovel—anything? This was my future Emmett was ruining. My chance at becoming the kind of musician I'd always wanted to be. My grade depended on this. My entire major. If I couldn't show the jury I deserved to be a composition major, I didn't know what I'd do. How could I show the rest of the world I had a voice that deserved to be listened to if I didn't succeed? I wouldn't be able to call myself a composer. I wouldn't deserve to be one.

Surprisingly, I didn't completely lose it by melting into a puddle of hangover-tinged self-pity. I bucked up instead and devoted the next hour to salvaging my music.

When I got to Kulas Recital Hall, my teacher and the other composition professor were in the audience, setting themselves up for the day. There were eight first-year composition majors, and all of them had to do their juries. I was the first to go.

"You're right on time, Quito," Professor Hoffer said, looking up from his semi-rimmed glasses. I was unable to look him in the eye. Instead, I fixated on the tiny ball-bearing chain that allowed him to take his glasses off and wear them around his neck.

Mr. Birnholz, a professor with curly white hair and bushy black eyebrows, asked, "Solo piano and accompanied vocal pieces today. Correct?" He looked at, then around me. "Where is your vocalist?"

I swallowed so hard that bile hit the bottom of my stomach. "He, uh, got sick. Real quick."

"Sick?" Mr. Birnholz said.

"I can still play all of my pieces for you." I took out my stack of sheet music and started spreading them out across the piano's music rack. The papers quivered in my jellylike fingers.

"Maybe we should postpone until later in the week?" Mr. Hoffer offered, his glasses sliding forward on the bridge of his nose.

"It won't help, Mr. Hoffer. My singer's from L.A. I think he left. I think he...went back home."

"Was he that sick that he'd just leave without singing for you?" Mr. Hoffer asked.

Mr. Hoffer had been working closely with me on my songs, guiding me all year. He'd been excited to hear them sung. Once he'd even said my style of writing reminded him of another composition student of his who'd gone on to win a Grammy. I was gambling that my effort to do the entire song cycle on my own would be enough to carry me through my jury, despite how bad it would sound without Emmett.

Then the images of last night came rushing back, whipping in rapid succession through my mind.

My hands on his body. My insistent groping. All while he lay silent and wondered how I could be doing what I was doing. Realizing that he never wanted to see me again. Emmett abandoned me because I did something I never should have even *thought* about, let alone gone through with. I didn't learn my lesson with Angela Asari. I should have accepted that Emmett was straight. I'd just pushed my own selfish desires onto him. Regardless of how he felt.

I'd betrayed him. And now I was paying the price.

"Quito," Mr. Hoffer said. "Did you hear me? I said, why would your friend just leave?"

"Because I'm a horrible person, Mr. Hoffer."

"Excuse me?"

"Sorry." I snatched the sheet music off the piano, crumpling the paper into my portfolio. One of the pages snagged on the zipper and tore. A violent rending of the paper filled the hall. I shoved it in regardless. "I can't play these for you. They're nothing without Emmett."

"Excuse me?" Mr. Birnholz said.

Professor Hoffer stood up and took his glasses off. "What about your jury?"

My face was wet with tears. "Fail me. I deserve it," I said and walked out of Kulas Hall.

I'd let down the Obertones. I'd failed Emmett. Why not my comp jury? It all seemed to be karmically correct. Emmett was my best friend. I loved him. So no matter how much I loved him or in what way, I should've respected what we had instead of forcing it into something it was not, like trying to push a square peg into a round hole. Now I'd broken the entire framework of what we used to be. I was blinded by lust. Or loneliness. Or I'd allowed myself to dream when I should have been content with reality. I didn't know. All I knew was that my life was going to be very different from now on. It was going to be missing a few things. Things that made it the life I wanted, *needed*, it to be. And I deserved all of it.

Back at the dorm, Jayesh and Melina were gone. So was my puke. One of them must have cleaned it up for me (probably Melina), though the smell of stomach acid still lingered. I didn't care. I crashed down face-first onto the bed. My tears turned my pillow into a sloppy, wet mess.

Chapter 22 — Now

WHEN I FINALLY get home later that evening, my dad, for some inexplicable reason, has on a top hat and is wearing a bedsheet on his back like a cape. He's holding a copy of *A Midsummer Night's Dream*, the play Emmett's rehearsing for.

"This falls out better," he says, "than I COULD DEVISE. But hast thou yet latch'd the ATHENIAN'S EYES," he recites, leaning into the rhyming words with a bit too much emphasis. "With the love juice. As I did bid thee DO?"

Emmett, seemingly unfazed by my dad's getup and halting line readings, says, "I took him sleeping, that is finish'd too—"

"What is this love juice he is talking about?" my dad asks.

"Ah..."

"Is this something dirty? Some kind of pornography thing? Wow. Maybe Shakespeare is more interesting than I remember," my dad says, flipping through the rest of the play.

Emmett looks at me briefly before realizing, rightly, that he shouldn't because we'll just bust up laughing.

"Hey, Dad, can I steal Emmett for a minute?"

He looks up from the booklet. "Ah? Oh, sige na. I'm getting tired now. I should go to bed. Did you eat already, anak? There's plenty of food there in the kitchen. I put it in plastic wrap for you in the fridge."

"Thanks, Dad."

I watch him shuffle down the hallway to his room.

"So, how's my father as a scene partner?"

"Incredible. I'm putting in a good word for him as my understudy."

"Don't actually ever say that in front of him. He would one hundred percent believe you."

"Well, I'm one hundred percent telling the truth," Emmett says, with that smile that says otherwise.

"Hey," I say, "I'm going to tell you something. But before I do, I'm going to ask you to not do something that you're usually really good at doing."

His smile fades. "And what would that be?"

"Act."

His face goes hard, unreadable for a moment.

"I'm just saying—can you promise to tell me the truth? To just be you?"

He nods.

I head back into my bedroom, and he follows without a word.

I close the door behind him and sit on the bed. With my lips, I motion to the spot next to me.

He smiles and sits down. I feel him so clearly beside me—that unique, familiar sensation that thrums through me like a chord.

We sit there, staring at the wall and outward beyond it.

"Mark cheated on me," I say.

"Oh," he says quietly. "And . . . how does that make you feel?"

"I'm not really surprised about it. Not that sad, either."

"I guess that's good," he says.

"How does that make *you* feel?" I ask.

"I'm sorry to hear that happened."

"Yeah?"

"Well, sure," he says. "I'm sorry that he was such a jerk to you."

"Really?"

"I mean—"

"Remember what I said. The truth," I say. "Are you *really* sorry?"

"No," Emmett says immediately. "Not at all. Not even a little bit."

"Why?" I ask.

"Because that means you can dump him."

I smile to myself.

I rest my hand on his knee. He goes quiet. So quiet I can't even hear him breathing.

"Is this okay?" I ask.

He nods.

I sink the tips of my fingers into the marble-like muscles of his leg.

"How about this?"

"Yeah," he says, his voice low.

I massage his leg with tiny, pulsing movements. "This?"

"Yes." A small moan escapes his lips. "More than okay."

My hand drifts upward, digging into the side of his inner thigh.

"Mmm."

I stop. I take my hand off him. A spark of panic flashes in my chest. My heart is racing so fast that I can barely spit out what I say next. "Emmett. Look at me. Are you sure?"

He looks me in the eyes but says nothing.

We stay there with time at a standstill, staring at each other.

Then, with the expanse of his hands, he takes the sides of my face, pulls me to him, and kisses me.

All the fear I have disappears. All the unallayed anxiety from the last time we'd found ourselves in this situation was now gone with the touch of his lips on mine.

Our kiss isn't only transformative—it's synergistic. Vital. Like being underwater or in space, out where it's just him and me. Breathing for each other. It's us anticipating and matching each other, pushing and pulling, flowing exactly when we're supposed to. Moving to the rhythm that drives us both. To the melody that has always been there.

In a way, our kiss is the natural culmination of what we've always found ourselves doing together: making perfect, glorious music.

I pull him down to the bed. His body presses against mine, all two hundred pounds of it like a blanket, surrounding me in strength and certainty. I asked him not to act, and I feel his promise to me now, the absolute truth of him on me, no curtain or facade separating us. There can never be barriers between two people truly in sync with each other. I feel that now, in a way I've never felt with Mark or anyone, really, before.

Our kissing becomes more urgent. I take his shirt off, and he takes off mine. Emmett places his hand against my chest— a caesura, a brief pause—as if bringing to a close the end of one phrase and the beginning of another. He kisses me deeply and then slowly begins to unzip my pants, pulling them down. I am somehow aware that I do not need to return the favor. I sense that he's now taken the reins and will do the same for himself.

Soon only the slimmest of layers separates us. As he continues to kiss me, now moving on to the sensitive ridge of my ear, tracing down the lobe of it and the sides of my jaw to the tender, vulnerable skin of my neck, I let him continue taking the lead while I do my part in the background and slip his boxer briefs down, past the rigidity of his hip bones, past the smooth roundness of his flawless buttocks, down, down, down the length of his legs and finally off his giant feet. I rip my own underwear off in seconds because I want to feel the core parts of us together, in perfect harmony, finally, after so many years of wanting it.

His hands are at the sides of my head, his fingers buried in my hair. I grasp my arms around his back, trying to claim the vastness of him.

The tempo accelerates, our metronomes ticking past the grounded, rational markings of time as every part of our bodies, including our erections, line up, matching each other, filling the gaps of each other perfectly.

We swell and crescendo.

And climax.

We stay there, holding each other, breathing, not daring to break the stillness in the afterward.

I hold on to him happily, knowing that this time we've gotten it right. That what came before this was just an ill-conceived, unprepared rehearsal. And as I lie there with Emmett, knowing that what we've just experienced will naturally, inevitably dissipate, I can't help but wish that the music we've made together won't ever fade away.

Through the open window, a breeze, warm with the promise of summer, carries in the scent of early evening. Cicadas click and buzz—the only other sound I hear besides Emmett's steady breath next to me.

"That was nice," he murmurs into the side of my face. "How was it for you?" His body goes slightly taut when he asks this. He's apprehensive maybe, afraid of my answer.

"Fishing for compliments?" I ask, butting my head softly against his.

He *tsk*s and wiggles his head *no*.

"I mean, besides the fact that we just did it in my childhood bed, it was pretty incredible."

Emmett's body relaxes, every part of him re-easing into me. "I've been thinking about doing that for a long time."

"Me too," I say. "For years."

"Ever since—"

"Oberlin. The night I completely fucked up."

"Quito—"

"Wait, Emmett. Just listen. Back then, the morning after, I was confused. When I woke up and saw that you'd gone, I was upset. Really upset. Your leaving me screwed up my composition jury." I pull my head away just enough to be able to look him in the eye with our bodies still completely connected. "But as angry as I was at you, I was even more mad at myself for chasing you away."

"You didn't. I had my own reasons for leaving," Emmett says. "I should have told you why. Or at least left you a note. Something."

"No," I say firmly. "*I* was the one who should've called you to apologize. But I didn't. It was easier to pity myself than to own up to what I did to you. For...*assaulting* you. I've done so many things wrong to the people I care about the most."

"I told you, Quito, you don't have to apologize." He puts his hand on the side of my face, caressing it. "Because you didn't take advantage of me."

Holding his gaze, intense and unrelenting as it is, is impossible. I close my eyes. The pain of the mistakes I made that weekend come back to me. I feel tears welling. "You don't have to lie just to make me feel better."

"You probably thought I was high and drunk that night. The truth is, I didn't have any pot at all. And I'd stopped drinking before you even arrived at that off-campus party. I was completely sober when we walked back to your dorm." He strokes my cheek, and a few tears drip onto his fingers. "I knew what was going on the whole time. I even pretended to be cold just to get you to hold me. Do you remember that? I was too chickenshit to touch you. So I made you do it instead."

"But you didn't say anything when I...when we started to...you know. You were quiet the entire time."

"*I* didn't say anything. But you did."

"I did?"

"After you put your arm around me, you said, *Is this okay?* I mean, you kind of mumbled it into my neck, but I heard you loud and clear. I only nodded in response. And I know you understood because you let out this little *hooray.* Even as drunk as you were, you still managed to do that cute little rhyming thing you always do."

Something unlocks inside me, letting go of a weight I'd carried for years. The relief makes me so happy I almost want to laugh. "Thank god."

I turn to him. "So why did you bail without saying anything to me? Were you really okay with everything that happened?"

"In the moment, absolutely. And I knew if I told you to stop, you would. No questions asked. But afterward, to be honest, I did sort of freak out. I thought I was ready for it all, but it was a lot to take in. After you passed out, I couldn't get to sleep. I just lay next to you, staring up at the ceiling. Thinking about what we'd done. Wondering if we did the right thing. The more I thought about it, the more I realized we crossed a line we were never going to be able to uncross. Our relationship was going to be different. Everything I knew had changed. About me. About us. I looked at all the ways we could move on from there, and all the options scared me. So I ran out. Threw my stuff in my bag and left. I couldn't think anymore at that point. All I remember was waiting at the bus stop for the first shuttle to the airport, thinking about how I wish we could've done that night over somehow."

"You agree it was a mistake, then."

"No. Not what we did. But maybe the way we did it. And the way I reacted, definitely. I'm the reason you flunked."

"I deserved it. Cosmic retribution. You were the one who always inspired me. I deserved not ever having another good song in me again for what I did to you."

"Whatever happened between us shouldn't have stopped you from composing. We might have approached it the wrong way, but that night? Us? The sex? Okay, it wasn't great. But it wasn't wrong. *You* didn't do anything wrong. I wanted it just as much as you did. So stop punishing yourself."

"I thought about you," I say. "All the time."

Emmett nods sadly. "Yeah."

"I wrote all these letters to you. Then threw them away before sending them. I'd pick up the phone. Dial your number to the last digit. Then hang up. I'd wonder why you never tried to get in touch with me. But then I'd remind myself it was because of what I'd done. And then I'd sink into a depression about the whole thing because I knew you'd never call me and I wasn't brave enough to apologize to you. It went on like that for months. Years."

Emmett smiles sadly.

"What?" I say.

"I wanted to talk to you, too. But I was too scared. I didn't want to accept the consequences of what we'd done. I was so stupid to leave you. I missed you. And your songs. By letting you go, I had to let that go, too. That love of music. That joy I felt when we did it together. I've never really felt that again with anything. Or anyone."

We lay quiet for a while in something not exactly like silence. Something seems to wind around us, a strain of some shared melody. Unheard but there.

"You don't actually want to go out with Emma Chen, do you?" I ask.

"I mean, you've seen her, right? She's hot as hell."

"I'm going to slap that dumb smile off your face."

"I can think of better things for you to do to my lips," Emmett says.

He kisses me.

Our reprise is even better than the first time.

Chapter 23 — Now

WHEN I REACH over for Emmett in the morning, all I touch is a cold pillow. I rub my eyes and, yawning, make my way toward laughter and conversation in the kitchen.

I'm confused when I enter. There are no smells of garlic rice or eggs being fried, no sausages on the pan. My dad is eating a bowl of children's cereal (mostly the colored marshmallow bits), and Emmett, wearing running shorts and a shirt damp with sweat (and smelling insanely sexy), is eating a banana.

"What, no silog?" I ask my father. "It's Saturday."

Emmett swallows the rest of his banana. "Oh, your dad was about to start cooking, but I told him we already had plans."

I raise my eyebrow. "Oh?"

"They have these incredible soufflé pancakes at Bette's Ocean-view Diner in Berkeley. Saw it on *Diners, Drive-Ins and Dives*. We have to go there."

I grab a mug out of the cupboard and pray Emmett's made the coffee this morning instead of Dad. "That place always has a long wait. Plus, I thought you were going incognito while you were in town."

"I was, but—" He looks at my dad briefly before saying to me, "I dunno, I guess I'm kind of tired of hiding. I'm not so concerned about being seen anymore."

My dad keeps on eating. I swear I can almost see him smiling, though it might just be the overzealousness of his mouth muscles as he chomps away at the marshmallows.

"Okay. If you really want to. When do you want to go?" I ask.

"I have to hop in the shower, but there's no rush. I called ahead and asked them to save us a table."

"But they don't accept reservations."

"They don't? Huh," Emmett says. He shrugs and walks off.

"Bring me home some of the famous pancakes, okay, anak?" my dad says, his mouth full of milk and cereal.

Emmett's got on his Ruth Bader Ginsburg hoodie (all black with DISSENT in white letters), a Lakers cap, and aviator sunglasses as we arrive at the café, already packed and with a sizable crowd outside waiting for their turn to be seated. When he approaches the person standing behind the cash register, though, he takes everything off. "Table for two under Aoki, please?"

The person—who doesn't seem to be a host or even a waiter but one of the cooks who just happened to be looking for something near the register—stares at Emmett with her mouth half-open. While the poor young woman seems to sort through endless thoughts without actually saying anything, the actual host, wiry and lithe with long blue braids, steps in front of us.

"Emmett? Hey. Welcome. Don't mind Liv. She's watched *The Hanoi Heist*, like, a million times." She grabs a few menus off the counter and walks back into the restaurant. "This way, please."

As we walk past the crowded tables, I can't help but be distracted by all the people looking up at us with expressions ranging from curious to incredulous, with plenty of surreptitious asides and not-so-subtle pointing.

The host seats us in the back. I casually slip into the seat facing forward so that Emmett can sit with his back toward the rest of the restaurant. He pauses for a second and then acknowledges what I've done by winking at me and sitting down.

Even with only the back of him visible, I can feel the weight of dozens of pairs of eyes on us. I watch them use the mirrors on the walls to look. Some even fully turn around. I don't understand how Emmett can deal with this kind of attention all the time. What must they all be thinking? Are they wondering what he's doing in Berkeley? Confused by the fact that he's grabbing brunch, not with some beautiful woman but with a sometimes-when-he-tries-really-hard-he-can-be-handsome-in-a-dorky-way-but-mostly-he's-just-an-average-looking Filipino guy?

I start to regret my decision to take the seat farthest in the back. I feel trapped. Everyone seems to be closing in on us.

"Emmett, wouldn't you rather just get something to go?" I whisper. "You can wait in the car, and I'll get the food?"

"Hey," he says. "Hey." He puts his hand on mine and squeezes it. The feel of it is initially comforting, but I eventually pull away, wanting to protect him. Or maybe myself.

He frowns. "Don't freak out, Quito. Okay? This kind of stuff happens all the time. It's not a big deal. People generally get over it after a minute or two. When they see I'm just like them, just a regular dude wanting to get some pancakes and scrapple, they calm down and forget about it."

I want to push back, to argue that being seen like this is something he's used to but utterly new and scary for me. Then he smiles. When his crooked tooth comes out, I think to myself: Just focus on that. On him. Block everyone else out. If he's okay with being watched, then you can be, too.

"What the heck is scrapple?" I ask.

"It's kind of like Amish Spam. I'll order us some. You'll see. It's going to be amazing."

"I can't wait," I say.

The scrapple is, indeed, amazing in an undefinable pork-product way. Also amazing are the pancakes—though the soufflé-ness of the ones I later bring home to Dad gets lost in translation by the time we get back. But as good as the food is, I just can't seem to let myself enjoy it fully. Even when most of the restaurant patrons stop overtly ogling, I can still feel the stings of their stolen glances like a hundred mosquito bites on me. The itch of it all makes brunch a joyless occasion when it should be a celebratory one. Emmett is mine. Finally. But not all mine, I realize. Someone like Emmett will never be just for me. Not when he constantly shares himself with the rest of the world.

After, I suggest we head straight home, but Emmett insists on walking off all the calories by doing an impromptu hike. Since my version of hiking is walking crosstown in Manhattan instead of waiting for the bus, I have no idea where we should go. He offers to find some suitable options on his phone. Knowing we'll be seen by more people in more popular, open parks, I steer him toward lesser-known options and more secluded trails. He seems to know what I'm doing but doesn't object. Perhaps because he's starting to sense that it *is* a good idea to stay hidden—and, in fact, when we return home and I suggest we just stay in for the rest of the weekend, he agrees without even trying to argue. In any case, my father is happy to have the both of us around to cook for, and we're rewarded with mountains of food.

Early Monday morning, as Emmett slips out of my bedroom to go for his daily run, I lie awake, unable to go back to sleep. Both Saturday and Sunday evenings, after watching TV with my father, we waited for him to fall asleep before going to bed ourselves, Emmett sneaking into my room only after we could hear my dad's snores echoing down the hallway from his room. We laughed about how silly it felt for Emmett to sneak around the house like that, not wanting to let my father know we were being scandalous under his roof.

But after the silliness subsided, the reality of our hiding begins to sink in to me. How much longer will we have to keep things a secret? From my dad? From the world? Will Emmett ever want to let people know about us? Coming out of the closet for a celebrity as big as he is would be a huge deal. It would change everything about the way the world sees him. It would change his entire career. The more I think about it, the worse I feel. I don't want to be responsible for anything bad happening to him.

And yet I also don't want to let him go. We had an amazing weekend together, when it was just us. As long as we keep it that way, we'll be fine. This afternoon, after school, I'll tell him that he has nothing to worry about. I'll stick by him but out of the way, where no one will ever see me, where no one will use me against him.

But before I do that, I need to get up and get into school early. To take care of something before classes start. A hanging thread that needs to get tied up.

Or, rather, cut off completely.

After a quick coffee run, I get into school and set myself up at the choir room piano. I pull the sheet music for *The Forever Boys* Act I finale out of my bag.

Unburdened by the need to push myself to do my best work, I finish up the last few lines of the bridge by scribbling in a repetitive three-note melody. I throw that on top of a repeating I–V–vi–IV chord progression, the most overused of all time. The lyrics were horrible. Why push myself to make the music any better? Certainly not for the guy who made out with my boyfriend.

I scan the music in the school office copier and send the sheets to Mark and Dinesh along with a copy of the picture of them kissing in the Twixxy VIP lounge. The email is short and to the point:

I'm done.

After rethinking it, I send them both one more message.

Ask J.B. at Broadway Baby for way better music than I could write for you.

Within minutes, apologies fly back from Mark. I'm almost inclined to write back to tell him off. To let him know what a jerk he was.

But I don't. He's no longer worth the effort.

I block his phone number and email address and shift my attention to my rehearsal outline for the day, trying not to sabotage myself with negative thoughts before I've even begun to plan.

As I stand at the podium sorting through sheet music and making notes, I feel a presence nearby.

The shy young tenor whose name I cannot remember is sticking his head through the door, staring at me with adorably droopy eyes.

I walk over to him. "Hi, Mel, Mel..."

"Milton."

That's it. "Milton. Come on in. What's up?"

He pushes the door open a crack and squeezes his body through, as if apologizing to the door that he's disturbing it. "I'm sorry I've been messing up lately, Mr. Cruz."

"What do you mean?"

"All those mistakes you keep hearing from the tenors. That's me."

"What mistakes? I never hear any mistakes," I say. He looks up at me with such clear awareness of my lie that I blush. "Milton, you're an excellent tenor. Really. You've got a lovely voice. You don't need to apologize for your mistakes. You're not the only one who makes them."

He shakes his head. "I just hate the way my voice sounds."

"Everyone feels that way sometimes."

"No. It doesn't feel good. I mean, it doesn't feel like my right voice."

His speaking voice has a high ring to it, sounding almost like a young woman's. There's no way he should be a bass. "Do you mean you think you're singing incorrectly?"

"Maybe. I'm not sure."

"Would you like me to do a little vocal coaching with you? Sometime after school, maybe?"

The bell rings. More students begin to enter. He looks around and fidgets. "I'll think about it."

"Well, I'm here if you need me."

He waves at me sideways as he rushes to take his seat, and I can tell that he won't be taking me up on my offer anytime soon.

After we do our warm-up, I decide to run through our trickiest piece—an English madrigal by William Byrd. Lots of problems with this one. The choir's musical skills are excellent, their pitches solid, and their rhythms mostly correct. Yet, for some reason, they seem to be missing something essential. The sound is sometimes muddled. At other times, sterile.

As I've been doing since I arrived, I run through the whole piece. I don't stop. Even during the rougher places. I know how hard they must have worked on the notes and want them to have that feeling of accomplishment by singing the song all the way through with no disruptions. They make plenty of mistakes, but I pretend not to hear them. I don't want them to feel frustrated.

"Very nice." I nod reassuringly. "Super duper, troupers."

Their faces reek of apathy. Even Celeste's normally sunny face is cloudy. Like every day since I've been with them, my anxiety level begins its gradual ascent. Can they not follow my conducting? Is that it? Am I really that bad? Am I not encouraging enough?

"You guys are great. Should we sing this one again? What do you all think? Maybe, with, I don't know, a little more joy?"

We do another run-through. I widen my eyes and grin, showing both rows of teeth. They respond by forcing smiles. This only makes them strain and sing louder. Some of their pitches push upward. They fall out of tune, which wreaks havoc on my sense of perfect pitch. I can't help but make a face. They see this and falter. Some of them stop singing altogether. I try to get them to keep going, but there's no escaping that it's a total train wreck. "Oops. Let's try that again. You all are doing so awesome."

None of them even bother to make eye contact with me at all after that. They must feel horrible. I have to keep being positive.

Celeste shoots her hand up. "Mr. Quitocruz?"

"Yes, Celeste?"

"Are you sure we did that okay? I mean, can you tell us what our mistakes were?"

"No mistakes! No mistakes."

"But, I mean, like on page two, when the tenors came in, they—"

"They were fine," I say, cutting her off. If she starts pointing fingers at her fellow singers' errors, it could lead to disaster. "We just need a bit more excitement, that's all."

Celeste slumps into her already rumpled dress.

I resume immediately to try to keep the energy going. The third run-through is worse than the first two. My head cramps up with stress tension. At this point, the choir will be worse for the concert, not better. I rack my brain, trying to think of some other ways to encourage them, when Celeste raises her hands again.

"Mr. Quitocruz?"

I sigh and brace myself for her question. Her instincts, musical and otherwise, have proven to be impeccable, but I just don't have the energy to deal with her suggestions when I can barely fix the problems I'm already painfully aware of. "Yes, Celeste?"

"Um, so I heard a rumor that Emmett Aoki is actually in town already. Is that true? Is he going to be rehearsing with us now?"

Shit.

Excitement surges around the room. Other students repeat her question out loud. They're all getting too worked up. I'm losing control.

"Uh, yes, he's in town. He . . . arrived this weekend. And he's just visiting with family and old friends. You all know he grew up here, right? And that he's an alum of Sunvalley? Yes, once he's done, uh, connecting with people, he'll be in to practice for the concert with us."

Unfortunately, my response does nothing to dam the deluge of follow-up questions that Celeste has unleashed from everyone.

"Isn't he your friend?"

"Mr. Cruz told us he was your friend."

"Your best friend."

"What's he going to sing?"

"Is he any good?"

"Is he staying in town all the way until the concert?"

"Is he staying with *you*?"

"How close are you guys?"

"Is he really dating Emma Chen?"

I hold up my hands. "Stop. He'll be here, okay? Just chill out!"

My inability to modulate my voice during stressful moments rears its ugly head again. They reel back. Some laugh nervously in response. The rest fold up like closed books.

Great move, Quito. Another in a long series of perfectly executed gestures.

My phone vibrates in my pocket. I pull it out quickly—a text from Emmett.

"Okay, everyone take out the Moses Hogan spiritual and take another look at all the words. Make sure you know them well. We're going to start rehearsing it from memory today."

They pull out their sheet music as I read Emmett's text.

Hey. Have to run a few urgent errands this afternoon. Might not be back this evening, so don't wait up. xo

I watch the kids silently mumbling lyrics to themselves and try not to be upset about the fact that I won't be able to talk to Emmett this evening—to tell him I've broken up with Mark and that he doesn't have anything to worry about with me keeping our relationship a secret.

But the more I think about his text, the more it begins to feel there's something else. Something he's not telling me.

It starts to feel familiar. Like he's telling me he's leaving me.

Again.

Chapter 24—Now

NORMALLY, HAVING TO get up at 5:00 a.m. to pick up Ujima at SFO would have been an utter impossibility for me, but considering I didn't sleep at all last night, it wasn't an issue. I tried not to stay up to wait for Emmett to come home from whatever he was out doing, but I did, fretting away in the living room, the kitchen, my bedroom, his. My father eventually got so tired of me pacing around everywhere that he actually forced me to sit down at the piano and play some music for him, which I was thankful for. It took my mind off Emmett—for about an hour, at least.

After my father fell asleep, I was back to wondering where Emmett was, what he was doing, and—most importantly—who he was doing it with. Visions of him cavorting around in some private hotel room in San Francisco with some woman or man—or both—raced through my head, making it coil up with metallic tension.

At around 2:00 a.m., I lay down on the bed and turned off the lights, thinking the worry would just burn itself out with me falling asleep from the fatigue of it all. No such luck.

Driving into Arrivals, I yawn so loudly, I startle myself. I smack my face a couple of times and scan the people waiting outside Terminal 2. Even a hundred feet away, I can spot Ujima. They tower above nearly everyone else.

I drive up to them and roll down the passenger window. "Aren't you freezing in those hot pants?"

"I got a jacket on," Jee says, as if I need my eyes checked. Never mind that it's a crop-top jacket that only goes down to their navel, and underneath all they've got on is a *She-Ra* T-shirt.

"Why all girled up?"

Ujima's loaded side-eye makes me blush. I was referring to their evening-ready getup, complete with platform heels and perfectly spherical Afro puffs. Not the fact that they didn't do the flight as Gerome. "I mean, why so fancy?"

"It's all for you, baby," they say, tossing my unintended slight away with a frosted purple kiss on my cheek.

"Get in. I'll take care of your luggage."

My knees buckle when I attempt to pick up the bags. "Were you planning on staying until Christmas?" I throw the luggage into the trunk, and my car sinks down. "Geez. That's my workout for the day."

"My gift to you," Ujima says, squeezing my biceps. "These munchkins need all the help they can get."

As we leave the airport, the fog clears. Glimpses of buildings and rolling hills become more expansive, and the majesty of the San Francisco Bay reveals itself. Jee turns the heat up and hums something low. "It is beyond beautiful here. Why did you ever leave?"

"To pursue all my unattainable, deluded dreams in New York. Just like you."

"We do make sacrifices, don't we?" Jee says.

"And speaking of dreams..."

They snap their head away from the window and look at me. "Yeeeeeess?"

"I slept with Emmett."

"Bitch, you better not say something like you both stayed up all night talking and fell asleep next to each other like fourth graders at a slumber party. If you're pulling my leg, I will slap you."

"No jokes this time. We did it."

"For real?"

"Yes. Several times."

"WHAT?!" Ujima slaps the side of my shoulder so hard that I almost swerve into the car next to us. "Ahhh, sookie sookie now! That's the best news I heard all month! Tell me everything. Don't leave anything out."

"I don't know, Jee. You know I don't like to kiss and tell."

"Girl, I will cut you."

"And the other thing is—I think we might have gone too far, too fast. I think he's bailing on me."

"What do you mean?"

"Well, he was out all day yesterday. And all night. He never came back home."

"I'm sure it's nothing. He's a busy man. He was probably meeting up with other friends from your old hood."

"He did say he had errands to run. But the choir got wind of him being in town, and now they're expecting him—today, actually. They're going to hate me even more than they do now when he doesn't show up."

"Why do you keep saying the kiddies hate you? What possible reason could they have?"

"The fact that I'm not my dad. He's their hero. I can't compete with that."

"You're helping them while he's gone. I'm sure they understand."

Ujima turns on the radio and surfs through the stations. Bursts of static alternate with music snippets as they try to settle on something. "Anyway, don't they have to be nice to you, considering you're the one who's bringing Emmett to the party?"

Old-school R&B blasts from the radio. Boyz II Men and Mariah Carey warble loudly for a few seconds before I turn the volume down.

"Jee, something doesn't feel right about Emmett being gone. I think I might have messed things up again."

"Were you that bad in bed?"

"Ugh, no, I—well, I mean maybe? No, that's not what I'm talking about. After the first night we, you know, slept together, the next day he insisted on going out to brunch. In public. Together."

Traffic flow slows down around us as we approach the Bay Bridge. The cars crowd us, hemming us in on all sides. Everyone eventually slows to a standstill. I look ahead at the long lines of cars ahead of us.

"It was his idea," Ujima says.

"Yes, but I should've said no. Now I'm sure he's regretting the fact that people saw us together. They could probably all see the afterglow of sex on my face and wondered why the hell Emmett was with me, and then he got embarrassed and remembered that he wasn't gay, or that he could do much better than me, or—"

A car changes lanes abruptly with no indication, swerving into a tiny open space in front of us. I plant my hand on my horn for a good five seconds. "Asshole!"

Ujima presses two extended middle fingers up to my windshield. "Y'all *better* be glad I don't get out of this car right now!"

"You know they can't hear you."

"Oh, they know what I'm saying. They can read my lips. They're too luscious to miss," Jee says, waving their fingers around their open mouth.

Ujima's set the temperature in the car too high. The steering wheel starts feeling like putty in my hands. I squeeze and squeeze, trying to somehow change the form of it into something else. I can't stop thinking about the possibility that Emmett has regretted his actions and abandoned me. Again.

Jee places their hand on my knee. The weight of it centers the floating parts of me, and I stop trying to alter the steering wheel into a different state of matter. "It looks like I got here just in time. You're falling down some kind of black hole, baby. And not the good kind." They sigh. "I'm going to have to snap you out of it."

The cars around us begin to gain speed. A red Dodge pickup with a flat tire takes up a chunk of the shoulder of the road as we get onto the bridge. Once we pass it, the traffic eases. As we drive over the bridge, the sky clears. We reach the end of the fog bank and coast into bright, sunny skies.

"Quito, you know you tend to overthink things, right? And that you're always too hard on yourself. So he was out for the night. So what? That doesn't erase everything that happened between you two this weekend—and by the way, don't think for a *second* I forgot that you haven't told me all about that yet. Y'all are fine. Just give the boy some space."

"You're probably right."

"Of course I'm right. I'm always right."

"Oh. And something I know you'll appreciate. I broke up with Mark."

"Hallelujah!" Ujima says, turning the music back up. "Time to celebrate!" They roll their window down, and the car's heat dissipates into the cool wind flowing in.

They start singing along with the Earth, Wind, and Fire coming from the radio. Their voice is a miracle. Unapologetic and real.

I join Jee in singing as we zoom across the bridge.

As we get off the freeway, I ask them, "Did you want to freshen up at my house before school starts? I know you can't check into your Airbnb yet. And you probably didn't get a lot of sleep on the red-eye over."

Ujima flips down the visor, checks their face in the mirror with a quick side to side, makes a kissing face, and snaps the visor back up. "I didn't, but a mug this naturally divine doesn't need as much beauty sleep as most other people would. I'll be fine. But I could use some coffee."

"There's a drive-through Starbucks nearby."

"Thank you, Jeeeesus," they singsong.

I switch lanes and change direction, heading for a nearby shopping center. "I'm sorry we don't really have room for you in the house with Emmett still in the guest room. Well, I hope he still is, at least. You know my dad would love to have you at the house."

"Your daddy needs his peace and quiet to recuperate. And I'm sure y'all already make enough noise as it is. I mean, *music*," Ujima says, snorting.

I drive us into Olive Crossing, a small outdoor shopping complex. Of the various stores and restaurants, only the gym and the Starbucks are open. We get in line behind the four other cars already waiting their turn at the drive-through.

As we wait in the queue, Jee perks up their hair with an Afro pick. "Have you told the kids I'm coming?"

"Oops. Sorry. I was just so preoccupied with what's happening with Emmett, I didn't mention it. In fact, they're expecting Emmett today, not you. I'm sure they won't mind."

"Right. Because anyone can see I'm a natural replacement for Emmett Aoki. Girl, you better be glad I already like you, or I'd be giving you some choice words right now."

A horn blasts from behind us. In my rearview mirror, an older woman with a transparent shower cap covering a headful of roller-curled hair throws her hands up at me from behind the wheel of her BMW. The cars in front of us have all moved ahead.

"All right, all right. Hold your horses!"

I jam on the gas. My car screeches forward too far. I don't brake in time and hit the bumper of the SUV in front of us. It's only a tap, but it's enough for a very large, very hairy man to jump out of the SUV and come at me, the edges of his lumberjack beard bristling with rage. I put the car in reverse and back up a few inches, careful not to hit the BMW lest I also get into it with the salon escapee behind us.

"Crap, crap, crap." I roll down the window after I've backed us up. "Hey, man, I'm sorry about that."

The man looks at his SUV's back fender and brushes it with his hands. There's a small smudge of dirt there from the impact. He turns around and looks as if he is about to pound on the hood of my car with his ham-hock-size fists. Instead, he says, "Watch where you're going, pendejo."

"Yipper, skipper," I say. "Sorry again. No harm done, right?" He's on the edge of arguing back. Before he can say anything, I add, "And please tell the cashier I'm buying your coffee for you."

The sneer on the man's face slackens. He shouts over his shoulder, "Then I'm buying coffee for the rest of my office, too."

"Great," I say. "You do that."

"Oof. What a beast," Ujima says. "Hit him again so I can ask him for his phone number."

I sigh and drive up to the speaker to order our coffee.

Our Starbucks trip makes us late. We arrive just in time for second period. I ask Ujima to stay out in the hallway so I can introduce them. The students are already sitting in their seats, looking more anxious than normal. Not surprising, as I know they've been waiting for Emmett's arrival. Still, some of them seem strangely out of sorts when I walk in alone, staring at me as if they've never quite seen me until now.

"Listen up, everyone," I announce. "First of all, I want to apologize. Emmett is here, but he's not here. I mean, he's not *here* here. He's in town, but he can't come today because he's busy with some...Hollywood stuff? He'll be here soon, though, I promise! Maybe as soon as tomorrow." I hope. "Anyhoo, in the meantime, I'd like to introduce you all to my friend. Who is, uh *are*...Oh, actually, you should know that they prefer the use of, uh..."

Ujima opens the choir room door wide. "Good heavens. Let me," they say and glide inside. "Hello, children. My name is Ujima Jenkins. Like Quito, I work in the theater business. I act, sing, dance, and MC every Friday night at Escándalo, Chelsea's hottest, sultriest, sexiest—"

"Jee!"

"What? Oh fine," they say, mock pouting. "Suffice it to say, I've been around a long time. I'm here to help y'all put your show together. But before we begin, let's just get it all out in the open."

They take a spare plastic chair from the side of the choir room and scoot it right up to the edge of the front row to sit with the students. They perch themself on the edge and cross their legs. "As I mentioned, my name is Ujima, but you can also call me Jee. And my pronouns are *they* and *them*."

I had expected that, out of the lot, Celeste would have something to say. Some sort of insightful, inclusive welcome. Instead, it's Milton who pipes up first. His chipmunk voice cracks from the back row, "You're the most beautiful person I've ever seen."

A few of the sopranos giggle. Ujima turns their head toward the girls, slowly, making the most out of every millimeter of movement. The girls sink down into their chairs so far their heads disappear between their shoulder blades.

Jee gets up and glides back to the empty-seat circle where Milton sits. They kneel down beside him. "What's your name?"

"Milton."

"Enchantée," Ujima says, holding out a hand.

Without hesitating, Milton shakes and holds on to it. "When did you know your pronouns were they/them?"

"You might not believe this looking at me now, but I wasn't always so comfortable with my body. It always felt like my skin didn't fit me quite right. It took doing drag for the first time— on a dare, mind you—to realize I felt better this way," they say with a flourish of their hand over themself. "More powerful. More myself."

Jee puts Milton's hand back onto his lap and stands in front of the choir.

"I know y'all might not understand this now. But the most important thing anyone can ever do is to truly see themselves and to love what they see. And at times, it isn't easy. But just hear this: No matter what people say about you, no matter how they try to define you, just remember that you get to decide who you are. *You* have the agency. Not anyone else. Not your mother, your teacher, your friends, or your enemies. No one." Jee looks at Milton and then back toward me. "Just you."

I see a variety of emotions on everyone's faces. Agreement. Admiration. And on a few, confusion.

"Questions?" Jee asks. "Don't be shy. This is a safe space."

I knew I needed Ujima's help to connect with the kids. Jee's always had an ability to get people to trust them, to let them in, past the safety of their hardened exteriors. I used to think this was because Ujima was like Emmett: an actor. Skilled at becoming whoever people needed them to be. I know now that it's actually the reverse of that. Ujima lives their life with no compromises. It's easy to put your trust in someone who so clearly believes in living their own truth to the fullest.

The kids are all smiles and wide-open faces, genuinely interested in Ujima's story. I decide to wait until tomorrow to figure out what to tell them about Emmett. Let them all at least have one more day.

After they're done talking, I clap my hands. "Shall we get started?"

"Now I know why so many people live here," Ujima says to me at the stoplight on the way back to my house from the school. They bite down into a burger. The pace is obscenely deliberate, like a slow-motion scene from a mukbang video.

"I thought you said it was the weather."

"No, it's definitely this," they mumble. "In-N-Out Burger? More like Put-It-In-My-Mouth Burger."

"Title of your sex tape."

"Charming." Jee holds the burger up to their face.

"What are you doing?"

"I'm taking a mental picture to save for later so I can fantasize about it when I go back to New York."

"Fanta...? Actually, never mind. Just don't eat mine."

"What kind of person do you think I am?" Jee wipes their mouth gingerly with the edge of a napkin, leaving a trace of lip gloss. "I'll just have some of your fries."

Green light. Warm late-spring air breezes through our windows, smelling of flowering trees. "Those kids adored you, Jee."

"They sing beautifully. Especially that little Milton kid. His instrument is damn special. The way it just sits up there? Child, I only *wish* I could sing that high. There's something off about the way he vocalizes, though. Feels breathy. Too loose. Tenor might be too low for him."

"You know tenor is the highest male part."

"And you know typical gender roles don't mean shit to me."

Ujima does it again. Reframes things in a way that's never occurred to me. Reminding me, as someone who has lived their entire life out of the box, that merely thinking outside of it is only the beginning.

"Do you think I should move him up to alto?"

"Possibly. Maybe even soprano."

"I just don't want to disrupt things too close to the concert."

"Quito, those kids are good. Really good. Even a music ed dropout like me can see that. They'll take anything you throw at them."

"My dad taught them well," I say. "I just really wish I could help them better. I've been trying to be supportive."

"Mm-hmm."

I groan. "Spill it."

They crinkle up their empty burger wrapper. "Do you remember that Cole Porter revue I did two years ago? At Peoria Playhouse?"

"Yes. You always knew it was going to be a lemon."

"You know why?"

"Because the director paid you with IHOP gift cards?"

"Because, during rehearsals, he told us that we were amazing, nonstop. The show was fantastic! We had nothing to worry about! Never gave us a single note about what we were doing wrong or how to improve the shitty sections. And believe you me, there were plenty of shitty sections. I mean, most of the cast was from New Jersey," they say. "When the person in charge tells you you're good, and you know you're not, well...There's only so much smoke up one's ass a person can take before they start gagging on it."

"I'm not blowing smoke up their asses."

"Yes, you are. Don't just run the songs and tell them they're perfect. They know they're not. They're looking to you to tell them what they're doing wrong. To tell them the truth. When you don't, they lose faith in you."

"I've had bad experiences in the past giving harsh criticism to other singers. Really bad." I slow down as we approach our house and park on the cracked concrete driveway. I make a mental note to mow the overgrown lawn. The grass has overtaken the meager bed of petunias Dad planted a few months ago. "I was just trying to keep their spirits up while my father was away."

"They don't need a cheerleader. They need a teacher."

With a tray of milkshakes in one hand and the sacks of burgers and fries in the other, I slam my door shut with my foot, a little harder than I intend. It startles a few sparrows from the ginkgo biloba tree shading the entrance to our house, making them fly off in a huff. "I'm not a teacher."

Ujima takes one of the bags from me. "Mm-hmm."

"Whatever, Jee."

Inside, the house is cleaner than it's been in days. Sun streams in from the open window shades, and the hallway floor smells of fresh Pine-Sol. "Dad?"

"Ah, you come bearing gifts." My father, dressed in a clean shirt and pressed trousers, hurries to Jee and goes in for a hug. "How have you been, Ms. Ujima? Or what is it, as the kids say these days? *Mx.* Ujima?"

"Either is fine, Mr. C." They pull back a bit from my dad and give him a good once-over. "Don't you look like a million dollars? Tell me the truth. You've been faking illness because you've decided to moonlight during the day at some secret new job." Jee rubs my dad's biceps muscle. "Are you running an illegal arm-wrestling ring?"

He titters like a little kid. "Ah, Quito, did I ever tell you how much I just love this one?"

"Yes, Dad." I hand the bag of food to him. "Eat up."

"Yum. Burger." He takes the bag into the kitchen. "Come, come. Eat with me."

The kitchen, like the living room, is unexpectedly spotless. The dishes have been washed, and the counters are tidy. I wonder if it's because Emmett's absence has made my dad so bored that he's decided to clean or because he wanted to impress Ujima.

We sit at the dining table as my father digs into his food. "Quito," he says between bites. Bits of lettuce fall onto the table. "How did today's rehearsal go?"

"Great. Ujima was there. The kids adore them."

They kiss ketchup off the side of their hand and reach for what remains of my fries. "Thank you. But the students were already in good hands."

"My son is a born leader."

I slap Ujima's hand away. "Dad, stop."

"You have a gift, anak. They sounded fantastic when I stopped by last week."

"That was the only time they sounded good. When you were there. Otherwise, I've just been making them sound like crap."

"Bullshit," my father says.

"Mr. Cruz," Ujima says, putting a hand on his arm, which makes him sit up embarrassingly erect. "I was just telling Quito that he might be taking it too easy on them."

"What do you mean?" he asks.

"He's not pushing them hard enough. They need to be corrected more often."

"Quito, you have to be honest with those kids."

"I just wanted them to like me."

"Ah, Francisco, Francisco." My dad sighs. "He's always been like this, you know," he says to Ujima. "He wants for people to like him so much, even if it means he has to refrain from telling the truth. Do you know what I'm talking about?"

"Yes, I do." Ujima tilts their head at me. "But it seemed to me like those kids liked you just fine, Quito. In fact, I caught a few of them shooting you some interesting looks during class today. I think some of them might have a crush on you."

"Actually, I sensed something weird, too. Like they wanted to ask me something but didn't know how."

"Or," Jee says, taking their phone out, "they *knew* something about you but didn't know how to bring it up. Didn't you say they already knew Emmett was in town?"

"Yeah?"

"Well, they had to have found out somehow. And they're kids, so it was obviously from something online." Jee swipes and types. The tips of their long nails click on their phone's screen. "Oh. OH."

"What?" my father and I both ask at the same time.

"Quito, there is a picture of you and Emmett trending on Instagram right now. And uh . . . " They glance at my dad. "Let me just show this to you."

Jee hands me their phone.

Someone at Bette's who had been sitting close to me and Emmett, with a view of the sides of our faces, snapped a shot of the exact five seconds when he put his hand on mine. From the angle, it looks like we are holding hands. The look on Emmett's face is less of friendly concern than it is utter devotion. The picture is tagged with #EmmettAokiOuted. It's been liked over 250,000 times.

I scroll through the comments.

Emmett has a boyfriend?

Always knew this guy was a homo.

Who is the mystery guy?

Time to quit hiding, closet case!

Seriously, Emmett Aoki is going gay for THIS dude?

"I need to call Emmett. Excuse me."

I push away abruptly from the table and run to my bedroom. The door slams more forcefully than I intend. I dial Emmett's number.

Thankfully, he picks up right away. "Quito?"

"Emmett, I saw our picture online. And all the things people are saying, and—"

"I was going to call you."

"Oh. Right. You must be pretty upset. I knew we shouldn't have gone out in public."

"Quito, listen. I'm going to try my hardest, but I might not get back in time to rehearse with the choir for the concert. And there's a slight possibility I might not be back in time for the concert at all."

"You . . . you what?"

"I just—it's important that I take care of a few more things here."

"Here? Where's *here*? Where are you?"

"Los Angeles."

"Excuse me?"

"I told you I needed to take care of some business."

"You didn't say you flew all the way back to L.A.!"

"I didn't want to worry you."

"This is about the picture, isn't it? Now that you've been outed, you're freaking out."

"That's not exactly right."

"Not *exactly*? Okay, why don't you tell me, then? Exactly."

"Quito, look, it's complicated. I just—"

"No, don't bother. I get it. You're running away again. Emma Chen is probably looking like a really good choice right now, isn't she? I should've known this was coming. I should've known not to try. I always end up here. I always end up in this place. Alone. Dammit."

"Quito, let me explain."

"Goodbye, Emmett." I hang up and then watch as my phone screen goes dark.

I drag myself back out into the kitchen and throw myself down into the wooden chair.

"Anak, what is going on?"

"Emmett left. He's not coming back."

"What?" my father cries out.

"He's got *urgent business* he needs to take care of."

"What does that mean?" he asks.

Ujima gives me one of their looks that says I need to tell my father everything.

"Dad, Emmett and I...we...um, kind of got together? As more than friends. And when we went out in public—well, it looks like people could tell we were kind of a couple."

My dad looks at me. His eyes, searching mine, seem clouded. "I don't understand."

"We hooked up, Dad. And people figured it out somehow. And now he's been outed. So now he's gone, and he's not coming back. Because he's afraid. Or he's crawling back to Emma Chen or something. I don't know."

"That's not possible," my dad says.

"Well, I'm sorry, Dad, but that's what happened."

"No." He massages his chest and gets up. "Excuse me. I need some antacids." He leaves the kitchen and heads toward the bathroom.

Ujima sorts through more social sites on their phone. "I don't think it's that bad, Quito. It's just that one picture. And a lot of gossip."

"That's all it takes to kill a career. You should know that."

They look up at me. Their face softens as my statement kicks in. Jee's part of the entertainment business. They know full well the damaging power of negative public opinion. And even though we've been blessed with so many more out and proud queer celebrities in the past few years, the ones that find it the easiest are the ones that come out early in their careers. For those who have been around for years, who have built a certain type of persona for themselves—like being a Hollywood heartthrob or an action movie star, for example—it can completely ruin everything they've so carefully crafted. They're afraid they'll be seen in a completely different way. Because they will. It's part of the reason people come out, because they choose to be seen for who they really are.

But some people aren't ready for that. Won't ever be.

Like Emmett.

"Just call him back," Ujima says. "Tell him he'll be okay. He'll be safe coming out. You'll help him."

"No," I say adamantly. "He has to help himself. He has to make that decision. Not me. I'm done trying to make decisions for us as a couple. What am I even saying? We were never even a couple to begin with. And where the hell is my dad, anyway? It shouldn't take him this long to get antacids."

"I'll go check." Ujima points at the mess from our In-N-Out meal on the kitchen table. "I'll leave you to clean all that up."

I start tossing things into the trash and reach for a kitchen rag to wipe up a few stray droplets of milkshake from the table when I hear Ujima scream out.

I bolt toward the sound.

When I get to the bathroom, I see them. Jee is standing over my father, who is lying down on his side on the tile floor. His body is convulsing, his right hand curled up into a ball against his chest. I quickly kneel down and cup a hand under his head. "Dad? Dad? Can you hear me?"

My eyes fill with tears. I look at Ujima. "Call 911."

Chapter 25 – Now

IT'S NOT FEAR or anxiety I feel the most in hospitals.

It's loneliness. Under the ice-blue lights, surrounded by chemical smells piled on top of an undercoat of decay, I'm reminded of the time when I felt the most alone. When, as my father drove hundreds of miles to get to us, I needed someone to tell me that my mother would pull through her six-hour surgery, that the surgeons would be able to siphon the blood from her brain, the pressure of it suffocating her just like the shrinking walls of the waiting room were doing to me. I needed someone to tell me my mother wasn't going to die.

And as my father now lies in the ICU, his body tucked into blue and white hospital bedding with an IV drip attached to his arm, the feeling of loneliness encroaches again. It makes me and everything around me feel tiny and insignificant.

I place one of my hands on top of my father's. The clamminess of it shocks me.

He stirs. A low sound rumbles in his chest, followed by a cough of water and gravel. He opens his eyes and manages a smile. "Mm," he grunts. Warmth ebbs into his hand.

"Hi, Dad." I smile back at him.

He tries to talk and is only able to open his mouth and rasp. His face stiffens into a scowl.

"It's okay. Don't try to talk. Just relax."

As usual, he ignores me. "Waa...water."

I take the pitcher on his bedside table and pour water into a plastic cup. "Here." I tilt it up to his mouth.

He takes the cup and tries to laugh but only coughs again. "I'm not an invalid, anak." After drinking the entire cup, he hands it back to me.

"More?"

He shakes his head and points with his lips for me to put it back on the table. I see now how wonderfully elegant the gesture is in its efficacy, how everything I need to know I can see in his face.

"Gutom ka ba?" I ask in my garbled Tagalog. *Are you hungry?* So typically Filipino of a question. That immediate instinct to feed our loved ones, the need to sustain them. I'm not sure he's allowed to eat yet, though, and I don't think I should be making the decision. I've already made plenty of bad ones for him. It wasn't a minor case of pneumonia he had. He's been seriously ill this entire time. On the verge of heart failure. And I should've seen it. Instead, I cooked him pork pancakes and brought him burgers and fries for lunch— when I should have been encouraging him to eat healthier.

"Hungry," my dad says as he closes his eyes. A restful calm falls over his face.

I reach for the phone. "Hi. This is Francisco Cruz, Mr. Cruz's son in room 138? He's awake and asking for food. Can you bring something?"

By the time I've hung up, Dad's already fallen back asleep. I'm tempted to turn the TV on to pass the time, to give him the soft background noise he always seems to have on at home, but I decide not to risk disturbing his slumber.

"Hi," Ujima says softly. They enter the hospital room with a brown paper bag smelling of shallots, ginger, and five-spice. Their face is creased with concern. "How is he?" they ask.

"He woke up for a minute. Spoke a little." I stroke my dad's hair, rearranging the brittle, errant bits into something more kempt. "He said he was hungry."

"Thank god." Ujima breathes out a sigh. "Speaking of which, I got your favorite."

"Pho ga?"

"Of course."

"Thank you," I say. When my dad visited me in New York, I asked him what he liked best about his visit. The Bach concert he'd attended at Lincoln Center? The *Godspell* revival? Or maybe even an evening at Broadway Baby during one of my shifts. He said, without even having to think twice about it, *the cheap and plentiful Asian food.* He wanted to try a new take-out place every night, and we did—Vietnamese, Chinese, Burmese, Korean. At the time, it pained me to think that the thing he'd remember the most about his trip to New York wasn't anything uniquely cultural but something he could just as easily get in the Bay Area. Now my fingers crunch around the brown paper bag, and I hold it there, not moving, thinking of how much I'd love to be able to share the meal it holds with him and not have to worry that I might be killing him with it.

I start to cry.

"Hey, hey, hey." Ujima pulls me in close. "Everything's gonna be okay."

A soft rapping sound on the doorframe makes me wipe my eyes with an embarrassed swipe of my sleeve. A nurse walks into the room, holding a small food tray. Or maybe it looks small because he's so huge.

"Thank you—" Jee looks up. "Sweet Baby Jesus."

The nurse, six and a half feet of Tongan muscle and tribal tattoos, says, with a smile on his face, "Sorry. Nurse Baby Jesus works in the maternity ward. I'm just Bryan."

Jee bats their lashes. "Last name? So I know what to engrave on our wedding invitations."

"Palu. Already married, unfortunately. But flattered!" He takes a look at the chart by the bed. "You said Mr. Cruz just woke up?"

"He did. For a minute or so," I reply.

"That's good. He was awake early this morning, too, when Dr. Sloan checked on him. His levels look pretty decent. You can take a break if you want. Go home for a bit. He'll be okay."

"No," I say. "I'm staying right here."

Ujima shrugs at the nurse. *Don't even bother trying to argue with this one*, their look says.

"All right," Bryan says. "But visiting hours are almost over. Family only after eight o'clock." He makes a few marks on the chart. "When he wakes up again, you can feed him his cherry gelatin," he adds as he exits.

"Jell-O?"

One of my father's eyes pop open, eyebrow arching like a comic book character.

"Hey there, handsome." Ujima pulls the rolling table with the food tray closer to the bed. "You had us scared there."

"Sorry." His voice croaks, though it already sounds stronger than it was earlier. "Can I have the food now?"

I take the small container of gelatin, pull the metallic covering off the package, and dip a plastic spoon into the bright red and wobbly mass. Something about the texture of gelatin is usually off-putting to me, but seeing the look on my dad's face, bright-eyed and childlike, makes me rethink my bias. He slurps it up like it's the best thing he's ever tasted.

I should be happy that his appetite is back so quickly, but a shiver of apprehension runs through me. I made a bad situation worse by making him worry about the choir's preparedness, constantly telling him I wasn't good enough, that I wasn't going to be able to get them ready for the concert. And then, on top of that, I told him Emmett and I had sex and that he decided to bail on me—*us*—completely. That last bit must have been what sent him over the edge.

That's why he's here. Because of me.

"Why do you look so miserable?" he says, laugh-coughing. "I'm the one who had a heart attack."

"I put you here."

"Hay naku, Quito. Be quiet. It's my own bad health choices."

"No. You got so worked up when I told you about me and Emmett. It made you sick."

"You're wrong. That's not the reason."

"If we hadn't done it, you'd be okay. I shouldn't have told you."

"Don't be stupid, anak. Of course you had to tell me. You should not hide things from me. It just makes you feel worse." He finishes the rest of his gelatin with a final slurp. "Ujima, did Quito ever tell you about how he came out as gay? To his mom and me?"

"Ooh! Story time." Jee leans forward, arms resting on their knees and manicured fingers interlaced. "Spill the tea, Mr. C."

My dad loves telling this story as much as I'm tired of listening to it.

"He was still in middle school. I brought him to one of my high school choir concerts. It was in the spring, I think. On a Saturday afternoon. We had this new boy who was a transfer student. Chad. He was very guapo, diba, anak? Very handsome?"

I groan. "Ohmigod, Dad."

Ujima is so far forward on their chair that only their impressive leg muscles are keeping them seated.

"This guy, he had such an effect on my son. Quito could not wait to talk to him after the concert. To congratulate him for his singing on one of the solos. You should have seen how bewitched he was! Like in that song. You know that song, Ujima? *Bewitched, bothered, and bewildered...*" he manages to sing in a thin, scratchy voice.

"Yes, of course you do. Anyway, I introduced them to each other while I talked to the parents of all the kids. I thought, well, he's happy. Then after that—susmaryosep! He was so upset. Their talk did not go well, you could say."

"Poor Quitolito!" Ujima says.

I roll my eyes in an attempt to diminish the event. But the truth is, I was devastated. I'd figured out I was attracted to boys by the time I was in sixth grade. Not wanting to deal with my feelings, I channeled all the unwelcome urges into playing piano and listening to music. Then, when I saw Chad sing at my dad's concert, everything that had been bubbling underneath came simmering up to the top.

It wasn't his voice, really. My crush on Chad had to do with his surfer blond hair and his Malibu tan. The fact that he looked like a boy band member straight out of a VH1 video. Most importantly, he seemed to be like me. The cute upturn of his lips, the almost unnoticeable flare of the wrist as he walked. All signs that we had more in common than just music.

"He was kind of a dick to me," I say.

"What happened?" Jee asks.

"I told him I thought his solo was great. Even though, honestly, it wasn't all that. But he seemed really pleased that I'd congratulated him. Really flamed out about it, to be honest. I thought, *That's his way of telling me he's gay.* So I took a chance and told him I thought he was really handsome, too. On top of being a good singer. All of sudden he shuts down, gives me this stone-cold look, and says, 'Yeah, I'm not into you. I'm not a faggot.' Then he just turned around and walked away."

The pain of that memory hits me harder than I expect. It was a mistake to reveal myself to Chad that day. It wasn't so much that I was afraid he'd tell other people. It was that I was horribly embarrassed by how wrong I was, thinking he could be like me. That a boy that beautiful would even want to talk to me. So much of that affected the way I'd go on to see Emmett—to be afraid of opening up to him, another boy who was so clearly out of my league.

I couldn't hide my shame and disappointment from my dad that day. But I didn't want to tell him the cause of it. When I got home that evening, I tried to erase the whole event from my head by doing the usual—playing piano nonstop. Hours of Chopin, Gershwin, Billy Joel, anything that came to my head. I played for so long, I managed to wear out my parents' threshold for listening to music. *Anak!* my dad shouted. *Cool your jets now, okay? Give your fingers a rest.* I got the point. Even they had their limits. I went to my room to listen to more music on my Walkman.

Then, after lying in my bed and humming along to the entire *Miss Saigon* soundtrack, something surprising started to happen.

All my tamped-down, adolescent hormones started sublimating, combining with the music I was force-feeding myself.

The notes came first. I remember seeing them floating, swirling in the air and then alighting onto the music staff in my brain. For years I'd been able to see music as clearly as I could hear it. This was just an extension of that.

The harmonies came next—a little more effort. Not much. It just took a realization of the accompanying bass. Filling out the harmonic structures was simple.

What was harder were the words. I'd never had much talent for them and might never have been able to come up with decent lyrics otherwise. But my blossoming desires pushed them to the surface, and they came to me, almost as easily as the music itself.

One day I'll break through
And do what it takes to
Be more than this simple disguise
Until then, it's clear
I'm giving in to my fears
By always hiding myself in these lies

I ran back out into the living room and started to work through it. My mother was preparing dinner, while my dad had fallen asleep on the couch watching the news. The song had so consumed me, needing to be let out, that it didn't even occur to me to hide any of it from them—the music *or* words.

They tell me the show must go on
So I'll try to be strong

And I'll say what they want me to say
But the person they'll see
Won't really be me
It's only a part I play

By the time I'd finished running through it, I wasn't even aware they'd been listening until I realized the TV had been turned off and the sounds in the kitchen had stopped. I turned around to see them sitting on the couch together.

The looks on their faces were hard to interpret. They seemed displaced. Confused. Their eyes searched for something to say.

"Oh," I said, embarrassed. "I didn't realize you guys were listening. Just a tune I came up with. I know it's not any good."

Those looks again, staring. Almost as if they couldn't place me. Like I was a curious stranger who'd just walked into the house out of the blue.

"It...it's very nice," my dad finally managed to say. "There's so much...so much...I don't know the right word." He turned to my mom. His face tried to squeeze out some sort of answer.

"Sincerity," my mother said. She rushed up and hugged me.

"So you like it?" I asked.

"More than like, anak. Much more than that."

My father hung back, so I was never quite sure if he felt the same as my mom. But though I didn't know what he thought of my very personal composition at the time, I did get the sense that he understood where it came from. And what had precipitated the creation of it.

I decided to go all the way. I told them both about my interaction with Chad after the concert. All of it. My mother said nothing in response, only taking me in her arms again and embracing me tightly against her, her tiny arms shaking, but with an excess of strength, not weakness. My dad nodded slowly. He came over, rested his hand on my shoulder, and said, quietly, *It's a good song, anak. A very, very good song.*

My dad coughs quietly now in the hospital bed. "Did you know, I made sure never to give Chad another solo?"

"I didn't know that."

"You're a good father, Mr. Cruz," Ujima says.

"I try." His eyes crinkle.

"I'm pretty impressed, actually," Ujima says. "Coming out to your parents when you were that young? It's never easy telling people, even the ones you love, who you really are."

My father, though still slightly pale, is more awake and alert than before. "Ujima, you are right. I continue to tell my son to be open with me, and yet I do not do the same. I am a hypocrite."

He coughs quietly. "Quito, this was not my first health emergency. One year ago, do you remember, during the summer? I told you I had a problem related to fatigue. I didn't tell you the whole truth because I did not have the whole story at the time. I thought maybe I was dehydrated. Light-headed from working too hard. But I was talking to Mrs. Ramos, the Spanish teacher, and all of a sudden I had such a hard time thinking of the right words to say. I couldn't even form a simple sentence. She told me I should go see the doctor. Just in case. Thank god I listened to her because I would not have known otherwise that I had a—what do you call it? A ministroke."

I fall into the chair next to his bed. "Dad! You should have told me."

"About the stroke? No. I didn't want to worry you." His face sags. "But the heart attack after that, yes. I should have told you."

"I was there for the heart attack."

"I mean the one before this one."

"You had a heart attack *before this one?*"

"When Celeste called to tell you I was sick, it wasn't from mild pneumonia. I was recovering from my first heart attack. Not too serious. At the time, I thought it was just acid indigestion. But, you see, I learned from my mistake! I called the doctor right away."

"Oh my god! Obviously you did NOT learn!" I jump up and begin pacing the tiny length of the room. "I should have been helping you get better. Buying you healthy meals. Making you exercise . . . I don't know."

He laughs, a phlegm-saturated sound. "We all die, Quito. That's why we have to make the most of the time we have."

"I don't want to hear this," I mutter.

"There's more. Sit down. Please."

I sit, crossing my arms and legs over myself like a strait-jacket. Whatever it is he's about to tell me, I need to be fully fastened in.

"I haven't been honest with you. I *have* been feeling better these past days, well enough to go back to school."

"Well, obviously not, since you're back in the hospital."

"What I'm trying to tell you is that I want you to take over the choir for me," he says matter-of-factly. Period, end of story. As if this decision of his has ended the discussion of how he's completely hidden the truth of his health from me.

The ends always justify the means when it comes to my father making decisions about my life.

In the aftermath of the Chad debacle, for example, after I came out, he asked me to be the accompanist for Sunvalley's choir. He said I'd grown in his eyes. I'd told them the truth about myself and shown great strength. It was time to claim more for myself. To do more. To be more.

I told him, *Hell no*.

I hadn't even graduated seventh grade yet.

But he'd already talked to the principal of my school. Everything was set for the coming year. I'd be given an exemption for one class period in the morning to play for the high school choir. Glenview Middle was just across the street from Sunvalley, so all I had to do was cross the road and—bam. I was an adult. That's when I realized it wasn't an invitation, really. It was him telling me what to do. Like when he "asked" me, at the age of three, if I wanted to start taking piano lessons. I wasn't even fully potty trained yet. How would I know what I wanted to do?

But, like the piano lessons, it was a good idea. I eventually became a better musician just by learning how to be a better accompanist. For an hour every day, I worked with him and the choir, watched his hands weave music, felt the breaths of a roomful of people come alive in my fingers. I became a part of something bigger than myself. And as a bonus (or was it the main goal all along?) I forgot all about Chad. My experience with him wasn't allowed to ruin choir for me. Dad got ahead of it. Turned it around. Prevented any bad associations with the choir by creating good ones instead.

He gave me the chance to be the director of my own life. To move it in a better direction. Even when he knew it'd be difficult.

"Dad, I don't know how to work with those kids. I'm just a pianist. I don't have any business teaching anyone how to sing. Plus, I live in New York. I can't just leave all my music gigs. Or my friends. Or Ujima."

He asks, "What about Mike?"

"Who?"

"Your boyfriend."

"You mean Mark."

"Whatever his name is. You didn't mention him."

"Quito broke up with him, Mr. Cruz. Before he and Emmett hooked up," Ujima says. "Mark cheated on him with the lyricist of the musical they've been working on."

"Thanks, Jee."

"What?" they say. "I thought we were supposed to be getting everything out in the open."

My dad shakes his head. "I always wanted Emmett to be the one for you, Quito. From that very first day he came into our lives."

I stare at him and attempt to respond, but I can't. I'm absolutely speechless.

I try to process what he's just said. I scan the kaleidoscope of memories from then, trying to remember what happened. I always knew that my dad has been a fan of Emmett since that first, irritating day that he forced himself on us in the choir room, with me nervous and upset and my father blissfully unaware of it, content that Emmett Aoki was gracing us with his presence. And certainly, I knew he'd grown to love him even more when he and I inexplicably became friends. But I thought it was just because Emmett filled a different sort of role as a son that I couldn't. I'd never had any idea he knew what was going on between

Emmett and me. How could he? I didn't even really understand it myself.

Time lengthens out while I sit and think.

"Dad," I say, finally, "I had barely come out to you and Mom. We never really talked about it afterward, either. I never realized how okay you were with me being gay. I mean now—sure—but when I was just a kid?"

"It was hard for me, Quito. At first. But your mother, she was the one who convinced me to be fully accepting. She told me, *If you're ever in doubt, just take a step back. And then look at our son. See through to the core of him, and you will know. This is who Quito is. We must make sure he wants for nothing in life, to get the chance to be who he was always meant to be. That is the job of a parent. To love their child one hundred percent, no matter what.*"

It's as if she's here in the room with us. I can see her so clearly, her deep brown eyes filled with steadfast resolve as she says these things to my father.

"But, Dad," I say, "how could you have known that Emmett had any interest in guys back then? Or in me, for that matter?"

"A parent knows these things. One day you'll understand." He shifts in the bed. Ujima and I instinctively reach out to help him. He waves our hands away. "That's why I asked you both to come here. I wanted to bring you together again. One last try."

"What do you mean, one last try?"

He coughs again, the edges of it so rough and wet that Ujima and I instinctively swallow. "I have been trying to get you together for a long time now."

This flies in the face of all the times I thought my father had seen us together. Seeing his expression when our bodies were too close or when our interactions seemed too intimate. I'd always assumed that he wasn't comfortable with the idea of me and Emmett being more than just friends.

"Dad, what are you talking about?"

He says to Ujima, "His mother and I, we always knew he was going to be different, you see. It came with the musical genius." He puts a hand on his chest and looks at me. "So much sensitivity in him. Seeing the world and hearing it so differently. I think this changed him, maybe. I don't know. I am not a scientist. I am just a father. I would watch them during choir rehearsal, you know? Or at our house for dinner. When they would work on music together. Emmett would watch Quito. All the time. That look on his face. I'll never forget it. As if there was no better thing in the world than to be near my son."

Ujima sighs in that annoying, dramatic way they do when they watch black-and-white movies. "So romantic."

"That was just the music," I say. "Emmett always loved music."

"He always loved music because he always loved *you*. And he always loved you because he loved your music. I don't have to know what famous actresses he has dated or has married. He will always come back to you because you are his home. We are his home. We are his family."

"You're right, Mr. C," a hooded man with sunglasses says from the doorway. "You were right. About everything."

"You're here," my dad says.

"I booked the next flight out as soon as I got the call."

Emmett takes off his sunglasses and pulls back his hoodie. He's holding a gift bag and an enormous bouquet of birds-of-paradise in full bloom, their orange beak blossoms on the verge of bursting into a tropical song.

He greets Ujima with a quick peck on the cheek. "How did you get here so fast from New York?" he asks them.

They take the bouquet and gift bag from Emmett, laying both on the table near the window. "I got into town early yesterday. To try to help that mess out over there," they say, waving in my direction.

"Who called you? How did you know we were here?" I ask Emmett.

"Don't look so confused," my dad says. "I asked the doctor to call him this morning while you were gone getting coffee."

Emmett hugs him, carefully, so as not to hurt him. "You seem fine to me." He ruffles the top of my dad's hair. "Are you sure this wasn't part of your master plan to get me to come back immediately?"

My father laughs. A much lighter sound now. "Even *I'm* not that dramatic. But...now that you're back, you can both make sure the concert happens as planned," my father says.

"The concert." My heart sinks. "We'll have to cancel."

"No," my dad says forcefully. "You have to go on. Both of you. They're all counting on you."

"Dad, there's no way we're doing this without you. This is *your* farewell concert."

"It's the concert I wanted, yes. But I never wanted this to be for me. My time has passed. Now is for you. You lead them in my place."

"I can't do that," I say.

"Yes, you can," my dad says.

"Do you think you'll be well enough to attend, Mr. C?" Emmett asks.

"Of course, of course," Dad says, dismissing the notion of his absence. "We have two weeks still. Plenty of time. I will be fine. I'll be dancing in the aisles. Happy I can enjoy listening to the music instead of having to be in charge of it."

Looking at him, he does look markedly better, his health some-how bolstered by Emmett's appearance. If he's able to come home tomorrow, he'd have plenty of time to rest and be well enough to attend the concert. At the very least, we could have someone live stream the event so that he could watch from home.

The bigger questions are: Do I have enough time to figure out how to get the choir back on track? Will Emmett stay? Is he done running away from me?

My dad has been looking at me, watching the gears turn in my head. "Quito," he says, "you haven't gotten a chance to eat the food Ujima brought you. And probably Emmett is hungry from the flight. Why don't you two go to the cafeteria? Ujima will keep me company."

"Are you just trying to get me alone, Mr. Cruz?" Ujima says.

"Maybe," he says, smiling.

Jee pushes Emmett toward me and takes his place by the hospital bed, shooing us out of the room with a flick of their wrist. "Go on. I'll stay here. And bring me back something tasty. Like Nurse Bryan."

Emmett and I stumble out of the room and meander the length of the hall. It's only when one of the nurses behind the desk lets out a gasp, pointing at an undisguised Emmett, that we're forced to move with purpose. We hurry down the hallway.

A room at the end looks to be empty. After checking to make sure it's devoid of any people or belongings, we close ourselves in.

The air inside has the heavy bite of bleach to it, and the beds have been vacated. Hopefully because the patients got well enough to leave and not the alternative. I begin to feel a little queasy. Or maybe I've already been feeling this way.

Emmett grabs one of the chairs and offers it to me. I hoist myself onto one of the beds instead. He sits in the chair and struggles to get comfortable, first sitting back, then leaning forward with his elbows on his knees, and then just resting his hands on his lap. A series of diminishing poses.

"Thanks for coming out," I say finally, cringing at the unintended double entendre. "My dad is definitely glad to see you."

"Quito, I'm sorry I left in such a hurry. Things were going on back in Los Angeles, and I needed to be there to sort them out in person."

The bed I'm sitting on is squishy and unstable. I hunch over in an effort to balance myself. "The picture," I say, "of us together. We weren't careful enough. We made a mistake. You needed to salvage your career. I get it."

"The picture complicated things, yes, but we didn't make a mistake, Quito. I knew being seen in public was a risk. That if I showed my face and if I showed any sort of public affection toward you whatsoever, people were going to come to some conclusions. Quito, I knew the person at the table beside us was taking pictures. I knew they snapped one when I held your hand. I didn't mind. In fact, I wanted them to. And I kind of expected them to post it online. That's just what people do."

"You...did?" I stare at him.

"As soon as the speculation started hitting, my agent called. I told him I wanted to make a statement coming out, wanted to get his help in crafting it. Maybe we'd need to pull in a damage control expert. I don't know. But he didn't want to hear it. He said I was at risk of losing a couple of upcoming deals. Stuff we hadn't signed on yet. He wanted me to refute the gossip. Make a statement saying I *wasn't* with you. That you were just some friend going through a hard time. He said my reputation depended on it. It's hard enough just being Asian American in Hollywood; it took me almost ten years to land my first movie as a romantic lead. Being gay on top of that? He said it was going to be a massacre and that I needed to do something to fix it ASAP. So I did. And I needed to fly back to L.A. to deal with it. To try to salvage some of the roles he claimed I was going to lose but also to be there so I could do it in person. So he understood how serious I was."

"Do what in person?"

"Fire him. Told him right to his face. He's been my agent for fifteen years, Quito. But he wanted me to stay in the closet. He's been wanting me to stay there for my whole career. I'm tired of it. Tired of not being seen for who I really am. Tired of not *being* who I really am. And tired of not being with the person I really love."

I sit quietly, trying to think of the right thing to say. Before I can respond, the silence is shattered by the ringing of an alarm and a garbled announcement from the hallway.

Emmett opens the door. Two nurses rush by. We watch as they run down the hall.

Into my father's room.

Chapter 26—Now

I NEVER REALIZED before today that my mother's closet has been empty all these years.

It took months for my father to go through her things after she died. A heartbreaking task for anyone to have to do, to go through the belongings of someone they loved, package them up, give them away. Every item another loss. I offered to help him, but he didn't think it was necessary or appropriate. Secretly, I was thankful. I didn't actually have the strength to follow through on my offer.

After he'd finally donated all my mom's clothing to Goodwill, I assumed he'd filled her closet with his own possessions. My father always had so many trinkets, inventions, and gadgets from thrift stores, sidewalk sales, or impulse purchases from infomercials, their promises of *getting things done better, faster, smarter* too much a part of the American dream that my dad couldn't ever resist them. He hoarded dozens of these things and stored them in every part of the house.

Just not, apparently, in my mother's closet.

The only things inside were his barong Tagalog—the classic Filipino dress shirt, gauzy and stiff, still in its packaging from a trip to the dry cleaners—and a pair of Prada shoes I'd given him three years ago on his birthday, which look as if they've never been worn.

I roam the bedroom. It feels as if he is still inside it, somewhere, if I only look hard enough. Everything is imbued with his smell, a combination of drugstore aftershave, unwashed shirts, and old music scores. His bedsheets are still crumpled in his familiar shape on the bed. I can see him waking up, putting on his tsinelas, stretching and singing a song on his way to the bathroom. The way he does every morning.

The way he *did*.

I've been lost in this one-hundred-and-fifty-square-foot room with nowhere else to go, replaying the last twenty-four hours in my head, seeing the doctor's sorry look of compassion as she walked toward us in the waiting room with her droopy eyes and mushy mouth, a face made of putty. I wanted to press my fists into it as far as I could go, pushing until I squeezed every bit of pity out of it. Pushing until I wouldn't have to see her looking at me the way she did when she told me, *I'm sorry, but your father is dead.*

I can't even remember how we got home. Ujima drove us, possibly. Or Emmett. They stayed up with me almost the entire night. I know that, at least. I sensed their constant presences, clinging to the periphery of my awareness and prodding me gently throughout the night. To eat. To drink. To use the bathroom. To sleep. Even when, every time, I'd shake my head in silence or just stare off into some void they couldn't pull me from. I know that they finally fell asleep on the couches toward dawn. I sat there with them for a while and then went to my father's room to escape their snoring. Something about the sound of it seemed obscene to me, a rude reminder of the constancy of life.

It's only when I feel the both of them stoop down onto my father's bedroom floor and hold me from behind that I realize they're awake again. I can't tell who is who, and I don't care. I let myself be tucked into an indiscriminate tangle of arms. We stay wrapped up like that for a while, rocking in time.

Later, at the kitchen table, I force down a lukewarm cup of coffee, finishing it in one bitter gulp. I push the empty mug toward Ujima. They brush my hand lightly and get up to make another pot.

Across the table, Emmett watches me intently. As if it's the only thing keeping me tethered to existence. Maybe it is. I don't let myself think of what I'd do, where I'd go, without the two of them here.

"How are you doing?" Emmett asks.

I don't respond.

Ujima stretches. "He's drinking something. That's a good sign. You need to eat, too, though, Quito. You haven't had anything since yesterday. Let me warm something up for you." They open the fridge and gape. The leftover containers filled with unfamiliar-looking Filipino dishes confound them. "Or I can go out and get us some doughnuts."

Emmett looks up. "Great idea. Doesn't that sound good, Quito?"

I trace the tip of my index finger on the edge of my coffee cup. "On Sundays after church, we used to stop by Crown Café and get apple fritters and maple bars. Dad used to eat at least three."

"That settles it." Jee stoops to kiss me on the top of my head. "Emmett, darling, may I borrow your car?"

He tosses them the keys to his rental. "All yours."

"I won't be gone long," Jee says to me. They catch Emmett's eye, communicating things to him in a knowing glance that I'm too exhausted to try to interpret.

The door thuds shut. My skin prickles from the sound of them revving up the engine and peeling out of the driveway.

The hard, heavy wood of my chair pulls me down. Gravity feels even stronger in here, almost inescapable, though somehow dust particles manage to float right in front of my face in the harsh morning sun. The slow impossibility of them signals to me that time is grinding to a halt. Like the world is increasingly refusing to spin on its axis.

The refrigerator door pops open. "Don't know why Ujima couldn't have just warmed us up some of this stuff," Emmett says. He holds up a plastic container of leftovers filled with a mixture of dark brown, lentil-size beans flecked with the red and green of diced tomatoes and spinach. I hear the low rumble of his stomach. "Looks like the monggo guisado from last week. Your dad was the best cook, you know? Even when he was sick, he was cooking for us. Taking care of us."

The thought of all the leftovers makes me sad in a way I can't explain at first. Then I realize that it's because the refrigerator is filled with remnants of my father. Time spent chopping, stirring, frying. Making things I've taken for granted my entire life. The refrigerated air creeps closer and corkscrews its way through me. I want Emmett to close the door, to shut it all back inside, but he just stands there, staring at the container in his hand, and I realize he's not turning around because he's crying. I can hear it in his breathing, the stilted rhythm that comes from trying to hide it, from not wanting to add his grief to mine.

He closes the refrigerator door. He's no longer holding the food but has, instead, taken out the carton of orange juice and goes to look for a glass in the drying rack near the sink, still being careful not to let me see his face.

Emmett says, "Hey. Didn't I give this to your dad that first time I came over for dinner?"

He picks up my father's favorite glass from the sink. It's wet, slick, and because Emmett isn't holding it carefully enough, or maybe because he's exhausted and broken, it slips between his fingers and falls, pushing through the thick, time-resistant air. The glass plummets for miles down to the countertop. I think to myself how surprising it is that Emmett still remembers the glass. How sad it is that he's the one to destroy it. And how my father will never see it again. Not just because Emmett is dashing it into a million jagged pieces. But because my father is dead.

The glass shatters.

"Shit," Emmett yells out, immobile.

"Leave it," I say.

"I'll clean it up."

I defy the sinkhole of my chair and push Emmett out of the way. "Just leave it!" Without thinking, I slap my left hand down onto the counter. A shard of glass punctures my skin.

"Dammit, Quito." Emmett grabs hold of my bleeding hand. "Let me see that."

I flinch. "I'm fine."

"You are not fine. This is a bad cut. Here," he says, rinsing my hand off in the sink and then pressing my other hand against the bleeding wound. "Apply some pressure. First aid supplies still under the bathroom sink?" Emmett says, running off to the bathroom.

I hold my hand up to my eyes, watching for a few seconds as blood sprints down my forearm. An iron-tinged tang fills the air. I tear a paper towel from the holder above the sink and press down on the wound. The blood pools quickly onto the paper, a crimson circle endlessly expanding. I'm surprised by how little pain I feel.

I find myself wandering out of the kitchen and into the living room. I slump down on the piano bench. I think back to my early childhood, watching my dad at the piano, wondering what wondrous machine he'd brought into the house and wishing I, too, could make it sound the way he did, coaxing the hard keys into creating a warm, round, vibrant sound that filled our home, that made my mother sing, that made me smile and sing along, too, even if I didn't know what words to sing. Those days of being together are long gone now, my mother missing for so many years. And now this—the backbone of our family dead, with only me to hold everything together. But what is a song without its structure? Without its beautiful melody, without the underlying bass line to support it? Just a lonely set of black and white keys with nothing to tie them together.

I smash my fist down onto them. The blood from my wound flows freely. The resultant sound is dissonant, ridiculous. I make the sound again and again. Red mixes with white and black.

Emmett comes running out of the bathroom, sets first aid supplies on top of the piano, and sees the mess of blood and tears. "Hey! Stop that. You're going to hurt yourself even more." He stands behind me and takes hold of my arms.

I collapse backward into him, crying.

"I'm going to patch up your cut, okay?" Emmett says. "Before you bleed out any more." I nod, still looking down at the mess I've created.

He sits next to me on the bench, peels the wrapper off a bandage, and moistens a cotton ball with alcohol. He pulls the bloodied paper towel off my hand, takes the wet cotton ball, and cleans the gash in tiny, tight circles. He blows on my hand to dry it and then affixes layers of gauze with firm pressure.

"Thank you," I say.

He says nothing, his attention focused on the squeezing.

"I'm sorry I didn't listen to you when I called. I was convinced you'd left me. Left *us*. I should have trusted you." I tug my hand away from him and continue the pressure myself, pushing my hands deep into my lap.

Emmett sighs. "To be honest, Quito, there was a moment there when I was tempted to do what my agent suggested. To go back into hiding. Back to how things were before. But being with you and your dad again, it reminded me of how happy I used to be. Here, in this very house. At this piano."

He takes both sides of my face in his hands and forces me to look at him. His eyes are wet with tears. He smiles. "What your dad said at the hospital was right. The two of you have always been my family."

My hand throbs, the wound pulsing from the blood racing around my body. I clasp my hands together, digging them deeper between my legs, as if that will somehow slow the pumping of my heart.

"All those years without music, without singing, without you—they were good, but they were never enough. And I knew I had to make a choice. With my agent. My career. My life. I had to choose to be the person you always saw me as. Because that was always the real Emmett. Not the one on the screen. The one here, that isn't complete without you."

When he says this, the previously shattered song of my family, with its plucked-away parts, winds through my mind and seeks out his words, using them to try to make itself whole again.

I put my arms around Emmett. We hold each other as the faint, unassuming threads of something new begin to stitch themselves together.

"Well, don't y'all look cozy," Ujima says, holding two large boxes of doughnuts.

Emmett and I are sitting together on the couch. His arm wraps behind my neck as I lay nestled against his muscled shoulder.

"How many did you get?" he asks, dumbfounded.

"I just want to make sure Quito doesn't lose his ample, curvy figure."

"Whatever. Your wig is a mess," I say.

"And he's back."

They put the boxes down on the coffee table and then pat their scalp with their fingertips, massaging their hair back into place.

"What? I had the top down. And I still look better than you," Jee says, sticking their tongue out at me.

"Gee, thanks."

"So, what did I miss?"

Emmett's hold around me tightens. He tilts his head down, touching his cheek to the top of my head.

"Nothing," I say.

"Mm-hmmmmmmm," Ujima hums, sliding all the way down the scale and back up again. I almost object when they sit down in my dad's recliner, tucking their long legs underneath them. Then I remember that it doesn't matter anymore who sits there. Jee glances over at me, their eyes scanning, reading the trail the shifting thoughts leave on my face. "Quito, what should I tell the choir kids?"

"What do you mean?"

"You're in no shape to have to deal with things with your dad *and* have to deal with the choir. Let me handle it."

We have only two weeks to go before the concert. There is no way the kids will be able to go on now. Not after losing my dad. It will destroy them.

And yet his last request, his last *demand*, was that the concert go on. No matter what. He'd want us to go through with it even more now. He wanted me to take over. Wanted me to take care of his students.

And he wanted me and Emmett to be together.

He's always gotten his way. Why change now?

"No, Jee. Thanks, but I'm going to take care of it. I have to. The show has to go on. I'll probably still need your help, though." I turn to Emmett. "And you, too, of course. It's time you came in to work with the kids."

"Will they even be able to sing?" Emmett asks.

"I won't force anyone to. If any of them can't because they need time to process everything, that's fine. Even if we just have half, or even a quarter, of the kids, I can make it work. It's what Dad would have wanted." I look at Ujima. "Help me rally the kids. I might even need you to sing if we don't have enough people left for the concert."

"And me?" Emmett asks.

"Just show up. They'll be heartbroken when I break the news to them. Just seeing you, meeting you—it'll give them a boost. I know they look up to you. Maybe you can help them feel more able to participate."

"Whatever you need," Emmett says. "I'm here for you."

I get up slowly, disentangling myself from Emmett's embrace. I stretch and yawn. The air in the living room smells old, stale. I pull back the curtains and roll open the window.

Ujima says, "I canceled the rest of my stay at the Airbnb. I'm staying right here on this couch for the rest of my stay, and I don't want to hear any arguments from either of you."

As sad as I am, I can't help but smile. "Of course."

"Wouldn't dream of it," Emmett says.

"And one more thing." With one deft move, Ujima flips open the top box of doughnuts and grabs a rainbow-sprinkled. "I can help out with the choir every day *except* for tomorrow. I have an appointment. With an old family friend, Dr. Sinclairé. She's the reason—the other reason—I came to the Bay Area. I'm going to be starting hormones, with her help." Jee's eyes begin to tear up. They smile, embarrassed. "Ooh, girl. I didn't think I'd get so emotional."

I go over and embrace them. "Oh my god. I'm so happy for you, Jee."

"Not sure if you've noticed, but I'm rarely out of my girl clothes these days."

I kiss them on their moist cheek. "Haven't noticed at all."

"Bitch, please." They laugh. The bright, unburdened sound of it is wonderful. "For the past few months, I've felt more

314

comfortable with my femme side. I've been seriously wanting to transition to being a trans woman and I've finally worked up the courage to do it."

"So would you like us to start using she/her?" I ask.

"I'm still identifying as nonbinary for now. But it's a journey. I see that. And I'm going to embrace it all."

I hug them tighter. "I'm so proud of you."

"Thank you," Ujima says. "I knew you'd get it. Now, about that concert. What exactly is the plan?"

Chapter 27—Now

EMMETT YAWNS. "REMIND me again why we had to get here so early?"

"So we can hide you before the choir kids get here."

"It still smells the same," he says, "like cardboard boxes and chalk. With a dash of BO."

He walks the perimeter of the choir room, taking time to look at the various wall hangings my father has put up. Music informational charts, inspirational sayings, humorous anecdotes, posters about tolerance and diversity. He runs his hands over the concrete walls and wooden shelves and pulls out one of the student's choir folders. Sheet music ruffles in his hands. "Hey, I think I remember some of these."

His face scrunches as he scans the pages, as if trying to recall something from his memories. Watching him makes me wish I can somehow make him experience what happens to me when I read music—how the notes stream off the page, key themselves into the waiting locks in my brain, and release specific sounds tactile enough to hold in my hands.

His brow smooths out. He *is* able to hear something. Maybe not as vividly as I can. But still, something familiar. Like the half-formed recollection of a dream, perhaps.

With a snap, he closes the folder shut and tosses it with unerring accuracy back into its slot. "Can we go into your dad's office?"

"Why not? I'm pretty sure he won't care," I say, more curtly than I intend.

"Hey." He comes up to me and squeezes my arm. The wound underneath the bandage on my hand wakes up. "I didn't mean to—"

"It's okay." The pain flares only briefly. I wait a moment for it to die out before entering the office with him. "Just messing with you."

Everything is how I left it—which is how my dad left it. The stacks of choral octavos, music books, catalogs, lesson plans, and sticky notes with jotted-down scribbles have been in their same exact spots since I first arrived. Moving any of them even a single inch meant that I was claiming his place, preventing him from coming back to take over exactly where he'd left off.

My dad's chair whines angrily when Emmett sits in it. He swivels around and leans back. His eyes latch on to something at the top of the green metal filing cabinet.

"That looks familiar." He jumps up and pulls down my father's tape recorder. A quick puff of his breath scatters dust into the room. He presses play:

. . . the part. You sing it back. We'll do that a few times, and you'll have it all on tape so you can have it to practice with at home . . .

It's jarring, the sound of my own voice as a high school student. So different from the way I hear myself now. I want to blame it on youth. And inexperience. The high pitch, the strain, the slight wavering of it. How what I'm saying doesn't seem solid enough to stand on its own, how the words seem inches from falling in on themselves.

Cool. Hey, thanks for doing this, by the way. I'd be lost without you.

When Emmett's voice emerges from the recorder, as unmoored as mine, I realize that it isn't because we were young. It's because we were afraid. Of each other. And of ourselves being with the other. Not the kind of fear that comes from the threat of being hurt but rather the kind that comes from wanting something too much, for too long, and then finally finding yourself possibly within arm's length of it. If only the right words are said.

And only if the other person can actually hear those words.

"You were never allergic to sawdust, were you?" I ask. "Why did you really join the choir?"

He sits back down in the chair. Metal parts grate.

"Hearing that song of yours freshman year hit me hard, Quito. I needed to find some way to thank you."

"Thank me for what?"

"For waking me up. For giving me permission to see something about myself I was afraid to look at before. For the hope that I wasn't the only person who thought that way about myself. It's just, I could never figure out how to tell you. We never really had any classes together. Didn't run in the same circles."

"I remember."

He laughs, the chair chirping along with him. "I figured I needed to take drastic measures. So I joined the choir. Even though it took me three years to get up the courage."

"Just to talk to me?"

"And more."

Looking at him now, I'm startled by what I see—a semblance there of something familiar. Some*one*.

A reflection of myself. My own desires. And needs. And fears. And love.

I touch the side of his face. He smiles up at me.

As much as I want this little trip down memory lane to keep going, I have to cut it short. "Come on. We need to go over the lines you'll be singing for this new arrangement I did for the concert."

Emmett's eyebrows go up. "And what new arrangement might this be?"

"You'll see," I say.

After about half an hour of practicing, I push Emmett into the office a few minutes before the bell rings. "Okay, now, be quiet," I remind him. "No more listening to old rehearsal tapes."

The kids start trickling in just after he hides himself. I wait at the piano, trying to maintain a normal look on my face. Every part of it is tortured and insincere.

I decide to let go of the facade. I've done them a disservice this whole time by not being honest. Now is not the time for sugar-coating anything. Now is the time for truth. No matter how hard it is. Even when my body starts to feel that familiar, inescapable weightiness.

As the kids settle quietly into their seats, Principal Higgins— normally a rosy-faced, ebullient man—ambles into the room without a single ounce of joy. He's accompanied by the mild-looking school counselor, Ms. Mulholland, and, surprisingly, Mr. Drummond, whose lips are so tightly pressed against each other, they look like one conjoined mono lip.

It's clear from their expressions. The students as well as the adults. Everyone is either worried or upset.

I steel myself.

"Everyone, what I'm about to say will not be easy. That's why I've asked Principal Higgins and Ms. Mulholland to be here. To help me, and all of you, with the news I need to share. And thank you to Mr. Drummond for also coming. And for subbing in for me the past two days. I didn't know you'd be here. I didn't expect you to..." My mind begins to drift, an effort to leave my body and go someplace else.

I close my eyes, take a deep breath, and exhale.

"My father, Mr. Cruz. He..." I hold on to the edge of the piano. I've never been so thankful for its faithful constancy. "He passed away on Wednesday. A complication from another heart attack."

Some of the students cry out. Celeste wails something loud and incomprehensible.

Ms. Mulholland moves swiftly to Celeste, who holds on to her. Principal Higgins comes to my side and says, in a loud yet calming voice, "Ms. Mulholland is here for any of you who would like to talk to her. And you are all excused for the rest of the day. Take as much time as you need."

The students are in tears. Some, like Celeste, are close to despondent, though Ms. Mulholland and Principal Higgins and even Mr. Drummond do their best to console them. I see that

Milton, alone as usual, is crying into his hands. I go up to him and, channeling my best inner Ujima, stoop down close, there for whatever he needs. Without a word, he leans over on to me. I hold him as he and the rest of the students continue grieving.

"Will we still do the concert?" Celeste manages to ask between sobs.

I let Milton go gently and swipe my face with the back of my sleeve.

I look out at all of them. It makes my heart ache to see them quietly breaking down in their seats, looking at each other, at us, down at the floor or out the window. At anyone or anything that might possibly tell them this is all some kind of trick. That they haven't just lost a teacher they love. That things can keep going on as before.

I move to the front of the room but still close enough to be able to feel them and our shared loss. The hardened, heavy wave of it. "As Principal Higgins said, if you need to take the next few days off from choir, or even not come back for the rest of the school year, you should absolutely do that. I know you all loved my father. Every student, every *person* who has ever known my dad has loved him. And you all know how much this concert meant to him. In fact, one of the last things he said to me in the hospital was that he still wanted it to go on, no matter what." I press a fist hard against my chest, trying to force it to slow down and steady itself. "So I want to honor my dad's last wish. I still want to put on the concert. With whoever can sing."

"I'll do it, Mr. Quito," Celeste says, her head still tucked against Ms. Mulholland's shoulder.

The other students nod. In their teary eyes, I can see determination replacing despair.

"Then I have someone I want you all to meet," I say. "He can't replace my father. No one can. But maybe he can help make the concert a better experience for you all. Emmett?"

Even before he emerges from the choir office, the kids scream.

It's the happiest sound I've ever heard in my entire life.

When he stands in front of them, I experience a brief flash of déjà vu—of Emmett appearing in this very space for the first time and everyone's reaction to him. How everyone was suddenly petrified. For someone unaccustomed to his presence, it's a lot to take in all at once. He can encompass everything in the room.

He opens his arms wide and motions his fingers gently toward himself. That's all the permission they need. They tackle him. He holds on to as many kids as he can. They're generally unable to speak, but the message is clear. They huddle in a mass of crying and laughter, the hopeful sound of happiness slowly wrapping itself around grief.

"So. You all really want to do this?" I ask.

"Yes," they say.

"For Mr. Cruz," Celeste says.

Emmett looks at me. "For Mr. Cruz."

Chapter 28 — Now

HERE'S SOMETHING NOT every pianist making his debut as
the conductor of his own father's choir will admit: the sight of a
packed auditorium can make the idea of adult incontinence pads
seem perfectly acceptable.

Standing center stage, I peek into the theater from behind
a tiny crack in the velvet curtain and watch the people stream
in. They crane their heads and gape at the camera crews,
newscasters, bloggers, and other paparazzi filling the back and
sides of the auditorium, angling to capture Emmett's performance (and breaking who only knows how many building fire
codes in order to do so). A barrage of thoughts nips at my
consciousness. Did we prepare well enough? Was two weeks
enough time? Will we fail completely? Will people like what
we've done?

Would my dad be proud of us?

Of me?

Honey-hued perfume winds around me. Ujima plants a quick
peck on my check. Their platinum-blond hair is tousled in a 1940s
glamour wave, their body snug in a strapless fuchsia evening gown
and arm-length gloves.

"Hello, Norma Jean," I say.

"Norma who?"

"Norma Jean? As in Marilyn Monroe?"

"Oh." Ujima pats all around their body as if making sure they have the right dress on. "I thought I was serving you some Material Girl realness."

"Right. You do know that Madonna was..." Something about the way they're inhabiting the dress, the way it seems to have always been there on them, waiting to be seen, makes me hold both their hands. "You know what? Never mind. You look stunning."

"Thank you, baby."

They take a step back and look up and down at me dressed in my father's barong Tagalog. Originally dressed in the black suit I'd brought with me from New York, I'd found my-self drifting into my dad's bedroom before heading to school with Ujima and Emmett for the concert, seeking some sort of last-minute guidance. The white barong hanging in his closet glowed like a halo and called out to me. I knew I had to wear it.

Jee's fingers fiddle with my hair. They look at me as if they've just found me after having lost me but fear they might lose me again if they're not too careful. "How are you doing?" they ask.

"I'm okay."

"Good." They pat the top of my head. "Now go talk to your boyfriend. He's wigging out in the bathroom. And not in a good way."

"He's not my—"

"Just go!"

"All right. Sheesh."

Jee gives me a quick satin squeeze before pushing me off, stage left.

When I get to the bathroom, Emmett is standing in front of the cloudy mirror. Staring, though not exactly at his own reflection. It looks as if he's mentally willing himself to do something. What, I can't tell. I'm too distracted by how his tuxedo pants hug his body so well that I can see his buttock muscles flexing.

"Hey. Everything okay?"

He nods. Adjusts his tie. Readjusts it. The tie ends up coming loose in his fingers.

I reach around his neck and take hold of the fabric, pulling and shaping so that the bow folds back into shape. He continues his unfocused stare and says, "Thanks."

"We have a huge turnout. The concert's going to be all over the news. The whole world's going to know about Dad and what a great teacher he was. What a great man he was. Because of you."

"That's great." He tries to smile and ends up gritting his teeth instead.

"Are you really that nervous, Emmett? You're used to being in front of hundreds, thousands of people."

"Quito, this is different. I feel super unsure of myself right now for some reason."

In the few minutes before any kind of show begins, when places have been called and the time remaining is announced, there's a mental pileup that can happen. A crash of worry and fear. Usually that means everything else gets squeezed out and left to huddle in the corners of our minds. Emmett's used to being in front of a camera, saying lines from a script, knowing that he can do another take if the first one doesn't go according to plan. But this is more like *Saturday Night Live*. And we both know that didn't go so well. He doesn't like being this vulnerable.

"Look at me, Emmett. Take a deep breath. Inhale through your nose. Fill your lungs as if you were filling your belly. Exhale." I massage the sides of his face. "Relax your jaw, your tongue." I hold on to his shoulders, pulling them upward. "Feel the air inside you rising up like a column of energy supporting you, giving you energy to propel you forward."

The tension in his body is replaced by a calm strength. His face relaxes. "Thank you. Looks like you learned a few things from your dad."

"I had a good teacher. But he had an even better one," I say.

"Mr. Cruz?" Celeste's voice pushes its way through the door. "Everyone's ready, and the box office said everyone's been seated. Should we start lining up?"

"Just a second, Celeste," I yell out.

"Quito, what if I can't remember the words? Like, I'm trying to think of them now, and they're not coming to me."

"That's because you don't need them now. The words will come when the time is right. If they're coming from the right place, they'll be there. Your body and mind can't just turn them off. The dependable parts of you will still come through."

Emmett smiles that wonderful, big, crooked-tooth-revealing smile.

Looking at him, I realize what I love about that tooth.

I love how imperfect and real it is. How small. How everything else about Emmett can sometimes be too grand when, really, these things are just a tiny part of him, a habit of staking his claim in the world. Or rather, of accepting ownership of what he's always been given—a capitulation to the privilege of being talented, and smart, and beautiful—whereas the tooth is who Emmett really is. Immoveable, unconventional, unapologetic. Never asking to be fixed because it doesn't need fixing. It has the ability to exist with every other tooth, straight and perfect. It stands out and says, *Look at me. I'm not like everything else. And that's amazing.*

I kiss him.

"Mr. Cruz?" Celeste squeaks outside the door.

Emmett chuckles. "Mr. C has got some moves."

"Ick. Mr. C is my dad."

"Well, you're wearing his Filipino shirt and everything. You look very handsome in it, by the way—"

"Okay, shut up now," I say, and redouble back on him, my second kiss even deeper than the first.

"Mr. Cruz?"

Dammit. I force myself to break loose. "We're coming!" I shout. "Are we ready?" I say to Emmett.

He laughs. "We're good."

"Break a leg."

"You too," he says as I open the bathroom door, trying to brace myself against the nerves sparking off Celeste. I walk with her to gather everyone else from the choir room.

They all follow me to the backstage area. Hushed conversations percolate as the kids take their places in the wings. The noise of the audience through the curtain is overwhelming. So much louder than the ambient conversations to which I'm accustomed. They're more excited than usual, maybe because of Emmett. Or maybe I'm projecting.

I take my position center stage behind the curtain and block out all the sounds. A vision of my father in this exact position forms in my mind's eye. His hands clasped behind him, a ruffle of soft belly gently overtaking his leather belt, his brow damp in its many creases, full of the same worries and doubts as mine, feeling the same low-sitting pulse of excitement in the gut, and I realize—everything is how it should be. All the details have fallen into place, coaxed into position by my father's unrelenting, well-intentioned machinations.

"Okay, Dad," I say, smiling to myself. "You win."

The curtain parts. The noise of the crowd decrescendos to silence. A spotlight shines.

"Whoa. Ah, hello. All you...fellows." The lights on me are unimaginably bright.

Focus, Quito. Focus.

I will myself to breathe.

"Over thirty years ago, my father, Mr. Cruz, became Sunvalley High's first choir director. During that time, he built up a choir so successful, they earned countless titles and awards, including last winter's first place win at the All-State Choir Festival. Tonight was to be his very last concert because he was going to retire. Instead, as you all know, he passed away unexpectedly."

I pause to look around at the endless faces, which, remarkably, shine back a strength of sorts. An energy to help me push through the sadness and keep doing what I'm doing.

"But as he told me in the hospital before he passed, this concert had to go on, no matter what. So while we are here tonight to celebrate the legacy he's created, to show my dad how thankful we are for so many years of being our director, mentor, friend, and inspiration, we're also here because this is what he wanted as his final note—his last gift. To *us*. Ladies and gentlemen, and everyone in between," I add, turning briefly and smiling to Ujima in the wings, "the Sunvalley High School Choir—with our special guest, Emmett Aoki—presents Mr. Cruz's final concert program, 'Stronger Together.'"

Chapter 29—Later

WHEN I LOOK back on that night, I will remember some things about the concert more than others.

I'll remember—after a week and a half of trying to get the boys to walk in from stage right and sing the entrance Gregorian chant without getting out of sync, slowing down, or tripping on their own shoelaces—how proud I was of the aural and visual effect they created. Exactly as my father must have intended. Dignified and hopeful.

How the chant was a perfect prelude to give everyone enough time to get into place for the Vivaldi, which went off without a hitch. Every section of the choir nailed their entrances with contained passion. How they'd taken all the prior notes I'd given them about the sopranos' unsteady pitches, the basses' overly covered sound, the tenors' tendencies to rush and the altos' to drag and transformed their merely okay practices into a glorious performance.

I'll remember how giddy I felt when Milton's solo as a soprano caught everyone by surprise during the spiritual, "Hold On"—a clarion treble tone coming from a young man. How it decimated their understanding of what the human voice could (or rather, *should*) do, the ringing out of his sustained soprano high C at the end of the piece soaring, sterling, so forward and bright that it knocked the wind out of everyone.

How Celeste's rich mezzo solo sprang from the heart of the choir as they sang "You'll Never Walk Alone," its melodies so stirring that it tested the choir's efforts not to cry. (Not at that point. Not so early in the program!)

And how, when Emmett took the stage for the first time, they were unable to hold the tears back any longer. How he sang "True Colors" with such sincerity that everyone felt stripped, deprived of their protective outer layer.

I'll remember how shocked I was to see that the accompanist for Emmett's second song wasn't some other pianist but the wind and string ensembles under the direction of Mr. Drummond. How he sidled up to me before walking onstage and said, *I never hated your dad, you know. I was just jealous that he took the best pianist I ever heard before I could recruit you for my jazz band.*

How they performed "You Raise Me Up," a song Emmett didn't so much sing as inhabit, starting from the inside of the phrases and propelling them outward, beyond even my own capacity to assign colors, shapes, or textures, the notes becoming mysterious and undefinable.

I'll remember how, after the strings wound their way around Emmett's final held note, he called me out onstage during the applause. How the audience's chant of *Quito Cruz, Quito Cruz* only ceased when I stood beside him. How Emmett then confessed to everyone that the song may have been in honor of my father (who was always more of a dad to him than his own) but was also intended for me. Because I'd always been the one to hold him up and see him for who he was. Who he should've always been.

How, then, Emmett pulled me into his arms and dipped me backward. Just enough to make my breath stop completely.

How he kissed me full on the lips in front of the audience and exponentially more, thanks to the countless cameras and phones memorializing every moment.

How Emmett finally, officially, came out of the closet to the entire world.

And how—even though the kids, the audience, and the press were going crazy, everyone trying their hardest to record, process, and celebrate the moment in a cacophony of gasps and excited chatter—everything crystallized around the two of us in utter silence, trapping us there like flies in amber, and how I wanted to sip the quiet sweetness of that moment forever.

Until I remembered that we had one more song to go. The finale. Which I'd reprogrammed to be "A Part I Play," but rearranged and reworded for not one person but many.

It started with me at the piano by myself, singing the first verse. Emmett joined me. Then Celeste. And Milton. The rest of the choir. Even a surprise appearance by Ujima, radiant in their gown, all of it building the song up to its refrain.

We know that the show will go on
'Cause our hearts all belong
To the person we sing for today
Yes, together we'll be
More than just you or me
We all have a part to play

And we all did. Because none of it could have happened without everyone's involvement. The kids. Rosie. Milton. Ujima. Even Mr. Drummond.

And Emmett, of course. And me.

And my dad.

And speaking of my dad, most of all, I will always remember this.

How, as I stood onstage, blown back by the onslaught of applause and cheering at the end, gripping Emmett's hand in mine and motioning the choir to take a bow, I was able to see my parents again.

My mother looked back at me as she did when I first played her my song, and the look on my father's face was the one he had when he'd walked in on me and Emmett sitting on the piano bench in our house that first night, our bodies so close that there was nothing between us.

Those looks on their faces I'd first assumed, from their resolve, were from fear, maybe. Or apprehension.

But now I see and remember. And know. It was always something so much simpler.

Understanding.

We see you, anak, they say to me.

We see you.

Coda

THE KIDS ARE just about there.

Their unison singing on the "Lo, How a Rose" section of Craig Hella Johnson's arrangement is impeccable. As close to sounding like one voice as it can get. No other high school choir can come close. Maybe because no other choir has singers who feel this close to one another, though I might be a bit biased.

The soloists need a bit more work. When they sing "The Rose," which intertwines itself with the Praetorius hymn, there isn't enough meaning behind the words. They're probably too young. Too inexperienced to understand the different images of love the song paints.

"Milton, Celeste. Could you stay after class for a few minutes?" I ask. "We'll work on this one together."

"Sure thing, Mr. C," Celeste says, looking lovely in a cardigan and a floral A-line skirt.

"Mr. Cruz?"

"You can't stay, Milton?"

"No, it's not that. It's just—it looks like you have a visitor."

I turn around. Emmett holds one of his infamous gift bags in one hand, the other placed casually on the doorframe; he takes up almost the entirety of it. But once he comes in, he scales back down to size. The same as everyone else.

"Hey, you." He gives me a quick peck on the cheek.

"Ooooooooooh," the kids say, giggling.

"All right, all right. Enough for today. Celeste and Milton, we'll work on this tomorrow. For homework, go watch *The Rose*. Or listen to Bette Midler. Or fall in love. Whatever sounds the least painful to you," I say, winking at Emmett. "Now get out of here."

The students stream out and wave their goodbyes at Emmett.

Celeste hugs him. "How long will you be gone?" she asks. "Will you be able to come back for our holiday concert?"

"Filming for the movie I'm in wraps in November, so absolutely. I can't wait."

"Awesome," Milton says. "I can introduce you to my new boyfriend."

"Ah! Congratulations. I'm looking forward to meeting the lucky guy."

"Cool," Milton says.

Celeste squeals, "Byeeeeee!" as they hurry out the door and merge with the flow of student traffic moving on to third period.

As soon as we're alone, I pull Emmett in for a long-overdue kiss.

"Too embarrassed to do that in front of the kids?" he asks.

"As a certain friend of ours likes to say, *I won't make a scene unless I'm getting paid for it.*"

"How is Ujima doing, by the way?"

"Good. The hormone therapy was a bit rocky in the beginning. But it's getting better. You should see how long their hair is now. It's crazy."

"Are they still doing that *Color Purple* tour?"

"Yes. They're in Pittsburgh, I think. They've even gone on as Shug Avery a few times."

"Can't wait until they perform it in San Francisco in a month."

"Speaking of which," I say, "did you end up putting an offer on that house in Pacific Heights?"

His eyes pop open. "That reminds me——" He bends down to pick up the bag. "For you."

"What's this?"

"Open it."

A bottle wrapped in pink tissue paper. It crinkles as I peel it away. Inside, a bottle of premium Dassai Junmai Daiginjo sake.

"Thank you?"

He laughs. "I know you won't drink it. It's for me. The other thing's for you."

I didn't notice the other, smaller wrapped object. A glass. With a familiar multicolored block pattern.

Like the one my father used to have.

"Took me forever to find it on eBay," Emmett says. "Macy's doesn't make them anymore."

A tug inside. No longer painful but there. And welcome more than not.

"This is so sweet of you. What's the occasion?"

"I didn't put in an offer on the Pac Heights house."

"Okay. I'm missing something."

"I think something closer to here would be better. Orinda or Lafayette, maybe? With a big enough garage for my cars. Maybe even space for that glass. And the rest of your stuff."

I nearly drop the glass.

Instead, I put it carefully on the top of the piano, next to the bottle of sake, and watch as the smile on Emmett's face grows, revealing the crooked tooth and every other part of him. All of it. None of it as overpowering as I thought when I was younger.

Just enough. Just him.

Not too much.

But still great.

A PART I PLAY (LYRICS)

VERSE 1

I get into place
Put a smile on my face
They're all waiting for me to begin
To get to this night
I've practiced all of my life
To change who I am to fit in

VERSE 2

I'll do what they want
And try not to flaunt
To be something I'm not supposed to be
Do it just so
So they'll never know
Deep inside I just want to be free

REFRAIN

They tell me the show must go on
So I'll try to be strong
And I'll say what they want me to say

But the person they'll see
Won't really be me
It's only a part I play
A part I play

VERSE 3

I'm tired of these games
Of not taking the reins
of my own life—to dictate my fate
But what else can I do
Gotta see it through
Can't alter the script; it's too late

VERSE 4

One day I'll break through
And do what it takes to
Be more than this simple disguise
Until then it's clear
I'm giving in to my fears
By always hiding myself in these lies

REFRAIN

They tell me the show must go on
So I'll try to be strong
And I'll say what they want me to say
But the person they'll see
Won't really be me
It's only a part I play
A part I play

BRIDGE

Be better
Try harder
Say all the right things
Play the role that was written for me
But one time, just once
I'd like to let go
And be the person I'm longing to be
Be the person I'm longing to be

REFRAIN

They tell me the show must go on
So I'll try to be strong
And I'll say what they want me to say
But the person they'll see
Won't really be me
It's only a part I play
A part I play
Yes, the show must go on
So I'll try to be strong
And I'll say what they want me to say
But the person they'll see
It's never been me
It's only a part I play
A part I play

ONE-DERLAND

Act 1

SCENE 1: WAITING IN LINE (THE RABBIT HOLE)

"Torn" (Natalie Imbruglia) .... Alice and Maggie

SCENE 2: ONE-DERLAND

"It's Raining Men" .... Alice and Ensemble
(The Weather Girls)

SCENE 3: THE CAUCUS RACE

"Macarena" (Los del Rio) ....Ensemble

Scene 4: The White Rabbit's House

"Baby Got Back" (Sir Mix-a-Lot) .... Off-White Rabbit

"I Want Candy" (Bow Wow Wow) .... Alice

Scene 5: The Caterpillar's Pad

"Ice Ice Baby" (Vanilla Ice) .... Mr. Caterpillar

"I'm Too Sexy" (Right Said Fred) .... Chester Cheshire

Act 2

Scene 6: Spilling the Tea

"Don't Worry Be Happy" .... Mad Matt and Martha Hare
(Bobby McFerrin)

"Closing Time" .... Alice, Mad Matt, Martha Hare, Off-White
(Semisonic)   Rabbit, Chester Cheshire

Scene 7: After-party at the Croquet Club

"Bitch" (Meredith Brooks) .... Ms. Queeny Hart

"Who Let the Dogs Out" (Baha Men)............................Ensemble

Tubthumping (Chumbawamba)................... Ms. Queeny Hart and
Ensemble

SCENE 8: BACK TO ONE-DERLAND

"Funkytown" (Lipps Inc.) .... Alice and Ensemble

SCENE 9: HOME AGAIN

"I Melt With You" (Modern English) .... Alice, Maggie, and
the Company

Sunvalley High School
Martinez, California

STRONGER TOGETHER

The Sunvalley High School Concert Choir
Mr. Manuel Cruz, *Conductor*
Mr. Francisco "Quito" Cruz, *Accompanist and Guest Conductor*

Ecce quam bonum .... plainchant
Tenors and Basses

Gloria in D Major, RV589 - 1. .... Antonio Vivaldi
Gloria in excelsis

"Hold On" .... arr. Moses Hogan
Milton Mathieson, *soprano*

"All Works of Love" .... Joan Szymko

"You'll Never Walk Alone" .... Richard Rodgers & Oscar
Hammerstein II
Celeste Gonzalez, *alto*

"True Colors" .... Tom Kelly & Billy Steinberg

Emmett Aoki, *tenor*

"Hiney Mah Tov" .... arr. Iris Levine

"Lean on Me"/..................... Bill Withers /Anthony J. Showalter &
Everlasting Arms   Elisha Hoffman, arr. Pepper Choplin

"The Tree of Peace" .... Gwyneth Walker

Altos and Sopranos

"You Raise Me Up" .... Rolf Løvland & Brendan Graham

Emmett Aoki, *tenor*

SHS Wind Ensemble & SHS String Ensemble

Mr. Jim Drummond, *conductor*

"We All Have a Part" .... Francisco Cruz

Francisco Cruz, Emmett Aoki,
Celeste Gonzalez, Milton Mathieson,
Ujima Jenkins, *soloists*

ACKNOWLEDGMENTS

To Gina Panettieri, thank you for helping to get my first chapter query ready for the perfect agent and then becoming that perfect agent.

Thank you to my editor, Alex Logan, for believing in my queer Filipino love story and for doing all the million things you needed to (and the million things beyond that) to help make this book a reality.

Thank you to the team at Forever—Beth, Leah, Amy, Estelle, Dana, Penina, and Anjuli—and to Caitlin Sacks for the beautiful cover.

To Dr. Hiyas Hila and Rhya Raymundo, maraming salamat for improving the authenticity of the details regarding Filipino culture, food, and language. And to Cleopatria Peterson, many thanks for your guidance on nonbinary and trans identities and issues.

To my Monday Night Writing Group—Esther Gulli, Barbara Jordan, JoAnne Tillemans, Steven Wight, Richard Kleiner, and Nancy Bourne (who I know is still cheering me on from the great beyond)—your friendship and advice over these past few years have meant the world to me.

Thanks to my teachers, Junse Kim, Joshua Mohr, Dan Coshnear, Roy Hagar (the greatest AP English teacher of all time), Margo Perrin (who gave me my start by publishing my first short story), Rachael Herron (without whose guidance this book would never have gotten off the ground), and Laurie Ann Doyle (whose mentorship has been a gift of pure gold).

And speaking of Laurie, thank you to my other fellow Babylon Salon cohosts, Lauren Johnson, Ryan Sloan, and Maury Zeff, as well as to the members of the Writers Grotto. You've all been my role models and inspirations.

To the two most gorgeous singers on the planet, Arwen Myers and Laura Thoreson, thank you for believing in my book and for watching trashy TV and eating junk food with me during my self-imposed writing retreat in Portland. There aren't enough heart emojis to describe how I feel about the two of you.

To my beautiful brander, Beth Carr—you are my Broadway Baby. And to Debbie Bidwell, my best friend of over thirty-five years—I love you "Always."

To my brother Joseph, music teacher and choir director extra-ordinaire, thanks for helping me with all the high school choir details. And thanks to Joe, Michael, and Theresa for being the best brothers and sister a guy could ask for. I hope you are proud of your kuya.

To my dad, you were gone from this world too soon. I wish you were still here to see this.

And so many thanks to my mom, who was wise enough to know that teaching me how to read would be one of the greatest gifts a parent could ever give to their child. Thank you for that and for the countless other gifts you've given me.

Finally, to Peter—you helped me create a story for myself I never thought I'd be lucky enough to have. You are more than just my rock. You are my love, my life, my everything.

READING GROUP GUIDE

Dear Reader,

Toni Morrison once said, "If there's a book that you want to read, but it hasn't been written yet, then you must write it." That's what I set out to do with this book. Growing up, I was an avid fan of romantic comedies. My favorite movie was, and still is, *When Harry Met Sally*. I also read all the gay novels I could get my hands on, particularly ones about Filipinos or other Asians.

What I could never find, though, was a combination of the two. Rom-coms were usually centered on straight white characters, while gay stories were often serious, focusing on the struggles of being queer. I wanted to create something I was never able to find for myself—an uplifting love story in which a gay Filipino, surrounded by other BIPOC and LGBTQIA+ people, finds his Happy Ever After.

Many of the people, situations, and settings in this book sprang from my own experiences studying and working in music and theater in the San Francisco Bay Area, Oberlin College in Ohio, and New York City. The Broadway Baby piano bar is a combination of Marie's Crisis in New York City and Martuni's in San Francisco. Quito is based partly on me but also on several composer and pianist friends of mine. The character of Mr. Cruz is a mixture of my parents and my brother Joe, who is a high school choir and piano teacher, while Ujima was inspired by a few singers and actors I've worked with in the past.

Emmett, however, is totally made up. I've never personally

known any movie stars, but that's okay. My husband, Peter, is far hunkier than any Hollywood actor could ever be!

And speaking of movies, when people set out to write a book, they sometimes say they envision theirs as one. Not me. I have always seen my story as a musical, complete with soul-baring solos, love duets, comedic numbers, and a big, showstopping finale. I hope that, after finishing *All the Right Notes*, you walk away with either a tune in your head or a song in your heart. If so, then I've accomplished what I set out to do.

Thank you for being a part of Quito and Emmett's musical romance. I hope you enjoyed reading *All the Right Notes* as much as I enjoyed writing it.

Yours truly,

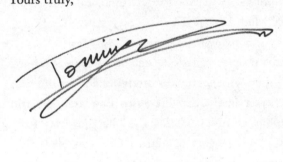

DISCUSSION QUESTIONS

1. Before Quito and Emmett start working together in Sun-valley High's concert choir, they already have preconceived notions of each other. What are they? Have you ever gotten close to someone who ended up being very different from what you initially thought they would be like?

2. Quito goes on to work as a pianist in New York but can't seem to find the love he once had for composing music. Why do you think this is? Have external circumstances ever changed the way you viewed something you were once passionate about?

3. Quito decides to reveal a part of his inner life by composing a song for the high school talent show. Do you think this was a good idea? Why or why not? Have you ever made yourself vulnerable by revealing something secret about yourself to the rest of the world? How so? Were you happy with the outcome?

4. The song "A Part I Play" appears several times throughout the book. What do the lyrics mean to you? Do you identify with them in any way? If so, how?

5. Ujima considers themself nonbinary and uses they/them pronouns. What does this mean to you? Have you ever met anyone who identifies as nonbinary or who uses alternative pronouns? How do you feel about the issues surrounding gender identity?

6. Ujima and Mark don't get along, but the reason is never really explained. Why do you think there is animosity between them?

7. Mark offers what he believes to be a great career opportunity to Quito—the chance to write music for Dinesh's musical. Why do you think Quito has conflicted feelings about this? Has anyone close to you ever offered you a gift that you felt conflicted about?

8. When Emmett auditions for a choir solo, the other characters in the room are impressed, even though he's not technically adept at singing. Why? Can you think of people who have impressed you with "raw talent"? How do you feel when you experience their work?

9. "Seeing" and "hearing" are recurring themes in the book. What are some instances of the characters seeing or hearing things that change the way they view other people?

10. Even though Quito is busy, he isn't able to say no to his father when he asks for help with his farewell concert. Why do you think this is? Are there people in your life that you find you can never say no to? Is this a good or a bad thing?

11. Quito and Ujima have a physical encounter when they are first getting to know each other, but instead of going on to have a romantic relationship, they end up being best friends. Do you tend to stay friends with your romantic partners or not? If not, why?

12. It's eventually revealed that the reason Quito hasn't spoken to Emmett since college was because of an awkward sexual encounter that Quito fears was nonconsensual. What do you think Quito should have done instead? Have you ever broken off a relationship as a result of a mistake you made?

13. Some problems arise from Quito and Emmett being seen in public together. Would you be interested in being in a relationship with someone who was famous? Why or why not?

14. Emmett chooses to come out of the closet publicly. What kinds of things do you think might happen to him because of that decision? What do you think might have happened to him if he had done so when he was just starting out in Hollywood? Do you think people are more accepting of

out LGBTQIA+ celebrities today? How do you feel about LGBTQIA+ men or women playing straight TV or movie roles and vice versa? Should LGBTQIA+ roles only be played by LGBTQIA+ actors and actresses? Why or why not?

15. Food plays an important role throughout the book. In what ways does food either bring people together or cause conflict?

16. The power of music is a major theme in this book. What does music mean to each of the characters? In what ways does music shape or transform them? How do they use music to communicate with one another?

Q&A WITH THE AUTHOR

1. This is your first novel. How did it come about? What inspired you?

I'd written a short story about a pianist who loses his boyfriend in an accident, which I'd wanted to turn into something longer. When I finally sat down to outline the details, the story shifted into something more optimistic and romantic. A lot of the short stories I'd written up until that time tended to be pretty serious, but I realized I wanted my first novel to be more of a reflection of who I am as a person—and I'm way more upbeat and fun-loving in real life! I'm always laughing and singing. I love to make music and celebrate love in all its forms, so all of that ended up inspiring the direction of the book.

2. Your novel provides a great slice of Filipino American life. Do both your parents have Filipino heritage like Quito? Or are you biracial like Emmett? How did your experience affect your portrayal of that character?

My parents were both born in the Philippines, and like Quito's parents, they met and got married there before moving to the United States. I was also born in the Philippines, but we immigrated to the United States when I was only a year old. So while I'm technically an immigrant, I consider myself more of a first-generation Filipino American. Many of my experiences growing up in a Fil-Am household informed Quito's story. Little things like Mr. Cruz's barong Tagalog, saying a prayer before eating, and the Last Supper picture above the dining table. But also bigger things, like his parents' struggle to establish themselves in this country, working odd jobs and making do with only the basics in order to provide for their child. My parents did that for me and my siblings, as did so many of my relatives.

3. The American dream is a big part of Emmett's plotline, and he succeeds beyond his wildest dreams while Quito struggles to find his place. In what ways have you been pushed to succeed? In what ways have you struggled to find your place?

From a very early age, I was motivated by my parents to do well in school, to make good on the opportunities they worked so hard to provide for us. My mother was an English teacher in the Philippines who couldn't find a job as a teacher when we immigrated to the United States, so she taught me instead. I was able to read before I even got into kindergarten. Early on, I wrote stories and poems that won prizes in local competitions. I always read a ton of books and did well in English classes. As I got older, my focus shifted toward music. My parents had provided piano lessons early on, which led to a passion for singing and acting. For years, I could never decide what to focus on—the performing arts or writing. In many ways, writing *All the Right Notes* is the culmination of my two great passions.

4. Your love of Filipino food is evident throughout the book. Who is the good cook in your family? Is it you? Are there special Filipino holidays to celebrate? What foods do you eat to celebrate?

I love to cook! I like to think that I'm the best at it in my family, but my two brothers, Joe and Mike, would probably disagree. They're both really great cooks, too. The three of us often make Filipino dishes for our family get-togethers (and my sister Theresa loves to eat them). Joe loves to make inihaw (BBQ), Mike makes a mean kare-kare, and I usually make adobo or arroz caldo. We all got our skills from our mother, who is by far the best cook in our extended family. She was the auntie whose dishes everyone would be excited about at family get-togethers. Our relatives always looked forward to her pancit or lumpia at Thanksgiving, Christmas, Easter Sunday, birthdays, and wedding anniversaries. The first thing we'd often hear when we'd arrive at any party was "What did your mom bring?" Nowadays, however, she's quite content to leave all the cooking to us.

5. Your love of Broadway is also evident throughout the book. Can you tell us a little more about where you got your knowledge of show tunes? In what ways has the power of music shaped or transformed you?

One of my most cherished childhood memories was watching *The Sound of Music* on TV during the holidays. When I was in middle school, my cousin played me her original cast album of *Les Misérables*, and from then on, I was hooked. I started performing in and musical directing the shows at my high school. (Fun fact: the person I codirected the musicals with was a young Craig Brewer!) I went on to Oberlin to study voice, and after college, I moved to New York to be a musical theater actor. I got my Equity card doing *Miss Saigon* at North Shore Music Theatre in Massachusetts and did a few more shows before I decided to go back to grad school to get my masters in music. Music has always been a huge part of my life. From musical theater, to playing piano, sax, and bassoon in school bands, to singing in choirs and early music ensembles, I've never not been making music in some way or another. I hope I never stop.

6. Your book is being published in June, which is Pride month. How do you self-identify? How do you celebrate Pride?

I usually identify as a gay cisgender male, though I sometimes just identify as queer. I'm thrilled that my book is being released during Pride month because I've always been so proud to be gay. I celebrate Pride in different ways. When I lived in New York, I'd always go to the Pride Parade and all the parties and clubs, but I was much younger then! These days, I'm more likely to celebrate it quietly at small get-togethers with my husband, Peter, and our friends. Lately, I've committed to reading books written by queer authors during Pride month. There are plenty to choose from, thankfully.

7. As your book is published, we are living through a period where LGBTQIA+ rights are being rolled back in many places. What do you want readers to take away from your story? Do you think that stories like yours can make a difference?

It's especially hard for me to see things sliding back because, over the past few decades, we'd seen so much LGBTQIA+ progress. That's why it was important for me to write a queer romance. There are a lot of stories about our struggles—and these are incredibly important to have—but we also need to have stories where queer characters can just be themselves. Ones where they aren't persecuted for being gay or feel afraid because they are trans or nonbinary. Stories are so powerful. They can be a way of wishing things into the world. If people can read about queer people and people of color being free to live their lives, finding happiness and love just like everyone else without having to worry about being hated for being who they are, then hopefully they can envision it for the real world, too.

8. Do you have a real-life coming out story that you want to share? It can be your own but could instead be someone else's experience that influenced your story.

The first person I ever came out to was my best friend in eighth grade, Debbie Bidwell, who is still my best friend today over thirty years later. It was over the phone and extremely awkward because she had a crush on me at the time, which I didn't know!

Luckily, she was extremely supportive. In high school, I came out to everyone, which, at the time, wasn't such a common thing and a bit risky. But, for some reason, all the "popular" kids decided it would be cool to have me as a friend, so no one ever gave me a hard time about it. I like to think that having such a good coming out experience helped make it easier for my sister and brother to do the same. They both also came out in high school!

9. Ujima seems to have the most fun in this story! What inspired their story? Does this character have a real-life inspiration?

Ujima is based on a few people but primarily on a very talented actor/singer/dancer friend of mine whom I met while doing a production of *Kiss of the Spider Woman* in Brooklyn. He wasn't nonbinary or trans, but he did do drag at the time. I was somewhat enamored with him whenever he transformed into his drag persona. Whenever we'd go out dancing, he would command the entire club's attention, no matter how huge it was, yet when we spent quiet times together, he was so sweet and funny and personable. I wanted to capture that feeling of someone who was both larger-than-life and down-to-earth, someone you'd want by your side during the fun times as well as the bad.

10. What are you writing next?

You've probably already guessed this, but I am a big fan of drag! And like most Filipinos, I also love karaoke. So I'm combining the two for my next book. It's about a Filipino drag queen named Rex who runs into his ex-boyfriend—the "one who got away"—now a bartender at a failing gay bar. Rex tries to help him by hosting a karaoke night to drum up business, except he doesn't want his ex-boyfriend to know he's a drag queen, so he trains a frenemy to be his doppelgänger. It's sort of a mix of *Kinky Boots* and *Tootsie*. I'm doing lots of research by going out to various karaoke nights at gay bars in the San Francisco Bay Area and watching lots of *RuPaul's Drag Race*, especially *Drag Race Philippines*. The hard life of being a writer!

TINOLANG MANOK
(SAUTÉED CHICKEN SOUP)

I'm lucky enough that my mother still cooks me a dish of my choice every year for my birthday. When I was younger, I'd ask for pancit or lumpia—more labor-intensive dishes usually reserved for special occasions. These days, however, I ask for her chicken tinola. It's an everyday comfort food, the Philippines' version of chicken soup. Tinola is easy to make and doesn't require a lot of ingredients, so I sometimes make it myself, but it never tastes as good as when my mom makes it. She manages to add that extra special touch somehow!

INGREDIENTS:

- 1 Tbsp minced garlic
- 2 Tbsp diced onion
- 2 Tbsp diced fresh ginger
- 1 Tbsp coarsely ground black pepper
- 1 to 2 Tbsp powdered Knorr chicken broth
- 2 cups of water (or more)
- ½ cup of green papaya wedges (or chayote or upo/green Filipino summer gourd)
- 1 cup or more cut-up pieces of cabbage, napa or bok choy

- Moringa leaves, mushroom, broccoli, or small wedges of celery are optional
- 1 to 2 pounds of cut-up fresh chicken
- 1 Tbsp of fish sauce (amount according to taste; salt may be used if preferred)
- 2 to 3 Tbsp of desired cooking oil

DIRECTIONS:

In a stock pot, sauté the cut-up chicken with minced garlic, onion, and ginger in hot cooking oil. Keep stirring the chicken until the garlic, onions, and ginger are transparent. Season with patis (fish sauce, according to taste).

Toss 1 Tbsp or more of powdered Knorr chicken broth into the chicken and keep stirring. When slightly browned, pour two cups of water and cover. Let chicken legs and thighs simmer for half an hour. If cooking an entire cut-up chicken, cook covered for at least 35 to 40 minutes.

Adjust the amount of the soup or water to the amount of cut-up chicken. Add the ground black pepper. Then add all your choices of vegetables and cook until soft. Serve hot with rice, and enjoy!

NOTE: If wedges of green papayas are desired, you may mix them with the chicken halfway through cooking until the chicken is tender. Papayas are our traditional choice, as well as cut-up green upo or summer gourd. You may also use wedges of potatoes if preferred.

The amount of seasonings listed may be adjusted to your desired taste. I like to add more garlic, onions, and ginger depending upon the amount of cut-up chicken, as well as the amount of soup to cover it.

ABOUT THE AUTHOR

Dominic Lim has enjoyed a lifelong love affair with music. Dominic holds a master's from Indiana University Jacobs School of Music, is an alum of the Oberlin Conservatory of Music, and has sung with numerous professional early music and choral ensembles. As a proud member of the Actors' Equity Association, he has performed off-Broadway and in regional productions throughout the United States. Although he probably shouldn't admit to having favorites, the thrill of singing "This Is the Hour" in the chorus of *Miss Saigon* still pops up in his dreams. Dom supports his local writing community as a member of the Writers Grotto and as cohost of San Francisco's Babylon Salon. He lives in Oakland with his loving and supportive husband, Peter, and their whiny cat, Phoebe.

YOUR
BOOK
CLUB
RESOURCE

VISIT
GCPClubCar.com

to sign up for the **GCP Club Car** newsletter,
featuring exclusive promotions, info on other
Club Car titles, and more.